THE LAND I LIVE

By Stephen Longstreet

Novels

DECADE
THE GOLDEN TOUCH
THE GAY SISTERS

Travel

LAST MAN AROUND THE WORLD
THE LAST MAN COMES HOME

The Land I Live

A NOVEL BY

Stephen Longstreet

> Passage to more than India! . . .
> Have we not stood here like trees in the
> ground long enough? . . .
> Have we not darken'd and dazed our-
> selves with books long enough?
> Sail forth! Steer for the deep water
> only! WALT WHITMAN

RANDOM HOUSE · NEW YORK

FIRST PRINTING

TO

JOAN AND HARRY

AND

ALL THE LITTLE PEOPLE

PREFACE

"THESE NOVELISTS are such children," writes Van Wyck Brooks in *Opinions of Oliver Allston*. "They are story-tellers, at bottom, whose true place is in the nursery; and, if they depart too far from this primitive function, they may become valuable as something else but they are not good novelists. . . ."

Well, the best stories I ever heard I heard in the nursery long ago, when I had a nursery, and of late in the nursery of my children. This book was an idea with me a decade or so after my own nursery days ended, and I have carried it a long time and the last two years have seen it written. I make no bones to be anything but a story-teller, and this story is the story of all of us and some of us and what it says is only a story. I started it in a period of armed peace; I wrote the last line with enemy bombers reported flying over my house; and the story itself goes on into a future none of us has yet lived and some of us may never see.

The story-teller should point no moral—but then the only moral I have been able to find in these days is that we had no moral or wanted much truck with one. This has been a hard book to write, and I hope it will be an easy one to read. I have invented nothing but the people, but what they say and do is true—or as true as I have been able to collect it and put it down. My "primitive function" is to tell a story. I have done so.

Chekhov once wrote, "Writers . . . are going toward something and are summoning you toward it too . . ."

I can think of no clearer reason for writing this novel.

Stephen Longstreet
California, 1942

THE LAND I LIVE

SOMETHING BEFORE

THE PACK HORSE went lame today. I shall camp here.

Yesterday a week ago a great many warm and excited men sat together in a huge, shouting hall and nominated my brother to represent their party for the office of President of the United States. . . .

The mantle of historian fits me badly. It bags around my bones.

The wire came to my father, and he showed it to us and we looked at one another and each of us retired to his corner and had his private thoughts about the message. Even earlier the radio and ·newspapers had begun their mad march across our lives and so in self-defense we have taken cover—all except Vicky, for whom this thing is caviar from Heaven.

Here in the hills nothing below seems very real. There the world is sick, and in the city and along the river bottoms the steel furnaces and mills and plants stand shoulder to shoulder, banging out the tools that everyone hopes will save us all from the blood lust that heats the day. It is a time of turmoil and lament and there are those fat mouths who speak well and shout loud. . . . But it is the little people that I understand—those who stand around in baggy pants and look at one another.

But I am not writing this to talk of the blast of things to come, of the loud winds that blow stupid and long over the airwaves. Nor of those with happy faces and broad bellies, who watch their dividends and heat the steel into shapes no plow should take.

Driscoll Ormsbee—my brother Dris—will most likely be the next President of the United States. What food did he eat, what words did he speak, to make him grow so big? Looking back, I can remember nothing to put into history books or carve into a firm stance in marble. So I have taken a pack horse and made for tall timber, and while the fire burns low and the scented wood smoke colors the haze over the lakes, I sit here writing it all down, trying to understand and remember and look back. . . . Dris is fine, noble, earnest, strong—but suddenly not very real. I must find him.

I do not know if I shall succeed. . . . I do not think it will matter much if I fail to remember him as everyone imagines him. History is not written by the confusion of little minds like mine. This is not history, anyway. It is a return to the weather and sunshine of my childhood and my youth. And through the tattered newsreel that I can create I shall perhaps see merging together the shifting facets of that thing—that moment—that destiny—which has taken Dris so far away from us all.

If there is here put down much that seems of no importance in the white halls of national history: a lot about women and love and art and steel ships and nasty little political intrigue; a low comedy of family bickering and small successes, of events that once seemed important and have now fallen away into footnotes since the beast sounds have begun to fill the sky, then I can only say that every man writes his own story in his own way.

There is a loon calling across the lake. The light is getting bad for writing. . . .

[4]

History will write other things of my brother. He may stand tall and firm against a sky in flames; he may creep away to hide and die in shame. That is for historians still unborn to scribble about. I shall begin at the beginning and write as long as I am able. . . . No one will bother me here among the old forgotten trees. . . .

The fire is low. The food is cooked. I have never seen such large stars. The wind is very cold. It blows from many directions. . . .

BOOK ONE

ONE

THE CITY OF ANTIOCH—and I can see its unquietly bright streets in my memory as I write—like most American cities had many strange examples of architecture, but I doubt if there was anything like my father's house: the house of the small bourgeois, the family home diffused in my mind in the glare of much sun.

It stood on a rise—a rise that I have heard had once been a windy farm hill and a grove of elm and poplar trees—but now it was a city street and the clanging trolley cars bounced past the door every twenty minutes, and from Polack Point the soot of factories and the whistle of the mills were always in the air. But it was an odd little house, surrounded on all sides by shoddily built rows of clapboard real estate bargains with their unwholesomely pallid façades.

My father had bought the house because he liked the garden and the old tired peach and apple orchard and the great oaks winging over the small, yellow house. My father was like that. A fool over nature—and my mother would tell him so very often with her usual sharp scarifying irreverence. Too often.

It was a solid little house, the foundation built of great field stones and the two top stories of reclaimed brick covered with yellow clapboards. There was a low attic smelling of mice and plaster, and three chimneys of old rose, weather-aged brick—most of which had been cemented up, for open fireplaces used too much wood and coal and gave no heat.

My father told everyone it had once been an old colonial farmhouse—I believed him for years. But my mother would snort, "Nonsense!" with a deprecating gesture and expand on the word. Then my father would go up to the attic where he did his cabinetmaking, and stay there until my mother had talked herself out. Once he stayed up there three days, but that was during a crisis when my mother was at the peak of one of her enormous tumults.

My father was an Ormsbee. . . . Peter Asbury Ormsbee. He came of a long line of outdoor people who theoretically despised wealth. Cattle dealers and lumbermen and farmers. He hated Antioch—as all men must hate the city that has taken them in when their fields have failed and given them a corner to lie in and hard bread in return for dirty city labor.

He had led a wonderful youth. Of his parents he knew nothing except that they had died young and had died in the open and been buried under living trees. He never wept for them.

He had been a timber topper—a logger, cutting the huge trees of the forests and trimming away the branches. He was a good story-teller and his version of great dank dripping woods with dead leaves piled into heaps by the centuries and left there so that he could be the first human being to wipe his feet on them was very good. Tales of warlocks and werewolves under ink-and-silver skies—and always the trees.

Then he had traded horses and cows and always he had saved his money to buy, some day, a wooded corner of land with just enough soil to plant some rows of corn and vegetables, enough to keep alive and happy. In spring he used to break log jams in the river and earn enough to last him until fall logging. He felt secure, armored, impregnable to the attack of the cities. Then a jam caught him and broke his leg and he limped slightly from then on.

It meant his river-riding days were over. A night-begotten fear told him the free days were past. They were.

My father was not a tall man. Too little food and improper living conditions as a child had, I supposed, taken a great many inches away from his height. Hunger had always been a tangible presence to him. All of his four sons were over six feet—but my father was a short man, made to appear shorter because of his heavy legs and his huge, muscled arms. He was handsome, with crisp brown curling hair worn over one eye in a fringe, and even his great hinge of a nose could not spoil his looks. Small teeth in a small mouth added to his attraction. And there were those who remembered his sensual explosion of laughter.

When I was old enough to understand him the best part of him was gone. He was a tired little cabinetmaker who had failed in everything, and his wife was always at his ear blasting away at his sanity with the most active tongue in six counties. She maltreated fidelity with a writhing, agitating voice.

My father had never wanted to marry my mother. It had been her idea. He had come to the city to set up as a cabinetmaker when his leg no longer let him ride the bucking river logs. She had come into his shop one day with a broken cane of her father's and decided she was going to marry him. She had a greedy avaricious desire for this handsome man pulling pine shavings out of his curly brown hair.

There was nothing my father could do about it. My

mother, Victoria Sewall, was a woman who knew her own mind too well.

Besides which, she was the daughter of Abner Sewall who held about twenty-five thousand unfarmed acres of land above the mines and fought law suits with Coppards and Cruikshanks over slag piles and increeping byways, so that he was always penniless on his rich land and swept his own puncheon floor.

My mother was a tiny woman with red-gold hair worn in a wavy bun—a sort of pre-Raphaelite hairdress. She had a soft rosebud of a mouth, a tiny, perfectly formed body and a way of tossing her head in a pleading, ingratiating way. She was thirty and my father at the time was only twenty-six. She had turned down every offer of marriage in town and had gone off to Boston to become governess to the New England branch of the wealthy Bancroft family of Antioch.

It was years before I ever found out something of what had happened in Boston—if anything ever had. My mother was a strange mixture of realist and romantic and never spoke the truth when she could make drama of herself. There was talk of a Bancroft son being a damn fool mooncalf.

Whatever had happened, she came back and decided to marry—and decided to marry my father. The poor man was hopelessly enmeshed before he knew it in a sort of sexual non-conformist piety. Vicky Sewall was beautiful, small and dainty, came of a fine old family and was very bright. The old faded photographs show great and fearful character.

She invited him to dinner at her brother's—Thoreau Sewall—and announced her engagement. My father sat numb at the table eating his big red fists and flushing painfully. He was not the talking kind in public, being a shy, silent man with a fear of people who bathed, and starched their shirts.

A week later my father walked up the high hill beyond the town and knocked slowly, cautiously on the door of my grandfather's house. Years later, when my grandfather would tell me the story, he would shake his great, bearded head and laugh. And my grandfather, before he felt the horror of death coming toward him, and before his fine body began to dry up and his marrow and muscles degenerate systematically into senile expectancy, was a fine figure of a laughing man. His white beard and his bright-eyed alertness gave him the look of God in Michelangelo's murals in the Sistine Chapel that I saw with a shock years later in Rome.

My grandfather was cleaning his shotguns at the time of the visit, he would tell; the teal and canvasbacks were flying past in vast honking V's, and he wanted a few wrapped in bacon and roasted in his Dutch oven. My grandmother was dead at the time and the old man was a fine cook—something his daughter, my mother, never was.

My grandfather answered my father's knock, came to the door and looked down at my father, squinting suspiciously at the shaking bridegroom-elect.

"Well, Pete, what is it?" My grandfather had the voice of a bull and an icy-blue eye, like a frozen gimlet.

"Well—I tell you, I'm not aiming to marry Vicky."

"Dammit man,"—my grandfather looked into the barrel of his shotgun—"the invitations are already out. Hand-printed and mailed."

"I know. None of my doing."

"She's a pretty girl."

"Very," said my father, pulling apart some hawthorne blossoms in the doorway.

[12]

"Comes from a fine family. If I *do* say so myself."

"Yes."

"I've ordered a steer barbecued and two kegs of hard cider and, hell, man, I'm not going to let you break a young innocent girl's heart." And as he said that, my grandfather said, he turned away and picked up his other gun—a single-barreled, silver-hammered shotgun and began to polish its walnut stock with his shirt tail, looking at my father as if he were a refractory lout.

"You go home, Pete, and get some sleep. See you at the wedding."

"Good day—sir."

"Good-bye, Pete," said my grandfather and went out to his mint bed to have a big laugh for himself and gather some greens for a drink. He said my father never had any more backbone than a banana and that the shotguns weren't at all necessary—he just happened to be cleaning them when my father called and they helped inspire confidence in the coming wedding.

Pete Ormsbee went down to the saloon and had two beers, ate two free lunches and went to his shop and filled his pack-sack, took out his bank savings and lit out for the tall timber just as night fell. Of course he was an honest man and so he stopped at the sawmill to settle his lumber account and my mother, driving my Uncle Thoreau's blind mare, found him there staring into the blinking rain puddles.

Vicky Sewall could talk. I have never heard anyone who could talk as long or as steadily as she could. Her voice was low and musical but as she went along, it beat on the sand bars of her temper, then it wrecked itself on her rage, grew high-pitched and then nothing could stop her or turn off her flow of words. The storm of absurdities and abuse had to blow itself out.

That night my father slept at my grandfather's house, and Vicky was up all night burning some cake she was helping bake for her wedding day. She never learned to bake.

My father and mother were married at my grandfather's house. My father was very flushed and wet and silent and only partly drunk, and my uncle would give him whiskey now and again and my father would swallow it and stand and sweat and eat his big red fists until my mother told him to stop and brush his hair out of his eyes.

My father was a churchless man. He had God always in mind, and feared Him, and later cursed Him, and then when my mother had pulled his character apart, he ignored God and withdrew into his own battered soul. My mother was high church, full church, holy church. Ready for the straw pen or High Anglicanism, just to have something to talk about. She loved the glitter and flow and the smooth prayer and high hymns and the holy clatter of people giving God a good reference. She was beautifully plastic with no need or respect for spiritual environment.

My father almost did not answer when the minister asked him if he would take this woman as his lawfully wedded wife.

But he did, after choking a few moments on his thoughts. *The goat call, the Pan cry, the fleeing forests were not as strong as the Sewalls.*

The happy couple went away to New York City for a honeymoon. My father was frightened to death of the grinding horse cars and the thunder of elevated trains and the rush of people all going to foul places in a hurry. He sat sullen in sodden apathy in his hotel room.

He thought of the spermy earth seeded and ready for spring and the bursting green earth seasons. . . .

But if my father didn't like New York, he liked Antioch less when he got back. The ape gabble of the streets made him shiver. The happy couple set up temporary quarters at my grandfather's house while my father went around looking for a farm with a ripe deliberation. He wanted to take up the thick woven fabric of his desires.

The soil was calling him again and now that he had a wife he wanted to feel again the soft loam of fertile fields and measure the length of a tree with an axe. Half articulate, sweating with hope, he tried to make Vicky understand.

Among other things, my mother's brother Thoreau sold farms. Day after day his blind red mare would trot out King Road, headed for valleys where the crops were ripening under a warm sun, and where sheep and good Guernsey cows stood in green meadows, watching them pass with chewing jaws and beautifully stupid eyes. There was something in the seductiveness of the waiting earth that thrilled my father.

My father had saved enough to buy a good farm and with his strong shoulders and sturdy body he dreamed of filled barns and cackling chickens and a writhing grape arbor over the back door. He never lost this vision—even later when he was head over heels in debt and was pointed out as one of the biggest holders of second-rate real estate in Antioch, when there wasn't enough bread on the table, he could walk into any of the Coppard Banks and get fifty or sixty thousand dollar loans to buy more shaggy, rotting street front property—but he still talked of the farm. He consumed himself—eating his own meat in bitter futility in a city.

He was a simple man who got simpler as he grew older.

There was something solid and firm about him, something calm and even about his outlook on life—an outlook he fumbled and faltered with. I never remember him saying a brilliant thing or gloating over the hopes of ever being wealthy in the sense of having real cash in the bank. His mind never worked in that way. He loved the land and I came to know the lost burial of his hopes on his face. He loved his children—and at times he admired the hot wired wonder that was his wife's mind—but he knew what he wanted and lost—a farm and fields and old trees and the scent of hay and the buzz of bees and the good earth like a night beast drinking in the rain. But when I knew him well the autumnal dusk had clouded all that from his vision.

He was surprised that Vicky had never protested his hunt for a farm. He would return at evening with bags of soil and samples of crops and eat his meal with loud animal noises that my mother could never cure him of. Then he would light his pipe and grunt it into burning clearly and he would look into the fire and say:

"Saw some nice land today . . ."

My father always started that way. I wasn't born then—but in later years I often heard that direful opening gun of a lost campaign. My mother would pucker up her small mouth and say:

"Land—*land*. Can you eat it—cook it, put it into your mouth? A big grown man acting like a child with a bucket of dirt on the front steps!"

I suppose in those days he still tried to dam the flood of words with a little touch of humor.

"Now, Vicky—you know you can't eat land—but land can feed you."

"Fiddle-dee-dee, Pete Ormsbee."

"It's a good farm . . ."

And then my mother would flood the room with her talk. Not directly protesting—just talking around the project, nibbling away any encouragement he may have got, driving his plans into a corner and taking them apart not by logic but by a flood of words. Of course she may not have talked too much before my brothers and I were born. She was very pretty and I think my father grew to love her very much. And she—although I couldn't swear—at that time she, too, must have been in the first flush of sexual experience and must have felt a glow of pleasure in the sturdy handsome man with brown curly hair and small teeth and big nose. She was of turbulent blood and the pulsing conduits of her body flushed her cheeks all her life.

The land hunt terminated one day when my mother said she was going to have a baby and *she* wasn't going to have it in the wilderness. Besides which, they were eating into their nest egg and my father had better get back to cabinet-making before his wife and child starved to death and they had to get charity to support them. My mother was always very dramatic at such times. I have often witnessed her performances when my father wanted to break away and do something he had set his heart on. Her emotions were always nakedly projected and her words flowed with a steady pace.

"Go ahead—go ahead—walk in cow manure over your boot tops. A peasant you are and a peasant you'll die! But my children are going to get educated and are going to be somebody. Not a farmer—not a clumsy cabinetmaker. Do what you want. I can take care of them. I'll scrub floors. I'll wash windows. Don't think I'll not. I've got no pride— not a thumbful. Let the town talk. I'll get a bucket and a brush and scrub floors for my children. I'm thin and frail but while there is still an ounce of strength in my feeble arms, they'll *not* want for anything. I don't mind scrubbing floors—not for *my* children!"

My father knew he was licked. When my mother's daydreams reached the floor-scrubbing stage he would light his pipe and pick up a walnut or oak dowel and rub it with sandpaper and say:

"Now, Vicky, don't chew so." He always called her talking "chewing the wind." "Don't chew. I was only thinking out loud."

"Well, I must say—a fine way to talk to a wife! *Chew,* do I?"

"Do what you want, Vicky. I've got a highboy job to finish."

And my mother would do what she wanted. That time she went out alone and roamed the streets and found the yellow house and made my father think he wanted it. It was old but well built—not that she ever knew anything about construction—and it was near the business section on Jefferson Street, and she wanted to be a mistress of a house and tie my father to the town, put his hopes into a state of spiritual refrigeration.

My father did not protest too much. He never protested too much against anything life did to him. He admired the old trees on the plot, the back stretch of garden and the old decaying peach and apple orchard. He sniffed at the outhouse, felt the old silvered wood of the tool and vegetable shed, and let my mother lead him to Jake Fry's office on Coppard Square, where he turned over his cash for a title to the property. Naked insurrection did not rise in him. Painfully he scratched his name as Vicky had taught him to.

He spent three days lettering a sign after a sample printed out by my mother. He had never had much education and could not read and write very well when he was married.

Vicky believed in education—up to a point. That week he hung out his sign.

PETER ORMSBEE
Cabinet Maker and Wood Work
of All Kinds
Estimates Cheerfully Given

The last line was my Uncle Thoreau's suggestion. Big business methods always. So the dream of land faded from my father's eyes—for a while, anyway. He moved his lathe and his saws and glue pot and shiny steel tools into half of the tool shed. He turned over the soil and tested it and nodded that it was good and planted it with tomatoes and corn and lettuce and turnips and potatoes. It wasn't much but it was something.

Then while business was slow he worked twelve hours a day in the steel mills taping vents and pouring slag and coming home to badly cooked meals and a lot of talk about how proud he should be that he was now a landholder and a citizen of a fine town.

A skeletonized love affair went on for a while and then Vicky felt other urges.

In time my mother had four children—all boys. The first in 1890. She was a tiny woman and we were all born good-sized babies. She never had any trouble. And only I was helped into the world by a real doctor. My mother didn't need a doctor but it was the proper thing by 1907 to have one in at a birth. There was even talk of going to a hospital for the event, but my mother would have none of those silly ideas. Even doctors she thought were unprincipled charlatans.

She named all the children with names beginning with D. Some dream she had once had told her that great men

[19]

would be born to her if she named them that way. (My grandfather said she had dreamed of the Devil.) Of course my father never was asked what we should be called.

My oldest brother was called Driscoll. Dennis and Douglas came as soon after him as they biologically could. I waited several years and then was born as a mere interruption of one of my mother's get-rich lumber schemes. I was incredibly imminent after the papers were signed. I sometimes think I wasn't planned—but happened because my mother was too entangled in a lumber yard deal to remember that I was being processed. I was called David —from the Bible—which Vicky had heard of, but never read.

Anyway, after that my father moved into the third floor, which had once been an attic and which he had paneled off and fitted out as a sort of special workshop where he could continue working at chairs and benches when cold weather drove him from the tool shed.

But all this, most of what I have put down here, was before I was born. I have thought a great deal of all the stories I had heard about my mother and father and have compared what they told of each other and perhaps I have not dealt fairly with their early life together. Perhaps.

My mother was very pretty and my father was very young and strong and they were very popular. The patterns that their lives were to follow may not have been too well molded—yet from all I have heard of this period of their lives they did not vary very far from what I have set down. In her way Vicky was always insatiably romantic about wealth and social position.

I remember my father telling of the early cold morning —a spring day in May—on which I had been born, and saying he went into the house to look me over and found half the bedding in front of the bedroom door and Uncle Thoreau's wife Netta—fat, round, gin-smelling, good-hearted Aunt Netta—whispering that Doctor Watson was in there and would my father be a good man and get his bedding up on the top floor before the doctor tripped over it. My father did. He guessed his life would be more sterile than ever now.

It is a scene I have often pictured yet there were no words to it. My father never said what he thought at this development and my Aunt Netta wasn't one to waste words. He knew he never would sleep in that bedroom again. Vicky was through with that *foolishness*.

I think he just threw the bedding over his shoulder and went limping up the stairs to his future bedroom. He always limped badly when something hurt or annoyed him.

TWO

MOST OF THIS happened before I was born. I arrived, a haggard transient, and stayed and howled away the nights.

I was one of those children who got along fine with himself and it was just as well. My mother wasn't very expert with children. My father loved us all with a gripping love tenderly expressed by his brown eyes and his soft kind mouth—but he was hard put upon to feed our hunger and keep the roof of the yellow house repaired over our heads. There were always bills, debts extending indefinitely into the future.

I remember first the goodness of sunshine and the great pleasure of soil and grass and my bare feet in them—wet with dew, and a luxurious buttery gluttony for life. But it was all emotion and I don't carry over any images beyond the swaying of the great oak that I lay under as an infant, and the hiss of wind among its leaves and dimly, far away, the lush tingle of the trolley bell. And the fear, the black-and-indigo of summer storm sounds.

I was four when images came and stayed and etched themselves in my limp foolish memory. I was pulling three little strawberry boxes tied together with string and I was howling like a train at a crossing. Already I had a yeastily stirring yearning for distant places.

One day I was eight. . . .

It was a fine sunny day, the heated tar street in front of the house gave off scent and heat haze. My grandfather drove up in his buggy, the little paint pony digging his newly shod feet into the soft tar pavement, snorting vague inarticulate sounds through his big yellow teeth.

"Hello, Davey," Gramp said, taking his pipe from his mouth and patting the flank of his pony. "Hot enough to fry a lawyer alive."

"Hello, Gramp," I said with awe and respect. For many years I was to confuse Abner Jonathan Sewall with God. His white dramatic beard—an Assyrian flood of pale ringlets—his loud voice, the icy-blue eyes and great knotted brown hands were to me signs of force and power. He had all his own teeth—big and yellow like kernels of corn. He was beginning to bend a little with the years and he had taken to hiding his left hand, from which the two smaller fingers were missing. He had lost them in action at Cold Harbor—and the more he thought of the people he had saved the Union for, the less proud he was of his war wounds. His eyebrows, stiff and thick, surrounded his eyes like heraldic lions.

"Come for a ride, Davey."

"Mom said stay in the yard."

"Come on, hop in and I'll buy you an ice-cream cone to hide your face up to the ears."

My grandfather opened the gate and I hurried across the brick walk, watching the paint-colored pony kick at flies with his little cruel hoofs.

Gramp lifted me up and I smelled good whiskey and old briar pipe and soap and clean linen. I sat on the buggy seat very frightened and very proud. I had never been that high over the street before. I was cantilevered over the cobblestones and felt anything but brave.

My mother came walking up the street on tiny heeled

[23]

shoes, waving a small handkerchief in her pretty warm face.

"Where is the child going?"

"I'm taking Davey downtown."

My mother stopped and smiled. I can see her as she was then, as I really saw her for the first time and remembered her. Tiny, red-gold hair worn in a wave and back to a bun, an abbreviated nose—very pert, very small—beautiful gray eyes and a darting glance and a rosebud mouth, her tiny, well-built body swaying, delicate wrists and ankles in motion.

"He hasn't been well. Delicate throat."

Gramp got into the buggy and took up the reins. "He'll live."

"Don't upset his stomach," Vicky said to the stonily impassive back. "It's very tender."

"Giddup!"

There never was anything the matter with my throat and stomach. But it gave my mother an excuse to take me over to Aunt Netta while she wandered over the town looking for bargains in corner lots, lumber or a scheme for a city bath.

"Wait."

"What's brewing?" asked Gramp, relighting his pipe, pulling in the waltzing paint pony.

My mother danced back on her small feet and waved her arms over her head. Behind her the shade trees looked Brobdingnagian and drowsy in their green leaves.

"I'm buying that stand of oak near Western Brook. I'll have it cut and stacked for drying and make a fortune in it. Oak is scarce and boards are sky high."

"That oak is no good—full of rot and mildew. You're a damn fool, Vicky . . ."

"Now, Father, I know lumber and I know cutting and

this stand should get me at least a hundred thousand feet of prime board. . . ."

"Lucky if it cuts half that. Well, it's your money—or rather, Pete's. Go on, Roger!"

Roger was the paint pony. Gramp flicked the shaggy back with a flip of the whip and we went down the street swiftly, Gramp looking at me from under a pale, decisive eyebrow.

I heard my mother talking. When we were half way down the street I turned and looked back. Vicky was standing in the middle of the street and shouting at us something about "a steam saw and carload timber lots . . ." that untrammeled expression still in her face. . . .

We turned a corner and the paint pony went along swiftly.

"You got yourself a mother, Davey. . . ." The finely cut aquiline nose was wrinkled in thought.

"Yes, Gramp."

"A hellcat for fair and a fool for money in the bargain."

"Is Roger a boy horse?"

"Huh—he's a gelding."

"Is that a boy or girl horse?"

"It doesn't make much difference, Davey, as far as Roger is concerned."

"We going to the woods today, Gramp?"

My grandfather turned a blue eye on me and with his mutilated hand pressed down the burning tobacco in his briar pipe. I could feel an inexplicable surge fill him with anger.

"Court today. God-damn lawyers are feasting on my ribs and pulling the lean meat off my bones. Giddup, Roger!"

Roger felt the old man's anger and stopped playing and swaying and got down to pulling. Antioch was a city of six hundred thousand then and hadn't been a village for a hundred years, yet it still clung to certain habits of life that belong to a town, any American town. But not for long. The Coppards and the Cruikshanks were bringing in more Polacks and Hunkies and black men onto the bulky escarped ridges to work the coal diggings, to stand over pouring steel and to sweat unloading ore boats. Solid bourgeois and mercantile families were coming up.

A purling, once-clean river, the Jefferson, far from its hill snows and pine slopes, ran through Antioch, dividing the business section of Jefferson Street and Coppard Square from the rank, weed-grown slag heaps and great belching gas-poisoned air of the steel mills and Polack Point where the workers lived. More and more the cheap little developments sprang up under the sooty snouts of the furnaces and pig-iron piles and railways—more and more the slum people of Antioch were being pushed across the river, cowed and apprehensive of the future.

Only King George Road was safe from the invasion of soot and progress. It stood east of the city and was part of it according to the tax board—an old road shaded in elm and shaggy tulip trees, almost parklike in its greenery, long lawns and the sprawling estates of the many Coppards and Cruikshanks and their in-laws and lawyers and doctors and henchmen. The old Yankee families made polite resistance and fled.

Slowly the steel mills expanded and the coal mines threw up more slate and rock, mixed with mill slag, and marched barbed-wire fences deeper into the city. Canning plants and carriage works and makers of pots and river boats added to the confusion. A few decades would see the city all one vast slum of workers and the miserable little shops and saloons that catered to them. But when I was a boy, only the threat and the growing slag heaps were the visible menace, slipping in dusty, tenacious ways along the old avenues. But always growing.

Roger pulled the buggy up Jefferson Street for the Court House Square. Gramp flipped his whip around in the sunny air and now he smiled at me and put it back in its socket after his vehement denunciation of lawyers.

"Never mind. I'll lick them yet."

"You will, Gramp. You can lick anybody."

For twenty years before I was born my grandfather had fought for his hill acres in the law courts. Abner Jonathan Sewall, everyone said, was a remarkable man to hold out so long against the interest of the Coppards and Cruikshanks.

He was a pioneer, one of those who, instead of going West in his covered wagon, had come East. History books have overlooked his kind. Coming East was harder than going West.

The Sewalls had taken up land grants long ago along the Sante Fe and in the Black Hills and along the California valleys. Just before the Civil War, my grandfather had come East, a pioneer beating farther and farther east of the Mississippi until he came to Antioch. He bought the high hills west of the town, the whole Monongahela Range. Here he raised ugly long-horned cattle near the rich Eastern markets and grew his own hay and corn. Here he raised many a ruckus, yodeled benignly in his cups, raised a brood.

The Coppards had invaded his holding while he was off commanding a section of Sherman's raiders, and after the war he had fought them and their interests and beaten them back from his acres in a vast scuffle of legal intrigues.

But in time, as the hills proved rich with coal and ore, they had come again with land claims and stream rights, and my grandfather spent his days in court battles. His wife died; epidemic carried off all his brood but Vicky and Thoreau.

The slag piles were maneuvering on the boundaries of his fields. The stink and heat of steel-making seared his fields and burned out his soil, and he fought on.

Sell out completely he wouldn't. Law courts and lawyers cost much money. He had lost the fertile acres around the city of Antioch. He had been driven to the hills. But he fought on. No one gave him much of a chance to hold on to his last hills. Intricate negotiations with the politicians were being used against him.

Roger pulled up before Blue Peter's Dutch Beer Garden and Saloon. Gramp tied Roger to the iron ring at the curb and went into the garden. We sat at a small table while Gramp drank two steins of foamy beer and I ate my first pretzel. And pigged for more.

A fat man with no hair on his head—not even eyebrows —came over, wiping his egg-shaped brow and his chins of whiskey-burnt fleshy wheels.

"Hell's bells, Abner—it's too hot to sit in court. Let's get a postponement and go after some brook trout. Luminous spotted blue ones fried in bread crumbs."

"No," said Gramp.

"I can just see them fat beauties leaping in bacon fat and a big pot of coffee coming to boil."

Gramp wiped beer from his white beard. "Damn it, Jake Fry, I've no time for that. I may die any day now and I want those land titles safe for my family. For Davey, here. Davey, this is Jake Fry—a lawyer and of course a skunk— but not too bad a fellow." (For years I remember them talking like this over beer.)

"How do, Mr. Fry," I said, nibbling around the edge of a fresh pretzel.

"How do, young man," said the fat, hairless face from between imperishable china teeth. "Well, I hope you have a better temper than your grandfather. He's pure rattlesnake crossed with bear and lacks a modulated courtroom voice."

"Have a beer, Fry, and stop talking until we get to court."

The lawyer opened the first two buttons of his vast, gutcovering pants and fanned air over his big belly with an old straw hat. Then he winked at me and buried his face in a mug of beer. I watched as he came out of it snorting, wiping his vast butter moon of a face with a careless gesture of the back of his wurst-fingered hand. He leaned over and tapped his nose with the biggest of his suety fingers, using an attentive, creepy touch.

"I've been talking to Ned Wonderly."

"I don't mix in politics," said Gramp, probing the rays of sunlight in his wide beard.

The lawyer tapped his nose again. "Maybe not. But he can do you a favor."

"Never ask for favors—never have—never will."

"He's on the outs with the Coppards. Judge Asbury is his man."

My grandfather looked away to where the river ore boats were making a great clatter among a silver chaos of lifting cranes.

"I've got to get Davey some ice cream. See you in court, Fry."

The lawyer opened another button and rubbed his gut with delicious agonizing stroking. "Look, Ned wants to make a ward out of your holdings and vote your cattle men in city elections. He can help you—if you help *him*."

My grandfather held me by the hand. He smiled down at me with a significant wink. "What will it be, Davey? Strawberry or chocolate?"

"Thank you, Gramp. Chocolate."

The lawyer had collapsed backwards in his seat and now, more unbuttoned and fanning and rubbing, he signaled the waitress for another beer with a grave serenity.

Shyly I pulled on the old man's arm.

"What, Davey?"

"Could I have nuts on the ice cream?"

"Hell, boy—of course. And a red cherry to top it off."

It was a long time ago—but I remember it all. The first clear series of events I remember—remember better than the things that happened last month. . . . The last time I saw Jake Fry was during 1929. He was a flabby thin old man, a physical outrage, living on buttermilk and gruel—a world-famous corporation lawyer and lobbyist for the steel and chemical companies. He was sitting behind gold-rimmed glasses in a big black Lincoln, the motor running, staring into space. My brother Driscoll had once been a member of his famous law firm. . . .

I nodded to him—not expecting him to remember me. He stared. Then he tapped one thin yellow-spotted finger to his skinny nose and winked a pious mauve-gray smile.

"Hello, Davey. Have any chocolate ice cream lately?"

I shook my head and for a moment did not remember. I had just lost my last five hundred dollars in the crash of the bull market.

Old Jake Fry tapped his nose again and said, in a suffocating voice, "And a red cherry to top it off . . ."

I smiled and remembered—and the past held us.

He died two months later and was buried with great honors after a special high Mass.

He left all his money to the Harvard Law School. Although he was a self-educated lawyer, they had given him an honorary degree after the Tea Pot Dome scandals . . .

My brother Driscoll went to Harvard to make the official address, setting up the Fry Fund.

Gramp lost his case in three hours—that first afternoon, I remember—which Jake Fry told us outside the courthouse was some sort of a God-damned record in my grandfather's dealings with the court. Gramp said the idea of God is too useful to bigots. The fat lawyer fanned his big belly with his straw hat and wiped sweat from his egg-shaped forehead while he admired a fine spaniel barking at Roger.

"Well, Sewall, you'll never learn to let your lawyer do your talking for you."

Gramp lifted up the iron weight that had held Roger in front of the courthouse and got up beside me in the buggy.

"I guess not, Fry. Now go swill yourself stupefied and send me your bill."

"Hell, I don't want your money. I'm attorney for the railroad now and I just fight your cases for the fun of it. I find them momentarily diverting."

My grandfather smiled. "Charity?"

"No." Jake Fry was suddenly serious, no longer lazy, lymphatic, he was a fat, wet, uncomfortable, serious man. "You haven't a Chinaman's chance of holding out against the mines and steel mills. But—well—I sort of want you to."

"Personal grudge fight with the Coppards?"

"No, Sewall. The Frys founded this city—stuck it out through rain and sleet and fire and the damnedest northwesters people ever saw. I have my embittered meditations when I'm full of beer. It was a pretty town once—well, just like I was a pretty boy once—nice hair and teeth and no big gut to carry around. I don't know. I guess I just get sloppy and sentimental over the old way and the good ways and hate myself for the corporation legal skunk I've become. See you in court next week. Slag-pile case on the calendar."

" 'Bye, Fry. Get on, Roger."

The fat dumpling of a lawyer slapped Roger on the rump and we clattered down to the Jefferson Street Bridge. My grandfather sat a long time, not saying anything, that hierarchical countenance of his very reposed. Then he pulled his great beard into some sort of order and let Roger trot slowly across the wooden bridge floor, his hoofs like sporadic thunder on the loose rattling planks.

"Something happening to people, Davey. They seem to be slumbering placidly and then they surprise you."

"Yes, Gramp."

"I don't know. The land and crops and the cattle and the fun of cutting hay and drinking cider and buttermilk seems to have gone out of them. Their comparative safety is in danger. The old books and the old gods and the little respects for their souls and for their neighbors' honor are going. Nothing has come in to revivify their spirits."

"Does Roger sweat, too, Gramp?"

"Huh, Davey? Oh! Yes, sometimes. I guess we've killed off the wrong people. They died in wagon trains and starved off in pine clearings and got slaughtered at Little Round Top, at Bull Run and on the deltas. The febrile clamor and agitation are empty sound now."

"Why does a stone make ripples, Gramp, when you drop it in water?"

"Because you can't stir up anything without sending out a lot of news of it to other people. Damn it—I'm thinking out loud. Boy, you ask the damnedest questions."

I asked no more—for five minutes.

We were out of the city now, moving toward the fields

and the slowly lofting hills. A hot sun ran ahead of us like fairy fire and heated the road we were to pass. King Road was once part of King George Road but had lost its manners and part of its name and was not the neat, rich, tailored part of valuable real estate. Tortoises and willow stumps and the woof and warp of weaving corn sat in the sun.

The road ran a long way back into the hills. It went past old farmhouses and stone walls too old to mind their manners while crossing fields. It went by very old trees, and my grandfather knew them all and could tell me their names, and some trees had special names and he told them to me. Old Moll and Shaggy Sam and The Hanging Oak and The Ghost of Elm Corner. There were red-berried poison sumac and honeysuckle.

Walking over the hills, the power cables led off to the muck of the mine shafts and the great lifting clouds of poison and gas of the smelting furnaces. Little cars of slag and red ore dust ran in deep wounds cut across the fields; and little engines drove dirty, steamy messes of scalding scum across mired brooks, where the stuff was dumped and pitched onto growing piles that added more evil boils to the green land. A ghoul fog of smoke donned its sheet and we were haunted by it until the last gash in the soil was past. Dead perch and breams and pout and pickerel floated belly up in the dirty streams. . . .

But as we came nearer to the Monongahela Range, the land lifted its head and threw off the pall of coal dust and mud and steel slag. King birds and indigo wrens met us.

My grandfather owned this Range and fought for it. Bits had been nibbled away from it—he had lost a forty-acre corner that day in court—but the backbone of the Range was still his. We passed his herds of Guernseys and big, beefy long-horns, his hay fields, yellow-gold in the sun, and his corn nodding like merry beggars on the hillsides.

Fennel and sweet cicely scented the air. I saw woodchucks.

Many old oaks led up to his house. The ground was good, dark, packed soil, the hedges were full of red flowers, and the barberry and whitethorn had never been clipped. The house was stone—field stone—built by my grandfather and his cowhands long ago. It was not in any style but a good thing. Popular Long Island real estate firms now mimic it and call it American Farmhouse.

Yew and boxwood and some china trees and willows grew in the front garden. There was no lawn, only this huge front garden and spreading fungi in bark crevices. The rose garden was L-shaped and ran around a corner of the house as if ready to invade the big barns. Rambler roses walked up the walls of the house and ivy wigged one of the south gables.

It looked as enduring as Roman aqueducts.

(*A swank golf club has a sandtrap there today.*)

Rip, the old colored man, came to take Roger to his stable.

"My, how the boy has grown, Major," said the Negro, giving me a searching, raffish look.

"Give the horse a rub-down, you black loafer and keep your lip buttoned."

Rip looked at me and winked. As if to say, "*We done lost that lawsuit today, white boy.*"

Inside in the big living room I drank warm milk which I disliked udder-fresh, but which I could not refuse under my grandfather's angry eyes. I swallowed the stuff and built a big wet mustache of it on my upper lip. I liked Gramp's house. No curtains, no drapes. Knotted pine walls (before they were fashionable, too), seemingly acres of hooked, hand-woven rugs—the great stone fireplaces and the Dutch oven—aged into a polished ebony by many logs. And the rifles in perfect order ranged over the mantel, and

[34]

Gramp's picture in his Major's uniform, with his beard some brown color and his eyes not so hurt or his mouth so narrow. And having all his fingers. A fine figure of man, my mother always would say—and so he was. Tall, broad, alive—full of life and a youth that had been toiled out of him by his troubles and his hard work on the Range. Eyes still staring defiantly, but old age working, too.

And a small painted thing of my grandmother, dead a long time. A small face with a pert nose and sad eyes and very thin hands—a little like her daughter Vicky—but with none of that flame-like darty alertness my mother had. None of that nervous unreliable joviality.

"Finished?" Gramp asked me.

"Almost."

"Last drop is the healthiest," he growled, lighting his briar until he looked like a fire god puffing white plumes from his wide nostrils. I gulped a cool translucent flow of spring water to settle the gagging milk.

"Yes, Gramp."

"Let's read, huh?"

I nodded and wiped my wet upper lip on a sleeve. Of all the family, Gramp was the only one to own books or read them. He was—until my brother Driscoll and I got the habit—the only habitual reader among us. Uncle Thoreau, Aunt Netta, my mother and father never read a book in their lives. I never saw them do anything more than open a mail-order catalogue or a magazine or *The Antioch Advocate*. They all had a serious hesitation about the printed word.

But Gramp had shelves full of books. Fine books. Good, well-bound books, dusty, antiquated volumes, cheap reprints. Treasures that he never sold, no matter how much he needed money for lawyers or taxes.

He pulled an old favorite of mine from the shelf, puffed

his pipe into a hot ember and began to gather momentum with his deep, solemn reading voice. Outside, the trees murmured in a hot summer wind and the brook talked to the pebbles on its bottom. I dug my face into a Golden Russet apple, chewed and listened. . . .

Travels into Several Remote Nations of the World. A Voyage to Lilliput. By Lemuel Gulliver, first a Surgeon, and then a Captain of Several Ships . . .
My father had a small estate in *Nottinghamshire;* I was the Third of five sons. . . .

THREE

I SPENT A great deal of the summer at Gramp's. My mother did not mind. The air was good for me, she said.

Although I was the youngest child, I was not my mother's favorite. My brother Driscoll—or Dris, as everyone called him—was. Not that he received any better care than the rest of her sons, but of him she was proud; she was sure that he would be the family success, its earner of great wealth and glory. She would tell of her hopes, talking like a denouncing prophet; so sure.

In some strange way she knew, she decided that he was the chosen one of all the Ormsbee boys. I don't think we minded very much—at least not until we grew older and saw that it was always Driscoll who got the new suit and watch-and-chain and the new bicycle. Even Dris came to hate himself a little, and he was not a dramatic hypocrite.

I suppose I resented it more than the rest. I was younger, smaller and a little bit out of their lives—a pudgy, diminutive brat always underfoot. My father would look at me with that moist eye of his, that cock of his head to one side, and take me on his lap and sing to me in a deep baritone the simple folk songs that he had picked up in lumber camps and cattle-trading centers or while working as hired hand in some sun-filled field. But he was a shy man and too much rested on his shoulders which he did not understand. Always he had to toil late, a smoky lantern sooting up the tool shed while he built chairs and showcases and cabinets, and felt smothered in the heavy cloth of straitened circumstances.

And if things got very bad and my mother's little schemes to get rich failed (and they almost always did) he would go to the steel mills and toil in the heat of burning coke and steel, churning the molten contents of the furnaces with long slice bars until he could hardly crawl home to wash and gulp some food, while my mother stood over him, banging down the dreadful cindery food she had reheated for him and shouting at him in sudden exasperation for not getting better-paying work.

"Here, eat. Fill yourself full. A fine pass things have come to. You going off to the steel mills like any Hunky—tracking the house full of dirt and rust—and what *good* is it? Have I a fur coat or a diamond ring like Mrs. Jackski next door? Oh, no. And you an American and Mr. Jackski five years in this country and still speaking English like a broken saw. I'd rather scrub floors than have people think I married a mill Polack or a no-account Mick."

"Now, Vicky. City taxes are due and people aren't needing cabinets. . . ."

My mother rattled the dishes. "Eat—eat your fill. If it comes to scrubbing floors, I'm not too proud for it. My children come first. They are going to be somebody—have money—open the eyes of this town. Driscoll will be a big man some day—and *no* thanks to you."

And then my father would crawl up to his attic room and groan himself to sleep. Gramp said he invited maltreatment—that he manifestly was born to be a victim.

All her life my mother threatened to scrub floors for her family, but I never remember her scrubbing even her own. None of us believed she would. No one but Driscoll. He understood her better than the rest of us, as they both were always tense with expectancy.

[38]

I never saw much of my second brother, Dennis. He was up before dawn with his paper route. Afternoons he delivered packages for the stores, and evenings he would go off to Bible classes and come home late at night, crawl into his nightshirt and bang himself to his knees and pray for our souls with insensate zeal. He was tall and thin with burning eyes and bitten-down fingernails and a habit of honesty that cost him dearly in this practical world. Then he would become fuddled with piety and play his flageolet for hours.

My mother would herself collect his pay, rubbing a little cooking flour over her rosy cheeks and go down to see George Pigot, editor and owner of *The Antioch Advocate*. After that she would march into Burnett's Market, talk fat, shaggy Mr. Burnett into a nervous breakdown, haggle over his three-day-old breads and unsold sections of meat, and come home loaded down with bundles of stale food and, usually, with at least fifty cents more in wages than was coming to Dennis, the fury of persistence still flaring her small nostrils. She enjoyed pay day.

She enjoyed haggling with tradespeople. No one ever presented a bill to her and collected it without adding, dickering, complaints of shoddy underweight merchandise, or evil, incredulously sly methods. The milkman and baker dreaded to come around for payment. Once, for spite, she ran up a bread bill of forty dollars. My father had to pawn his best set of tempered steel tools to pay it off. Arrogant— a *femme fatale* to tradespeople, Vicky took her revenge on life from the meager morose peddlers of foodstuffs.

She was always at the tax office insisting her water meter was wrong, and the gas utilities and later the electric company always had to shut off service to collect their bills. But she never became passive to their routine. She remained persistently a bad debt.

[39]

Dennis never seemed to mind being stripped clean every pay day. He would make notes for his Bible classes and nod his colorless hairy head and kiss my mother on the cheek and go out into the cold of night to pick up empty milk cans for the farmers' market. Naturally my mother said she only invested this money for Dennis. And Dennis would roll his noncommittal yellow eyes and play his flute, not even grieved.

She bought chickens and sold their eggs until some guests came and then she would invade the hen house with a heavy axe and chase the clucking poultry with a helpless, hic-coughing leer until my father came out and took the axe away from her and killed off the egg layers for her singeing cooking. I never ate a good, well-cooked meal until I was old enough to sneak over to Aunt Netta's.

Or Vicky would buy up empty beer kegs, waiting for the summer brewery rush to get a high price for them. Very clever of her. Usually they had been used for kerosene and were, of course, worthless to the brewery. How she would seethe and hiss in agitation against the Beer Trust.

Driscoll also got a job after school as soon as he was tall enough to stand behind a counter with an inquiring look. He had a weak heart, my mother told all his employers (he was a young ox), but was bright as a whip and was a demon for figures. He swept law offices, collected for credit houses and hunted old furniture for Mrs. Alexander Cruikshank. He was too proud to have Vicky collect his wages— he saved them and presented them to her neatly folded, the silver coins wrapped in rolled paper, once a month. He resented being pampered by her but loved her too much to hurt her feelings. Driscoll was a beautiful, meaty child. He wore blond curls until he was six and then Gramp came along and cut them off down to the pink scalp and they had to send for the doctor because Vicky collapsed when she saw her shorn lamb.

My brother Douglas was the only one of us who took after my father. He was solid and square—not as tall as the rest of us—with a big nose and a habit of chewing his fists when angry. But he had a backbone and a droll, elfin way of speech.

He had more courage than my father—a bold, strong child with not too much loud laughter, but enough of a sense of humor to rub people the wrong way with odd, lazy sentences. He made a rhythmical vibrating sound at his work—a sort of tuneless hum.

He was the only one who ever stood up to my mother and let her talk at him while he smiled sweetly—like a stupid cat—and went on with whatever he was doing, carving a boat for me or stringing beads on a leather belt or cutting out little wooden figures with his jigsaw.

When I first remember him, Douglas was too young to work, my mother feeling that no child under ten should be forced to labor too hard for his bread. But when he was older he went into the steel mill against everyone's protest and became a water boy, then a screw boy and later a chipper. He said he wasn't going to horse around for peanuts; if he had to work, he would work in the mill and earn a man's wage. For years he and the truant officer played out a series of street wars that were famous in the city. Douglas hated school like Englishmen hate an epidemic among the Parsees.

It was rarely that we were all together. I remember one such evening. The snow lay thick on every street and a wind howled around the roof of the yellow house with oaths of depredation and forced its way through the paddings and wedges that had been placed around all doors and windows. We sat around the red-hot pot-belly stove in the dining room under the stained-glass gas fixture which my mother had salvaged from the bankruptcy of a Greek soda parlor.

Pete Ormsbee sat with his work-worn hands on his knees, smoking his pipe, looking at the stove's red surface, brooding over pedestrian facts. Dennis was polishing his shoes and Driscoll and Douglas were counting their collection of beer caps. I was watching my mother botch a length of cloth that she was trying to shape with blunt shears into a copy of a dress from *The Ladies' Home Journal*.

Dennis sometimes read the Bible but not for pleasure— only to light a monstrous piety. (Driscoll said he did it to sandpaper his soul.) But for the Bible there was not a book in the house except the Sears Roebuck catalogue. My father was a fine teller of stories but tonight the mood was not on him. He sat as if in a lethal chamber.

My mother at last gave up dressmaking, snipped the cloth into lengths for washcloths and threw the magazine into the stove. I sat on my haunches, tasting the full heat of the stove on my body.

"Damnation, taking people's good money and lying about things that can't be done in their pages! I've a good mind to write them a letter and ask them to pay for the cloth I ruined. Those rich fat magazines . . ."

"Now, Vicky," said Pete. "I told you to buy a dress."

"Well," said my mother, at last having something—some-one—to talk to, "throw it up to me I'm not stylish like other wives. That I work my fingers to the bone sewing my own rags means nothing. Go ahead—tell me what other woman scrimps and saves every stitch on her family's back—don't sit there like a stone wall. Tell me how wrong I am—how wasteful—how I ruined your life by not loving cow manure and hillbilly squalor."

My father did not relish the thought of his cold attic bedroom at the moment. He did not answer but put his fists against his mouth and looked at the stove and began to sweat profusely.

"Sit there. A log you are and a log you'll remain. Men are doing things, making fortunes, dressing their families, educating them, being proud of their wives—and I had to marry a log like you. I don't know why I ever did it. Victoria Sewall doing a thing like that."

We children went on with our tasks. This was the steady stream of lives. The torpid vindictive phrases left us cold.

"But it's no use, *Mr.* Ormsbee," went on my mother, growing very impersonal suddenly. "You may drive *me* to scrubbing floors—but my children are going to be educated right. Driscoll is going to become a lawyer . . ."

"No," my father said calmly.

"You'd rather have him a rich cabinetmaker like his father?"

My father got up, knocked out the dottle in his pipe on his fist and made for the door leading to the attic. "No lawyer. Not my son. The scum of the earth—that's what lawyers are. Leeches, sucking the life and happiness of the country away into their fat pockets. No lawyer—no, thank you."

My mother crossed to him, her tiny figure angry, almost dancing in rage, her eyes enormously distended in her small face.

"Once a peasant, always a boor. Don't *you* yell at me. In my father's home no one yelled at *me!* You hear me?"

My father raised his voice—one of the few times I had

ever heard him shout. It was a yelp of ruin and desolation—
the naked man in agony.

"NO LAWYER! ! !"

The next week Driscoll had a new suit and repaired shoes
with copper toes and he went to work for Jake Fry, sweeping out the offices, running out for food and whiskey for
the vast gut of his boss and learning how to fill in legal
papers in the meager light of the mahogany-colored legal
library.

My father never again mentioned his repugnance of the
profession. He never asked Driscoll how he was getting
on and how he liked his work. He had had his shout.

My mother was very proud of Driscoll. We knew now
that she felt that of all of us he was the most likely to
have the success he wanted from life.

When Driscoll had been working in the law offices a
year my mother called on her brother, my Uncle Thoreau
Sewall, and I then had the first inkling of what she expected
of my brother Driscoll.

"Now, Thoreau," she said, handing her brother some of
her bitter coffee and her rocky rock cake, "I'm looking for
a bit of something good. Want it to buy land in Driscoll's
name. Want to send him through college on what it in-
creases in value by the time he's twenty-one. Well?"

"Now, Vicky. You ain't planning to make that boy President of the United States, are you?"

I saw my mother's eyes open wide. "Don't be a fool. Not
that he isn't smarter than that fat fool, Teddy Roosevelt."

"What just are you aiming to make of him?"

"A success. A rich man. Someone to give his old mother
comfort in her old age. A place to lay her old head and
maybe a car and a fur coat and everything that goes with
having a bright son. He's a smart boy, Thoreau. I say I

want comfort and wealth—that's just part of it. Little part of it. Dris is a great man."

"Well," said my uncle, draining his huge mustache out of the dreadful coffee, "all mothers got dreams like that. Netta feels that way about all our kids."

"How many have you now?"

"Eleven and one on call. Netta is carrying again."

My mother looked up to where I was leafing through the mail-order catalogue on the floor.

"For shame. You're not a man—you're a menace."

"Ain't I, though." Uncle Thoreau leered.

"Well—can you find me a plot of land—not too dear—but something that will be worth a lot of money in ten, twelve years?"

"Might have something at that. For the future President of the United States. Ha ha!"

My mother refilled his cup with a smile, a smile astute and secretive.

"You pick up Davey and me ten o'clock tomorrow morning and we'll look around. More cake?"

"Well, Vicky, I'm always a little down on my feed when I come here. . . ."

But he didn't dare leave before he had finished his second cup of coffee and had, with extreme propriety, let some splintery cake into his stomach.

Next morning my Uncle Thoreau called for my mother and myself in his early brass-bound sputtering flivver. He earned a living, of sorts, selling real estate, insurance, coal, washing and sewing machines and a little item called "The Handy Dandy Handy Kitchen Kulture," which was a huge, badly printed book of wonderful secrets that would help the housewife in her tasks without toiling too much over a hot stove.

[45]

My Uncle Thoreau was in his early forties in those days. And even his father said he was the spitting image of Rudyard Kipling. And he was—a small, mousy little man with a fuzzy baldness and heavy—very heavy—black eyebrows and a huge mustache over a weak chin. And heavy, thick-lensed glasses. A yellowish, bilious man who always seemed distraught by his hairy, chubby fists.

My Uncle Thoreau was married to a big fat blonde woman whom I called Aunt Netta with much respect all my life. I was very fond of her. She mothered all of us brothers, wiped our noses, fed us well on her fine cooking and I think loved us as much as she loved her own wild and snotty brood. She was large, very fair; she was no doubt not very wise, but she was very kind and I even grew to forgive her her habit of gin drinking: the deplorable defect in a fine, generous nature.

With the years she became more and more a slave to the drink habit—yet she is the only person I ever met who did not drink because of emotional or neurotic reasons. As a young girl her teeth had been bad and the family remedy for toothache was to swish a mouthful of gin through the bad teeth. In this way, by such treacherous ambush, she had become a gin addict.

When she married she had all her teeth removed and replaced by the most perfect white uppers and lowers I have ever seen. With strangers she was shy. She would lower her head and try to bite her clavicle.

Poor Aunt Netta never could have her gin habit replaced like her teeth.

Uncle Thoreau had no bad habits. He did not drink or smoke or play cards or visit the houses above Polack Point. He only hated two people in his whole life: Henry Ford and J. D. Rockefeller. He had once had the local Ford Agency and the motor company had ruined him by forcing him to take more cars than the town could afford to buy. In three seasons he had a garage full of dated models and a drawer full of notes coming due. Henry Ford made him a militant atheist. Later he had been offered a job with an independent oil driller as field boss but the oil magnates had the independent's oil line cut, their oil cars set on fire. From then on my Uncle Thoreau never had a good word for the Rockefellers either. Every time they gave away a few millions to some front-page cause my Uncle Thoreau would say, "I wonder how many people died for that cash and how many independents were smashed for all that sweet newspaper gush *and* appropriately scoundrelly begging to be let into Heaven."

But my Uncle Thoreau was not a bitter man and did not believe in Heaven. Life was hard and Netta was on the gin more and more and the brood needed a lot of food and clothing and he was paying up his notes—but life pleased him. The atheists lost him and he became a radical agnostic of the Henry George school. . . .

As he drove us out toward the mills he was telling us about the future.

"I tell you, Vicky, we are living in a wonderful time. Our children will see the stuff that progress and machinery have done for the world in an era of easy living and good housing and clean, healthy people."

"You sound like a street-corner shouter, Thor," said my mother. "Where is this corner lot? At the North Pole?"

"Easy, Vicky. Another ten minutes. See that flower, Davey? That's myrtle—the flower of Venus."

"Drive on, Thor."

I didn't mind how long it took. I liked riding in a car. Even in a 1914 collection of rattling nuts and bolts.

The lot and buildings were on a grimy corner—a part of

the city still half country. A place of goats and tin cans and hovels built of city refuse and near a smoldering dump. Three little clapboard and tin-roofed shacks stood on the land from which were sold fly-specked canned goods, moldy remnants of yard goods and a typhoid-tasting ice cream (I had a cone of it).

"I don't think much of it," said my mother, sniffing the dump odors.

"Driscoll will make a fortune out of this in about ten or twenty years, Vicky. Trolley cars and parkways coming this way. The dump is filling out the neighborhood nice and level and this is a corner that's going to coin money with a two-story taxpayer in a few years. A & P stores and cheap cleaners and maybe a saloon downstairs. Dance hall, dentist or even a sewing-machine shop upstairs."

"It's not very pretty," said Vicky, looking over the bold-faced Hunky and Polack kids, some playing football with some tin cans, others behaving atrociously with some dirty yellow dogs.

My uncle removed wax from his hairy ear with a pinkie and laughed and was as happy as if he were creating a sonnet sequence.

"It's paying property. The rent from them shacks covers taxes and you don't do any repairs. No siree, not on these shoe boxes. Fifteen hundred dollars for the shebangee—one hundred and fifty feet by two hundred and all corner property. Five hundred down and the Home Loan will see you for the rest. Until the Single Tax comes, you're safe."

"Well," said my mother, sniffing a handkerchief touched with camphorated oil to hold back the dump.

My Uncle Thoreau prided himself on being a good business man. He pulled out some papers and slapped them in the palm of his hand. Tangible reality, he always said, got results.

"Signed, sealed and delivered in the name of Driscoll Ormsbee—with you his guardian until the proper age, as soon as you put your John Hancock right here."

"Don't be vulgar, Thor," said my mother, whose knowledge of American history was dim and chaotic.

"Huh, Vicky?"

"I'll take it."

My uncle got out to grind the flivver into life. "Get a horse," howled the Hunky and Polack kids as the motor dribbled away ingloriously. Uncle Thoreau spun it alive again.

"Got forty of them right here," yelled my Uncle Thoreau patting the heaving bonnet of the flivver. A sale of any kind made him very happy. We drove off with a snort and a stench of unburned gasoline.

"A happy moment, Vicky. You'll make slathers of money on it. What a world our children are going to inherit! I was born thirty years too soon."

Vicky—a bad scholar—was doing mental arithmetic with her eyes closed. "Keep still, Thor. I'm adding."

"Stop adding. In ten years—in 1924—nobody will know this part of the town—it will be so stylish. In twenty years nobody will know the world—it will be so different. It will be a fine place for everyone. The brotherhood of men on earth . . ."

A long time later I found out how right—or wrong—my Uncle Thoreau could be. The world did change. In 1931, when my brother Driscoll was running for the office of United States Senator, he sold the corner lot for fifty-two thousand dollars.

There was talk of having Vicky's stores and lofts condemned as fire traps, and Ned Wonderly, the political boss, didn't want the Democrats to pin that on my brother's record. My mother always said she lost a hundred thousand dollars on the deal. During the boom years, 1925 to 1929, Driscoll had refused to take a hundred and fifty thousand dollars for the corner.

But Vicky's arithmetic was always more from emotion than from Euclid.

Vicky didn't buy land for the rest of us. We didn't expect her to. Dennis read his Bible lessons and I would spend much time with Doug after working hours, watching him file his photograph collection of steamships and ocean tramps and cargo boats. Doug had no interest in Spanish pirate ships or Roman galleys. He admired the sleek, steel sides of modern shipping and collected hundreds of photographs of them.

He was proud to work in steel, proud to know he helped make the steel to weld and rivet these ships together. Like Pete, Doug loved solid, firm things, and a picture of a steel ship pounding through high seas thrilled him. When his collection grew too large, Vicky tossed it into the yard and Doug built himself a cabinet in the tool shed and carried on his collection.

Yet, except for several short river trips on brick and ore barges, he had in those days never been on water—never seen the sea.

It is cold. Sitting with a blanket around me, writing all this down, waiting for the late spring to color green the hills, I wonder why it is that, writing of my family, I can find none of those direct patterns laid down that were to lead all of us to whatever goals we were to go to. I can see faintly something stirring, but that clear wide road most novelists find—no sign of it yet. The light is bad. It will rain chill wetness soon. The tent leaks. . . .

FOUR

ANTIOCH WAS GROWING. Even I, in a black astrakhan cap, could not miss the fact. That August of 1914 the steel mills and mines, efficiently organized, were very busy. Yet the old country charm of a big city set down between hills on a fertile plain was still there. My brother Driscoll had me in charge and we wandered far over the grotesquely inconsistent city.

I was growing—like all my brothers—into a tall, wide male but I was not very bright. I was the fool of the litter, my mother would say—and perhaps I was. I touched life with deplorable results. Everyone was older. I was always running on shorter legs after someone older and taller. I was always losing my hats and handkerchiefs and mittens. I was a dreadfully tangled child, always on the knife edge of petty disaster. So Driscoll was appointed to take care of me after Dennis had left me to the world one wintry day, lying in a snowy gutter digging snow trenches, and had forgotten my existence while he went off to a church rally that was levying tribute to salve the souls of black children in Africa.

I was found at midnight—frozen blue, blubbering cold tears, my shoes full of icy water. My father found me, took me home, hugging me tight against his warm beating heart, and I went to bed and did not die or even catch a cold. Dennis was beaten to within an inch of his life in the tool shed in one of those rare mad rages my father sometimes had. I remember Dennis praying to God to forgive my father for walloping the prayer's behind.

I liked Antioch as Driscoll showed it to me. He was tall, handsome, well liked but a little too nosy after causes and effects. I never developed his natural fluid quality of charm. He had discovered books and was trying to make me read. I preferred to walk with him down to the river and watch the humpbacked boats come lurching along loaded with red iron ore. The hill ore was still not produced fast enough for the furnaces.

Driscoll and I would lie in the tall river grass, eating and chewing on sour grass seeds we had picked, kicking our heels on the hard, sun-baked clay.

"Once this was all ice and then the ice piled up and big rocks came down with new ice caps. Millions of years ago."

"Dris, how do you know?"

"I read it."

"Gramp reads a lot, too."

"And then the ice went away."

"Why?"

"Never mind, pipsqueak. Just listen to me." There was a bit of the martinet in Dris when he had me in tow.

"I like ice and them juices the Wop squirts on them."

"And then the valley was left when the ice went away and the hills were pushed back and all this was deep in good rich mud and the things grew and people came and built a city across the river banks and then they dug out coal and chopped down timber and the mills were put up and now Antioch is a great city. . . . Stop throwing rocks in the water, sprout."

"I like it—the way they skip across—bouncing sort of. . . ."

"Come on, brat," said Dris, "you've got no culture, just like the rest of the Ormsbees. . . ."

So even then I could see that my mother had put over the idea that the Ormsbees were peasants and not cultured like the Sewalls. Although, except for Gramp, none of the Sewalls had much education or love for books. Uncle Thoreau said he preferred raising flowers. He knew all their names and taught them to me.

I was learning to listen and not to talk too much, so I didn't question Driscoll's remark about my father's family.

I was beginning to understand the feuds between my parents, the simian sarcastic emphasis of their life together. There was always that sense of truce that could at any moment break into verbal warfare in which my father had no chance at all.

My father was doing well. He had hired two men to help him among his wood-shavings. He was busy all day and far into the night, yet we were always hard up for cash. Debts seemed to rise perpendicular all around us—like cliffs.

Vicky's schemes were not working out. The war boom had started, yet nothing my mother touched seemed to have any sense or knowledge about it. She rummaged the markets furiously and her appetite for gain was like a preposterous romantic lover.

Everything we could spare went into her schemes. Dennis handed over everything; Douglas had gone into the steel mills as a screw boy and was now a stripper, working his full time and overtime and coming home dirty and red from the great fires of the smelters—but proud of himself and his work, speaking in gushes explosively of the number of tons rolled.

Dris read law and drove Jake Fry around the state. Jake was busy with corporations in the war boom.

My father hated the war boom. Everyone else was all elated and ready to see millions of men die in great locked

[53]

combat, men now positively indignant at being kept out. I don't think in those early days anyone cared very much which side should win. But as the propaganda came through and the English cut the enemy cables we began to read *The Antioch Advocate* closer and grow hot and bothered over rapes and violated nuns and little children with their hands cut off. And women with their breasts torn out and their men marched off to be shot. The Kaiser took on a personal dreadfulness and we all came to hate him as an incarnation of all the evil of all the world.

And the mills never stopped dividends.

I remember when Dris pinned up a huge colored map of Europe in the dining room and began to tack it full of colored pins. Gramp had been over to have my father fit a new stock to his best shotgun and we had gathered around the hot stove to listen to Gramp read Charles Dickens.

Tonight the reading was not going so well.

Gramp kept looking at the map and then back to his book. It was *The Mystery of Edwin Drood* and Gramp had figured out an ending for the unfinished book and wanted to test it on Driscoll. But something bothered the old man and I saw it was the map. His voice, usually so calm, spoke in martial asthmatic tones.

"Whose idea of wallpaper was that?"

"Vicky's," said Driscoll. As we grew older we, for some reason—I think because they were so unlike other parents we knew—called our mother and father Vicky and Pete. "Vicky thought we ought to follow the war closely."

Vicky looked up from some wrong arithmetic she was working on. "I want them to understand what the times mean. It's a time for big men and big doings. The world is shaking and growing up. We'll all make our fortunes."

"You always were a hellcat and partly a fool, Vicky,"

said Gramp, closing his book and pulling off his silver-rimmed glasses. "It's the time of Antichrist *if* there were an Antichrist. The world will never recover from all this. We shall live out our time under dreadful artificial lights."

"Fiddlesticks," said Vicky. "You've been to court too much."

My father knocked out the dottle of his pipe on his work-worn palm. "We'll be in it soon."

Vicky threw her figures into the stove and tossed a shovelful of coal after them. "Nonsense. My boys will never be soldiers. That's all right for the slaves whipped into battle in Europe, but . . ."

I sat on the floor and looked up at all these people and I saw myself as a general and took an old paper bag and tore it open and began to draw a battle. For some time now I had been marking up every scrap of paper and, only a week before, I had been beaten with a broom handle in Vicky's hands for drawing in colored ink the most delightful mustaches on the fly-proud enlarged and hand-colored photographs hanging on the cold wall of the always-closed parlor.

I was drawing now while Gramp closed his eyes and ran his long white fingers through the curls of his carefully tended beard. A habit he had when he wanted to show his genuine ill manners.

"I've brooded and spawned out a lot of fools. I think I'll pack a horse and head for high timber and stay up above the fir line until the world comes to its senses or is forever irrevocably damned."

Pete Ormsbee shook his head. "I think we'll never see ourselves free of all this killing. It's going on and on."

Vicky stood up and rubbed her small pretty hands together. Then she looked at my father, her little head cocked to one side. "What you don't know about things would

fill a mill stream. Old men and farmers warming their be-
hinds by a hot stove while the world fights it out so that
their children shall all have a chance. By God, if I were a
European, I'd roll up my sleeves and go in there and knock
some sense into Kaiser Bill's head. I'd not sit here groaning
over bad dreams. To bed, Davey."

Gramp snorted. "You just said only whipped slaves are
soldiers."

"I'm going to enlist in the Canadian Army," said Dennis.
"I want to fight to keep God free."

My mother leaned over and slapped Dennis on the side
of his head. "Oh, you'll enlist and leave us all here to starve
on what your no-good father scrapes out of his lumber
shavings. You go to bed too, and when your country needs
you you'll enlist—and *not* before! The idea of going away
like this and helping them dirty Canucks . . ."

Gramp got up and reached for his old wolf pelt coat.
"Damn it, Vicky, he was only listening to you. Can't you
ever stop chewing your tongue?"

Vicky was in her element. "By the thumb of Daniel
Boone, there aren't enough men in this family—real men—
to hold a candle to a cider barrel. Vision—you none of you
have it. Well, except Driscoll and he's always got his face
stuck in them books. I think of what the world can give a
real man and then look around and it's enough to put skirts
on all of you."

"You don't make much sense," said Gramp, pulling on
his gloves. "Never did. But I guess you get the savage
ardors from some damn fool in my family history."

"I've got more sense in my little finger than your family
ever had in all its born days. And you, Papa—hiding out
there on the Monongahela, trying to get the better of smart
live wires like the Coppards and the Cruikshanks. Court-
fighting away your trees and cows for a bunch of mangy

[56]

man-eating lawyers and letting your family—your daughter
—live in rags when you *could* be a big business man and
cut more mine timber than anyone in the state. And don't
tell me there ain't enough meadow and hay for ten thousand more cattle up there, either . . . A fine hell of a thing
when a woman's own father thinks more of his pet oak
trees—and meadow flowers—than keeping the wind from
off her naked body. Well, I can take care of myself. I can
go out to work if I have to. . . ."

My mother was almost alone. My father had gone up
to his attic. Gramp had slipped out after giving his book
to Dris. And I was following my brothers upstairs to our
bedroom. Obstinately, loudly, Vicky's voice battered the
subject. . . ."

Douglas and Dennis slept together in one bed and Dris
and I shared another. I stripped to my long underwear and
shivered into bed and against Dris, who kicked me away
with a discourteous heel.

"I'm no stove. Warm your own side."

I shivered and closed my eyes. Vicky was coming up the
stairs with the oil lamp held high. Its rays shone into our
bedroom and I felt its light beat softly against my eyelids
and then it remained adamant once it got in focus.

"Gentlemen I'm raising, fine gentlemen! Leaving their
mother alone down there to shut up the house."

Dris gave a low mock snore. I wriggled my rump and
buried my head in the pillows. The window slammed shut
near my head as Vicky worked energetically on the ill-
fitting frame.

"Fresh air—you'd think it was good for you. How many
times must I tell you night air isn't healthy? You've all got
weak chests as it is. A fine thing if you all took sick and
I had a hospital on my hands. I'll raise you alive and kick-

ing and make something of you all yet. It's all right for old men and your fool of a father to talk about trouble—but you are all going to make something of yourselves."

She tucked Driscoll in and rubbed his head. "And a little respect from you, Dris—and be sure and pick up Davey from school tomorrow."

School was hell to me until I was transferred to the Indian Avenue High School. Dris would wait for me until I came out and walk me home as a precautionary measure.

Before that, I would have to fight my way home through the tough Irish and Polack kids and, after having my nose bloodied and my behind well kicked several times, I refused to go to school. I was no hero.

I was not the stuff that heroes were made of. I could give as good as I got but there was no hope of ever knocking down enough of the snotty-nosed dirty-pants Micks and Polacks to live in peace.

They ran in packs—dirty, undernourished, leering, foulmouthed and very wise to all licentiousness for their years. Their fathers worked in the mills or held small political jobs, and their sons were healthy and brutal and grasping. They pillaged milder children incessantly. Most of the children paid them tribute in the form of pennies and candies and ice-cream cones—but I couldn't, as we never got any spending money. Vicky needed all the loose change for her schemes.

Dris would call for me every afternoon and see me safely home. That duty had once belonged to my brother Doug—but he was now working full time at the steel mills. Doug's method of protection had been to grab two of the worst offenders and bang their heads together. Then he would boot them hard in the rear with his heavy shoes and send them off with a cuff on the ear. It was impressive and it got respect from the hoodlums.

[58]

My brother Driscoll handled matters differently. He would appear with a pocketful of buttons asking for the re-election of one of Ned Wonderly's old whiskey-soaked war horses and ask me which was the toughest gang at the school. I was asked to pick out the gang and then Dris would give me the buttons to hand out to the proud little thugs. He also got them invitations for free food at the political rallies and jobs handing out circulars and throwaways. In time they became his personal army and greeted him with jubilation and loyal verbal foulness.

Of course I was no longer molested. I became their "pal." I was even invited to their orgies. Their joy was bushwhacking, a disgraceful, happy expedient. At dusk they would form into gangs and run wild through the parks creeping up on lovers or yelling odd words at passing girls.

During the day they smoked cigarettes and gambled for small coins and picture postal cards of ball players or actresses. Their talk was disgraceful and filthy and given much to gloating sexual glee. They must have been dreadful liars or wise beyond their years. I was an absolutely monstrous innocent.

I knew nothing important to tell them.

They were strange, hard little people who in time became Driscoll's loudest political supporters. I can still remember them, unkempt shaggy little children with warped, leering faces usually dirty—and headed for the dismal predictions of the social reformers in broken shoes and torn pants, with great holes in their stockings. Yet not all went bad at that. Some of them I pass every day. Respectable citizens growing old—a little tired and sullen, or happy in simple pleasures.

Most are dead. They died in the great bootlegger wars of the twenties, died blithely in that bedlam of beer . . .

In gambling raids . . . In little alley shootings . . . In industrial accidents . . . In drownings at sea . . . In the electric chair. Several are still behind bars.

One became Father Bevins. Stick Novak and Neal Joyce are big powerful men in Ned Wonderly's political set-ups, peculiarly susceptible to government contracts. But those I remember best are almost all dead. . . .

Piggy Tone, leader of the huge beer caravans, who died in machine-gun ambush, and Bugs Neffski, who took someone's rap and ended in the electric chair, taking three shocks to still his calloused soul—and Eddie Baron, who died in Spain fighting for the Loyalists and who would not have had a Mass said for his soul if my brother Dris hadn't pulled wires . . .

But best of all I remember Turtle Travis, who stood, even at fifteen, six feet tall and had a cast in one eye and could knock down a steer with his bare fists and did, at the local slaughterhouse, until Piggy Tone took him into the prize ring and he almost became world champion, only they hit him once too often on the head and he ended up sweeping out Blue Peter's beer garden and saloon, very punch drunk and a little slug nutty from the old hammerings on his skull. He would yell in Gaelic, *Sigle nid Amhlaoible—* to hell with England.

Perhaps I remember Turtle Travis best because he was the cause of Driscoll's meeting Linda Coppard.

I had noticed that Driscoll met me every day after school when there was no longer any need for it. I was in solid with the gangs because I always had a handful of buttons to give out. But Dris still met me every day.

It was Piggy Tone who explained it all to me. He was smoking a cigarette in the school lavatory, eaten by devouring jealousies.

"Dris kinda goes for that Coppard tomato, huh?"

I said, "Who?"

Piggy rolled his blue eyes. "That sweet little dish, Linda Coppard."

"Oh, her."

"Yeah, her. Ain't you got no yen to . . . ?"

"You say Dris likes her? I don't believe it."

Piggy threw his cigarette away. "Oh, so I'm a liar."

"No, Piggy. Honest I didn't mean that."

"I oughta murderlize ya . . ."

"She is pretty . . ."

Piggy spit and put the lavatory to its proper use—or, as he always said, shook hands with an old friend. "Pretty. She's the best tomato in the whole place."

I let it go at that and went back to brood over American History. Linda Coppard was not a public school pupil. She attended private schools in New England and Europe. But this year her mother had taken ill and she was kept in Antioch. There were private schools in the city but Hartley Gould Coppard was involved in some legal struggle with the only two acceptable private schools, trying to drive them off their estates and pile slag and mine shafts over their landscaped snobby acres. So Linda for a short while attended public school and stressed her consonants a little too much.

I had admired her myself—but of course never felt enough courage to address her. As a matter of fact, I had no desire to. Looking at her and thinking of her in connection with the books by Dumas I was devouring was enough. I saw her as a lady—with just a touch of the spirit of a Parisian *gavroche*.

I was a very young fool.

She was fourteen at the time—a tall, slim, blonde girl with polite manners and a silver laugh and a way of carrying herself as if she had never had an awkward age. I don't think she had. She had no use for that ferocious responsibility most of the old families had trained into their broods. . . .

The school let out with a shout—many feet clattered over the old polished hall floors under the plethoric eye of the janitor. Blobs of color ran away from the building, mothers bundled the small fry into extra jackets and the gangs went their way, tearing each other's coats and kicking tin cans before them.

A few luckless and feebler students were set upon and kicked and bloodied, called "foureyes" or "jewboy" or "yankeedoodle," and the history teacher—Bean Belly Browder—rushed as usual out to his waiting farm, on his rusty bike, his pendent fair mustache fluttering.

And there at the curb, neat and smart in mended clothes with his patched shoes blackened, stood Dris, passively smiling.

I thought of what Piggy had told me. "Hello, Dris."

"How's the scholar today?"

"All right, I guess."

"Pull up your stocking."

Dris had been reading law seriously for three years and he had two heavy volumes under his arm. He pulled on his frayed tie that had once been Pete's and I saw Linda Coppard coming down the front steps.

She was chatting with Betty Sewall—one of my Aunt Netta's brood. Turtle was standing with Piggy, his big hands in his pockets. As Linda passed he stepped forward and threw her off balance with his shoulder. He turned, reached for her and grinned.

"Careful, Sugar. Ya almost took a cropper, head over teakettle."

The girl was still smiling. "I'll thank you to keep your hands to yourself."

Turtle grinned and pawed her throat. "Ain't we high and mighty 'cause Papa owns the bank?"

"Keep your filthy hands off me."

The other children made no move. Piggy and Turtle were tough and most of them had felt their hard hands, been the butt of their jokes and ridicule.

Dris stepped up and laid one hand on Turtle's shoulder. "Cut it out."

"Hello, Dris. I'm just bein' sociable with a lady."

Dris turned to Piggy. "Tell him to stop it."

Piggy spit. "Tell 'im yourself. I ain't yer butler."

Dris said, "Stop it."

There was a sound of tearing cloth. Linda did not scream. She kicked Turtle in the shin. Turtle stepped back and my brother hit him hard on the head with the heavy law books. Turtle, angry now, swung and hit Dris under the right eye. Dris went down and I was suddenly around Turtle's knees, pulling him down. I felt a blow on the back of my head where Piggy had rabbit-punched me and when I cleared my mind Turtle was spitting blood from a cut lip and my brother was on the ground beside me rubbing his fast discoloring face. Turtle was not angry; humbly, with servility, he said:

"Aw, Dris, whatsha make me do it for?"

My brother rubbed a skinned knee. "You're a dirty dog, Turtle."

"Aw, Dris," said Turtle, rubbing his big fists together, "whatsha make me do it for?"

Suddenly Linda turned to my brother, inhaled and closed her eyes. "And I'll thank *you* not to start brawls over me. I can very well take care of myself. You're *no* better than he is."

[63]

She swept past us and went along to the sidewalk. I rubbed my sore neck. Piggy spit and said, "Cheez it. Here comes Wooden Pants."

Wooden Pants the janitor was coming toward us. Turtle brushed dirt from my brother's jacket. Dris held a hand to his fast coloring eye and watched the girl walk up the street to where the family car usually waited for her.

He turned, winked at me and smiled. He did not seem very annoyed. Turtle, almost heartbroken at what he had done to his idol, was almost in tears.

"Whatsha make me do it for, Dris?"

Dris admitted no grace, no penitence.

"Skip it, Turtle."

The eye darkened. The flesh around it took on a stale purple hue. I remembered suddenly another time Dris had gotten a black eye. One morning Vicky had sent Dris downtown to the Roscok Meat Mart to bring home an order of meat for pot roast.

It was a warm day. Roscok's was a square box painted a peeling yellow with a damp slimy floor covered with sawdust (in which chicken feathers and chewing tobacco always seemed to get mixed up). Great flayed cadavers of steers hung headless and limbless from rusting iron hooks, and plucked chickens, their slit necks placed against barbs, stood on tiptoe and seemed to dance a strange *Danse Macabre* in time to the buzzing of big blue flies that filled the rest of the window.

Jack Roscok stood behind his oak chopping-block, looking at his black broken fingernails. On his head was a straw hat with the top ripped out, and the warts on his face were wet and large. Everyone knew Jack was mad as a hatter, had been since his wife hanged herself in the icebox between two stiff cold bodies of sheep.

[64]

Jack kicked at his fat brown cat and banged his cleaver against the oak chopping-block. . . .

"Ormsbees, huh? Well, it's no meat for you until your mother pays up that last meat bill."

Dris looked at the hanging bodies of tormented cows. He turned pale green. Something in him rebelled against this hanging of flesh on iron hooks, this displaying of naked chickens by their long slashed necks. He could not look at the pink stupid pig lying on a marble slab, his blind blue eyes staring into the meat grinder where gouts and clots of red tissue were chopped into sprouting worms of flesh. Dris ate meat, liked it, enjoyed it—but he never could look at a butcher or a hanging cadaver without becoming ill. It was his nature—confusing to me who felt that if I could enjoy eating meat I could certainly look at it hanging raw.

Dris said, "But Vicky said it was all packed . . ."

Jack banged his cleaver on the oak block as if he had the tender white neck of a virgin there. "Out of me sight you begging little bastards and not a sliver of beef until that bill is paid. Now *git!*"

And with these words Jack came toward us with his tool. We ran, and Dris smashed into a dripping cow hung by her heels from the ceiling—and so got his first black eye.

And the second was for love.

FIVE

DRIS HELD HIS eye and my hand.

Walking home from school I liked to loaf, stopping to eye-shop the store windows, enjoy the skates, the toy trains and the shotguns I would not get as gifts that year.

Or, pressing my wet nose against the window of Minsky's candy store, I would stand drooling over the views of licorice sticks and soggy sugared bars and sourballs. Ben Minsky, a warped, kind little Jew with jolly brown eyes and a shiny expanse of baldness, would stand at his window, expressing in every kind feature his newly learned American policy—*no purchase less than a penny and everything for cash only.*

But the day my brother Dris got the black eye over Linda Coppard there was no slow walk home. Dris was in a hurry to get off the streets with his shiner, and brood over his discolored cheek. But he did not appear angry—not even ashamed. I think he rather enjoyed getting a drubbing over a pretty girl. Such was Dris in his youth and I, who felt that no lady, no matter how charming, was worth a mouse on the eye, could not understand him or the rhythm and chemistry of his blood stream that drove him on.

As we walked home—he dragging me by the too-large coat sleeve (it had been Dennis' coat three years before), I noticed for the first time how the city was changing: 1915 had led into 1916, the city had gone over to the Allies bit by bit and even I spent my time in the schoolrooms drawing dreadfully ill-matched air battles between brave English fliers and evil-faced tusk-mustached German aces.

There were more strangers in the city. I had never seen such people before. Hillbillies with great yellow mops of hair and Adam's apples all in working order, Polacks and Hunkies and Spicks and Greeks—not like our own second-generation foreigners, but jabbering husky giants who spoke strange tongues and wore oddly cut clothing and who only said, "No spik Ennglish, tank yo so muchhh," when spoken to. Answering only the rich benison of bells and whistles of mines and mills.

The steel mills were creeping like boiling fire-fungus past Polack Point and chewing away the hillsides near Gramp's land. Leaving behind raw red gullies and bleeding muck and clay. New pits were being torn from the bowels of the earth, and the coal trains ran all night and grew in length until a hundred-and-ten-car load was nothing to see pass along Railroad Avenue, and we kids would stop our games and count the cars that sometimes took twenty-five minutes to pass.

And there were new factories mushrooming up along the filthy dump-fringed outskirts. Plants that ground out airplane motors and shell casings and bandages and army cloth. New flivvers were appearing in a great many places, and tool sheds and coal huts and vegetable houses were being remodeled into garages. The rich tapestry of fertile field was disappearing into tar-paper boils.

"Vicky wants a car," I said to my brother, who was examining his eye in the mirror of Hayes's Haberdashery.

"We've got no money."

"Vicky can get it on time."

Dris scowled. "I don't believe in that. Come on."

We went on in silence. I pictured myself behind the wheel of the flivver with my cap on backwards and the wind going past my face. A hundred and ten miles an hour.

As we turned up our street I suddenly forgot about my racing career. There was a loud-talking gathering in front of our house. Aunt Netta and a few of her brood and Gramp and the minister of the Church that Dennis had joined after losing Faith according to Mary Baker Eddy and recovering it in a Baptist dipping pen.

My brother Dennis stood very tall and earnest on the sidewalk, wearing a sailor's uniform, and I remember I envied him his little white hat. My mother—tiny and angry —stood next to him talking very loud and fast—and in not too lyric ecstasy.

"Well, a fine lump of meat I gave birth to! A fine specimen I suffered for and went hungry and worked myself to the bones for. A sailor—a poolroom loafer, he's turned into. Great day in the morning, look at him! A fine thing —the navy needs men and they take a boy who isn't dry behind the ears yet."

"Now, Vicky," said Dennis earnestly in his heavy, honest way, "I felt the call to go. I thought it out. There is nothing wrong in it. We need a fine navy—no telling when we'll be in the war—and, Ma, what I'm doing I'll do, because . . ."

The minister, a pale man with too many teeth and a habit of hissing when he smiled, patted my mother on the shoulder, thrumming the ill-matched notes of his vocal strings.

"My good woman, it is all for the best. We are on the side of all that is good and . . ."

"Don't 'good woman' me, you fraud! I've seen you lurking late at night around the cigar factory gates making love to the Hunky wenches in the tall grass! Don't *you* play holy Joe on me!"

The minister tried to turn paler but failed. Vicky had invented the last statement but it was to do the minister no good. He pressed Dennis' hand, faded from the scene. Gramp took my mother by the arm and led her indoors. Aunt Netta shooed her brood ahead of her, like a herding hen, and we all got indoors and out of the public eye.

In the kitchen, Vicky collapsed and Gramp got her a drink of water and she sat at the table moaning—her arms folded, rocking her small body from side to side.

I was surprised to see her carry on so. She had never shown any of her children, except Driscoll, any great affection; had neglected us and fed us on her bad cooking and always said, "Oh, they'll grow up strong and husky." And we had. But today I suddenly saw that perhaps I had misjudged her. In that luscious almost obscene passion for possessions, she was showing her love.

When my father came in for his early supper, so he could go back to another four hours with his work, Vicky did not lash out at him with her usual mouthing. She spoke of the past. Of what Dennis had to live for. She just half rose from her chair, sobbed, put on a moan and waved a small arm in the direction of Dennis, spoke of his forefathers—notching off his ancestry like killings on a gun.

"It's all right, Pete," said Gramp. "The boy is doing what he wants—even if he is a fool to go and be fish food. Forget his great-grandfathers. They died in wars, too."

Vicky moaned. My father sat down and rubbed his fists against his mouth and ate quickly the stew Aunt Netta placed before him. Coarsely he ate, his eyes looking at Dennis with a seductive tenderness.

"Well, son," said my father at last, rubbing the lemon-colored stubble on his unshaved jowls.

"I'm doing what I want to do," said Dennis.

"So," said Gramp, picking cake crumbs from his beard, "I suppose young fools always will do that when they become surfeited on torpid stagnancy and hunt trouble."

My father filled his pipe. "You think you're going to make the world safe for Democracy?"

Driscoll spoke up from the depths of the evening paper. "Wilson is going to keep us out of the war."

"It's a good slogan," said Gramp. "Men are no longer even masters of their tongues."

Pete lit his pipe. "Dennis, I love you. I can't do much for you. We aren't rich people. This is my country too. I want to see it go on. But, son, if it means . . ." My father wiped his face and puffed on his pipe. The long speech had been hard to get out and now he was through talking for a while. But he touched a sore subject with my mother.

Vicky lifted her head. "And why aren't we rich? Why? I should have married someone with more spunk and backbone. A fine husband I've got, standing all day in shavings like a millhand while fortunes are being made every day. Fortunes, I tell you! It's poverty that's driving Dennis from us."

"Stop chewing, Vicky," said Dris. "Let's give Dennis a swell send-off."

Aunt Netta beamed, smelled far-off grapevines. "Let's have drinks all around."

Vicky was looking at Dris. "Where—what in Heaven has happened to your face?"

"Turtle Travis," I said, "hit it."

"Shut up, Davey," said Dris, turning his head away.

"It was over Linda Coppard," I said, proud of myself.

My mother looked close at the fast-closing eye. "Linda Coppard?"

I nodded. "He was protecting her from the fresh guys."

Dris scowled. "I'll murder you, Davey, when I get you alone."

Vicky grabbed his head and inspected the eye.

"Let go, Vicky."

Pete had finished his pipe and he now looked at Dris with plaintively worried glances and shook his head. "I don't like fighting. Well, I've got to get back to the shop."

"How about a drink—to send Dennis off?" said Aunt Netta, who had been busy over the jug of hard cider Gramp had brought down for us that year.

Vicky was rubbing Driscoll's eye. "My poor boy. It's all right. A gentleman should always protect a lady. Linda Coppard is a fine girl. It's a fine thing you like her."

"Aw, stop it. I don't like her—much. . . ."

"Not much," I said.

Aunt Netta sipped the cider. "Flying high, boy."

My mother was off, enjoying visions. To her, to like was to love, and to love was to marry, and to marry into the rich Coppard family was something to keep her dreaming for weeks.

She was no snob. She made no pretense. She worshipped wealth and position and honestly thought that all life was molded so that those who were best and handsomest and brightest would get their share of it. That Driscoll would get his eye blackened over a Coppard girl was enough for her. "*She could dream, couldn't she?*" Gramp would say of her. And she was dreaming now, a dream most likely that explained why she never saw hope in the straitness of Presbyterianism.

She bathed the eye and kissed it and put a pad on it and asked all sorts of questions about Linda and the fight. Dris hated the attention and poor Dennis was almost forgotten and Aunt Netta drank a great deal of hard cider and Gramp had to lead her home surrounded by assisting, shoving members of her brood.

And late that night while I could still hear the rip-saw in the tool shed cutting into lumber, I lay in bed with Dris and listened to him tell Doug and Dennis about the fight.

[71]

Doug, his face burned red by the blast furnaces, yawned. "Stow the gab. Turtle Travis could break you in half with one hand if he wanted to. He likes you too much to hurt you, that's all."

Dris said, "Maybe—but it's mind over matter. I can handle him just with a look. Like Jake Fry handles a judge."

"You lawyers," growled Doug. "I'm glad you didn't handle him until he got one over your eye. Now shut up —I'm on the early shift at the furnace. We're pouring twenty thousand dollars' worth of steel every time we knock out the furnace plug."

"I'm sorry," I whispered to Dris, "that I told about Linda."

"That's all right," said Dris, sighing magnanimously. "I don't mind. I love her."

I could not speak. To love someone was not the sort of thing a manly boy did. It was sissy stuff—in my mind. It was nasty and sticky and bred on male gutter talk. It was something no one would ever admit. Yet here was my brother calmly saying he loved a girl. A tall, soft, limber girl with rye-colored hair and a pretty mouth and a taut, lovely voice. I had strict ideas of propriety at that age. Love a girl! *Pooh!*

I turned on my back and did not say anything. I was afraid. Dris might tell me he wanted to kiss her and hug her and hold her panting breasts against his chest the way they did in novels. No, I wanted no more of this confession. I was a formidable young blue nose.

I was almost asleep when Dennis tumbled out of bed to pray a last great clot of a prayer because he was going to the naval training station in the morning.

He prayed for his soul and his family and his mother and his father and all his brothers by name and his relatives and his grandfather, and I think he would even have prayed for his pastor, but Doug threw his heavy steel-worker's shoe at him and just missed his ear. And this would have started a fight but we heard my father's heavy, tired step on the stairs, creaking the loose treads, so we lay very still.

Pete stopped outside our door and stood there, breathing hard. I knew he wanted to come in and say good-bye to Dennis, who would leave before Pete was up in the morning. But after a while we heard him going up to his third-floor room. My father never did what he wanted to do, but he never regretted it—except this time, I think. This time he did not come in to say good-bye to his son, Dennis, praying mechanically to his Maker for a leading light, a word of Faith.

For the Dennis who came back from the war wasn't his young, trusting, believing son. Dennis came back a tall, dry-eyed man with a mistrust of all the values he had once believed in. All he saved out of the war was the stark covenant of his stern God. But he was a stranger to us forever after.

And my father was very shy with strangers. . . .

The war drums rolled now in torpid indecision. I could hear them. The city could hear them. Destiny in bad press engravings marched on the front pages of *The Antioch Advocate*. There was coming a tide that would sweep us into battle. The beat of indecision was to pass.

But I was young. I was in my first new fully-owned suit of clothing. We were—it seems strange to write it down even now—we were, in a way, rich. The war boom had caught up with us and cast us into paper wealth.

My mother had nothing to do with it.

After Dennis went off to bounce around on the wet, cold sea, she tried harder than ever to work herself into a social success and a fortune—but it was my father who pulled the trick. Or rather, he and Uncle Thoreau between them—two innocents in a machine and corporation age stumbled into success in a world too busy with great spending and pocket picking to bother about the crumbs these small fry picked up.

Vicky had cut lumber from condemned wind-blown woods, and the stuff was no good. It was rotted and molded and spoiled by weather. Uncle Thoreau had failed in chicken farming on a mud flat outside the city and his brood ate pale, watery chicken stews until they gagged at the thought of their little feathered friends.

It was my father who saved the day.

He was lighting his pipe when the only brilliant stroke of business genius in his entire existence came to him. He never repeated it.

"Now, Vicky, you have that condemned lumber . . ."

Vicky blew air through her pretty pug nose. "Condemned, my eyeteeth! It's just a frame-up by the Coppard Lumber Yards to keep me out of the business. That wood is better than the stuff Ned Wonderly is selling to build City Hall. Great ball of fire—it's wood, isn't it?"

Pete took a big puff of smoke. "And Thoreau has that mud flat where he tried to raise chickens. About twenty acres of it. The mills and mines are bringing in people faster than they can be housed. Think of a lot of cheap houses, each with its little garden patch that would be just what they would want. They get good pay at the mill and the mines and they could grow their own food and have enough land to stretch themselves. . . ."

Vicky turned slowly and looked at my father with a saturnine face. Even I stopped drawing in my scrap-book to look at him. He ducked his head—confused and shy. Even to himself it was incoherent for him to come out of his shy inertia.

[74]

"It was *only* an idea. Forget it."

Vicky was hunting her hat. "It's a sign from above, I tell you—a sign. I've been dreaming—dreaming all these nights of a great thought. I knew it was near, would come to me . . . And it has—through you, Pete."

"It's a gamble," said Pete. "All that lumber—not much good, true. But we'll have to go in debt with the banks, up to our necks—and Thoreau may not want to build."

"You stay here—both of you," said Vicky, hunting her gloves. "I'm going right over to Thoreau's. Don't you talk to anyone, do you hear? Not to *anyone*."

The back door banged and Vicky was gone.

My father sat smoking, picking little slivers of wood out of his great square thumbs. He looked at his heavy silver watch. Time he was back in the tool shed seeing what his helpers were doing with a special order of first-aid cabinets for the steel mill. A methodical man, Pete got out the last splinter and stood up.

"We going to be rich, Pete?" I asked.

He brooded himself to the door. "I hope not. I hope not. It'll turn your mother's head completely around like a squirrel in a cage."

"All the way around?"

He patted my cheek and looked at my drawings of soldiers and knocked out his pipe against a hard palm.

"I never could keep my mouth shut when I should have. Vicky is going to go through with this—*if* the bank will give her money."

The next day Driscoll, Vicky and myself entered the Antioch Trust Company and waited in a small marble room for Hartley Gould Coppard—one of the three important Coppard brothers—to see us. The frosted glass set in fumed oak said: H. G. COPPARD, PRESIDENT. PRIVATE.

[75]

and we stared at it with pleasure and respect. We admired the hatefully efficient pace of the place.

Driscoll had been brought along because he was reading law and he was to assure Vicky that nothing underhanded was going to be put into the mortgage contracts she was hopeful of signing.

"This way, Mrs. Ormsbee," said a clerk.

At last we stood on the good thick red rug of the private office. The room was paneled in walnut. And oil paintings —the first good ones I had ever seen in my life—were on the walls. I can still remember a small, jewel-like Corot and a square Cezanne that puzzled me, for in those days most people in Antioch did not know of Cezanne and I wondered why anyone would paint in such solid forceful squares.

At the cherrywood desk sat Hartley Gould Coppard himself. When he saw my mother, he smiled, stood up and shook hands with all three of us as if he held us in special esteem.

"Well—always like to see a pretty woman in a bank."

"Thank you, Mr. Coppard. These are my sons. Driscoll —he's going to be a lawyer. And this is Davey."

"Pleased to meet you."

Hartley Gould Coppard in his late thirties wasn't at all the fat money-bag with the dollar signs on him that I had seen in the Art Young cartoons which I had been copying in India ink. He was a great gentleman with a reputation of loving all pretty ladies, and I could see Vicky had pleased him. He was the only man in Antioch who went to Europe to buy paintings, the rest of the town being satisfied to clip a *Saturday Evening Post* cover for framing. He inclined his head graciously and motioned us into chairs.

Jake Fry used to say he was the last of his class—the landed and estated gentry who had no use for money just for money's sake—one of those who lived lavishly and had no interest or hate for the workers. He had a fine wit and a sense of humor, and when the new rising tide of business men—crude, powerful, politically strong and low in manner and foul in tactics—came and tried to engulf him, he stood his ground and watched them pulse and moil, and all he said once to Dris was, "Well, so goes the cycle. I took it away from the pioneers like your grandfather, Abner Jonathan Sewall, and the riffraff that stayed safe in the cities while the country was being developed are rising out of their mulch to put dirty hands on the throat of the wealth and resources of the country. If the workers didn't like *me*, wait until they see what these babies are going to do to them."

But at the moment he was seating us in big smooth leather chairs while listening to my mother talk. After she had run out of wind and was tacking back into the breeze, he nodded at her and smiled, impressed, I was sure, by her tiny, perfect beauty.

"All right, Mrs. Ormsbee. You don't have to sell me on the idea. Housing for workers will be a problem, and the value of any kind of new building will go up. You are a good risk. You go ahead and build. When you've got the walls up, we'll give you mortgages on them, and to start we'll advance you enough on the land to begin foundations. I'll have the papers ready for your lawyers tomorrow. Who are they?"

"Thank you," said Vicky, proudly putting an arm around Dris. "Dris is working for Jake Fry. He's the lawyer in the family."

"Vicky, I'm just finishing night law."

"So," said Hartley Gould, smiling down at us, "the young man is going to be a lawyer?"

"Yes, sir," said Dris. "I'm going to be a fine lawyer. An

honest one. I'm going to see that justice is always done and that for which the Bill of Rights was written is what will be done to all people."

"Imagine that," said the banker.

Vicky said, "He's the only one in the family takes after me—in a brainy way, I mean. Davey wants to be an artist. Silly shillyshally—stinking around in paints."

"I like that," I said, pointing to the Cezanne. "But why does he paint like that? Broken up . . ."

"I don't know, Davey. But I like it, too. Well, I wish you all the success you want. Now, if you'll excuse me, Mrs. Ormsbee, I've got to go and watch a merger hatch out another head."

Vicky didn't even smile. (She prided herself on having no sense of humor.) And so we all shook hands again, and I liked the way the banker's hand was dry and soft and smelled as if bathed in shaving lotion.

Dris turned from the door. "Oh, I know your daughter —I mean Linda—Linda and I went to the same school for a while."

The banker was far away, deep in some rolls of type-written onionskin paper. He had forgotten us. "Did you, now? H'mmm . . ."

We went out and walked along Coppard Square. Little dirty birds pecked at the horse-dropping under the bronze frown of the Civil War soldier on his granite base. The summer heat shimmered off tin roofs and the sky was bluer than it has ever been since. Country men in washed, faded cloth stood at the store windows inspecting things they would never buy. The trolley wires over our heads sang with unction, like a muttering prayer meeting.

Vicky was walking as if in a trance. I think at that moment she was happier than she had ever been in her life. She was all that she would ever be—all that she would ever want. She had met the social heights of the city, she had all the money credit she wanted, her sons were growing into tall manhood, and as she walked she knew that *that* day the city was hers. . . .

And those times did something to Dris too. It was not the building of houses that mattered to him. He never had any property sense or cared much for the making of money. But there stirred in him some strange emotion, some love of change and chance. That night—on the day we signed the loans—I remember being punched awake and finding the world dark. Dris stood over me, dressed and scowling in the light of a small flashlight.

"Get dressed—I want to walk. . . ."

I protested, but looked at the sleeping bulk of Doug and got into my clothing. The chill night air brought me alive and we walked slowly downtown, Dris staring around him as if he had never seen this night world before. Great pools of yellow still flooded the street corners, and then they went out except on every fifth block. A late piano rattled its wired soul and drunken voices were heard in alleys. Late street cars passed, swaying, and there was a scent of river and river boats and the good green odor of the farmers' markets beginning under the flares that drew steel reflections from the cobblestone market squares.

Dris walked and I followed and he seemed to hunt for something, but what I never knew—for he never found it. There was a feel of throbbing night. And the wetness of the streets was helped by the water trucks that soaked it and the tap-tap of a late horse driving past with a bundle nodding over the dashboard. Cars passed too. But they seemed unreal—bug-eyed monsters—great ants crushing past in a wind and snarl of white gas.

The shadows walked and tossed, the old buildings looked older, and the night girls hissed from doorways and the mill night crews crept along the curbs and there was a tang of new-baked bread in the suddenly still air.

I looked at Dris and some excitement held him. Near the river we sat on old silvered wood and watched the waters slip by like gray wolves—(or what I thought of as gray wolves, for I had never seen a wolf).

And I must have slept. For at dawn Dris shook me and we went home to our bed.

The next day we started building.

S I X

VICKY, OF COURSE, took charge of the building of the houses. Every morning she would pack some thick-cut bread and singed meat and fill several bottles with her muddy coffee and I would join her on the trolley car. We would go along, swaying and grinding past the business section, past the slums, the great groaning black-spitting steel plants and come at last to the end of the line.

Here in a wide wilderness of burr and barberry thickets, the conductor would get down to drink his can of beer, light his pipe and swing the long, wire-touching pole around. Then Vicky and I would take up our bundles and walk along the rutted clay road while to our left the river ran steady and even, cooing like a dove around the wooden supports of the many little piers.

In a muddy drop between two hills men were busy erecting square little shapes, while tired horses pulled scrap plows and dug shallow cellars. Here my father's ideas were taking shape. It was muddy and damp and the few trees had been knocked down and murdered with axes and shoved aside to form platforms for the cement mixers and gravel loads. It was dismal and it was shoddy. It was sad to see the line of boxes go up the slow loft of the hill until they seemed to run toward the pine woods for shelter from the cruel rays of the sun.

Yet already there were customers. Big heavy Polacks and lean, tobacco-eating Yankees, men with dirty, oil-marked faces who, off from the night shifts at mill and mine, were gathering to look over these *"Small country estates at a price to fit your purse,"* as my Uncle Thoreau's broadside said.

Uncle Thoreau was busy now as we came upon him, sucking the ends of his great mustache, polishing the thick lenses of his heavy glasses and talking—talking in that happy voice of a man who knows he has something to sell and is selling it.

He could only spare us a hand wave as he went on, pointing to a huge roll map on a packing case set in the mud. A wide Central European steel puddler stood solid and square-faced in front of him, while behind him his wider wife and three tow-headed children chewed gum and shifted from one muddy foot to the other while big blue-bottle flies hunted on their red necks.

"Gardens?" said my Uncle Thoreau. "A hundred feet behind each house. Good soil free from acid and sourness and just waiting to snap at any seeds you drop in the soil. Watered? Look at it. Did you ever see such well-watered soil?"

The steel worker and his family looked over the muddy, churned, Elysian fields.

"Is plenty water. Maybe *too* much."

"It got terlet?" asked the wife, spoiled by American luxury.

My Uncle Thoreau covered his eyes and said softly, "We have a full plumbing system. All it needs is an outlet and cesspool which can be added by yourself on any day off."

"It got terlet?"

"The plumbing is as modern as money could buy at these low selling costs. Now take the house itself. A huge kitchen—you could live there and close up the rest of the house. And if you take in boarders you can live like a king with no cost to yourself."

"Yah, boarders. They help."

"Yes, sir."

"I ask you—it got a terlet?"

"And take the view. Cozy with plenty of neighbors. But the river just two hundred feet away. The hills behind you —and only a stone's throw from the trolley line."

"It got a . . ."

Vicky pulled me out of the mud and we went up to the houses, beginning to stagger along the convolutions of the valley. Twenty were in work. They were almost no bigger than our tool shed. Set low in the mud—boxed in with Vicky's condemned lumber, covered with tar paper, roofed with a red-painted scalloped tin, and hammered together by a crew of five men under my father's watchful, worried eye. He wasn't used to such shoddy workmanship and such dreadful material. He was a craftsman and yet he knew that he had to build these houses quickly and cheaply to keep always one step ahead of the bank or the whole scheme would collapse into defeat and complete poverty for all of us.

Vicky nodded. "Wonderful, Pete. Aren't you using too many ceiling rafters?"

"Vicky, if I used less, the whole roof would come down. This lumber is mildewed and flawed with rot. It's warping the walls as soon as we get them up."

"Smear them with red paint," said Vicky. "You're too slow. Red is a fine color. Strong looking."

"I've got to nail them right. The joints don't hold in a lot of this trim."

"Keep it up. I've got a lot of people coming this afternoon to look at them. How many sold?"

"I don't know. Ask Driscoll."

"Where is he?"

"In the office making out deeds."

Vicky ran up and down a set of front steps.

"H'mm . . . Too much wood. Why don't you fill them in with fieldstones before you cover the steps?"

Pete sighed and went back to a struggle with a door that would not fit into a square shape. The office was a tar-paper shack set on stilts in the mud. Driscoll sat at the badly behaved typewriter filling in forms. Uncle Thoreau was the Notary Public, but Dris was searching the fine print in the printed deed forms to make sure.

"Hello, Vicky. I'm starved," he said, looking up.

Vicky handed him the badly cut bread and meat and while he ate she counted off the squares marked SOLD on the wall map I had drawn so carefully with colored crayon. I had invented green trees shaped like malignant carbuncles.

"H'mmm . . . Fifteen sold. That's fine."

"Only twelve. But Uncle Thoreau marks up more to show to customers. He says it shows our financial stability."

"We've got to sell more so we can build more. Build, *build!* The steel mills are putting in three eight-hour shifts starting next week. Got a ten-million-dollar shell order for the Allies. I tell you we can fill these hills and river fronts with a thousand houses. It's a gold mine—and I should know. I've a head. The only business head in the family. If I hadn't worked this out, your father would still be making his damn fool cabinets. . . ."

Dris winked at me and opened a law book. Vicky cocked her tiny head to one side and stood looking out at the men and women inspecting the half-finished houses. Then she took a pile of bills off a nail and scowled as she added with no definite coherent bookkeeping plan.

"The prices! Oh, the swine—the dirty swine! Look at these prices for cement and nails and hardware! Why, we'll lose our shirts. That's the way it is. Great day in the morning! An honest person can't make a living any more without the wolf pack coming in to take the bread out of his mouth. Hell and high water, the mangy wolves!"

Dris said, "Wolves don't eat bread. Anyway, we're raising the prices from three thousand to three thousand nine hundred. That covers the cost in rise in materials. More than covers it."

Vicky was figuring with a huge yellow pencil on a cement bag. Wetting the heavy pencil on her small, rosebud mouth, leaving black marks on tiny lips, she was adding figures.

She looked up. "Damn them! On fifteen houses—a thousand dollars lost on each to the supply people. Fifteen thousand dollars lost. Dris, we've *lost* fifteen thousand dollars on those houses!"

Dris closed his law book and took a bit of gristle out of his mouth and looked at Vicky's occult and mystic science of arithmetic.

"Look, Vicky. We're *not* losing any money. We're adding a thousand dollars on to each house to cover the rise on material. We make the same sum of money we planned."

"But, Dris," Vicky was weeping, "we could have kept that extra thousand on each house for ourselves. Now it's got to go to those Judases in the supply yards. Dris, Dris, you're only a child. You don't see that we're really losing fifteen thousand dollars, and the more we sell the more we lose. A thousand dollars on each house. Say we build a thousand houses—a thousand thousand dollars—is that a million, Dris?"

"Look, Vicky. We haven't got land for a thousand houses."

Vicky was back, figuring with her pencil. I sat on the steps watching the people come up the lane from the trolley stop. It was a fine day. The sky hung high and tight and a hunting hawk dared to beat his wings against the wind. In the woods on the hills it looked cool and restful.

Vicky was looking at her figures. "I get a different answer every time. I still can't figure out how we are not losing a thousand dollars a house if we pay it out in higher costs to the supply people. . . ."

Uncle Thoreau entered with a fistful of small bills. He was breathing hard.

The thick lenses of his glasses were fogged with sweat.

"Another sold, but damn this love of flush plumbing among Polacks. We've got to put in an extra toilet."

Vicky groaned. "Twelve more dollars to the plumbing wolves."

Uncle Thoreau marked up three plots as SOLD on the map.

But Gramp did not build on his lands. He watched his beef herds and grew corn and hay to feed them and felt no glow when he got more for them. It all went into his lawsuits anyway. The courts were a formidable force in his old age.

I saw a great deal of Gramp that year. Vicky was busy and he would send his overseer, Cap Roc, to bring me up to the range. I liked Cap. He was slightly insane. The normal buoyancy of life had seeped from him.

Cap was a square hard old man with a red face covered with crimson warts. His nose was square—as square as his thumbs. He was a navy man who had fought off Cuba in the Spanish-American War and had a shell split his young head, and then they brought him back to a hospital ship and set two silver bands around his skull to keep his poor head together. Then they turned him loose, for it appeared he had never properly enlisted in the Navy and had just joined up and thought that was all there was to it. He was treated as a meddling civilian. And so he would have died by the roadside if Gramp hadn't taken him in and fed his red face and trained him to love cattle. And he had stayed on and helped Gramp and now he had the title of overseer and loved Gramp with a crazy crack-headed love that was more dangerous than people thought when he smiled so solicitously. Cap Roc never drank or smoked but every so often blinding headaches would come over him and Gramp would bind cold cloths around his shattered head and lock him in the spring house until it was over and poor Cap no longer foamed at the mouth, was no longer dissociated completely from sanity.

Once he got out and ran loose for a week and Gramp went after him with ropes and irons and had him hauled dirty and nude back to the range across the back of a horse. But Cap was getting older and calmer and it was only talk about lawyers that brought the mad look into his everyday eyes. And when the eyes rolled back and were almost pure white, then Gramp would unlock the spring house and lead Cap sobbing into it. . . .

But he always gave plenty of warning before his madness climbed behind his eyeballs and he never would harm a child. Many times we drove to Gramp's. He would look behind him at the houses my father was hammering together, chew his eating tobacco, spit into the road and rub his numb red face with a ham of a fist.

"Pappy still a-building?"

"Yes, Cap."

"People crazy to build more than one house. Only live in one at a time. Crazy thing to do, huh, Davey?"

I would look at the mad man's battered red head and nod. "Yes, Cap."

[87]

I think Dris was a little mad that year too. It was the madness of a young man, the madness of the fullness and feel of life. He was tall and in him there stirred, I was sure, the full understanding of the power that pulsed in his loins. Young manhood—the rising of juices in the young body—the filling of the young mind with stronger blood. It all drove him into a pitch of fury and desire that made him appear mad to me.

I was a clod. I had no understanding at the time of anything. But after a day at the houses Dris would brush back his hair and shine his shoes and drift off, against the shrill protests of Vicky who suspected the worst in the way of Polack girls and Italian-brewed wine.

One evening he handed me my cap and asked me to come along. We walked a long time and came at last to the great barns of the Horse Terminal. Here the farmers and breeders brought their stallions for stud; here the Army came to buy horseflesh that was soon to rot in Flanders. Hundreds of horses stood here in the mellow reek of their own manure, eating hay and crushing oats between velvet lips, waiting to be sold or bred.

Dris entered and I followed. Old Sarg, an odd little man with only one ear, was night watchman here, and I saw Dris slip him a pint of corn whiskey.

I tapped Dris on the shoulder. "What's the idea?"

Dris looked at me and winked. "Mug—I've been coming here for weeks. Come on."

I followed him into the cold yard. Under the light of several yellow bulbs I saw the backs of many horses. They stood in groups making that snickering horse-talk that means so much to them. Younger horses playfully nipped each other's flanks, colts did silly things with their long red legs. Dust rose, scented with dropping. Hay was bunched into forms and a great black stallion with pink-flared nostrils was topping a cream-colored mare with all the passion of any strong young lover.

It was a strange sight, this gathering of horses. Their legs and heads made patterns in the lights; their big bellies and slim feet mixed in the strangest shapes. And I knew no one, no man, could ever be as beautiful as a horse. The mare shivered and made low bubbling sounds. . . .

I turned to find Dris with a saddle in his hands. He patted a red gelding and fed it sugar. He saddled it and leaped on its back and went round and round the yard. I stood watching him. He rode well and moved in time with the horse, and the whole strange sight of my brother on the horse was unreal. I knew where he had been all these weeks. But why?

In a half hour the red gelding had had enough. Dris unsaddled him and rubbed him down and then turned to me.

"Well, *how* was I?"

"Pretty good, Dris. But why all this love of riding?"

Dris looked at a small colt nuzzling against its mother's taut brown pelt. "Davey, I don't know if you'll understand—but there are a lot of things I want to do—and do well. And just now, well, I want to ride like a gentleman. Would you understand that?"

"No," I said, but Dris was not listening; he was looking at the horses stir in the night, restlessly lifting their hoofs, pushing one another about.

Dris wasn't thinking at all about the houses that were to make us rich. . . .

SEVEN

PETE ORMSBEE went on hammering together his houses.

As the times dragged on swiftly, as the nation moved toward war, there was so much myth in everyone's outlook that now I can wonder how we fell for it. We believed everything; wanted to believe—as in a religious conversion.

I was only nine—but even I took pride in the long horse face, the bad teeth and the solemn textbook prose of President Wilson. *He had kept us out of the war. We were too proud to fight.* And it pleased us. Pete Ormsbee was no great thinker, but he would light his pipe after a day at his development, yawn, and fold his newspaper and declare he was going to vote for the re-election of Wilson. Uncle Thoreau, a Socialist with enough of Henry George clinging to his ribs, was swayed, and agreed. He was a Wilson man, too, and wore a huge button declaring it to the world. We failed to see the truths behind the great potential dangers we were supposed to be menaced by.

Vicky took no part in this talk. She cared very little about politics and suspected, I'm sure, that they were evil doings run by a male society for its own no-good purpose and besides, it mattered little to her what kind of shenanigans went on in Washington as long as it was still a country where a poor boy could become President and a manly lad could marry the squire's daughter. And Dris would scowl under her fond glances and drag me off to help organize the Ned Wonderly political clubs.

Dris was a Wonderly admirer because Jake Fry was— and because Ned Wonderly, the state boss, had picked Dris out as a likely lad and had put him in charge of the lads to heckle Wilson meetings and parade with banners and cheer at the proper moments. Dris in those days was a sort of intellectual desperado.

I remember the first time I met Ned Wonderly. Dris had dragged me out of a welter of Wilson talk at home to help tack Republican posters up on telegraph poles.

Our work done, we had crossed town to the Union Club, the stronghold of G.O.P. calmness and hope.

It was built of solid red stone in the shape and style of some French prison before the Revolution and suggested to me the storming of the Bastille. The tall, narrow windows were always full of beefy, white-haired old boys smoking good cigars and reading the conservative New York City newspapers. Their club ties were somewhat awry.

Inside, the paneling was very old and very polished, the rug smelled of some delightful bug spray and rubber trees in brass and bronze pots brought back from China by a rich traveler stood around under the most dreadful oil paintings that were ever placed on canvas and surrounded by too much gilt frame. (But, frankly, at the time I first saw them, I thought them respectable and famous efforts by men who were magicians and creators of master works in oil paint.)

As Dris and I entered the club and walked down the turkey-red carpet in the hall, I could just peep into the huge reading room, past the fog of good Havana leaf and the tacking of many newspapers as they shifted in the breeze of polite and well-fed conversation. Fat legs were crossed and I admired cordovan bluchers and oxfords.

Then a tall oak door opened and we were in a fine, blue-papered room, simple and not overfurnished with a golden oak desk and a small painting of the Virgin big with Child.

The drapes were robin-blue silk and carefully pleated. Behind the desk sat Ned Wonderly. Few people saw him at that time, and only Jake Fry and Dris, as his errand runner, really knew him well.

Ned Wonderly was very tall—well over six feet—with a narrow head going nude, the thin, colorless hair plastered down against the lean skull. The eyes were hard and green and the mouth a mere slit, the nose very sharp and thin. Gray ties with a black pearl were almost a uniform to him, as were gray double-breasted suits with a faint white pin-stripe. He had long narrow feet and I never saw him wear anything but smooth black leather shoes.

His voice never had much energy, but he didn't believe in talking, anyway. Action was his method. He was, I found out, a realist—there was no sham to him, and he had little hope in the human race. He was, however, betrayed at times into being almost a mystic and at such times a great giver of Masses and chapels. He looked like a man who loved horses—and he did. Women were nothing important to him. He did not drink or smoke. His gambling was fabulous, as were his high, stiff, linen collars.

He had come up the hard way, everyone said—the son of an Irish roofer and a Scotch waitress in Blue Peter's Beer Garden.

The city remembered his father's carbuncled nose and his thirst. At an early age the roofer had one beer too many on a hot day, stepped onto a projecting roof that was not there and the parish buried him, and Ned Wonderly went out to peddle papers. Less admiring people said he was the look-out for a floating crap game at an early age. But Democrats would say anything, the Republicans said. Ned ignored the murmurs of deprecation.

What is known is that, as a young man, in a hard black hat, he took the river wards away from the Coppard machine and voted them to defeat the quaintly silhouetted Senator who had been Coppard-plated for years.

The Coppards knew Ned's worth and his menace and made peace, and Ned went out into the state and came back and organized the city, and the Coppards rested easy, feeling they had a fine-edged, steel-nerved tool. But Ned was not ready to take orders and so now that another election was coming up the Coppards were again wondering what of these hoodlums they picked up and made powers, and *if* they would proceed according to regular business methods.

There had been a new break between the Coppards and Ned. Ned was pushing his Polack and hillbilly and even Negro aldermen into key positions in the city government, instead of the old-guard, broken-down colonial families that gave lip and backside service to the Coppards. Ned knew he could trust his own lads, break them if they stepped out of line, but he could not depend on the stiff, tattered pride and the snobbish remnants of Boston, New Amsterdam, Philadelphia and D.A.R. riffraff that polished its worn medals and talked as if silk breeches were still in style. They lacked loyalties and funds, these sweepings from history, and did not repay all the bother they caused. . . .

So Ned was weeding out the Coppard old guard and bringing in his brash hungry hordes from Polack Point, from the red-clayed Nigger Hills, from the fringe of slums and factory belts that rimmed the city. They were right guys and willing workers—and they would take orders and carry them out. To hell with the Coppard anachronisms!

Jake Fry, his great convex countenance panting, was reading a letter as we came in, but he put it down and winked at Dris. Ned Wonderly smiled that thin, hard smile of his as we entered.

"Well, Dris? Mr. Fry tells me your boys covered up every Wilson poster in the Sixth Ward."

"Yes. We worked all night."

Ned nodded and looked at his ceiling. "That's fine— very fine. This your little brother?" A green eye turned to look at me.

Dris grabbed off my ragged cap. "This is Davey. He helped."

I stood and waited first on one leg, then on the other. I liked this atmosphere of richness, of good rugs and solid cigar odor and furniture polish and shaving lotion and good Bourbon whiskey. This to me was then the high life, the good life, the full and fat life that Vicky held up to us boys as goals. I stood nervous and arrogant—a hopeless nonentity in all this splendid living.

"Well, Davey. It's nice to have you with us."

I said nothing and Dris almost let me have his elbow in my ribs.

"Sure," I said.

Jake lifted his massiveness of padded limbs, sat down on a corner of the desk, patted his fearful stomach, tossed off a whiskey and shook his chins in pleasant agony as the liquor went down.

"Dris," he said, picking up a green-leaved cigar, "you've been reading law and history. . . ."

"Yes, I have."

"You know Napoleon often changed his plans—plans the lower ranks couldn't understand. By the way, can Davey keep his mouth shut?"

"You bet!" I shouted. I did not want to be sent from this place of ostentatiously magnificent promise.

"Good. Dris, we want you to uncover all those Wilson posters—and put up a lot of new ones. . . ."

Dris made a face. "I don't understand . . ."

Jake Fry put out his cigar in the belly of a bronze goddess on the desk and nodded to Ned Wonderly. Ned came around and faced us leaning against his desk.

"This is man-to-man stuff, Dris. I want to make a test. I can't use my regulars—they wouldn't understand yet. The clubs *may* switch over to Wilson. I want to study some public reaction. Can I trust you?"

Dris nodded, serenely impartial. "Yes—but I don't get it. The Coppards are against Wilson and . . ."

Ned said. "Let me worry about party lines. Jake and I know what we're doing."

"All right," said Dris. "I'll get Piggy and the boys moving."

"Good," said Jake. "But I guess you know, Dris, we can't be connected with this *yet*. Can't be too careful of consistency. . . ."

Ned pressed a buzzer on his desk.

"I want you boys to have a big meal—on the Club. Anything you want. But no liquor. I'm against it for kids or anyone else."

"You bet," said Jake Fry pouring himself three fat fingers of Bourbon.

The dining room was sumptuous. I saw my first starched tablecloth. I studied the sauces and chilis and pickled onions and the glass containers of spices. I admired the slaughtered heads of deer and wild boar and bear on the walls. I sank back in my big chair and watched the colored club waiter bring in the silver tray of olives and celery, and shyly I dug out a wedge of white butter and smeared it on the crisp roll, my mouth watering painfully in anticipation.

Dris was more at ease. He spoke directly to the darky. "And after the soup, the porterhouse steak with fried onions and mushrooms and French fried potatoes. With plenty of pickles and skip the salad and, oh—a pot of coffee."

"Coffee?" I asked in awe.

"A big pot of coffee," said Dris, infuriated that I should think him a *poseur*.

At home we boys drank a concoction of badly merged milk, powdered chocolate and sugar under the name of cocoa. To have coffee in this place was beyond the hopes of mortal Ormsbees. Yet Dris acted as if it were a negligible essential.

I have never since eaten such steak—such red, flavorful meat—such glory of onions and mushrooms, such dark, scented gravy, so good to sop up with many rolls. I envied the privileged their inherited privileges.

I finished every morsel, soaked up the last tear of gravy and gobbled up the remaining sliver of fried onion that clung to my fork. I had no compunction about wiping dishes clean.

I was full. I was sated. I had known great happiness and had for the first time tasted the full wonder of what life could give to a man. Good, well-cooked, rich food. I sat, my jaw dangling distractedly.

I looked across at Dris, still slowly chewing. He winked at me and poured the dark Mocha and added what looked like half a pint of cream, tossed in three lumps of sugar and slid it across to me.

I swallowed the hot, gold-brown drink. I opened my eyes to see the darky shove a huge wedge of apple pie un-

der my amazed nostrils. I ate, I drank and at last I wiped my
mouth on the stiff, rich linen (crested with the club seal)
and sat back moaning with pleasure. I was ready to bust
wide open and start all over again. Holding my hand a little
higher than the Medici Venus, I belched.

Dris held up a pack of cigarettes and I took one, trem-
bling, and the darky held a silver candlestick over me and
I set the tobacco on fire and I inhaled and my inner man
signaled all was well.

I had smoked before—but never so brazenly in public.

I watched Dris use an ash tray.

Imagine saving the ashes! There was a lot I had to learn
about the higher life before I could meet an Anglican
bishop as a table equal.

Dris frowned and looked across at me.

"Have enough?"

I could not answer. I could only roll my eyes.

"Next time we'll try lobster."

I grew frightened. "Lobster! Dris, *you* had lobster here
once?"

Dris shook his head. "Not yet. But I will!"

"Dris!"

Vicky had impressed on us the lowness and vice of the
sort of people who ate lobster and drank champagne.

"It's all right, Davey. They bring it packed in ice from
Maine. But, Davey, what do you think about this business
of Mr. Wonderly going over to Wilson?"

"Uncle Thoreau is, too."

"Uncle Thoreau—he's an old crackpot. . . ."

"Oh, no, Dris."

Dris paid no attention to my defense of my fine uncle.
"You know, Davey, I've been reading a lot of books. I
don't get it. This business of men like Mr. Wonderly and

[97]

Jake Fry controlling so many votes—making something the people are supposed to decide for themselves . . . Having it done by clubs like this . . ."

I was shocked. "You mean, Dris, people really don't vote and elect people like the civic books say?"

"I don't know, Davey—maybe it's better this way. Big leaders like Mr. Coppard and Mr. Wonderly telling people, helping them make up their minds . . . But again, suppose there were no people like Mr. Wonderly—and bad people got hold of the clubs . . . That wouldn't do, either."

I was feeling sleepy. "I guess Mr. Wonderly knows what he's doing. Didn't he give the city Washington Park and that house George Washington slept in? And isn't he giving a big picnic to open the house to the public right after election? A man that loves George Washington can't be so bad. I bet they have free frankfurters and root beer at the opening!"

Dris looked at me and said calmly, "I'm taking Linda Coppard."

I said nothing. The last roll and gravy had really been too much. Besides which, I knew nothing to say. When it came to girls, a pathetic silence was my reaction.

Dris mashed out his cigarette in the cut-glass tray. "Come on, we've got a lot of new posters to put up. Wilson can't be such a bad egg, either." Dris smiled at me. "He admires George Washington, too."

The darky brought in the fingerbowls. I used them but felt as lewd as a French novel.

But to Antioch the election was more than a fine dinner. Hartley Gould Coppard, his brothers George and Nesbitt, wanted bigger and better dividends from their steel plants. They did not trust Wilson, wanted no Princeton frump still starry-eyed from teaching a polite version of American history. They wanted no college professor. They wanted a Republican and a friend of the business man. That they wanted war, I did not believe. They had a lot of back orders to fill for the Allies.

And the Cruikshanks . . . Old Alexander and his Scot broods wanted the coal and iron mines to go along as they were, tariffs left as they were. And they, too, did not want Wilson—and together they feared Ned Wonderly.

The city did not much care except that it wanted to stay out of war and Wilson had said he would. Dris and I worked hard getting Wilson posters up—and Ned Wonderly's ward heelers and two-bit bosses got ready to swing their polls 'whichever way he asked.

Doug laughed at us. He was growing bigger and surer of himself at the steel plants. There was talk of bringing cheap and hungry workers from the South if the steel puddlers and crane men and chippers and rollers really demanded enough pay to keep pace with the high cost of living. But Doug was not scared. Steel was paying huge dividends. The plants could afford to keep the men strong and well fed.

All this I heard and tried to forget. I was only interested in the victory picnic to come and the rare and spiced food I would put away.

I was growing and never had enough exotic food to eat. It was thick bread and butter and potatoes and burned beef and soggy greens when Vicky could get around to it. I dreamed of the mustarded foods that Wilson victory would bring me.

And the gangs sat around smoking cigarettes, speaking of the great hollowness they were building up for the picnic. Dris carefully combed his hair every morning and polished his shoes twice a day on the back steps and he, too, seemed to look forward to victory, but with him it was not the stomach but the heart. I was shocked to find out one day while inhaling a soda at the corner drugstore that he spent a nickel a day calling Linda Coppard on the booth phone.

The booth door did not fit very well and I heard enough to spoil my soda. Seven days a week—seven nickels—enough for seven sickening pink acid sodas with big balls of rancid-tasting ice cream.

And Dris wasted them on phone calls!

The late Indian summer was very hot. Dris and I used to go to Slavin's Slide below the lumber mill, where the river made a great pool after leaping and stirring the big mill wheels.

We would strip and go tumbling into the water and sputter and turn and splash. Dris was a fine swimmer and would go way out into the channel where the river boats passed, bringing their wild waves. Very few people knew about the pool below the mill. It was hidden by private barbwired land and gated by the mill yards. But we went along the old tow path and had the place to ourselves until the Polish girls who stood all day in the steam of the paper box factory also found the pool.

We never spoke—but all that heat spell we shared the pool. Just as dusk would fall, about ten of the girls would appear—tall wide women with red hair and firm white bodies. We all swam nude. They stayed near the mill wheel and we held the tow path. And we swam and bathed. They had wonderful bodies. Large, heavy with work, yet too young to be warped by endless childbirths, or beaten red and blue by drunken husbands. I had a strange feeling as I watched them circle the pool, cooling their tired bodies after a day of pasting together paper boxes. The clear waters of dusk held their bodies, floated them just above and just below the surface. Arms, thighs, full breasts cooled in the waters of the pool.

Dris and I circled our tow path and advanced toward them and moved back—and then again hugged our tow path. And one night we dressed and met the girls on the steep path they used behind the lumber yard.

Their clothes were cheap and shoddy and the gay little ribbons and Woolworth stuff they tried to color their persons with were unworthy of them. They were big women and beautiful women and very young. Soon they would get blowzy with the wrong kind of food; soon someone would marry or seduce them, and they would grow shabby and mean in cheap housings, and annoyed at the tugging of many brats at their nipples. But now they were very fine and we passed each other, nodding and laughing that dark laughter of youth at night.

Dris liked them and often spoke about them, but it didn't make much sense to me. Something about the fullness and honesty of life, and the wonder and decency of people not yet made dirty by greed. I suspect he got it out of a book.

But this period of bathing did not last long. Piggy Tone and his gang found our nude bathers. They stopped coming. It grew colder. Dris was too busy with the coming election. I went alone once. The water was very cold. No girls came. I went home to listen to election talk. Dris never told Linda about that pool. He never told anyone about it. . . .

EIGHT

ALL ELECTION NIGHTS of my youth I remember were almost the same—all except the re-election of Woodrow Wilson. Usually there was the big talking and tub-thumping and the free tobacco and shouting and flares and the town brats out with buttons and banners, gathering barrels and fences for bonfires, stealing outhouses and howling through the lanes with purloined building lumber, usually with a sputtering Dutchman or Hunky hot after us. The morass and incoherent stammer of politics bothered us not at all.

But the night of this election, I remember, my Uncle Thoreau and Aunt Netta were sitting in our dining room drinking hard cider, Aunt Netta as usual overdoing it and Gramp and Pete reading the late editions of the newspapers, Vicky just rocking in her rocking chair, almost lost in its large, polished oak arms. There was a definite pattern to our waiting—a family calmly waiting for news.

Douglas came up from Blue Peter's carrying a tin of beer, the suds falling away down the sides of the growler, sweated with moist, cold tears. He put down the beer and shook his head.

"Hughes all the way—it looks . . ."

"Damn them Republicans!" said Uncle Thoreau, wiping beer foam off his Kipling mustache. "They have jobbed Wilson and are preparing to get war orders. It's the sign of the machine age."

Pete shook his head. "Well, I hope we keep on selling those houses, costs going up all the time."

Gramp, in solid gauntness, angular, stirred and rubbed his great arms where a stiffness of age was beginning to settle. "It doesn't matter. We are all lost anyway. The good men died at Gettysburg, at Cold Harbor, at Atlanta. The others stayed at home and grabbed everything. Now the world has grown too small for the grabbers and they have met other grabbers from other lands . . . and we are going to fight a hundred-year war over the greed of the grabbers. There is an ominous sound in all this unsound strategy. . . ."

Vicky grinned. "I'm a grabber. So are you—only the lawyers have soured you on life. Well, me and mine, we're going to grab and hold on. Where is Dris, tonight?"

Douglas looked up from the newspapers. "Down at Ned Wonderly's place. The club stinks with lawyers and big bellies and I know tomorrow there are going to be speed-ups at the steel furnaces. How they are rushing us! They don't even let the stuff cook enough—pour it every eight hours and roll it. Some of that steel plate is like cheese."

Gramp stirred. "We fought Second Bull Run in paper shoes."

Vicky said, "Supply and demand, and when you've got demand you've got to rush supply. I keep telling Pete we've got to get more houses up. I've taken an option on fifty acres beyond the old hen houses."

Uncle Thoreau polished his glasses. "It's a swamp most of the year."

"It's dry now," said Vicky, "and I'm having drainage canals cut in it and I tell you that land is going to be full of developments within a year. Wilson or no Wilson. I can't understand this yammering over one man or another. They are both Americans, aren't they?"

Gramp hunted his hat. "So was Paul Revere's horse."

Pete got up and made for his attic bedroom. He saw Vicky was a person developing an opening for a grievance.

We all went to bed thinking Hughes had been elected. It was only when Dris came home near dawn that we knew different. I was sleeping when he banged into bed and pulled me erect by my scalp lock. I yawned out of a terribly arduous dream.

"Hey, Davey. Wilson carried California!"

"So what? I'm sleepy."

"It's an upset. It means that Wilson is *still* President!"

"That's nice."

"Ned Wonderly knew it all the time. *Never* lost confidence."

Douglas sat up in his bed across the room and lifted a heavy steel-worker's shoe. "Shut up, you political bums. I'm making steel in three hours. . . ."

The picnic in the park after the Wilson victory was very fine. I had phenomenal success in acting the glutton. I ate myself into bed with a high fever and an upset stomach. I lay a week in a hot dancing mist, feeling very light in the head and drinking chicken broth which Aunt Netta brought over every day at noon. There were wonderful Uneeda crackers soaked in the broth, and I ate them with a crude popping sound and much relish, and Aunt Netta, on the superb hams of a matador, drank gin and told me folk tales.

The rest of the time, I lay alone in the house, Vicky being off at the buildings in the sanguine immersion of fever lights. I grew to like it, this spinning lightness in the head, the buzzing red wheel that seemed never to stop spinning and, as I lay there in the late fall of the year, I would think of many and fearful things.

[104]

I wondered, I remember, about space. How could it *ever* end? Always, no matter how many universes there were, there would always be more space beyond it. Yet how could it go on forever and yet how could there be an end? It was before I ever heard of Einstein, and now that I still know nothing of Einstein I have stopped worrying about space. Another fear was that the Grand Canyon would go on cutting into the earth's surface until it cut the world into two halves like a knifed apple and the shattered globe and poor little me would go falling through space done in by a mean river. I was a great little thinker in fever and boredom, egged on by a selfish, indulgent nature.

Another thing was Dris and Linda Coppard. Before I had eaten myself into illness I had seen them in the little bandstand in the woods. Dris was looking very dapper in his neat new suit and Linda was dressed in some tight-fitting white dress with blue bows over it. They were standing very close together and he was kissing her rather obviously on the mouth and cheeks.

I stopped in my tracks—a huge roll and frankfurter half way to my greasy, eager mouth. He kissed her again and again and she leaned against him, and he leaned over and kissed her neck and she looked at him and began to cry. I got ready to run. But Dris didn't seem to mind her crying and neither did Linda, for she stopped crying; and then, very close together, they walked off down the path toward the lake after she graciously accepted his arm around her waist.

Mustard fell from the roll in my shaking hand and down my black stockings, and I looked at the long brown shape of meat and soiled roll and suddenly threw them from me. I was ill. My standards were Antioch's standards—or rather, the public virtues hammered into us at home and school, and those times I had been captive in Sunday School. Sex was evil and that was all there was to it. A reticent vulgarity. It was something one's parents were tarred with and no one but a nasty-minded, foul and evil fellow would admit that those stomach-churning emotions that came over me when I saw a girl, with the wind behind her outlining the young limberness of her figure, were anything but dirty and mean. I carried well hidden my sediment of adolescent viciousness.

Piggy and Turtle and their gangs were deep in sex—but everyone agreed they would come to no good. Piggy was wise and evil, and he was expert in luring willing factory girls into the shrubbery. Amazed, we small fry would sit around roasting spuds in a fence-rail fire listening to him, the master of us all, the teacher of things, telling us of the details of sexual pleasures to be had by the few bold ones among us.

I tried in my reading to reach the bottom of this mystery of life that was hidden and condemned, but it was all pretty flimsy and untelling in the books I got hold of. In translations from the French, one could find a man who would strip a woman naked and kiss the nipples of her lovely breasts—but usually that was as far as he went before these little marks appeared * * * * *

No—when Dris kissed Linda on the mouth and cheeks and walked with her down the path, his arm around her hips, and then held one palm dangerously near the French nation's kissing passion, I was made ill. That and soda pop and too much ground-and-peppered cheap meat and ice cream and the other truck that Ned Wonderly was giving us victorious workers in his causes.

Pale, with sweat bathing my vision, I came home and was dosed and bedded, and so I lay there for a week. When I got up I was feeble and my limbs shook and I sat in the sun, pulling grass with numb fingers, glad to be alive. The first time I had ever felt that desire to remain on earth, rather than merely accept life as something that *was*, and that was all there was to it. I accepted sun and life without passion, rancor, heroics or hypocrisy.

The sun poured down and I lay in the yard-grass and the cats walked the fences, bees buzzed among the flowers and the old oak overhead was shabby with many bird nests. I felt like that line in one of Gramp's books: *"Old, cold, withered and of intolerable entrails."*

Dris came up the path and saw me and stood over me. He looked very handsome and serious and he turned me over with a toe of his shoe—like a puppy.

"Hello, Davey. How's the inner man?"

"Fine."

He patted his meticulously parted hair, looked about him and then sat down beside me. "Davey, have you thought much of marriage?"

"I don't think I'd like it. Look at Vicky and Pete always chewing away at each other."

"Not everybody is like that. You're the only one I dare talk to. You'll marry some day."

"Not me. I'm going to be a great artist, maybe work on a newspaper and do drawings like Barney Google."

"Davey—do you think a man is too young to settle down at my age?"

I looked at him. "You and Linda Coppard?"

"Huh!"

"I saw you kiss her at the picnic."

"I oughta kick you bowlegged, you Peeping Tom."

"Didn't mean to. It was kinda public."

"I'm taking my law exams in two months and Jake Fry says he could fix it. But I don't want him to. Law is easy. But Linda—well, I guess it's one of those things just sweeps over a fellow."

I hated to spoil this. But I had begun to respect certain genealogical trees. "What about Mr. Coppard? He hates Antioch people. They aren't high-toned enough for the high-and-mighty Coppards."

"Linda doesn't care. She's going to Florida with her folks. And then, when I've passed my law exams and Jake Fry has taken me into his office . . ."

"Partner?"

"Law clerk, you mutt. But don't worry, I'll be partner yet. Well, Linda and I are going to run off and get married."

There was nothing I could say. It was hard to see a clean-cut young fellow like Dris involved in this stickiness of sex and girlish beauty. I thought of the slim young body of Linda and then of Dris and almost I was foul enough to envy them—but the banality of my social training saved me. I shook my head.

There was a *clop-clop* of horse's hoofs down the street and Gramp's buggy swung into view. Gramp was driving as if he were at the helm of the Sun Chariot, and one arm held up my brother Douglas, still in his dirty, burned, oiled, steelmaker's clothes. Doug was very pale, one eye was covered with a bandage, his face was caked with blood and his arm was tied in a gory rag.

Dris turned and snapped at me, "Remember. Keep your mouth shut." I nodded and we both ran to the gate. Gramp was helping Doug down, elbowing his pony to keep him still.

"What happened?" asked Dris, leaping to Doug's side.

Gramp rubbed his white beard, soiled with his grandson's blood. He was full of immeasurably righteous wrath.

"They beat Doug with steel bars. Niggers—with steel bars—hillbillies and white trash and niggers brought up from the South. And I found him in jail with wife-beaters and thieves."

"But why?" I asked.

Doug groaned. "The bastards, the bloody bastards! We'll show those scabs . . ."

"Easy, Doug," said Gramp. "Doug and his crews were getting ready for some wage-increase demand because of steel prices and the high cost of living. Well, the Coppards didn't wait. They brought in their scabs and when the boys objected to lower-waged help, they let them have . . . How's the arm?"

Doug grinned through his pain. "Never mind the arm. I've heard the last of their promises. We'll get an A. F. of L. charter and organize. . . ."

"Waste of time," said Gramp, carrying Doug up the steps. There was still great strength in that huge body. "Why don't you come up into the hills with me? We'll take Davey and Dris and get some stuff on a pack horse and hit for high timber and let the world go smash as it intends to anyway. You can't stop it with A. F. of L. charters or unions or hillbillies or real estate developments. A wind of formidable dimensions is going to blow cold for a long time."

We got Doug to bed and put in a drugstore call for Doctor Watson and then just stood around and watched Gramp wash Doug's wounds. They were nasty cuts but not dangerous; and when the doctor came we went back into the yard and stood there a while, all naturally reticent to talk of this thing that had shocked us.

Gramp went out to his buggy and climbed aboard and whipped up his horse. "I'm going to see if I can get some warrants out for a few arrests. They *still* have a Bill of Rights."

We watched the buggy roll off down the street. Dris kicked at a mushroom growing shyly under the oak tree.

"This is going to make it difficult. But, after all, Linda isn't to blame for what the steel plant does. Still, Doug *is* my brother."

"Well, Mr. Coppard didn't go out there and personally hit Doug on the head. . . ."

"No, Davey, he didn't. And there *is* a Bill of Rights. . . ."

It didn't seem to matter very much—the Bill of Rights, the cost of living, the color of the sky—when the United States declared war on Germany and her allies. I do not think anything mattered very much in those days except the excitement and hustle and bustle of going to war. I was ten then and I know there was a spell of joy in the air at the idea of going into battle with the foe. No one said anything of its loathsome, odious details. I have seen other wars since, but the glow, the desire, has not been in them. No, not that impetuous torrent to get into the brawling.

It was Gramp who explained it to me. We were sitting under the oak tree in the yard—just the two of us—eating fresh-picked pears from Gramp's orchard. Pears sliced and placed in a bowl of chipped ice. The rich juices ran down my chin while Gramp threw his head back to keep his beard dry. With his head back, the last remnant of a huge pear sliding down his throat, his eyes up toward where a foolish robin had nested three shrill young gullets (who had come through the summer and were now old enough to fend for themselves), Gramp studied the tree for a while. Then he said:

"They like this war. It's got fine posters, fine slogans— but mostly they like it because it's a long time since the last one. They are desperately happy—ravenous for battle. Mr. Hearst's and Teddy Roosevelt's little charade does not count. The old gaffers in blue who yarn about Grant and Lee are too much like jolly characters out of Dickens. The blood and sweat are too far away to remember. This is going to be a popular war—for a while—until physical nausea sets in."

I wiped pear juice out of my eyebrows. "Dris wants to enlist but Vicky is against it. Pete says a lawyer knows his own mind, so-called. Pete hasn't learned to like lawyers yet."

"Dris pass the bar?"

"He was first—top of the lists."

"Shame to waste a good mind among foul law books and perverted minds scrimmaging for vices to smear over public stones."

"Jake Fry says Dris can be President."

"Jake Fry is an old windbag carrying around a good mind full of mistakes he is sorry for. Any more pears?"

I ran my fingers around the lumps of ice. "No more pears."

Gramp got up and wiped his huge jackknife on his shirt front and put it away in his pants pocket. "I've got to get to court."

"Still fighting the mines, Gramp?"

"Yes. And it's no good. Government behind them. We've got to build and build, they say, and nothing else matters. Well, Davey, don't you go enlisting."

"Hell," I said, knowing Gramp didn't mind swearing, "even the Boy Scouts won't take me."

The day Dris enlisted, Vicky had sold six houses at the development, now known as Ormsbee Vista, and so she really had little time to give him the tonguing she had promised him. She just boxed his ears with dramatic abruptness and hugged him to her.

Pete took it hardest. He sat smoking his evening pipe under the grape arbor he was painfully raising outside the back door. He was a hurt man who felt he had lost his son, Driscoll, twice. Once to the law and now to the Army. I think of all of us only Dris at that time had reached any real understanding of my father's character.

Dris understood him—yet of all his sons, he was the one who was farthest from him. Dennis, in his inane sheepishness, was a stranger in his own family but a dutiful one—and loved us all. When he came home from the Navy on leave, he ate a few meals and went off to his church meeting to talk of "Sin in our Fleet" or collect old dime novels for the Navy.

The young lawyer, Driscoll Ormsbee, newly enlisted, stretched himself and looked into the yard, then slammed down the window and turned to me where I was messing up a water-color study of three ash cans and a garbage bucket being attacked by three foul-colored cats. I was rather a realist in those days and the painting of garbage appealed to me.

Dris looked down at my painting and said in a querulous voice, "Have you seen Linda lately?"

"Linda?"

"Linda Coppard, you goon, and don't talk as if you didn't know."

"No, I haven't. I thought you two were going to sort of get married once you passed the bar."

Dris shook his head. "The war and me enlisting. And—well, you know her father—and all that. Davey, she has been avoiding me."

"No." I put down my brush.

"Hell! I can't say she has—but every time I call her house she is out at a flower show or shopping with her aunt. It's hell, Davey—hell on a man in love. She doesn't understand why I enlisted."

I nodded. Neither did I.

The painting stared up at me. I thought the old fragment of fish had come out rather well. Dris sat down and faced me. "Davey, I want you to do me a favor."

"No."

"You haven't heard it yet."

"I know, but . . ."

"I can't go near King George Road—we'd be separated forever if her family ever got wind of it. But you can go. I want you to see her—and ask her to—ask her . . ."

"Ask her what, Dris?"

Dris bit his lip and snapped his fingers and shook his head. "Well, ask her if she has been avoiding me. I'd rather know that than just wait around and hope."

King George Road was well cared for. The tall elms and oaks were tailored and trimmed and the houses with their baroque façades stood well back from the road behind the barberry and privet.

Hartley Gould Coppard's, flanked by the English stone houses of his brothers, sprawled over the center of a landscaped block, a mere forty-room French Provincial house guarded by some grinning stone lions brought back by Mrs. Coppard from a trip to China.

I was not foolish enough to walk up and ring at the doorbell. I just sat on the curb drawing faces in white and red chalk. Waiting. A great car passed purring now and then, its red wooden wheels and solid thin tires sneering at me. At four I was about to give up.

Then someone dressed in white came out of the side entrance with two tennis rackets under her arm. It was Linda, white silk stockings on her splendid legs and a white silk patternless kerchief bound around her honey-colored hair.

I stepped into the drive and stood in front of her as she was about to cross the flagstone court to the tennis courts.

"I'm Davey," I said.

"How nice."

"I'm Dris—I'm Driscoll Ormsbee's brother."

"Oh," she frowned, "do you want anything?"

"Driscoll sent me."

"He did?"

"Yeah. He wants to know, *you* avoiding him?"

The girl looked at me, flushed and looked down at her tennis rackets. I felt a fool. She smiled then and said, "Davey, he shouldn't have sent you."

"I didn't wanta come. But Dris is kinda proud and, well, am I to take back an answer?"

"No. No answer. I shall speak to Dris—in good time."

"It's your old man, huh?"

"What do you mean?"

"We ain't—aren't—good enough for you. Well, my brother Dris is going to be a great man some day and your family will be proud to say you knew us—so there! Or is it because he enlisted?"

"Why, Davey, I believe you're angry at me, too."

"Well, I'm not happy about it. Your old man—he thinks . . ."

"Let's leave father out of this, Davey. We're all so young. The world is in such a mess. It's hard to think and get a good answer—a girl or a boy could trust. I love Dris, but if he wanted to be in the Army, he should have waited for the draft. I love him. . . ."

I blushed. It was a rather daring conversation, I thought.

"Well, all I gotta ask, are you avoiding Dris?"

"Yes, I have been. It's unfair. Tell him I'll meet him at five at the public library. He knows where."

[114]

"That's an answer?"

"That's an answer. You're rather cute yourself, Davey."

I walked away, cheeks on fire. I couldn't see what Dris saw in this sort of stuff.

I had forgotten about Dris and Linda and how joyfully Dris had taken the answer. That night in bed Dris kicked me away from the center of the bed and folded his arms behind his head and looked at the ceiling.

"Everything is just fine. Linda is a very sensible girl. We're going to wait a while. Maybe even six months. Linda said she would wait for me."

"That's nice," I said, disgusted.

Dris had hurt his father by becoming a lawyer and now by enlisting. But Dris was proud and he was so sure where his paths lay that he regretted he could not bridge the simple human values and differences that would have brought these two—father and son—together. Dris was too young, Pete too apologetic to life.

I was the runt of the litter—always underfoot and wrapped up in my drawing and my own dull little emotions —and so I, too, failed Pete.

It was only Douglas who managed to live with him in normal daily existence. Doug had opened a gas station after his beating at the steel mills. He had hoped to organize the plants but he was told by A. F. of L. officials that now that war was here it was un-American to put pressure on the steel owners who would fight back. It would give the A. F. of L. a bad name and of course Doug wouldn't want that, *would* he? Doug had told them to go to hell and had opened a gas station on part of the business corner that Vicky had bought for Driscoll.

Every night Doug and Pete would sit smoking under the

grape arbor with loose masculine nonchalance and talk of lumber and gas prices and three-ply paneling and transmission grease as if that were all that mattered in the world— and by 1919 even I began to think they were right. By then the carcass of civilization lay rotting in the viscid mud.

The day Dris enlisted, my father sat a long time alone under his grapes. It was Saturday and Doug had to stay late at his service station. I think Pete cried a little—that soft, soundless sob that I heard from him at least three times before I was full grown.

Gramp did not cry or sob when he heard about Dris' enlistment. Dris had two weeks before reporting for duty.

Gramp kidnapped him and me for a camping trip into the high tall timber behind his range. Out of the mad expanding crystal of the war world, he said. He hated to show emotions, did Gramp, but when he packed a horse and hit out for the pine and lake belt it was his way of going on an emotional jag.

He said, "Life is aphrodisiac, diuretic and emetic up there. And a damn lot of fun. . . ."

Getting ready to go with Gramp was simple. I packed while Dris sat and talked about the hills and wonder of the mountain meadows. Then feeling he should do his share of the packing he would tear open the packs and toss everything back on the floor and repack.

Cap Roc would call for us and we would toss our packs into the buggy and go singing up to Gramp's house. We slept in a sort of rabbit hutch under the great roof on low cots and I usually slept well. But about nine o'clock when I was ready to turn in Dris suggested we crawl out on the kitchen roof and sleep on the low-pitched roof. I felt it was a damn fool idea, but Dris had his way and soon we lay on the roof, arms folded behind our heads, staring up at a silly moon.

The roof was rough and hard and I didn't like it. Dris tossed aside his blankets and sat up. His nude body was a dark shape in the moonlight.

"Davey, people go mad under a moon—go walking along the roof ridge and nothing can make them fall."

"You feel mad, Dris?"

Dris stood up. "I don't know. I don't think so. But I would like to feel mad—to be insane *just* for a while to see what it feels like. Maybe we would all be happier that way. Not that I'm unhappy. I just like to know how people feel. . . ."

"Well, if you walk the roof ridge you walk it alone."

Dris was looking up at the moon. He held his arms up toward it and began slowly to climb up the high house roof. I saw him above, standing balanced on the roof ridge. I grabbed my blankets and got back into our rabbit hutch. Over me feet hissed and then something rolled away toward the low side of the house. It wasn't much of a drop. He wouldn't be hurt. I yawned and tried to doze off. I never had any moon madness in my whole life.

NINE

AT GRAMP's the dawn was always cold and smelled of honeysuckle vine, and it bit into the bone when the first rays of the sun came walking across the hills. Gramp would throw open the windows and rout Dris and me from the beds with a howl of wild, exultant jubilance.

This morning the mist was crawling along the fields, trying to scare the cattle. And everything was seen as if through a veil dimly from our humid morning bedroom windows.

Dris was up first and he dragged me to the pump and doused me and I howled while he dug into my ears with a rough huck towel and polished my neck red until I yelped. The water was ice cold. The hound dogs barked and blew their great rubbery cheeks in glee and bounced off our chests. We beat them off with our fists and went in to breakfast through the clucking, addle-pated hens.

Griddle cakes and sides of lean bacon were ready, and the colored cook grinned and begged us to tuck in as Gramp drove a fast pace in the hills. Gramp sat at the head of the rough table stuffing his foul tobacco into a huge pipe and shouting at us to gorge ourselves while he gave last minute orders to Cap Roc.

The pack horse was already at the door and I had but time to pull apart my scalp lock that I had dipped into the maple sugar, when the dogs began to howl and Dris kicked out at them and brought them to heel. Gramp was in checked flannels and high leather shoes and an old sweater full of holes and his faded yellow cotton hat was strung with feathered fishing flies.

He pulled the diamond hitch tight on the packs until the horse grunted, then he looked Dris and myself over and inspected our shoes and patted us across the rump and handed me the draw line and I started the pack horse along the trail. The dogs, all except Major who was to come with us, were locked howling in the house. Roses and nasturtiums bordered the path going up.

The sun was still cold and below us the bustle of war-making and a people full of war and war talk and war business seemed very far away. By noon we were beyond the range of the factory smoke and the last hint of chimney stink against the sky. Splendid ranges soared above us in the sun, loamy dewy fields wet us.

We walked into the afternoon, the horse having a fine time tearing up with his ragged teeth the slim green bough that was stupid enough to dare the open path of the trail. The going was hard—turning from packed clay to shale and from that to a carpet of pine needles and the remembrances of old oak leaves. We passed men hewing tan bark. The path was rising all the way and the trees grew taller and the wind was wiser and didn't bear soot and slag dust. Even the dog, Major, sniffed the pungent, maddening blossoms.

The lakes were silver and the birch matched them tone for tone, but later in the day the water turned darker and the crayon-blue sky held a steady cobalt blanket between the few cotton clouds. There were flagroot and sweet fern and Gramp gathered some.

Dusk came suddenly but Gramp was ready for it. We were soon against a great out-jutting castle of a rock and our tent was up and the coffee pot bubbling and sending maddening odors into the fast-darkening air. A hedge of hemlock broke the wind on our back.

Dris came back from the lake with a hatful of leaping fish, and Gramp had the fire roaring itself out into a bed of embers and soon the fish were dipped in crackerdust and jacketed in bacon and frying and we ate them with beans and hot bread freshly made in a closed pot. We all ate sitting among ginseng and yellow violets. The coffee was too hot and I swallowed it until tears came and then we all leaned over and wiped out the frying pan and had more coffee and then Dris and Gramp lit their pipes and the night sounds and the night moths closed in. We sat, three dark shapes against a darker night-rock and night-wood, and all we did was digest and look into the fire and then we went down to the lake to wash. It was a grand night. A primordial vapor haunted the lakes.

I hunted big roots and logs and banked the fire, and Gramp had laid the blankets over fresh cut pines and slowly we sank back and with arms folded behind our heads we looked at the stars brushing the tree tops. Across the lake, a loon sounded. And something crushed its way through the woods and we heard the picketed pack horse chewing grass, tearing with his broken teeth the earth surface and pulling nourishment into himself. Then the dog came back, mouth open, tongue out, laughing about something he had scented near the dead patch of lightning-struck trees. And then I slept.

I awoke once to find Gramp pulling the blanket closer around me, and the fog was drifting in over the lake and the moon was bigger than it could ever be. The dog sniffed the ashes near the dying fire and I was asleep again—asleep until the morning wind made seaside sounds in the birch leaves. I sat up yawning and looked about me and I suddenly knew that life was very good. The piny air tickled my throat. A small male happiness stirred me.

Gramp was skinning a rabbit, and the bread baking in the

closed pot was the most wonderful thing I had ever smelled. Far out on the lake Dris was fishing from the rubber folding boat. He shouted something and waved and it took a long time for his voice to reach us. Higher, I saw coarse mountain pasture, a world-remote house, cows.

I closed my eyes and lay back on the blankets and wriggled my toes for joy and it was not until the dog came over to run his cold nose over me that I got up, mother-naked, and went down to the lake to bathe, stretching and yawning and groaning. I dried myself on wrench grass.

I was hungry.

We did not stay at the lower lakes. We gathered our stuff and banged the load onto the pack horse until his knees shook, but we drew in the ropes until his eyes rolled and then we went higher. The going was rough, the trail less marked among laurel and rhododendron.

I have never seen such trees. They were Gramp's trees and he was fighting to keep them out of the lumbering saws' evil teeth. They were ropy, obscene trees and the moss was on them like the coating of age on a turtle's shell. It took almost a full minute to walk around them through the clinging underbrush. They filled the sky and made a darkness, a green-blue underworld like a sea bottom, for us to walk through. In some places we broke away from the trail and there we found twenty and thirty feet of dead leaves and vegetable matter and old limbs and seed pods that had been piling up for five and six hundred and maybe more years. Ours were the first feet to cut into this mold, to break the surface of this great, piled-up wealth of fungus and festering mold and fertile soil. Trees that had never seen man before sheltered us and earth that had not seen the sun in almost a thousand years of tree-made darkness formed our beds.

But the big trees passed and we were on the backbone of the world where only rocks had families and the little, twisted, warped versions of trees were out of fairy tales, evil fairy tales.

But that, too, was soon passed and we crossed the ridge by a tumbling iron-rock trail and waterfalls wet us and spindrift and spume from great columns of dropping water wet us to the skin. Below were the fat golden sheaves of corn, the torpid haze of cultivation.

At noon we stripped and lay on pale red rocks and let the sun dry us and Gramp told us tales out of his youth and we fingered a scar on his thin ribs that a certain evil day had brought to his body.

He was a giant grown old, a perfect machine running down, and the strength was still in the hard calves and in the stony biceps; but the flesh of the belly—while still lean— was beginning to sag, and the pucker around the throat crisscrossed like a road map. The beard was very white. It was sad to see a man's body betray him, to see the steady dreadful tearing down of tissue and form that would be completed only when the soil takes over the one you love. But I was younger then and callous, and not so full of ethical instincts as I am now, and so perhaps I did not think too much of old age that day. I was self-conscious in my nudity.

Driscoll was a young man of perfect mold and when he yawned and kicked the ground with his hard heels, the body muscles rippled. I didn't pay too much attention to myself. I was at the age of string-bean thinness. The pubic pride in body hair was about to begin (I prayed).

But a chill breeze drove off the sun and so we dressed and dug the horse's face out of the green gage bush, whistled for the dog and pulled the whining horse away from the bad taste of a tree marked by polecats and went on. We passed many Lombardy poplars.

That night we camped on a sandbar alongside of the rushing stream. In the eddy it was calm and the sandbar was bone-white in the moonlight. Fish leaped and turned over in the air all around us and the dog treed something and did not let it rest until dawn. Then he lay down and snored in the sand until I kicked him and he yelped. The sky of morning was one golden disk of light. The sandbar and the stream and the green edges of the world were all merged into one eye-blinking glare. And closer it became wild grape and savin, walnut, spruce.

I swam a long time in the lime-green water and Dris came and ducked me and I choked and swallowed muddy bottom water but I got away at last and I tied Dris's shirt into such wet knots that a week later he was still puffing and chewing at it with his teeth.

We made permanent camp against the friendly back of an old tree that could no longer stand erect and we built up a platform of stones and covered part of it with elm and pine branches. And I set up the tent. Gramp and Dris plastered up a stone pit for cooking and sent the horse up a close valley and fenced in the opening with saplings so he could eat crimson sorrel and crowfoot blossoms in safety.

The next morning there was a mist rolling on the earth. And later the sun would tear it away and we would go down to the lake and it would be very cold. Cold enough, Gramp said, to hurt brass monkeys, but it was fine too, to float around and lash out with chilled arms until I could feel the blood pounding through my chest journeying to warm my toes and my shivering body. I wished I had a bigger set of muscles.

Dris was best. He had developed. A tall wide young man with a barrel chest and long brown limbs. Gramp and I would float in the water, watching him swim away out into the middle of the lake and back again, his head flashing like lacquer in the wet morning, the long hair flicked back over his shoulder by a laughing head and then we would come out of the water naked and stand in the sun drying by the shadbushes and harebells. I sketched them on a paper bag.

Gramp, all muscle with a slack belly and a brown, hairless chest and long limbs that showed almost in outline what a fine figure he had once been and still was. Dris, filling out, and the buttons on his paps were hard and brown and the water ran off his smooth hide into the hardness of his belly and down his legs. He was a man already and I envied him his powers and regretted my own soft belly and hairless state. But I was growing and could chin myself four times to Dris's ten on the limb of the pine tree that grew with crazy pride over the lake.

Dris fished and I gathered wood and dug a peony bush for Vicky. Gramp stirred secrets in a pot and we ate and ate and Gramp had a few bottles of beer cooling on strings in a spring-bottom and we drank them down and I belched gas up through my nose. After the first week, the beer was all gone.

Then we had no more tinned milk. Gramp fixed dough and baking soda and wound it around sticks and toasted it. Soon we were down to coffee and potatoes and a side of bacon and so we hunted small animals and skinned them and salted and peppered them and ate them with relish. And the dog grew wilder.

Our hair grew and Dris and Gramp had beards and I had, I thought, a mild fuzz. We lived off the land and it was good. Dris said nothing about his enlistment but I would catch him brooding over his fishing lines although we never spoke about it. And once I ducked him deep in a spiral of phosphorescence during a night swim.

[124]

We moved high on the ridge and were beside a leaping, chortling stream. The fire was low—rabbits came to stare at us but we were too full of a hot day's bathing and hunting and fishing to bother them. The last of the coffee bubbled in the pot, tossing the lid like a chatter of wild teeth. A pulsing feline silence brooded over the wilderness.

Gramp was carving a cane out of a knob-rooted bit of hickory. Dris came toward the coffee pot, lifted it off the fire with his old hat and poured coffee into our tin cups until the pot was empty. There was no sugar left. We looked at each other and smiled. We knew that tomorrow we would break camp, find the hobbled horse grazing below somewhere and head back to Antioch and the world full of madness and production and war. We looked into our cups with an amicable quietness.

Dris sipped his coffee. "Gramp, you're wrong—wrong about this war. . . ."

"Am I, boy? Maybe I am. I've lived a long time and seen a lot of battles—a lot of conflicting reality. There isn't any good in it and never will be. Not in any war. It isn't all recruiting posters—not by a long shot."

"I don't mean that," said Dris. "I'm thinking of why we are fighting. Oh, to hell with the slogans and all that! It's deeper than that. Deeper than the Morgan loans or a safe fifty-percent investment in death-dealing toys or Henry Ford or Rockefeller oil boats. . . ."

Gramp took out his old briar and cut plug into its bowl. "Is it? Are we fighting for the men who starved in covered wagons once—are we fighting for the land and the green trees and the rivers and the little people on the dirt roads —or are we fighting to keep the sales charts going? I don't know for sure any more. I fought a long war—four years full—I got a belly full. They say we saved the Union, but the stink of the new millionaires who made a good thing out of poisoned beans and rotten shoes and broken guns is always in my nostrils. I saw the banks take over the farms of those who walked in the Wilderness with Grant. I saw the railroad crooks and the Goulds and Fisks and their ilk steal the valleys from the mates I slept with before Five Forks. I saw the lethal smothering of little storekeepers. And now there are the Du Ponts and Astors and the Vanderbilts riding high over the production of the tools of war and sending boys like you out to get your heads split open for the finest moral reasons, with the greatest hope for a fine peace. *But . . .*"

Dris looked a long time into his coffee cup. "You're wrong, Gramp. I've been reading history. The swine and wolves may hold their dirty teeth in the hides of all of us —but they'll die and everything they ever stood for will be just marked papers in vaults. They can't last. And let them have their little day in the sinking sun. You, Gramp, and all your friends were bigger than they."

Gramp picked up a coal from the fire and held it in his horned hands and set fire to his pipe again. "That's a hell of a way for a young boy to talk. Book talk, *that's* what it is."

I nodded. "He's reading all the time."

Dris grinned and playfully pinched my stomach. "Maybe I'm all wet. Maybe I talk like a book. But, Gramp, underneath we are fighting to keep ourselves clean. I don't hold much with England and France. Anything they are getting they deserve. But the Germans are worse. They just don't want trade routes and all the money in the banks. They never have been anything but bloody savages since Caesar found them—mugs with working minds and a way with official bloodshed on battlefields. They'll come over here and take us over like a fish pond. They'll give us their so-called *kultur* and bind us to their ideas of bone-eating living and exploit the world around us for their God-damn Seat in the Sun."

"Maybe," said Gramp. "But they reproduce like other people, they get hungry and die and while they may like following orders a little too easily, their big ideas are stupid and childish and only dangerous now because the rest of the world has drifted about hunting dividends and holding companies instead of standing a little humble before the wonders of the universe. . . . And eating camp cooking for a week or so."

Dris scowled. "I know what I want to know and I feel I'm right. I swear, Gramp, we've got to stop the Germans before they make this a German world—and then no more camping out or going where you damn well please."

"Oh, hell," said Gramp, blowing smoke rings into the wind. "I don't know everything—I don't want to. I want to live a few more years and see my children and my grandchildren play alive in the sun. I want to eat and sleep and shoot wild game and walk under tall trees. I want to see the sun rise and a good horse run and I want to re-read a few old books. I'm an old man sitting by cooling embers and the taste in my mouth is good. I'm not full of hot blood and I don't want to understand the reasons behind the tearing of human flesh by human hands and tormented steel. Maybe after you've seen war, Dris, you'll understand. *If* the Huns are loose again let's round them up and put them behind barriers they'll never come out of again. But let's not talk of crusades and battle banners as if this is just a bank vacation. And let's live a while and enjoy something of what we have. . . . I'm going to make a duffelbag stew. . . ."

I stirred with interest. "What's a duffelbag stew?"

"It's the last night in camp. You empty all the remaining tins and cans and paper bags—and get some nice young ducks and rabbits and young deer, maybe, and stir them all together and eat it at dawn after a night of simmering, just before you pack up. And it's the best thing to remember and the *last* thing you enjoy before getting back to the city. . . ."

The wind rose, and the old man took us down to the lake and we stood at the lake shore watching the sun die a clown's death. The waves were white-capped on the lake and bird calls and boughs rubbing together made a soft background for the splendid garishness of the sunset. We stood against an unbranched bole of a great tree in the russet-bronze light.

At our feet the lake waters lapped over smooth pebbles and a squirrel overhead scolded us and frisked his tail in disdain.

Slowly we went back to camp and I shall never forget it. The round-shouldered tent against the great boulders and the fire winking in the dusk, the scent of pine needles and the packs resting on tall, wild-grown sod. And somewhere the night insects were playing soft music in the silver chaos of birches on the subsiding hills below. . . .

Two days later Dris went away to war. I did not go home. I went to live with Gramp. Fall was howling through old silvered fences. Our home was broken, scattered by the demands of war. Dennis was in the North Sea sweeping mines. Doug was running gas stations and giving Pete a hand with the buildings.

Ormsbee Vista was growing; standing in mud, it spread its shoddy housings up the valley and nothing could stop the war boom. No matter how high rose the costs, the demand for houses went on.

The mines and mills grew dirtier, smokier and worked faster. The slag heaps and mine refuse grew taller, and the river ran yellow and deadly poison on its way to the sea.

Gramp and Cap Roc bought more cattle and ranged the hills inspecting his herds. He never accepted the war talk and war hates and the war cause but he did not talk any more about his own battles of long ago. Dris and Dennis were facing battles now.

He was still as strong as ever but his limbs hurt at times and I would rub his knotted aching muscles and he would read to me from his books to keep what he called *"the ape gabble of the press"* out of his ears.

Night air and night sounds I remember, and the cattle crossing the dark brook to drink and hunt for salt among the rocks and the loaded ore trains and ore boats and coal freights whistling far away. And there were trucks marching along the dusty roads, loaded and heavy like pregnant women, groaning over the ruts. But I only heard Gramp read . . .

I, rubbing Gramp's stiff arm while he read to me—the long, white beard in place and the lamplight gilding the solid planes of his face . . .

And I can remember word for word the lines he read one night from the big volume of William Herndon's *A Natural History of the World:*

"In the body of the female of the great deep-sea turtle the future of the horny-shielded race is kept safe in the twenty to forty thousand eggs that the plastron shells of her green body holds together. She lays four or five hundred of these eggs a year and so the smallest egg is not to be laid for almost a century yet. In the body of the giant deep-sea turtle a slow steady pregnancy of fifty to a hundred years goes on . . . In the hard shell the future generations lie waiting to spawn . . .

"In the night the creeping turtle comes out on the sands and digs by some subtle reasoning of nature a hole, and lays her yearly deposit of eggs toward the continuance of the race of deep-sea turtles, and covers them with sand, and goes back to the sea. leaving the future to take care of itself. Those broods the sun warms into life on the lonely shore.

"The first young turtle breaks out of the egg and comes out into the light of life and day. Clumsily the small life waddles out of the nest followed by brothers and sisters and in single file they make for the shallows of sea wrack and kelp. Here wait hungry fish who have tasted young turtle before and have great hunger and no mercy. Of the few hundred little turtles that leave the nest, not more ten or twenty reach the reefs leading to the open sea. The rest are gone from life into the maws of the fishes, have lived a short space and served their purpose: holding and delaying the hungry turtle-gulpers so that ten or twelve brothers and sisters can reach the reef.

"Once through the breakers, where half their number is lost to gobbling spotted eels, the few survivors plunge into the swirling sea where bigger fish wait. One or two may escape to their destiny, to life; and from their inner organs will the race of deep-sea turtles go on living over the face of the earth . . .

"Some day, perhaps, the sea-teeth will be too many, and no young turtle will be able to struggle through into life . . . and in a turtle generation or so, the sea shall be empty of plastron shell.

"That it has not happened so far in the natural history of the world is no sign that it *cannot* happen. . . ."

BOOK TWO

TEN

THE WORLD, persuasively unrationalized, was slow to awake from its dreadful dream. It stirred, groaned, and even in Antioch the newspapers had long since forgotten the unimportance of the Peace Conference and shoved it off the front pages.

It was a dull, logy peace with a sense of no peace at all. The slogans and the cheering were locked away, perhaps for another crusade to come. A cold brittle light came up on a tired desolation. No one felt anything had really been done across the seas.

"The mangy, shouting statesmen," said Gramp, "stamping their heels on each other's stomachs and sharpening their knives for each other's throats. Ready for new wars as soon as the little people have bred another crop of soldiers. And the foul diplomats have again reached the ends of their ropes in their lying, face-eating, gentlemen's game of politics and markets and safe divisions and dividends."

Gramp was growing very old. His limbs were twisting. His features were dissolving away until his bones seemed almost to break the skin of his face. One got a disquieting impression of the shortness of life. But his beard was still a white flame and the pride of his life. I think that the care of his beard and the battle of all his lawsuits was all that kept him alive. He was still a giant among the short bulbous men of the law courts.

There was no pleasure to be found in the family's progress toward that social and fortune-filled plane Vicky had planned. Ormsbee Vista stood knee-deep in its river mud— a crumbling, peeling development of stench-filled streets and stony gardens and sagging, warped timbers. But it did not matter. It now belonged to the bank, and a receiver with a nose like a hinge ran it.

Vicky had overbuilt. The Peace had caught her unexpected and so, with a hundred new scabby little huts on her hands unsold, the end had come to her bright hopes. Her warped vista careened tipsily. The mills had stopped grinding out planes and trucks and shells and great guns.

Uniforms, army shoes, gun carriages and bayonets were no longer needed. The Peace Conference tables were to be a more deadly set of weapons. But the Polacks and the Yankees and hillbillies and Negroes and Hunkies and hodcloppers were no longer wanted by the hundreds of thousands. The smoke went out of most of the steel furnace chimneys; not so many men crawled underground to hack out coal. Rickets and scabies appeared among the children in the company houses. And panicky-eyed fathers slapped them. Then wages went down. Strikes broke out and heads were split and the state troopers and National Guards and company thugs and finks went through Polack Point breaking men's bodies. And for a week tanks rumbled across the Jefferson River and through Coppard Square. Barbed wire was locked in ugly welts across King George Road. Then it was all over.

The strikes were broken and that was the end of the revolt of the little people whose sons had died in the Crusade and whose arms had built the fighting tools and whose savings had gone into a stupid installment-buying trap. There were, after that, no more of those industrial wars that bloodied the streets in the rest of the big industrial cities. The Coppards and Cruikshanks had strangled all such violence in one fast, brutal assault on the little people who had quivered rebelliously for one mad minute.

Gramp said it was better so. Once the little people had their lesson they were better off to be still and take what was handed out, rather than go again and again to the gates of the masters to get their heads opened. Vicky would have none of such talk. Her hopes broken, wiped out, she was back to living off the wood carving and cabinetmaking my father could pick up, yet she still had the tongue and spirit that would never leave her. And from which we ducked defensively at the first sound.

"Well, a fine thing to hear from my own father. Talking like one of them Bolshevikies—dirty rats with their bombs and filthy habits . . . I tell you, things are going to boom again. The soldiers are coming home, people are going to have to eat and live and have families and go places and do things. I'm not licked *yet!* Great day in the morning! *If* the war had lasted another six months we would have been worth a half million dollars. . . ."

Pete got up and put on his jacket. "On paper. I don't understand such things."

"On paper. Stop talking like an ignorant Hunky hoarding gold pieces in his smelly socks. Paper—that's credit. And paper—that's commerce. And paper—that's something that keeps us going. Do you think Hartley Gould Coppard carries his millions around in old torn greenbacks?"

"No, Vicky . . ."

"You're a damn fool, Pete Ormsbee, and always will be. A clod, a stick of the field and it's a good thing my boys still have their mother to take care of them."

Gramp snorted. "They're pretty big—big enough to take care of themselves. When is Dris coming home?"

"Any day," said Vicky. We all turned and looked over at the mantel on which stood an enlargement of a snapshot

[134]

showing Dris—very tall and handsome, even in a badly fitting army uniform—his overseas cap tilted over one eye. He was standing on a bridge and behind him a Rhine city was marked against a river hillside. Dris was with the Army of Occupation.

Gramp shook his head, flexed his fabulous nostrils. "Now he's a policeman collecting the swag for the bagmen. Helping the carpetbaggers with the most laudable motives."

"Nonsense," said Vicky, "he's going to college and learning to *parlay vous* and speak German. What a nasty way of talking *that* is . . ."

Pete turned from the window. "There is a cab stopping in front of the house. . . ."

"Our house?"

"It must be Dris," I said, leaping out of the door and across the yard. The battered taxi stood breathing weakly at our curb.

It was not Dris who fumbled for the fare. It was Dennis. For the first time in three years out of his sailor uniform. He was wearing baggy, belted tweeds of some moss-green shade that did not go very well with his earnest tanned face. He smiled as he saw me and I took his hand. Tiny pimples lurked in the corners of his thin mouth and his colorless hair had thinned out, showing a bumpy forehead. His eyes sat—as ever—deep in his head, sombrously contemplating.

"Well, welcome home," I said. "We thought you were still at the Boston Navy Yard."

"Discharged a week . . ." Dennis turned, handed the cabby the fare and pulled a small, thin girl from the cracked leather interior of the cab. She had a spotted complexion, very wonderful blue eyes and full lips, slightly open so that she moved them with every breath she took. She seemed to have some bronchial condition—breath came very heavy for her—so that she had a heavy, stupid and sensual look.

[135]

"This—this is Davey. Davey—this is my—this is *Mrs.* Dennis Ormsbee."

I stood very still and just stared. And then Vicky was upon them. Behind her with less hurry came Gramp and Pete. Dennis flushed so that the pimples around his mouth turned white. Then he repeated his little speech in his high, febrile voice.

"Ma—Vicky—this is *Mrs.* Dennis Ormsbee."

And so Dennis came back from the wars—a laudable husband—but sombrously afraid of his mother. . . .

Her name was Rose. She came from the fringe of an old Boston family but not from Back Bay. Her father was a minister who had lost the faith so many times and tried the true light so often that at last no church would harbor his wandering hopes of discovering the true, indefinable mystery.

I met him once. I have vague recollections of a tall, honest man with a good mind encased in the lard of theology, who spent twenty years proving (in an unpublished book) that Christ would have been a follower of Karl Marx had he lived today. Such thinking lost him his last pulpit and so he set up a mission in an old store near the wharves of Boston and sent his vast brood out over the city with cups and booklets and tracts begging for a living while he brooded over future incarnations and *Das Kapital.*

Rose's father liked Dennis the first time my brother appeared in his mission and offered to lead a group of broken-down sots and sods through a Bible lesson. Rose showed him his classroom and that week-end he took her out to tea (on the Charles River) and told her of his pagan family and on the way home (he once told me) the devil entered his flesh and he put his fingers on Rose's breasts and kissed the slightly open, puffy lips and a great desire came over him and then they both cried and promised to be good. And Dennis worried away another week and little pimples formed on the corner of his mouth. The flesh, with delicious, original talent, tormented him. And so he went and spoke to her father of what he had done to his daughter's breasts and the father said the only thing to do was to get the sinners together in holy wedlock. And so they did.

Three days later they came home, after they had spent a honeymoon visiting the old whaling churches—between which visits Dennis managed at last to plant the seed that was to be the first of their eleven children. A colorless, dull-eyed spawning of soggy brats that I never relished being uncle to and to whom Dennis taught the higher things while he beat on their bottoms and put the fear of a jealous God and three hundred Bible verses into their little scrawny souls. In his ferreting, lamenting manner, Dennis enjoyed the wedding bed.

Naturally, Vicky never thought Rose was good enough for Dennis. Two weeks after the return of the bridal pair —who thumped out hymns and a greater understanding of each other in what had formerly been our bedroom—we got the War Department announcement that Captain Driscoll Ormsbee was coming home—*honorably discharged*.

The bands no longer played *Hail the Conquering Hero* when the soldiers came home at the Antioch station. The time of music and joy was over and the crystal air was cold as ice. The soldiers were beginning to slip home unnoticed, and too many of them were finding no jobs held for them. They stood around in wrinkled Army clothes watching the city walk past them. They stood with stolid patience at first. Then their stoic gestures turned to limp fear.

Dris was due in on the noon express. And Uncle Thoreau had tinkered with the metal gizzards of his flivver and got it moving and Vicky and I and Dennis went with him to welcome our Captain home. Pete couldn't leave his work bench because of a sudden rush of seven coffins for influenza victims and Doug was pumping gas—alone, now that he no longer needed a helper.

We all went up on the top train platform and stood around waiting. It was the first hot, gritty day, with far-off distances of silver tracks dancing in the spring heat and the repair gangs in bright shirts toiling like ants on the local rails, while gandy dancers swung their picks and drove the ballast under the ties. And in the hills beyond there was the quiet weather of country silence. Then there was the distant pencil scribble of smoke and the signal arms broke away and became set in a new position and the express was seen far out on the garden-patch plains, struggling very quickly to mount the stone elevations that carried it through the city of Antioch.

"There he is," I shouted.

"Late as usual," said Vicky. "Never do give a taxpayer any service. Heaven knows they get enough fares."

Uncle Thoreau leaned way over and nodded and the train came closer, a brown-streaking, chocolate-colored shape and its noise grew louder, air brakes hissed, iron groaned and the train thundered in, car after car—Pullmans deep in plush, with well-fed faces looking down at us. Then we saw the day coaches. People began to pour from the train.

A cloth-covered bag fell at our feet and over us stood Captain Driscoll Ormsbee, still in uniform, peaked cap, shoulder bars, Sam Browne belt and little cane. And a smudge of a mustache under his tanned nose. I felt an immense vitality and a big hand waving.

"Hello there!"

"Dris!" shouted Vicky, and he leaped down and pointed

to some bags, and he caught Vicky in his arms and lifted and kissed her. Then he turned to us and patted Uncle Thoreau on the back and winked at Dennis and pulled my ear as I collected his bags. Complete intimacy had been renewed among us. Dris had a specific talent for it.

"Well. You're all looking well."

Vicky stood back. "You're thin. That damn Army food. Starving you boys while the fat Congressmen eat like pigs. Did you have enough underwear?"

Dris laughed. "That's no question to ask a Captain. Where is Gramp?"

Uncle Thoreau helped me with the bags. "As usual, in court. Said he might make it."

Dris frowned. "Still in court?"

"Yes. Tough old bird. They've got him pushed way back on the Range. Land titles all wrong, they claim. And he's had to sell a lot of acres for back taxes and to recover from hoof and mouth in the herds . . ."

"Dennis is married—Dennis is married!" I said.

Dennis shook hands with his brother. "It's good to see you back. I prayed we would all come back—us Ormsbees."

"That's fine of you," said Dris, taking Vicky by the arm. "Now let's get home to Pete. And Doug—how's he?"

"Broke," said Uncle Thoreau. "The oil king put up two fifty-thousand-dollar gas stations on his both sides and they do everything but escort you to the toilet."

"Thor!" said Vicky, acting incredibly naive as she held on to the big Captain's arm.

"Anyway, he doesn't sell much gas any more. Collecting pictures of ocean-going boats again."

Dris suddenly stopped and turned around. "You've got to excuse me. I crave indulgence. I've got to make a phone call. . . ."

He went into a booth and Vicky waved her tiny hands. "For heaven's sake, who can he be calling?"

I smirked. "His girl—that's *who*."

"Who is she?" asked Vicky.

"I ain't telling."

"Who is she?"

"I *ain't* . . ." and Vicky cut me short with a strong slap of her little hand against my ear.

"Pick up them bags. I never had any use for a tale bearer. You're an exasperating fool, Davey. If it's anything serious Dris will tell his mother in good time, I'm sure."

I picked up the bags, brooding over the discrepancies in human nature a growing boy runs into.

Gramp was waiting for us at home. Everyone was there. Aunt Netta, buoyant and optimistic, and her growing brood, Pete in from the tool shed and later Doug came home, having recklessly locked his gas pumps, saying no one wanted his gas, anyway. There was a great deal of talk and Dris walked around giving military orders to show Aunt Netta how it was done and then everyone ate a great deal of the rich food Aunt Netta had been cooking all day and by the time the sun was down we were exhausted from welcoming the hero home in a mellifluous flow of preposterous opinions on the post-war world.

Dris had grown into a huge man—very tall, with wide shoulders and a thin waist, long strong arms. The planes in his face had gone serious and he had a habit of walking around with his hands clasped behind his back. On his neat jacket were pinned two medals, the Distinguished Service Cross and some French order with green ribbons. From his bags he unloaded some presents. Some perfume for Vicky, a nude wooden woman carved in the shape of a pipe (which Pete hid at once), a German trench helmet for me and English military hair brushes for my brothers. And a great deal of unwashed linen.

Uncle Thoreau kept winking and asking for French postal cards and Aunt Netta boxed his ears and thanked Dris for the set of plates with the Eiffel Tower painted on them.

I saw those plates last week—or the four left of the set. They had been cracked and mended. They hung on Aunt Netta's dining-room wall. But I lack that spiritual vitality to connect anything of moral value to their survival.

It was upstairs in the room we all used to sleep in that Dris broke his complacency. Pete sat at the window, smoking. Doug had gone back to his gas pumps and his brooding over ships' plans. Uncle Thoreau had driven his brood home. But Gramp had stayed and Dennis had gotten out some snapshots of Navy comrades while Dris opened a small bottle of French brandy and toasted the inevitable collapse of the world, yet to come.

We were all drinking it from cracked mugs—even I had an inch of the stuff. Gramp wiped some beads of brandy from his beard. His beard and his thought were inextricably tangled this day of Dris' return.

"Well, Dris, now that you've helped save the world, what are you planning to do? If anything."

Dris frowned, swallowed his brandy and refilled. "Saved, my behind. We didn't save a thing. We were sold out by a lot of dirty dogs in wing collars and cutaway coats at the Peace Conference."

Dennis nodded and put down his brandy untouched. "It was nothing like we were told. I was at Brest with the food convoys. The harbor floating with millions of dollars of foodstuffs, thrown away by Army commissions because the French grafters would give us no docks to unload the stuff.

And then we took one convoy to Russia—one-hundred-million-dollars' worth of food and supplies sinking into a swamp at Archangel and as soon as the stuff disappeared in the muck we threw other loads on in. Food, lumber, tents, cars, wheat—everything—and in the town the girls were selling themselves for a slice of bread."

Gramp held out his mug.

"It's of no use—this war. They started the war to put away the German tribes. But they haven't locked away the savages. They are just starving the Germans and letting them yell among themselves. They are trying to work them like slaves and squeeze out of them what they can't give. You can't treat barbarians like that. The Germans are like Indians. They'll never learn to live like men. Happiness is of secondary consideration to them. You've got to put them on reservations and guard them while you feed them and give them blankets. They are the evil spirits that will haunt us all like a guilty conscience."

Dris shook his head. "The Heinies aren't so bad. I met a lot of their rank and file. They seemed glad it was all over."

"The rank and file doesn't matter," said Gramp. "You can't march a lot of little men around, removing their minds while you do it for a thousand years, and then suddenly change their way of looking at things. The Junkers and the landowners and the steel masters will rise again and the herd will follow because they are conditioned like—*like*—Davey, what's that fellow who works with dogs?"

"Pavlov, the Russian."

"That's the man. He had dogs reacting to bells. One bell means food, two bells means pain, three bells means a walk. The dogs don't think any more. They just react to the bells. The Germans, the little people of Europe—they just wait for the bell. All Europe is bell-trained. Dinging dismal bells in a glutinous, reeking slime. Damn the bell makers!"

Dris emptied the last brandy into the mugs. "It's not that bad. There are men all over who count and mean something. Even in England and Germany and among the French high-bourgeois grafters. It's men that count, Gramp. Give them time in Europe, they'll figure something out."

"I hope so," said Gramp, "but you still haven't told me what you're going to do."

Dris began to take off his jacket. Then he pulled off the shirt. A long, red welt ran down his right side. He fingered it tenderly.

"Shell fragment still in there some place. Hurts like hell when it rains. I'm going into the firm of Fry, Rogers, Coppard and Ormsbee. A *full* partner!"

Gramp snorted. "A lawyer. Better if that shell had gone in higher. A lawyer, with belly bulging pronouncedly and Blackstone in your hair!"

Dris grinned. "But first I've got a date with a girl."

"Liquor and women," said Gramp. "Soldiers don't change much."

Today the brown rabbit came very close and watched me cook lunch over the stone-built field oven. Every day he has come closer and today for the first time he did not turn his white tail toward me and run for home when I spoke to him.

I had to speak to someone. Even a rabbit. Writing is all very well, but a man likes to hear his own voice, and the rabbit is a good listener. The first grasshoppers are springing about and at night the tree frogs sing to me of love. The trees are madly going green.

The rabbit is still there. I don't think the other rabbits like him. He is hunting company too. I hope I can resist the desire for rabbit stew. . . .

ELEVEN

THE BEER WAS BAD now at Blue Peter's. Men with hard faces were appearing on the scene and delivering barrels at midnight. But the citizens of Antioch drank it and asked for more. I saw my old school gangs—Turtle and Piggy Tone driving through town on huge trucks covered with dirty canvas but smelling of stale beer hops. Others of the gang walked around knocking on rusting iron grills of basement doors or were peddling alki and cut hair-tonic to nervous little Wops and Polacks who didn't understand yet that everyone looked upon them as saviors and not lawbreakers. We were willing to pay a great deal of money to gulp the foul stuff and groan about the good old days as nauseating revulsions welled up in our stomachs.

When Dris entered the firm of Fry, Rogers, Coppard and Ormsbee, Jake Fry and Ned Wonderly gave him a party at Blue Peter's. But not in the beer garden. The garden stood empty and dirty. The front entrance of the house had been closed and everyone drove up the alley under the glazed cupola of the place and knocked at the closed kitchen door and felt damned brave and excited about the romance of the thing.

I went to that party. Dennis was away from home looking for work. Doug, solid, angry, hurt Doug, had joined the Honest Citizens' Group and cursed Ned Wonderly and his damned machine. Uncle Thoreau was back with Henry George. Gramp never went to parties any more. And my father would not sit down with lawyers. It gave him a psychological satisfaction to think them bigger failures than he was.

But I was willing. I was anxious. I even took a bath.

The great cellar of Blue Peter's Beer Garden had been decorated by paper grape leaves, and some stained-glass walls were put up to make booths. A new yellow bar was staining fast with spilt beer, and the barmen were new people with glassy green eyes and warped jaws. Only Blue Pete hadn't changed. He remained a Bavarian-Alpine type, looking like a neolithic man in modern dress. He was a square yellow brawler with a cocky tobacco-stained mustache and a voice to match. He wore checked pants, had baggy knees and hard little red hands like bung-starters. When excited, he would flutter his lips wetly and wink at everyone for no good reason with a blank, reptilian stare.

He was excited now as he stood with Jake Fry at the bar, trying to talk up the price of the extra wine. Jake was gulping Old Fashioneds and not giving way with an inch of his vast gut, tonight clothed in formal black and chained into place by many gold links holding their assortment of Lodge trash and emblems of phallic shapes.

Jake shook his fat neck and came toward me, a drink in each hand, a design in fat, wet black and ochre.

"Where's Dris, Davey?"

"He went to get a shave."

Jake finished one glass, then gulped the other and handed me the empties. "Keep an eye on these. Christ, what whiskey they use! Oh, dry desolation and blistering drought! What's happened to an American's right to drink his liver into a state of stone with legal permit?"

"I wouldn't know, Mr. Fry."

"No, I guess not. Have some food, Davey."

"Thank you, Mr. Fry."

I liked Jake Fry. He was a product of some river tribe of yellow-haired, flat-chested poor whites who, in desperate ferocity, had produced this seed—this one spawning of talent out of some secret fund of ancestry, long hidden by ignorance from the world. He had educated himself, flung his fat, twitching body around and become the biggest lawyer in the state.

He was a kind man tormented by a vast, buttery body and ideas that he had failed the little people he had sprung from. He spoke Latin and read good books and knew more about good painting than anyone in Antioch except Hartley Gould Coppard. Yet I was to find out later that in that lard that surrounded his soul there was fire hurting him, flaming up with a thick, choking smoke to stench in his own nostrils the fact that he sold out his folk and his birthright to walk with rich men and argue bought judges into verdicts for the vast corporations that blotted out the city sky for his kinsfolk. A grandiose hopelessness sat on him thicker than his fat.

It was this sad ineptitude, this voice, that had made him take Dris to his vast soft bosom, that brought my brother into the firm. Time was to show that in Dris he saw a handsomer, slimmer version of himself—a poor boy from a descending family who had been born with a good and hopeful future. But it was all ahead. That night I was only to know that Jake Fry loved Dris and was giving this wonderful, illegal party in his honor.

Men came to the chained door of Blue Peter's cellar and were admitted after a little stage-play of words and whispers. Many I knew already. Ned Wonderly in tailored black with his black shirt studs. Allan Coppard, a Coppard nephew—a Harvard bum, a Palm Beach tennis expert—a white slug with a cultured accent who handled the family estate in the firm of Fry, Rogers, Coppard *and* now Ormsbee. He had a great love of farming and had created a model farm out of fields wrung away from Gramp. There he would have been happy breeding beef cattle while walking the fields in manured boots, but his wife was a Bugsbee and suffered from a gall bladder that took her often to Carlsbad and into the arms of titled lovers—and the Coppards would not leave him on the farm but forced him to sit in hot courtrooms reducing tax assessments. And so Allan Coppard never amounted to much more than a white slug of a snob.

I also knew the other partner in Jake Fry's law firm—Biff Rogers. Biff came from the Southlands—from Dixie—and spoke with a lush lisping slur of words. He was a little man with a fire-red head of curly hair and had a dramatic limp gotten in an air battle in France. He was never sober and never drunk and he beat his wife with his small, hard fists —or so the servants told everyone. He was a brilliant lawyer and hated labor unions and had six children—all giants —and he would beat them, too, until they grew old enough to gang up on him.

Dris appeared, in polished patent-leather shoes—the first time I had seen him out of uniform. He had shaved off his mustache and he was more like the old Dris, the brother I had camped with on the lakes with Gramp and a pack horse and a dopy hound dog called Major.

"Well," said Dris, stepping up to Blue Peter's bar, pulling on his wing collar, "I am a law-abiding citizen and was dragged here against my will. Bourbon."

Ned Wonderly called for soda water for himself, and the rest of us held our poison high. It was my first big drink. Ned lifted his soda water into the air, a poignant expression on his gray face.

"Well, Dris, welcome home to Antioch. Welcome for Jake and all the boys. I don't make many speeches. I don't make long ones. But here is one I want to be remembered: to the day we see you Governor of the state."

I popped my eyes and pulled Biff Rogers' sleeve. "What does he mean?"

The little red fighting cock stood on tiptoes and let a glass of beer flow into his hard little body.

"Where you been, boy? Dris is going to run for the State Legislature."

"I didn't know."

"Hell, Ned's been spreading it all over town."

I put down my glass and went up to my brother. "I didn't know. The best of luck."

Dris put down his glass. "Nonsense, Davey. I don't think I'll run."

Jake Fry was high. He hugged Dris to him. "You gotta run. Just gotta run. Every American citizen got the right to run and none smarter than you, Dris. Best little lawyer in the whole land. War hero—local boy—good God-damn old American stock—God-damnedest candidate I ever saw! *Who* wants to fight?"

Jake was peeling off his coat from his wet linen arms. He stuck half way and stood there swaying, intrinsically ugly and fat. No one paid him any attention and Ned Wonderly refilled his glass with soda, obviously pleased.

"Not running, Dris? You've got to run. The whole district is behind you. It's not just a local issue. It's state-wide. We're putting in boys who fought for their country in France. We're tossing out the rum pots and whiskey noses and giving young blood a chance."

Dris frowned. "You've made up with the Coppards?"

"Yes. The Wonderly Clubs are all solid Republican now. It's a good party—a fine party—and no more local fights.

We're solid G.O.P. in Antioch now. No more splitting of forces to let any dirty Reds in to stir up trouble."

Dris rubbed his chin. "My father—he's always been a Democrat. I've always sort of thought I was one, too."

Ned placed his arm around Dris' shoulder, still sure of himself. "Look, Dris. You know me—short and sweet and no beating a bush to death. You love your father, I know. Every son should love his father *and* his mother. But the new world—the new way of life—the American way—is going to go ahead and it's our party that is going to make that way. Build America. Take this man Harding . . ."

"Who?"

"Warren Gamaliel Harding. A real American. Small-town boy, a newspaper owner—plays poker on his back porch, goes fishing, no silk hat or cane about him. That's the kind of stuff we're going after from now on. Dris, you love your country. You proved it—fought for her—hell, you were wounded for her. Don't you want to be part of her—help make the laws—put your brain to work where it will do the best good?"

Dris turned very white. He lifted his head and looked at the glaring lights. I could see he was impressed by Ned Wonderly's voice, his words, his manner. He turned back to the bar. Ned went on . . .

"It's like this, Dris. You *know* what . . ."

I didn't hear the rest. The waiters rushed in then and Blue Peter beat his bung-starter fists on the bar and roared, "Food's ready. Come and get it or we'll dump it in the alley."

The waiters pushed aside a lot of screens and everyone hung back a moment and then piled over to the tables, and I found myself staring at a big plate piled full of red boiled lobsters, the stigmata of stupidity on their cooked claws. Jake Fry, now very drunk, tossed one on my plate, piled on a shovelful of slimy potato salad and pounded me on the back with a flipper while he shouted:

"Happiest God-damn moment of my life—happiest God-damn moment of my life. Live to a hundred—never have a moment like this again. I crave indulgence. Eat, Davey, eat."

I turned around and saw Ned Wonderly and my brother still standing at the bar. Dris was calm but very white and Ned was looking into his soda water and talking very low. Futility, apathy, spoiled my lobster.

It was not subtle poison that Blue Peter served. It hit you hard, but once the first shock was over, the recovery was quick. Walking home with Dris after his party, my head cleared. I failed lamentably to make small talk.

It was a cold, moonlit night with foolish stars peeping down from between large goblin clouds. The sky made serious patterns. The city at two in the morning was still stirring. Cabs crawled past with people leaning back in their seats, eyes half-closed or limbs locked together. Trucks went past, hooded and snarling, and the last lunch wagons were turning down the extra lights. Milkmen clucked at their shabby horses and the early street-cleaning details were already unrolling their black rubber snakes to wash down the main streets.

Dris walked quickly, his head turtled into the collar of his topcoat, the leather heels of his shoes clicking against the night walks. I paced him step for step and as my head cleared I looked at him. His face lacked any expression under the melodramatic lighting of arc lamps. His susceptibilities to food and wine were much less than mine.

"You going to run for legislator?"

"No dice, Davey. But I'm sending you to college."

"No. You turned Ned Wonderly down?"

"Yes. I'm not sure I like public office."

"Ned runs the state. You could go far with him."

Dris fumbled in his pocket, put a cigarette to his lips and set fire to the tobacco. A shell of light picked out his features and I saw that he was scowling. The discrepancies of his nature puzzled me. I saw law no better than politics.

"Davey, I want to get married. Politics is slow and unsure. With Jake Fry I can make a lot of money fast. I'm young—I'm in love—and I'm tired of being pushed around by brass hats. The Army cured me of a lot of pretty illusions and other things. One was the idea that men serve best that thing they should hold most sacred."

"I don't understand, Dris . . ."

"Politics is lousy with graft and easy picking and lobbies. They crept into the Army with arm-chair officers and the spur-scarred desks of the dollar-a-year men. I don't want to touch any of it. I'm going to be a big lawyer and have a beautiful wife and raise up a brood of kids. And educate you, you shaggy young wolf cub."

"You mean Linda and you are getting married?"

"Soon, Davey—soon."

"Vicky sort of hoped you'd be Governor or something some day."

"No. I'm going to be a lawyer—a damned good one—and you are going to college. As soon as I get some cash in hand."

I looked at Dris and his quickly burning cigarette. "I don't want to go to college. I want to go to art school."

"Maybe you will. But first get an education the right way. I had a year at Oxford while in the Army's Officers' Training Group and while I didn't care for the tea-taking frumps, it was fine stuff. Jake Fry and I—we've had to pick up our education on the run—but you, you lug, you're going to a real college."

"I'll think it over," I said as we came to our house, lime-yellow and still in the night. Dris tossed away his tobacco and grabbed me by the seat of my pants and hoisted me up the stairs.

"I'll do your thinking—*you* do the studying."

Dris and I were sleeping on day beds put up in the seldom-opened parlor. Dennis' bride still held the bedroom—but they were leaving in a week for a general store that Dennis had bought upstate with his Navy pay. Doug slept behind his gas station and dreamed of boiling the Rockefellers, one by one, in his unsold oil and of a fleet of little ships under his orders.

As we were undressing in the dark, the door opened on its shrill hinges and Vicky came in behind a huge oil lamp. She looked smaller than ever in her long white nightgown as she reined in the too-long cuffs.

"How are my boys?"

Dris yawned. "We're all right and almost sober."

"Was it a fine party? Tell me who was there." Vicky sat down on the big black horsehair sofa and folded her arms. Her eyes were alert and excited. Dris grinned and began to expand. He knew how to juggle colored reflections for Vicky.

"The damnedest party you ever saw. Lobsters bigger than a tea kettle and more roast suckling pig than Gramp has in his sties. Davey ate three meals—one on top of the other—and then went out and had a new mouth drilled in the back of his neck . . ."

"Who was there?"

"Everyone. Ned Wonderly. The Governor. The Mayor. Oh, hell, Vicky—you know who goes to these stuffed-shirt brawls. A big covey of important muckamucks."

Vicky rubbed her small hands together. "My boy is a big

man. My son is an important man. I knew it. I always knew it. Did you get overheated?"

I pulled the sheet up to my nose and said, "He refused to run for the State Legislature."

Vicky stood up—stood as in suspended animation. "You did, Dris?"

"Yes. And don't start chewing at me. I want to practice law a while and make a lot of money—a great deal of money. Don't make me give you evasive answers."

Vicky nodded, grinned inscrutably. "You're right. Who does Ned Wonderly think he is, offering you a place in his two-penny legislature—his herd of Hunkies and drunken Micks and busted ward heelers. You'll be a Senator or nothing."

"I think I'm too young to be a Senator."

"Then you'll wait and make a lot of money first. You will make a lot of money, Dris?"

Dris opened his mouth and relaxed with a barnyard yawn. "Vicky, I'll make enough money to smother you in diamond-plated frying pans . . ."

Vicky stood up and blew into the lamp. From the sudden darkness her voice floated up.

"You're a good son, Dris, a fine son. Do what you want. Don't listen to me."

My brother Dris was a fine lawyer—although I didn't like lawyers as a rule, having had my eyes opened by Gramp to the tactics of the "tribe of pompous Latin-rancid pigeons." Dris was an honest lawyer, which Gramp said was about the only good thing he could say about his career. Fry, Rogers, Coppard and Ormsbee was a distinguished firm. A well-thought-of, well-liked, important set of legal talents, nicely calculated to purr majestically in the proper courts.

They were corporation lawyers who kept the Coppard

and Cruikshank utilities and railroads out of the clutches of tax collectors and trust investigations and labor boards. They selected and worked the state and national lobbies for steel and coal and power and saw that their clients died well heeled and with enough power of executors and trustee-ships in their wills to give the law firm a stranglehold on their estates for a long, long time. It was all tradition and all very legal and very, very profitable.

My brother Dris accepted all this as normal, and it was. When I was to hear of the crooked doings of other firms, I could understand how noble and upright Fry, Rogers, Cop-pard and Ormsbee was.

But I never grew to admire the lawyers' profession and I could never understand the need for lawyers, anyway. They were so unnecessary in Antioch and in the state. The judges were all Ned Wonderly's boys anyway, the legisla-tors were all machine cogs and the State Supreme Court judges and the Appeal Court judges all held huge handfuls of Coppard stocks. Why lawyers? I was too young to under-stand that gentlemen like to commit their little mergers and shut-outs and holding companies with the fullest of legal blessing. My temperament was singularly ill-adapted to understand such things.

Dris did well, and like a brooding mannequin *I* packed for college. I heard him argue his first case. A matter of a railroad protesting a land fraud pulled by one of its vice-presidents who had refused to resign. I found it rather dull but everyone said it was brilliantly handled. Even the preoccupied mien of the judge grunted approval.

That afternoon a huge Studebaker pulled up to the front door and Dris got out and honked the horn until Vicky stuck her head out of the side window and showed she was susceptible to awe.

"Hey, Vicky! Look!"

"Dris! An automobile—a *real* big one!"

Vicky came out and tried out the seats and fingered the wheel and looked rather lost among the soft sinking upholstery. "Yours, Dris?"

Dris shook his head. "Yours, Vicky, to have and to hold and smash into poles with. Like it?"

"Yes!"

Vicky tested the horn again and put her small head out of the window to see if the neighbors were staring. They were. Pleased, she turned to Dris in rising enthusiasm.

"Well, that's something! Thinking of your mother. I'll have to get Pete to learn to drive it and Davey can keep it polished. . . ."

Dris shook his head. "Davey, as you know, is going to college. Princeton."

"Them sissies!" I said.

"That's a high-class place," said Vicky.

"The best," said Dris. "And now let me drive this crate into the yard."

Vicky shook her head. "Let it stand out front. So people can see it. You're a wonderful son, Dris. I love those gray and red stripes on the wheels."

"Wait until I get real big cases. I'm going to appear before the Supreme Court in Washington one of these days—assisting Jake Fry. But you just wait. There is more coming to you. . . ."

Vicky ran the car window up and down.

The whole street watched.

There was no more coming to Vicky from Dris. The car was the first and last big gift Dris ever bought her. Two days later I was awakened by a hammering on our front door and found a messenger boy standing there staring at the door, a telegram in his hand.

A telegram was a rare thing in our house in those days and I opened it and read it and banged on the landing until Vicky appeared. Even Pete came down from his attic, giving a disquieting impression of a man walking in his sleep.

"You sick?" asked Vicky.

"Telegram from Dris—from Maryland—listen: LINDA AND I MARRIED TONIGHT SEE YOU IN TWO WEEKS DRIS."

Pete rubbed his eyes and shook his head. "It isn't proper going off like this without even bringing the girl home. First Dennis and now Dris. It isn't proper."

"Oh, Dris!" said Vicky.

Pete shook his head again and looked at Vicky as if he wanted to hug her, thought better of it and slowly went upstairs again, limping badly. This had hit him harder than I imagined. Sometimes his non-resistance and passivity was badly bent.

Vicky sank down on the stairs and began to weep.

"I was so looking forward to a big church wedding. With real old lace and a full choir and the Reverend Reuben Doll in his golden robe reading the services. It would have been *such* a big social event. And we could have had someone drive us to the church in the new car. My boy married— with a wife!"

I placed the telegram on the hall table and went back to bed. The wind howled across the rooftop and I thought that a few hundred miles south Dris was lying with his bride under the same dark sky. I felt so alone. Buoyancy seeped from me.

In the hall Vicky stirred and I went out and wrapped a blanket around her shaking shoulders. She took my hand and held it and I knew suddenly that she loved us all very

[156]

much and that in her burned a fire that is seldom lit in most women. I was shocked to think that Vicky was a very odd and remarkable woman. Smiling solicitously, I kissed my mother. I loved her very much.

It was Pete who took hardest the idea of Dris leaving our yellow house to go off with a Coppard bride. There was some strange yeast in him that none of us knew. I never knew Pete. He was always a stranger to me. I think he was too simple and direct for me. His dislike of the lawyers and the Coppard interests was more real to him than bread to me. They acted on him.

The morning after the wire came he was in his garden digging. Dirt was flying—he had scraped off the garden soil and was piling the red underclay into hills. All that day he dug and it was dark when he came in, wolfed his dinner, and went up to bed I heard his shovel scraping rock the next day.

Wet, dirty, he stood in a hole in the garden, digging. He attacked the packed clay and rocks and hoisted them up on his hills and dug on under a broiling sun. He tore up his corn plants and mashed out his prize beets. The holes grew deeper and he connected them with trenches. He ate no lunch and Vicky was too busy downtown gossiping to come home and force him to eat.

Late that night I heard him drag himself to his attic. The next morning he was again attacking the earth. His face, wet and covered with unshaved stubble, was blank—only his eyes seemed larger and rimmed with red. He tossed shovel load after shovel load out of a growing pit.

He saw me and looked up. "Plant cellar—very good for plants—in winter . . ."

I went down into the pit and took Pete's hand and led

him into the house. He sat on a kitchen chair, staring at his soiled hands. I fed him meat and bread and he ate and went up to his attic. He stayed there for two days . . .

It took me a week to get the garden back into some sort of order. I never found out why Pete did not approve of Linda.

T W E L V E

I DID NOT get to know Linda very well until Dris and she
had been married two years. I had seen her around since
childhood, when her trips over town were protected by a
marching formation of chauffeurs, governesses or maids. I
had been closer to her romance with Dris—that is, closer
than anyone but Dris—but the night she eloped with my
brother I knew little real about her. She was pretty—no,
she was beautiful—her father was a very rich man and her
family owned Antioch and the state and a great deal of the
resources of the nation. They had a social appetite and that
Boston impassivity of manner.

She and her mother lived a great deal of the time in
Europe. Linda attended very choice private schools and she
rode horses like a demon. That was all she added up to until
I knew her better. Oh, and I had seen her kiss Dris several
times—and she performed the deed as if she meant it. And
she once said I was cute—but I forgave her, for her voice
was like a Latin benediction. But of the real Linda—nothing.

Hartley Gould Coppard's reaction to his daughter's marriage with a poor young lawyer was typical of the man. He
went home, poured himself a drink, called in the reporters
—and said he was very happy. Linda had an income from
her grandmother and now he hoped the young couple would
be very happy and he washed his hands of them. They
would have to make their own way in the world. He had

three sons to carry on the Coppard fortunes. He loathed public eloquence.

Linda had an income of about twenty thousand dollars a year. She had certain interests in her father's companies, but they were so manipulated that they brought in no income.

Linda was sweet, kind, and very much in love. But I think Dris forgot her background. She was used to luxury the way I was used to bread and butter. She never thought of her clothing as anything but covering acquired in smart New York and Paris and Palm Beach shops. She liked horses and fast imported cars, but she was not a snob. She really must have thought of a cottage small among the rose-bushes when she married Dris. But it didn't work out that way. Her high-strung fastidiousness functioned quicker than her mind.

Dris and Linda were away from Antioch for almost two years after they were married. Jake Fry sent Dris South while his honeymoon was still on, and Dris spent two lovely hot summers handing in briefs to hillbilly and cracker judges for the foreclosures of estates which had been foolish enough in the lean years to sign certain papers while taking loans from Coppard banks. Their legal chaos achieved exactitude in Dris' hands.

It was dangerous work. Dris was facing an enraged citizenry, he was a damnyankee bloodsucker come to take over men's lifeblood for the bank. He made a good job of it, but he hated it and never again did he do any foreclosure arguing for the firm. He could not honestly be vindictive and ruthless.

Meanwhile, Hartley Gould had presented the newlyweds with a plot of ground on King George Road and soon a sort of French Provincial house of field stone and pale-gray stucco and rough slate was going up. It was known as the "new Ormsbee place," my father's yellow structure being the "old Ormsbee place."

Dris was paying for it out of his earnings and advances from the firm. In the end, with alterations and tennis courts and stables and landscaping, he was to sink fifty-two thousand dollars into the gift lot.

Of course with Dris so involved in Southern lawsuits and building expenses, his big gifts to the family stopped. I know that within the next five years he and Linda were spending so much on just living that at times he didn't have enough change to buy cigarettes. Yet he was not credulous or shallow—just in love, I guess.

Vicky at first was disappointed that the big car wasn't followed by a fur coat, by a gramophone or a diamond pin —but as the house on King George Road went up, she took greater and greater pride in it and would rout my father out at all hours and have him drive her to the building site where she would examine the beams and test the doors and raise hell with the contractor (although she had no authority). She paced the spacious, high-ceilinged rooms and rubbed small hands on costly mahogany trim.

And Pete would wait at the curb in the big car, smoking his pipe and scowling at the radiator cap which was in the shape of a nude silver woman. Vicky never drove as her small feet could never have reached the pedals—or her strength turn the huge wheel. No. She sat in back, squirming her lithe body and talking.

She had forced Pete to take out a permit and learn to drive the lusty gasoline giant and for years, until the car went into mechanical decay, he drove her. He never learned to love this iron machine—hated it always and drove bent way over the steering wheel, staring ahead of him with careful gaze, blowing his horn at every corner, plying his arms in hand signals and sweating fearfully at every busy crossing. He advanced in jerks, took corners clumsily and never reached that state of driving when it becomes mechanical and easy.

In time the car began to give trouble. Pete learned to tamper with her innards and when the hour came when there was no hope of moving her, she was stored under canvas in the back yard. For years when Vicky referred to "my car" she meant the tireless, broken heap of molding junk that was a nesting place for lovesick cats in the backyard.

I saw it, still there, only the other day—its paint finish all gone, the great cold motor exposed and red rusting and the wheels sunk deep in the soil. Vicky could still have said, "My car."

One day there came a letter saying that Dris was finished with the land cases. He and Linda were coming home. Their new house was ready. It had been furnished by Del Hooper—the local decorating talent. Del was never like other boys. He was sensitive and went to Paris for years to study decorating. He came mincing back to Antioch and opened a shop and did the most lovely things with blue linen and old hand-rubbed furniture. Del prospered and his wavy blond hair grew white, but he never got over his fondness for blue linen and the posterior beauty of passing waiters. Dris' house was his masterpiece.

Del had been given a free hand, and he filled the house with hand-blocked wallpapers and leather bindings and Chippendale tea tables and a black walnut bed—once used by George IV himself at Bath. I have seen a great many of these rich collections of good taste and delightful color schemes. I always felt I was intruding at a museum collection of historical buildings. I never felt they were a home. Only sterile atmospheres . . .

I was away at college—at Princeton—when the young couple returned to Antioch and moved into their own home. I was busy being bored with snobs, and protesting against the sort of essays they expected me to write in the style of Henry Van Dyke, and Chris Morley. I didn't care for the prissy stuff the English prof liked and I wasn't dumb enough to think I could say anything of importance in the prose pants of Emerson. I cut classes and became an omnivorous reader and beer drinker.

I enjoyed Princeton because I liked the New Jersey landscape. I wallowed in the books stacked on its library shelves. I met an art instructor who had known Renoir and who drank too much gin, so that I often helped him into his classroom. I enjoyed the morning walks around the land and I kissed my first girl—a wretched debutante down from Tuxedo Park, who mistook me for one of the North Carolina Ormsbees and let me touch her hips while I quoted T. S. Eliot at her.

One night she drove me far away and talked to me like a mother and said something about a man named Freud, and I shivered because it was very cold and the frogs were dancing in the water—and I tried quoting something of Ezra Pound and she kissed the words off my mouth.

But she reminded me of Linda and I drew back.

I suppose I was ashamed of myself for almost a week, and then she found out I wasn't the right kind of Ormsbee at all—and she slapped my face the next time we stopped for cokes and I never saw her for ten years. She had married a South American swine, been divorced, married a publisher, been divorced, had a breakdown and six months in a sanitarium, and one day I met her on Fifth Avenue coming out of a gallery that was showing an exhibit of my black-and-white drawings made on a trip around the world. And we went to lunch and held hands and drank sixteen cocktails between us. But it was all over—everything except that hollow feeling that we were older and much nearer to the grave than we had been that first night at Princeton. And she no longer reminded me of Linda.

Anyway, that's the reason I wasn't in Antioch to welcome Dris and Linda home. I had several letters from Vicky about what a gay party it was, how much every stick of furniture in the place cost. But what I really wanted to know was how Dris was doing, how he felt, what success, marriage and travel had done for him. I couldn't get much from Vicky's letters.

She didn't look for cause and effect. She took inventory. I was reading Proust at the time and I made a note on the title page of *Swann's Way* that Vicky would have been a fine writer on the subject. She could line a class, show the decay of an individual or a cause, by pricing the bedroom curtains or naming the color of the toilet paper.

It was during the Christmas vacation of my second year at Princeton that I first saw Dris and Linda at their new house. It had been snowing, but not very actively, and the lawns. of King George Road were lightly blanketed in white. The luscious green of fir trees was dimmed. I remember the way the nude elm trees struggled to hold on to the thin silver edges of snow on their twigs and the way the walks had been quickly cleared—so quickly that no snow was left on their smooth surfaces. It was a gracious, white, polite day.

I walked up to the front door and pulled a bell stop that gave off a refined dying wail somewhere in the thick brick-work. A butler opened the door—one of those constipated-looking, lower-class Englishmen who was born too near the village horse pond to go into the Foreign Office, so his constrained nature made him a servant.

He showed me into the living room and I stood carelessly (in a studied pose) under the white stone fireplace, smoking a cigarette, trying to look very worldly-wise and *just* a touch tired. My heart was pounding against my shirt, as my apprehension about Dris had increased.

Linda entered and she smiled and we shook hands. I had suddenly a feeling from her of an introspective cult of boredom.

"Hello, Davey."

"Hello," I said, assembling some thoughts.

"How have you been?"

"Very well."

"You're looking splendid." She took a long, foul-looking cigarette from a jade box and I hunted for my matches but caught them too late. She clicked off the dull silver lighter and smiled at me again. I tried to exhume some small talk.

"I feel fine."

"You've grown, Davey. Why, you're almost as wide as Dris."

"Doug—he's the wide one in our family. How is Dris?"

"Fine. Busy as usual. Will you have a drink?"

I nodded—as if I always had a drink with a pretty lady. An emerald pendant gleamed. She was very beautiful. I stood with stolid patience.

"Vermouth? Or would you care for a Martini?"

I fumbled. "Oh—oh, just a straight drink with a chaser. Rye."

A cabinet opened under her fingers and I poured and she had one, too—and another—and we fizzed soda into them and we looked at each other over the rims of our glasses and I suddenly discovered she was shy, too!

We sipped our drinks and watched our cigarettes die and gave each other ridiculously sad glances.

Linda was in her very early twenties then. Later she grew a little drawn and thin, but she always retained that glowing, flame-like beauty and those stoic gestures. Yes, she was beautiful. Even then in the cold afternoon light, her hair piled up with golden pins and her dressing gown of soft silk, like a Greek vase painting. There was something about her that caused me to suck air into my lungs and I could see what she was to Dris. Something rather exotic in a healthy way—yet so much above what he had seen in the hard, bickering, brawling little yellow house of Vicky and Pete. Her manners were good without that lush overdevelopment of the snob, and I don't think she gave a hang about social position. And I felt a freedom from conscience.

She had her faults—yet Dris always said they were not faults. They were ingrained in her by her birth, her childhood and her family and perhaps by the lonely life Dris' house forced on her.

A coal miner's face is ingrained with blue seams of coal dust under the skin—ingrained so that no soap can ever remove them. That was Linda. Her faults were so deeply ingrained that she could not change them—even to forestall disaster. She would always expect grand houses and many servants and rich surroundings and imported clothes. She had her own income and I suppose there was a point where it ran over in debt and she borrowed from Dris' law-won loot.

There was something else, too, my foolish, book-drunk mind saw. You see it in race horses and wolfhounds—those elegant creatures bred too close and true, so like hothouse fruit, that some nerves seem rubbed out of them and other nerves are swelled all out of proportion. Linda was like that. She dressed in an armor of planned breeding. The Coppards were not an old family as families go. They had avoided most wars by sitting home in their counting houses and cultivating gout and high-colored skins. But they bred among themselves and produced a stately race of people who were very fine and very noble and very much given to stateliness as long as the world was suppressed and held in bondage for their wishes. But there was a wild wind blowing up and the high places were the most exposed, and the Coppards would show freak strains in the weary times ahead, I thought audaciously that day.

In those days I was reading too many dull theories by wise old birds with big white beards who wrote so often about what a fine world it was. I was younger then and if I thought of Linda in a muddle of such biological slush, it was perhaps that I was a little put out by her taking my brother Dris away from me. And maybe I thought of that girl at Princeton who had offered me Freud on the libido.

We had finished the drink and I poured another and Linda swung to her feet. She looked at me and twirled the delicately fluted glass.

"You're an artist—I forgot. I want to show you father's gift on our first wedding anniversary."

She led me into one of those terrifyingly big rooms—almost dining room, part library—and often mistaken for a lobby. Over a wax-polished highboy hung a theatrical English painting that did so much to spoil the healthy art of men like Hogarth and Constable. A flashy, whorish duchess in carefully primed silk and lace suggested with that dainty brushwork that suggests nothing more nor less than a male hairdresser fussing over an oily head of dyed hair. There was a lot of Royal Copenhagen and Haviland china, too.

"A Gainsborough. An original. Daddy bought it at Christie's in London last summer for fifty thousand pounds."

"Cute," I said, swallowing the drink.

"Cute! Oh, Davey, you are a wit."

I frowned and was about to say some such word as "gamy" or "adequate" but Dris came into the room just then looking very dapper and tired in blue pin-stripe tailoring, a neat hairline, watch chain across his thin flanks, and—Lord help me—a bowler in his hand—and spats. I opened my eyes disproportionately large and grinned.

"Hello, mug," he said, patting me on the shoulder. "You're getting uglier than ever. Do you like college?"

"I'm polite to it."

"You work hard or, by God, I'll make you scrub floors."

I grinned on. "Vicky been offering to scrub them *again?*"

Dris nodded and I saw Linda make a *moue*. Dris shook his head. "There is no holding Vicky down. Do you know what she has done? She has opened a pot-cheese factory and delivers pots of the stuff all over town in that car I gave her—Pete at the wheel and the ice blocks dripping out of the doors. And a sign—ORMSBEE'S AWFULLY FRESH POT CHEESE."

I looked at Linda Coppard Ormsbee and said, "How undignified of Vicky!"

Dris nodded. "I've tried to buy the herd of cows from Gramp—that she works with. But Gramp—he's changed, too."

"Older," I said.

Dris nodded. "I've tried to take over his lawsuits and get them into some sort of shape, but I regret to say he thinks I've sold my soul to the vested interests and so he doesn't want me to help him."

"But Jake Fry is his lawyer and you're a partner."

Dris fingered the lapel of his well-pressed suit. "Jake Fry got his notice two months ago. Some land lawyers from Jefferson Point are handling Gramp's affairs now. Good,

[168]

honest people—but no drag with the courts or judges. But hell, it's good to see you, Davey. Like old times when we sat among the guitarists in society and ate our first well-done steak. Remember, fella?"

I felt the remark singularly inappropriate.

"Let's celebrate," said Linda. "We could go down to the Bay for a lobster dinner—then to the Yuma Club for dancing, and we'll show the lad the inside of Tony's Four Hundred Club. . . ."

Dris rubbed his chin. "I'm sorry. But I've got to be at Ned Wonderly's house. Arrange those mail contracts for those steamships Ned is taking over on Harding's say-so."

I said, "Got to go anyway—and help Vicky deliver pot cheese."

Dris looked at his collar and tie in a mirror and kissed Linda. "I just dropped in to see Davey and change my shirt and collar. Drive you downtown, Davey?"

"It's been very nice," I said, offering Linda my hand.

"You must come again—and tell me all about Princeton."

I looked up at the girl. It suddenly dawned on me that she was not only bored—very bored in this big house and this original worm-bored furniture, sporting the duchess that had cost fifty thousand pounds at Christie's that summer—but she was frightened, too. I didn't know of what. . . .

I went to see Gramp that evening. He was sitting all twisted up in a low chair, and Cap Roc was rubbing his warped arms and begging him to drink some warm milk. Cap looked as mad as ever—as if the silver bands set in his skull were pressing on his mind. But he was very gentle with Gramp and left us alone as soon as Gramp had swallowed the warm milk.

"Learning things, Davey?" said Gramp, rubbing his beard.

"Too many things. I saw Dris this afternoon. You angry at him, Gramp?"

"No. I pity him. Young, brilliant and the wrong beam in his eyes. He doesn't want wealth or that junk shop of a house or all those fat friends and those nasty little legal jobs he does. . . ."

"No?"

"No, Davey. Dris wants to knock out about him. He wants to bend a few horizons, see a few other places besides Antioch. But what has he got? A museum to live in and a powder puff for a wife. Jake Fry and his foul crowd pat him on the back and Ned Wonderly whispers what a brain he has. Dris is worth twenty of any of them. Dris is a great man—but no one worthwhile will ever know it in those slumbrous law courts."

"He's making a lot of money."

"So does a breeding cow. So does a whoremaster. Dris doesn't need money. . . ." Gramp sat sombrously contemplating the leaping fire.

"That house costs a lot of cash."

"It's a burden. Full of puerile prettiness and bric-a-brac."

"They have a Gainsborough—Dris doesn't seem to care for it."

Gramp stirred his old bent limbs. "Why should he? His father-in-law hands him a solid chunk of gold and all it's good for is to hang on a wall. Why, every time Dris looks at it he must boil to think how much he would have preferred the cash."

"Why?"

Gramp pulled his shawl closer around his thin shoulders. "That house and furnishings and nigger chauffeur and English snob are milking Dris dry. Dris is about fifty thousand dollars in debt, Jake Fry told me. That's why I fired the ball of suet—letting *that* happen to a young man!"

I was impressed by the sum of Dris' debt and whistled. I could respect a man who didn't have enough money to pay such staggering bills.

Coming home from Gramp's I saw how the city had grown. It was no longer the country city of my boyhood. Its shacks and mills and slag piles had lapped over into new meadows. Downtown streets glowed like bright twisting worms from my view on the high hills.

The steel mill furnaces were burning bright in the night, and the gush and drive of their flames reflected on the river, and when they poured a batch of molten steel, fairy fire ran across the yards and made golden letters in the molds.

It was a pushing, growing city—a city for young men like Dris to take and hold and grow rich in. It was the time and the place for bright young men in neat business suits and Buick cars and only a fool would have it different.

As I walked I smelled the night-blooming vines on country houses fighting the last rearguard actions against real-estate developments. And the gas stations and hamburger stands were advancing in the night with glowworm neons making show over their shapes. Then the city began—first the row on row of mill workers' shacks, then the factories, and at last the paved city streets. It was a growing city where a man's debts didn't matter. . . .

THIRTEEN

But I am afraid I did not worry too much about Driscoll and his debts or envy too much his great home. His beautiful wife was another matter. I was young and home for the holidays, and even Vicky and the pot-cheese business did not annoy me. I was drafted to drive the big tan car and I sat many an afternoon behind the wheel, very aware of the oil-cloth sign tacked to the door: ORMSBEE'S AWFULLY FRESH POT CHEESE, while Vicky toured the villas and colonial developments with a basket of balled cheese, some-times disappearing for hours and returning with all the cheese but with a new social conquest made. She did not pique my curiosity any more. I knew of what she talked.

No. I wasn't very interested in the family problems. Pete was in a bad way, living in mental abasement. He was again standing alone in the tool shed, knocking together his little cabinets but the demands on his talents were few. The little business lay prostrate.

He and Vicky were part of that great army of minor war-rich whom peace had ruined. Little shopkeepers and petty market plungers and small hoarders of grains and sugar—little people who had managed in idiotic conceit to build and hide and borrow and mortgage, and had seen paper profits and inked bank balances go. They had been wiped out where the wheels of war had stopped and crushed them . . . crushed all these little people and their mediocrity. And in so doing, slowing the wheels *just* enough to let the big fish escape.

For the Coppards and the owners of motor plants and shell-filling factories and the clothing mills and the canneries of filth and food had not been wiped out. They were safe and had their two hundred percent war profits safely tucked away—and were closing up some of their plants and laying off the workers. The scaffolds stopped climbing—the caldrons grew cold.

To the small enterprisers like my parents, it was stark ruin—and wooden cabinets and furniture repairing and peddling a nasty pot cheese from door to door was only just keeping their heads above water.

The bureaucrats took their spurs off their desks and returned to Antioch.

Uncle Thoreau was standing on street corners, talking to passing strangers, demonstrating his kitchen gadgets. Three fat, giggling daughters with strong bodies went into housework and spent hours, their warm pink hands in dirty dishwater, earning a few dollars to fill the gullets of their younger brothers and sisters. Gramp took pity and invited Aunt Netta and some of the smaller fry up to the hills and fed them well and kept his liquor locked up. But pickings were slim—even for Gramp. He was cutting timber and selling it for less and less. His herds were growing smaller, beef prices were down at the packing houses, and the lawsuits went on. Gramp tended his *by bloemen* tulips.

As for Doug, I spent two days helping him pump gas into the maws of rattling, shoddy flivvers. But there was not enough work for two—and so I left Doug reading old *Sea Adventure* magazines and was not very surprised when two months later, for a Greek junk man, he went off on a freighter bound east for Port Said, to inspect some tramp freighters being sold for scrap iron. The great gasoline companies had licked him.

They grabbed his corner and put up a fifty-thousand-dollar white palace and hired a lot of the unemployed ex-War Heroes, Coppard Post of Antioch—who wiped windshields and wore white monkey suits and were glad to get the jobs. Doug still loved steel—and buying scrap iron for Greeks pleased him.

Dennis I didn't see. He was upstate in a general store with Rose, his wife, singing at prayer meetings and planting the new seeds of a large and hungry family in her willing body. He was an honest, earnest, trustful, godly person. He failed in life and went on failing, went on paying his debts, impregnating his wife; went on praying, opening little stores that failed, moving on, trusting, honestly doing his job, paying his debts, failing, moving on—increasing his hungry flock. The finest character anyone ever met, yet lacking any talents to live in this wolf world of sharp teeth and sharper methods.

Gramp said Dennis was not for this benighted age. "He was made to be nailed to a cross. But he suffered from debts all his life, when he should have borne coagulated wounds."

But Antioch was full of hope. I liked to walk its streets and see the high-school girls pass, flicking their young muscles and looking back with thick laughter to see who was staring at them. I enjoyed the river hills and the sight of clouds hiding the tall chimneys that smoked rarely these days. Yet there was hope in people's faces. And everyone knew that Harding was a great man and wonderful and everyone forgot the war—almost—and started to pile up a little cash again.

It was good to see people who had just been wiped out by the collapse of the war boom begin all over again to gather in their little bundles of savings bankbooks and un-important stocks, their land deeds and hopes in oil wells and patent medicines or shares in a company to run an auto motor on water. The city was peculiarly susceptible to the offers of the Stock Exchange gentry.

I was born in 1907, a year of great depression. But Vicky and Pete had kept going and had repeated the mistakes that had almost ruined them then and several times since I had seen them done in again by the same methods that had pushed them under before. The Twenties were times of instability and envy and Vicky led all the rest.

Harding and Coolidge were to see Antioch gather in another store of prosperity—a prosperity to go under dur-ing the pink-baby-face rule of the surly Mr. Hoover. Only that time I couldn't be very amused, as I was wiped out myself, and since then I haven't bothered very much with piling up a store of tainted nuts in the hollow tree of eco-nomic hopes. Like the Church's weakness for rich old women, I lust for luxury but no longer feed myself from my own bankbooks.

The new rich were the bootleggers, the cutters of bad hair tonics, the makers of horse-brine-tasting beer. I was walking past the old Fire House—a Civil War relic of tor-mented brick and Walter Scott towers, when Piggy Tone and Turtle stopped me and gave me the office with much laying on of hands. They were dressed in what was then known as "sharpy." Small, tortured felt hats, wasp-waisted jackets with slant pockets and narrow, pipe-stem trousers that suddenly flared out into huge bags around the shoe tops. It was all, I suppose, a vague furtive fumbling for double-breasted respect.

"Whatta ya know," said Piggy. "The college boy."

"Ain't he," added Turtle.

"You boys look fine. Where was the fire sale?"

Piggy admired himself in the dirty glass pane of the Fire House door. He felt like a dragonfly coming out of its larval shell, I knew. "Nifty. Cheap John Spitz's best stuff. Handmade buttonholes, look."

"Mighty nice. Since when has rushing around for Ned Wonderly paid off like this?"

Piggy winked and his little eyes sank back into his fat cheeks. "We ain't with Ned no more—full time. Here, have a card, sport."

I took the square bit of pasteboard and read:

THOMAS TONE

"Call me Piggy and call me often"

Wet goods. All standard brands. Bottled in bond.

ANTIOCH 200

"You're a bootlegger."

"Yeah. Me, too," said Turtle. He held an imaginary machine gun in his paws and made a *tat-tat-tat-tat* sound with his lips.

"Isn't that dangerous?" I said in my innocent early-Capone state. "It's a Federal law you're breaking."

Piggy spit. "Law, my ———. Them Feds is taking *schmaltz*. We grease them all. Come on in, pal, and see the plant."

Piggy knocked on the side door of the Fire House and a scarred face looked out of the first Volstead Law peephole I had ever seen, and let us in. Four huge old Liberty trucks, still showing signs of army work, stood on the Fire House floor. A lot of the old gang—most of them old friends in quasi-juvenile vices—from our bushwhacking days, were loading beer kegs. They winked at me and went on loading. All looked happy and most of them wore cheaper versions of Piggy's sharpy tailoring.

[176]

Below stairs, Piggy showed me his cutting rooms, his dreadful brews stirring in huge vats and the method of refilling unrefillable bottles. A printing press clanged off "genuine" Haig and Haig labels.

"This is something," I said in admiration of the rising, young, not very clean-cut, business man.

"Nothin'," said Piggy solemnly. "Kid stuff. Wait until I get some real dough. I'm goin' to set up a still in every Hunky and Polack and Wop and Mick bedroom. Give 'em the stuff and let them cook it for me. I'm goin' to hist the stuff in over the Canada border in me own trucks and Turtle is linin' up some sub-chasers to contact the rum boats. But that's all going to take china—a lot of it."

"I should think so."

Piggy brightened up. "But—I'm gettin' the ward heelers in line and oncet I get the wards set for our side—see—it will bring in enough to hire protection. Not local hoods but mugs from New York—real torpedoes."

I looked at Piggy as if he were talking Latin. *Torpedoes, hoods, protection, china.* It was an argot that the motion pictures of the Twenties were to make familiar to every innocent tot—but in those early days it was new to everyone. Even Piggy used it with a conscious pride. Piggy, an important little blowfly laying eggs on the carcass of a Federal edict.

"But the law," I said. "Don't they bother you?"

"I tell you we grease them! Federal men, local bulls and even the Internal Revenue mugs. Where do you think we get them real genuine Federal tax stamps? Care for a drink?"

Piggy picked up a bottle that was a masterpiece. Men took care in those early days, before the mass production of bootleg poison broke down people's morale and they drank anything. Piggy opened the bottle, explained the seal and the tax stamps and proper corkage, and showed me the salt-stained label and the cob-webbing.

I said, "You're a cockeyed artist, Piggy."

We drank and I shook but kept it down. Piggy expanded.

"Of course, I'm just a little guy. I'm really only set up here by the guys who sell me most of the alki I cut. But onct I'm gettin' enough out of my own stills, I'll be bigger than they . . ."

"Who are *they?*"

"Don't ask . . ."

"But suppose you get in a jam—get in jail . . ."

"Don't make me laugh—I got stomach ulcers. We got a revolving door on that jail. We got lawyers that spring us in twenty minutes."

"But what lawyers would take that kind of work?"

Piggy looked at me over his bottle. "What are you doing, pal, playing dumb? Fry, Rogers, Coppard and Ormsbee are our mouthpieces. Dris has a pocketful of habeas corpuses always on hand."

That evening I was sitting in the living room, watching Vicky and Pete weighing pot cheese into three-pound lumps. Pete was very honest, giving each ball just the right amount and an added little lump for good measure. But Vicky always took his lump off and stood scowling down on the scale, picking up grains of cheese until the marker was just right, muttering until Pete was distressingly conscious of his limitations.

"No business head. No business head," she said to Pete. "The money in this business is in the crumbs—and you give it away! Davey, you weigh—and no extra crumbs. Remember."

[178]

Pot cheese is pale, soft, insipid stuff. I mushed a ladleful onto the scale. "Vicky, Linda doesn't like you to go about the city with a sign reading: ORMSBEE'S AWFULLY FRESH POT CHEESE."

"That's just too bad. Her in that big, beautiful house with all that real china and silk curtains and me trying to earn bread for my children. A fine lot she cares—Dris takes good care of her."

I slopped more of the mess onto the scale. "You think Dris is happy there?"

"Hell's bells, watch those crumbs. Happy? How can you not be happy in a house like a palace with servants to wait on you hand and foot and never a worry about water pipes busting or termites eating your floor beams out . . ."

Pete was loading his pipe and he looked up with a classic gravity. "I don't think he is so happy."

Vicky turned and waved the cheese scoop under Pete's nose, so that there was an ingenious distribution of crumbs on him.

"*You're* happy—living like a pig in an old yellow house dogs wouldn't take. *You're* happy playing with wood shavings all day and scratching your behind while the world goes by in silks and furs and I've got to sell this stinking stuff to keep a little bread of life in our mouths. *You're* happy, *I'm* happy. *Davey* here is happy—but Dris, with everything in the world—he *isn't* happy! Great day in the morning, what a fool I married! Davey, get away from that scale!"

She attacked the lump of oozy white on the scale and trimmed it down, the crumbs falling and splashing back into the pot and over the tablecloth. The way she handled the spoon prophesied disaster for Pete.

Pete had his pipe burning and got up to go out under his

grape arbor. He was retiring from Vicky's nightly squabble. "I'm as happy as I can be—here. I'm contented, anyway. . . ."

"So is a cow," howled Vicky. "So is a frog in his muck. A fine fool you turned out to be. First you ruin *my* real estate development and now you try and turn your own sons into woodchoppers and loafers fit only to sit under that damn fool grape arbor. I've a good mind to get an axe and cut those vines down!"

Pete went out of the door and said no more. It was the great fear of his life that she would cut down his grape vines and dig up his garden and build garages in the yard. His eyes would go wide and remote and his face furrow with fear.

Vicky went on stirring the pot and weighing out the lumps. She was angry, her tiny body stirring and moving and her breath coming from her small mouth in angry jets. I looked at her closely. She was as intense and emphatic as ever. Middle age had not calmed her spirit. She was the same Vicky who had stormed and planned and hoped and dreamed of the future. She was speaking in gushes, explosively, loud and fast. She was still slim—in fact, growing thinner. Her hands were no longer smooth and pale, but brown and hard. Her hair was still strong and wavy, but there were silver signs in it and little crow's-feet were creeping into the corners of her eyes. But she looked younger than her age, her tiny figure alert, and her face could still be mistaken for a young girl's. And as she stirred the fearful dripping pot, I suddenly understood her the way Dris understood her, understood the significantly intimate facts about her.

She was noble—she was strong—she was something rare and wonderful, for all her bite and fury. There was in her a great, driving love of family—a little driven into wrong channels, perhaps, a little given to false values—yet to her all values were romantic and wonderful.

Yes, Vicky, I decided, was a romantic, one of those rare souls who lived a full busy life in a world of his own making with no time for sloth and sensuality. I do not think she ever saw the real world, the full hard surface of the things as they were. She was a spirit like those men and women of the medieval times who never touched the earth but existed on a plane half spiritual, half fantasy. She, too, was a creature of fierce savage visions and rare moods.

"Davey! Someone at the door. I declare college has made you stupid. Answer the door."

I got up and went to the front door. It was Dris. He filled the doorway, well dressed and nervous but, as usual, intense and emphatic.

"Hello, Davey. How's everything?"

"Full of cheese. Come in."

Vicky beamed and kissed Dris as he leaned over and she held her wet hands high in the air. There was almost something lascivious—inordinate—in the way Vicky always greeted her favorite son.

"Well—a stranger come at last to see his old mother!"

"Hello, Vicky. Still messing with the dripping stuff?"

"You look piqued, Dris. But glad you remembered we were alive."

Dris nodded and sat down. He was used by now to Vicky's way of greeting him with reproaches. She always protested his visits too much and made much of him for at last remembering his old mother was alive. It was her way.

She was turning into an actress producing little pathetic follies and fatuities.

Dris looked up. "I've come to borrow Davey for the night if you don't mind."

"Of course not. Time he got around and took his nose

out of those books. Maybe you can find him a nice girl—someone cultured—perhaps one of the Cruikshank girls . . ."

I nodded gloomily. "The one with the pimples and the gold-wire teeth braces and the half-million dollars."

"Nonsense," said Vicky, "*all* my children marry for love. Anyway, what's the matter with Betty Cruikshank? She's steady and she's good to the poor and . . ."

Dris waved a deprecating hand. "You sure you don't mind my dragging him off?"

Vicky went back to the cheese scale. "No, dear. The little birds are beginning to leave the nest. The last little bird is Davey." And she began to cry into the cheese pot. But I knew damn well she was thinking of Betty Cruikshank.

The Packard car crossed town and Dris kept his strong hands steady on the wheel, but I could see his mind was not on his driving. He held out a pack of Luckies and I took one and he pressed a gadget that shot out red hot and we set fire to the tobacco with it. I felt he was in some awkward situation and I said nothing.

For a while we sat there smoking. Dris looked straight ahead at the streets which passed like a sonnet sequence.

"Davey—I need you tonight."

"Anything wrong?" Sudden agitation had placed a cat in my stomach.

"Nothing and everything. Davey—I've made a wrong turning. I don't like what I see and I don't like what I do. I've always been honest with myself—I've always done things because I've believed in them. Davey, that's why I became a lawyer—that's why I went into Jake Fry's firm—but law has changed since Lincoln rode the circuit, and the tangible reality makes a eunuched cat of the tiger I wanted to tame."

"Dris—Lincoln was a railroad and corporation lawyer in his time. He wasn't the plaster saint they teach in school. He was a great guy for all that and one of the fine Americans—like Gramp. But he knew the ropes and didn't let his legal practice get him down. Buck up, Dris."

"Would he have defended bootleggers?"

"No—no, I don't think so."

"Do you think I do?" He glanced surreptitiously at me.

"I know you do. I met Piggy Tone."

"You did?"

The car rolled on and Dris tossed his cigarette away. Dris wasn't one to go howling his self-lacerations. I wondered.

"Davey—I'm getting out. I'm taking a leave of absence from the firm and I'm going to run for the legislature."

"Ned Wonderly going to back you?"

"Yes."

"Then you're *in*."

Dris turned up the pine-clad drive of his house. "You don't like Ned Wonderly?"

"I don't dislike him. But he's a political boss. Hell, I guess college gave me a moralist's eye."

"If I run for office, I want to be elected—I'm an honest man, Davey, and Ned knows it. He knows I'm no fool—and he's no fool either."

"Sure," I said.

"Lincoln played ball with the politicians, didn't he?"

"Sure. So did Wilson and Webster and Clay and Jackson. They were all great men in their way. I suppose that's the wonderful thing about Democracy. The right people get on top—everything is built so well that no matter what the ward heelers do, it still works. Doesn't it?"

Dris stopped the car outside the French windows. I could

not see his face. He couldn't see mine. My center of the universe was in flames.

"Maybe, Davey. Maybe. Anyway, I want you tonight because Jake Fry and Hartley Gould Coppard are coming here to talk me out of going into politics . . ."

I pressed Dris' hand. "And you want a member of the family around to back you up?"

"You always were a conceited little pup, Davey. The going may get loud and hot tonight and I want you to serve the drinks and cigars. The servants are too nosy as it is."

You lie badly for a coming political power, I thought.

F O U R T E E N

"WELL, DAVEY," said Hartley Gould Coppard coming across the living room of Dris' house, "you still going to be a great artist?"

"I will if I ever get out of Princeton."

"H'm. Busted out of there myself."

Jake Fry and Dris came into the room together and I put the cut-glass bottles of Scotch and rye whiskey on the end tables and opened the ice bucket. Jake Fry was getting baggy. He no longer fitted his skin well. There was a yellow tint to his rosy surfaces and some illness seemed to run through the oily liquid that filled out the empty spaces under his great pelt—between the flesh and bones and guts and the balloon that was the man.

He took his whiskey almost neat with only a polite belch of soda and swallowed it smoothly and refilled. I could see that he and Hartley Gould Coppard had been having a few before they got there. I had some rye with ginger ale (just to keep from looking like a butler) and settled down. I had a feeling—a sense of some sort—that these men had come to use words, arguments and even force on Dris. No, not force—for they were gentlemen. At least Jake Fry had rubbed elbows with the habits of gentlemen. But they would go beyond perverse dalliances.

Dris was drinking, too. But I knew it never affected him and he didn't seem to like the stuff.

The lamps—jade china figures—and the old waxed services and furniture were reflected in the cut-glass bottles. Dris put down his drink and looked up at the nobly classic proportions of the ceiling.

"I'm happy you gentlemen could come tonight. Linda has gone to a play with her mother."

Hartley Gould smiled, a smile redolent of a good cigar. "Don't be so grim, Dris. We haven't come to flay you. We're friends."

"Friends, old friends," said Jake Fry, eying his drink as if it contained pestilence.

"I know," said Dris, getting up. "Well, I've just about decided I've had enough of the law. Maybe I'm six different kinds of a damn fool, a weak wit and a mental Boy Scout, maybe—but I didn't pass the bar to defend bootleggers, foreclose mortgages and steal land from busted farmers, or babble incessantly before bought judges."

"No," said Hartley Gould.

"No. I haven't even the decent excuse that I'm earning it for myself—for my family. I'm earning it for the railroads, for the big corporations, for holy holding companies of holier holding companies."

Jake Fry said, "You mean it's a distaste of *what* and *who* your legal talents work for?"

"No, Jake. For myself I wouldn't ask anything. I come from people who never had anything. I could get along without land schemes and bootlegger fees and foreclosures. It's just I don't even want to do it for others. Maybe I'm an honest fool or just a fool honestly—but it's no go."

"I see," said Hartley Gould, refilling all the glasses. "We are unclean. We are the fat cartoons of trusts and takers of public swag and you don't want to mix with us."

"Yes. No," said Dris. "As people you are fine. As associates—well, I'm not trained or born to accept it. I don't want to go into the complexity of it."

"Understandable," said Hartley Gould. "But you forget we are related. You married my daughter. I was grand about it. I didn't howl from the house tops. I didn't become a snob and bring in our different social destinies—I accepted you. As a matter of fact, I like you. But to hell with these evasive insinuations. Dris, *don't* be a fool."

"Thank you," said Dris. He refilled the glasses. "But this law suddenly isn't what I want. And, as for Linda, I wonder if she wanted it or the money it brought in."

"Yes," Hartley Gould said, "she did—she expected it. This is her world and it would be unfair to take her into yours. She didn't make the system you don't like. I didn't create it either. You can say we inherited it, but that isn't true either. We just accepted it—because only a damned saint in our position would reject it. It's painfully apparent, Dris, that you're not full grown yet."

"And I'm a fool," said Dris.

"You're young—young—young," said Jake Fry into his glass, those amethyst eyes of his swimming in fat. "Love you like son—love you as if you were carved out of the pure butter over my heart. Dris—Dris—*listen* . . ."

"I'm listening. My mind is made up, but I thought I would give you a chance to see what made it up. I'm listening."

Hartley Gould ate the end off a fresh cigar and set fire to it slowly. He had the instinctive aversion of a gentleman to a scene. He turned, looked up at the painting on the wall. "Dris, my standards are my own. I'm honest. I'm clean—and I'm the kind who plays the game fairly as *I* see it. You may not like my labor methods, my price fixing, my way of trimming dividends from waiting stockholders. But I've something more in mind than mere money. Those steel plants give men jobs—keep the farmers' fields green in the valley—dig from the earth and shape such things as cars and iceboxes and iron horses. Perhaps I enjoy that power of creating these iron tools. In doing so, I may push the Hunkies and hillbillies a little hard but—*damn it*—maybe they'd starve in the hills and in slums if I didn't make the best God-damn steel in America! It's yours, boy—all of it—some day. My brothers are childless and all I've got is Linda. Don't you see you can have more real honest earned power in the plants than you can get running around with a lot of dirty political bums at the State capital?"

"I'm going to avoid power," said Dris, looking very ill suddenly. "I don't want power. I don't want power—or money."

Jake Fry stirred his vast gut, looked at his swollen fingers. "Yes, you do, Dris. You want power—you want the stuff money can buy. You like good things—good food. Look about you. This house, these chairs, that painting. It's just your pathological obstinacy making you act like this."

Dris gulped his drink. "No."

Jake Fry went on. It was painfully apparent now he was ill. "You fight it. You fight it better than I did. I was just a poor, fat boy from white river trash and I used to stand outside King George Road houses listening to the music and, Jesus, but it drove me. I had a good mind packed in lard and I made something of myself and I got power and money! Boy, I *got* them! But I didn't have what you've got. You've got a goal and a purpose for your power. You'll go farther than me—higher, faster. I'm too fat—too wind-filled. Dris—Driscoll, my boy, I'm as drunk as a Federal judge— and my back teeth are floating—but *don't* give up the law. You'll sit in the Supreme Court some day, and I'll lie like an empty wineskin under my tombstone and laugh with glee at the fat fine worms that drill me; I'll laugh because I put you there, on the Supreme Court bench. One of my kind— see—one of the little people. And you'll reform the law and make it a tool of justice and a wonderful thing of kindness —not the foul nest of special pleading and legal trash it is now. Dris—Driscoll, fill my glass, as I die slowly everything is a monstrous unreality—except you."

Dris sat down. "You two aren't talking of the same thing. You're both asking me to remain a lawyer for opposite reasons. You, Hartley Gould, want me to take over power —power that can ruin America—and Jake wants me to re-form the Supreme Court bench and the Federal law codes. Come, gentlemen. I expected hard-headed business logic and I get fantasy."

The cigar in Hartley Gould's hand smoked calmly. "That's it, Dris. Only the common man grubbing his shirt for lice is a realist. Only the country-corner real estate agent can call himself a hard-headed business man. I am a mystic. Jake—Jake—well, he is a glutton and a romantic. We live by the grand coup and a card trick called Wall Street. We are the men who have moved worlds—in our own unbusinesslike way. We have imagined what could be done and have done it. And what Jake wants and what I want is the same thing. We want to keep you out of the hands of Ned Wonderly and his retinue of rat-trappers."

"What," asked Dris, "has Ned Wonderly got to do with my life or my plans?"

Jake groaned as he watched Dris' face covertly. "You want to be elected. He's got the only organization that can put you into office."

Hartley Gould nodded. "I support Ned Wonderly. I have made my peace with him and his districts. But I always make my peace with what hinders me—in one way or an-other. But that doesn't mean I trust Ned Wonderly or like him. He'll ruin you, Dris. You're a new problem to him because he's never had anyone like you with him. You're something like a Ming vase in his big paws and you puzzle him. But in the end you'll be one of the fat boys with cigar ash on your vest taking orders from Ned Wonderly and, through him, from *me*. And my orders, Dris, to the State capitals are not very pleasant for earnest young men to take. You'll never make a good intellectual *déclassé*."

"I don't think you understand me," said Dris. "I took orders from Jake and you in the law firm and did a lot of things I didn't like because I felt I was only a student of the law and what to me was unpleasant was the right and proper way to justice for everyone. But I've grown since then; and as soon as I saw how sorry a thing the law really is—how foul and low and loose and one-sided—well, I'm getting out and away from the carnivorous orchids corporation lawyers are."

"And politics?" asked Jake Fry. "That's pure and smells of lilies and is as poetic as unrealized passions?"

"No," said Dris, regaining his sense of humor for the first time and smiling. "No. Politics isn't as pure as laundry ads. But understand this—I've talked to Ned Wonderly. I've put my cards on the table. I'll run for office with his organization behind me. I know it's the only way to election. But I made it clear I wasn't going to be his hot-chestnut puller. I would stand for what the party stands for—I would support its honest candidate and honest bills—but I would at all times think for myself and be accountable to no one."

"Spoken like a fine Republican," said Hartley Gould.

I moaned. "We've been good Democrats for a long time."

"Democrats will never sit in the White House again," said Jake Fry. "Any financial tip sheet will tell you that."

And so we all sat, a little heated by alcohol and the thought of ethics. Then Hartley Gould got up and killed his cigar in a china tray. "I'm through fighting you, Dris. Do what you want and be happy. You and Linda. I can't agree with you—but go on. And don't be too proud to ask for help. I mean *money*. I wouldn't lift a finger to help you politically You're poison to what I want from politics."

"No money, either," said Dris. "I never took a thing from you direct except that damn painting. And I never will."

Jake Fry stirred himself to his feet and almost fell as Dris caught him in his arms. "Driscoll, boy—my boy, my son— I'm a dirty fat old sonofabitch—but I'm behind you right into the White House. Be good and kind and always remember the little people—like you—like me. *Sure*, I'm one of the little people, even if I do weigh over three hundred pounds. I was born on a river barge and my mother never learned to read or write."

I don't remember much more. Emotions and whiskey and talk of high principles mix badly in my gullet. I passed out —cold.

Vicky the next day brought me out of my hangover. I went fishing.

I suppose that some day some smooth young genius will write a book on how Driscoll Ormsbee stood on a mountain top and had a vision or heard a voice—and ran for the State Legislature, beginning a noble political career. But the facts are as I have put them down or rather as much of the facts as I can remember (being at the time a little warped by drinking and confused by the talk of three men who had exposed a little corner of their souls). With Pecksniffian smugness, I went fishing when I should have played historian.

Dris was nominated and Ned Wonderly's boys saw that everything went smoothly. There was no more talk of my returning to Princeton and I became Dris' private secretary one fine rainy day and went with him to muddy crossroads and sat on his left hand when he spoke at ladies' forums and joined him in wilted potato salad and sticky cake at the club socials. I saw every cog in Ned Wonderly's machine perform its wonders.

I registered at the Antioch College for something called Liberal Arts—(the nearest thing to a Liberal being the Dean of English, a hardshell reactionary Baptist—and the Arts were some dreadful casts of Roman statues with the plaster genitals hammered off by Miss Bonifeather, the art teacher, and their manhood replaced by tin fig leaves that she herself had cut from tin cans in the interest of pure thoughts among farm boys and corn-fed girls who had seen animal fornication since birth). That year the earth was very green and the city was always under a blue sky.

It was not a very good school and I attended very few of its classes. I was mostly with Dris, tacking his banners to ant-eaten poles and retyping his speeches in my peck-and-hunt manner on a lisping old Royal. On the river the sailboats and barges moved as always.

I was doing a lot of learning. The Antioch College Library had been left a great many books by old Judge Flanger and no one besides myself and the librarian had ever opened most of them. I read Darwin and Spencer and Mill and old bluffers like Kant and poets like Keats and Shelley and aped their lines and failed dismally. I ate up volumes of H. G. Wells and became slightly ill, and shifted through Dickens and Mark Twain and caught my mind on Tolstoy but broke free and dipped into Spinoza and retreated in fear. And like all young jackasses I wallowed in Voltaire until I discovered the Machen translation of the complete Casanova. . . . And after that I lived in a warm fantasy of flesh and lust and brittle dialogue until there was nothing left but to tackle Henry George and Plato and Karl Marx and the novels of Stephen Crane, Joseph Conrad and Frank Norris and Balzac's large and fertile world—and a strange book called *The Red and the Black*. Even Dris was fed up on my book-nosing.

Slightly ill after all this undigested stuff had numbed my mind, I gave up reading for a long while and went out into the wards to line up the voters. Ned Wonderly explained it all to me in that dining room of the club where Dris and I had so long ago put away our first well-cooked steak with such devastating integrity.

Ned and his henchmen and Jake Fry and myself sat eating curried chicken. Dris was off in the northern part of the state, speaking. Ned, thin, paper-gray face, gray-clothed, his black pearl in place, sipped his mineral water and spoke softly.

"It's all right. I've got the wards and the districts set for Dris and all I want from you boys is a little talk about how much we've done for the people—and we have done a lot."

Outside I went over to Piggy Tone, who was reading a tabloid in the smoking room of the club, bravely dressed in a silk shirt and fawn-colored tie.

"What's Ned shooting us a line for?" I asked.

"What line?"

"To remind the voters what he has done for them."

Piggy took out a cigarette case and held it toward me. He looked at me as if I were manifestly born to be a fool. Piggy was developing manners and soft habits but he had retained a certain hard honesty of character.

"It's on the up and up, Davey. Ned's a wonderful guy. I hate them goons what say he's a grafter and a crook. Ned don't graft and he don't steal. He don't have to. His trucks and lumber and paving companies and brickyards are honest stuff, see?"

"Yes. But what does he do for the people?"

"Plenty," said Piggy with a shrewd plausibility. "You

live in one of his districts, see. And your kid breaks-and-enters and they want to send him to reform school. Ned gets him off if the kid jerns the Navy. Or you got a lotta old shacks you make a livin' from, see, and if you repair them or worry over fire laws and stuff you're sunk. Ned, he fixes so the inspectors don't bother you. Or you want a gas-station corner or you got a lot that the city chewed off the corner. Ned's boys get you justice and a good price."

"What about the courts?"

Piggy spit daintily into the brass pot as if I had said something invariably vulgar. "Listen, fella, if you drive a truck all day and knock down twelve bucks a week and your daughter she gets caught in a cat-house raid, see—and you gotta hire lawyers, the leechin' sods, and you gotta bring witnesses and you can't beat the rap anyway. But Ned's ward heelers—they'll see you through—smash the case before it opens . . ."

"*But*," I began, "there are charities . . ."

"*But* my hind teeth! Go live in them cold-water flats and ask the Salvation Army for food and see how they pray your knees off before they hand out a lousy crust of bread. Go lie at them charity places and get examined for fleas and asked questions and be labeled and pushed around for a lousy shirt and a patched pair of pants. But not Ned—he don't ask no questions. You a club member—and it's a ton of coal and a turkey and a basket of eats any time you need it. And you don't have to break your knees in prayer and you don't even have to ask for it, if you're shy. Ned's captains make the rounds—and if your furniture is on the curb, he pays the rent, and if you look hungry, a bag of grub is home before you are."

"I know," I said, very confident of my point, "but, Piggy, it's selling your *vote*."

"No, it ain't. You don't have to work for the party. Nobody is begging you. But if you're smart, you'll see Ned Wonderly is one of your kind of folk. Go vote with the muckamucks and reform boys and Christers and see how far it gets ya."

"But the reform people will change laws and see that people are taken care of without a political boss handing it out."

"Yeah? Then why don't Dris run on the reform ticket? Why don't he back up the screwballs? Why? Because they ain't nothing but a lot of hot-mouthed flannel heads shooting hot air. Ned Wonderly—he does things. Dris knows it . . ."

"And you think Ned is an honest man?"

Piggy nodded. "Sure he is. Maybe he has to have bootleggers and hoodlums and fat aldermen doin' his work for him —because nobody wants anythin' to do with him. Maybe he takes it away from the rich taxpayers—but Ned Wonderly don't graft." Piggy spit again, leered. "He don't have to. He makes his."

I wondered how Dris felt about Ned Wonderly and the brazen self-assurance of the man. I knew that Ned ran a rotten and corrupt political machine that sold anything anyone wanted to buy. True, Ned himself was honest and ran his companies on the level—but his firms depended on public works, and how did he always get the proper bid in? Never too high and never too low. Perhaps the graft was cut up among his captains and he didn't touch tainted money. But he *was* buying voters, free Americans, body and soul. I went out and saw it for myself. People loved him and blessed him and felt no shame at giving him their vote. Perhaps, I felt, Piggy was right. These people were getting a little back for their votes. They were not being bought but were trading a little of what the system kept from them for their mark on the ballot. But it all had the dimensions of a national crime.

In the end the taxpayer paid for everything. Even I was made an election-board clerk at seventy-five dollars a day, and I worked three days filling ink-wells during the election and registration periods. I took the money, but I wasn't as grateful as most of the people in Ned's organization. I gave the whole matter too many subtle interpretations.

One night I went to King George Road to find Dris to get him to sign some papers. Linda was at the piano, playing Debussy's *Girl with the Flaxen Hair*. She looked very lonely and appeared very happy to see me. I always felt an elusive, indefinable quality about her.

"Hello, Davey. Dris is out. Let's make a night of it."

"Where is he?"

"Speaking at some Polack social club. What shall we do?"

"Play some more music."

She didn't play well. Linda was not a trained musician. But I was no critic. She played a long time and then I saw she was crying. She stopped playing and looked at me. I suppose I answered with an inappropriate expression of my own.

"What's the matter with me, Davey?"

"Nothing."

"That's what I thought. I'm young—I'm not too ugly—and I'm damned desirable. Don't you think so?"

"Well . . ."

Linda came over to me and put her arms around me. "Tell me, Davey—you ever slept with a woman?"

"Well . . ."

"Have you?"

"Oh, hell, Linda—what kind of a way is this to talk!"

"Davey—I just wanted to know. I just wanted to talk

to someone who could understand. I had to talk to some-one before I went off my mind. Davey, I'm no fool. I'm no prim little thing with a mind all Sunday school. What's the matter between me and Dris?"

"Nothing. I mean—how should I know?"

"He hasn't slept with me in a month."

I got up and walked to the window and looked out at the intricate stippled shadows. "I'd rather not hear any more."

"Davey, do you think he's unfaithful to me? Do you think some pretty little bitch has gotten hold of him? Davey, Davey—I'm going mad. Tell me anything—*anything* at all. One way or the other—but I'm not going to sit here and think mad things—lewdness, pride, cruelty—I don't know what has come over me."

I turned around and tried to be very calm. "Linda, I've been with Dris more than anyone else these last few months. I swear there is no other woman. It's—it's hard to put into words. It's so damn lousy-sounding when you say it right out—so like something out of the Rollo books—but Dris—well, he's really honest and noble and earnest about this business of being in politics. I don't want to make him seem a prig—a noble prig—you know, working for the welfare of the little people. But, Linda, he's in this deep emotionally and it would kill him if anything went wrong. Linda, don't ever think *that* about other women. Don't ever say it—not to him."

Linda looked at me, her eyes abnormally lucid. "Why not, Davey?"

"Maybe I'm a sap," I said. "I'm a little too cynical about life. You know me—good-natured. But I don't expect too much from anything. Dris isn't like that. You and he—well —you're something from another world to him. Purged, clarified and of trenchant beauty. Christ, that's a stupid re-mark. You're someone from above. After all, we Ormsbees are not much. But if you showed you lacked a certain faith in Dris now, it would break him up. He's real, Linda. He's very real. And people like you and me—we're not. We're daydreaming souls. We're what we read in books or imagine in art or music. But Dris is real. You know, sometimes he's as real to me as Lincoln. Not in the cheap plaster-saint way of the story books but in the way Lincoln was real before history distorted him. Rooted—deep—and honest at the core. Like few men are these days. Oh, hell, Linda. I can't keep up talking important. Play some Chopin."

Linda looked at me. "Davey, you've been reading too many books. Dull ones."

"Yes, a great many. Too many about an esoteric universality."

She smiled. I could see the firm resilience of her throbbing breasts. "But there is *no* other woman?"

I gave up. "No."

"What can I do, Davey? I don't want to be like Mrs. Lincoln. She went mad."

"Why don't you appear with him on the platform, pose for news pictures with him or with housewives? It will help."

"I'll try. I'll honestly try. Oh, Davey—sometimes I worry about Dris. And myself. You can be close to a man. Like you, Davey, some day can be close to a woman; love her, lie with her, stay with her, be part of her fully, warmly, with passion and yet you'll feel alone maybe. The closer you try to get the farther the other retreats into his own passion to gloat over it alone. Am I that way? Davey, do you understand what I mean?"

"No," I said. But I knew of that firm elastic caressed obsession, of the lustrous rhythmical peculiar feeling of doubt and desire, of the strangeness Linda felt.

Odd, we were both saturated with it. I looked down at her.

"Ravel," said Linda, beginning to play.

I went too often after that to hear Linda play modern French music. It was a brooding unreal sort of friendship. It was unspoken and gave little satisfaction. I was young and I think I tormented myself a little that here was a pure love, free from the cloying twisting demands of bodies, of crushing passions. Only the very young or those covered with an aspic of poets' soft words become involved like this —and I knew it—and went back for more piano music.

I spent most of my time visiting either Linda or Gramp. The old man had something that I missed among the people I met every day. Sometimes I felt I had found out his secret —then I knew I was foolishly expecting him to act like an oil painting of a pioneer.

I would spend a great many nights at Gramp's, reading to him from his old books. Books no one reads any more. Books that are illustrated in color now and given as Christmas gifts. Books by Smollett and Dickens. I lived on a diet of Dickens and Ravel. . . .

FIFTEEN

"It was the best of times, it was the worst of times, it was the age of wisdom, it was the age of foolishness," I read from Gramp's tattered volume. The old man sat deeply in his chair, wrapped in detached personal composure, plucking at the strands of his thinning white beard. A twisted, knotted pale hand waved me back to my reading. I went on. "It was the epoch of belief, it was the epoch of incredulity, it was the season of Light, it was the season of Darkness, it was the spring of hope, it was the winter of despair, we had everything before us, we had nothing before us, we were all going direct to heaven, we were all going direct the other way—in short, the period was so like the present period that . . ."

"What time is it, Davey?" said Gramp, leaning forward, his lean head highlighted into dynamic planes by the lamp light.

I looked over at the banjo clock on the fireplace. "Getting near seven. Shall I go on reading?"

"No. I've read it twice before. You'll be wanting to get back to Antioch. Driscoll must be elected by now."

"Yes, the results should be almost certain by now." I put aside my book and went up to Gramp. "If he's won, they'll be giving a big dinner for him tonight. Why don't you come? You're like Pete, Gramp. He doesn't approve of what Dris is doing, either. Why?"

The old man looked at his thin hands. "Davey, I'm an old

man and as an incorrigible rationalizer, I see I'm going to die—sooner or later. *But* sooner than most people. The world has gone to seed and only I seem to care. Here is our era. Life with no hardships but counting bank balances—life without Indian raids and tree-chopping and blizzards and cattle stampedes—life with fat dividends and imitation whiskey. It's no good. Can't last, Davey. Dris wants something but he doesn't know what. He's adrift in a world that can't be changed but for the worse. It's off like a snowball down a mountain, and a man named Harding sits in Lincoln's chair. Dris isn't going to find what he wants in politics—not yet, he isn't. The world will have to burn at both ends—and it will, irrepressible, indefatigable. And then perhaps Dris will find work to do."

"Dris wants to serve the people."

"What people?" said Gramp, giving me an inscrutable, swift look. "The oil crowds cheating the nation out of mineral reserves? The Wall Street crooks with Harvard watch charms building up a Bull market? The people doped with installment gadgets? The intellectuals full of Freud, foul wind and their little vices softly performed in steamheated flats? The writers and artists standing around in popular poses, patting their breast pockets in which the latest check from Hollywood is? Those people? Dris couldn't serve those people. He can only run with them—be part of a tide."

"That's all everybody is—part of a tide."

The old man sat a long time very still. Silver light rays danced on his bowed head, the loose raddled flesh under his eye sockets twitched.

"Better get along, Davey. How old men rave! Maybe I'm too full of what Jefferson and Andrew Jackson had in mind. Maybe. But what they built—is it strong enough to stand this stupid lust after the yellow butter they dig out of the earth—this worthless dental filling? And this rushing with machines toward a new Thirty-Year—Fifty-Year—Hundred-Year War?"

"I'll be up next week, Gramp," I said. "Maybe we'll fix up a pack horse and hit for tall timber again—like we used to."

"Ask Dris to come along, too."

"Sure."

Outside, the wind was moving slowly along a row of elms. Cap Roc was standing at the stables watching the field hands drive the milk herd in for the night. He saw me and came over wiping his mad red face with a huge red sheet of a handkerchief. His scarred skull was more welted and wrinkled than ever. I could see the ridges where they had placed the silver plates to hold his poor hurt head together.

"Evenin', Davey. How's Gramp look to you?"

"Old."

Cap Roc nodded and set his teeth in a wedge of tobacco and tore off a section and shaped it into his cheek. "Notice anythin'?"

"No. He's getting older. That's all."

The big, wide, mad man shook his mutilated head. "That ain't what I mean. Has he talked to you—about the world? I mean, what's happening to it—how it's going up in flames —stuff like that?"

The little insane eyes looked at me. "Cap, Gramp is an old man. He's read a lot, and lived more and maybe he's adding it all up and getting a bad answer."

Cap Roc spit. "I dunno. Them land lawyers is talkin' of seizin' the whole Range with the help of sheriff posses. I'll blast daylight out of them first with shotguns. But it's affectin' him—affectin' him bad." Cap Roc put a stubby black-nailed finger to his temple. "It's here it's affected him. He ain't right sayin' them things about the world. But I'll take care none o' them land lawyers get near him."

"Do that, Cap," I said, wondering if there was any serene lucidity left in the world.

All the way down to the road I kept thinking how strange it was that a poor crackheaded creature like Cap Roc should think Gramp was off his trolley. Yet what else could one think in this age of Harding, this time of progress and of Stock Exchange fever, this world of coupon clippings and Kredit Klothing? No Thirty-Year, Hundred-Year War faced the world. There was talk of a disarmament conference in Washington and kindness toward the German savages who were being broken on the wheel of inflation by the British and French industrialists and bankers.

At the bus station the road was crowded by flivvers and Chevvies going to Antioch to see the fireworks spin up on a brave new happy world.

There were special police in front of Driscoll's house on King George Road. The lights were on in every room and all sorts of people were being admitted. The furniture had been removed from the entire downstairs and a large number of plank tables covered with white cloth and bunting had been put up. The austerities and decencies had been packed away for the night.

There was a great deal of food—a great many kegs of foaming beer and too many people talking too loudly. They were party leaders, society speakers, the first Buchmanites, and gentlemen from the State and National Legislatures. The small fry had not been admitted. They, the poll watchers, ward heelers and party workers, were celebrating in the Ned Wonderly clubs where they did not have to conduct themselves with propriety.

I found Ned Wonderly himself in Dris' library, three phones ringing on the walnut desk and some important party people standing around, smiling at the ends of their glowing cigars. Piggy Tone sat on a white-covered Chippendale chair, his square derby on, his long black overcoat buttoned. He was looking at the paneled ceiling with his little, wavering, half-facetious eyes.

Ned looked up as I entered, and put a phone back on its hook. He had a melancholy, apprehensive look.

"Hello, Davey. What happened to Dris?"

"He's been elected—I gather."

Ned grinned and rubbed his paper-gray face with well-cared-for hands. "*That* I knew weeks ago. But what's happened to him tonight? The boys want him to say a few words—with Mrs. Ormsbee—for the press and cameramen. And he's disappeared."

"Was he here tonight?"

"Yes, yes. Said he was going to get Mrs. Ormsbee, and disappeared."

"Maybe they are upstairs. I'll see."

"Do that," said Piggy benevolently. "We boys from the old Fire House wants to present him with a watch. Solid gold. Twenty-one jewels."

The house had been built in the shape of an L. Linda had placed the master bedrooms in the short arm of the L, away from the street. As I went up the stairs, I found Linda's maid and the fat cook standing at the head of them with their hands under their aprons.

"Have you seen Mr. Ormsbee?" I asked, having sudden painful premonitions.

They rolled their heads toward the master bedroom. I went along the soft yarn rugging and came to the polished walnut of the big bedroom. I knocked, then turned the handle and walked in.

Dris sat on a footstool, looking at a strange, wobbling Linda who sprawled on the bed, kicking her bare feet, waving nude arms and letting her taffy-colored hair flow in front of her face. She was wearing a blue, lace-trimmed dressing robe, the front gaping open, exposing her solid little breasts. Her voice was shrill, in painful ascendancy.

"Hello, Davey," she said, grinning. "How's the sweet little brother? How's the boy? The cute little boy?"

"I'm all right," I said, almost adding, "you look fine, too."

"I'm swell. I'm sitting on top of the cockeyed world. Dris and I. Aren't we, Sweet?"

Dris shrugged his shoulders and got up and walked to the bathroom and came out with something in a glass which he handed to Linda. She took it, thanked him and threw the glass against the wall. It broke, blotching the pink and gray flowers of the wallpaper. Linda faced me in sullen exasper-ation, then grinned.

I said, "Dris, the newspaper reporters—the cameramen are waiting."

"Let 'em wait," said Linda, blowing her hair from her face. "No. Better still, let them interview the lucky candi-date and his happy wife. Who says I'm incapable of grati-tude to the stupid voters! *Who?*"

She stood up and swayed on her feet and then fell across the white rug on the floor. Dris picked her up and lifted her in his arms. He turned to me. His face was very white, the brow dewed and twitching, his eyes sad in a dark opaqueness.

"Davey, get me a woolen robe for her. She'll catch cold like this."

I went to the wall closet and opened the double doors. It was dark. I moved in to find the light cord and kicked aside some glassware underfoot. I pulled on the light. I was standing in a scent-filled closet of dresses, wraps and shoe bags. And under my feet was a fine collection of whiskey bottles. Dozens of them. All empty.

I knew suddenly what extenuating circumstances bothered Linda tonight. *She was dead drunk.*

Somehow I got rid of the press boys and cleared the house.

It was half an hour before I came upstairs again. Linda was still lying sprawled on her back, her beautiful face flushed, breathing through her mouth with a sucking sound. Dris hadn't moved from his footstool. He seemed incapable of action.

"It's all right," I said. "Ned got the boys on their feet and pointed them toward the door and he invented some yarn for the press about you and Mrs. Ormsbee slipping off to an old country house to be alone on this great night of nights. How is she?"

Dris looked at the bed and said nothing. If anything his glance was despicably sentimental.

"Vicky called," I said. "All excited. I told her you would see her in the morning."

"Thanks, Davey. Christ, this has been a shock. I never had any idea of anything like this. Had you?"

"The liquor?"

"Yes."

"No, Dris. I never had any idea she was hitting the stuff on the sly. It isn't all her fault. She's been lonely. You've been away a lot."

Dris turned to me, rubbed his capable-looking hands. "She knew where I was—what I was doing. I was running for public office. But there is no excuse for me. I feel so stupidly naive, muddled."

"She broke down once and asked me if you had another girl."

"She did!" Dris was amazed and showed it. "Good Lord, whatever put that idea into her mind?"

"Dris, it's none of my business. I'm just the kid brother and what I don't know would fill several houses—but it kind of looks to me as if you and Linda got off on the wrong foot in this political business and you've stayed that way."

My brother nodded and looked at the sleeping girl. He got up and pulled the sheet closer under her throat and kissed the warm brow. He seemed suddenly ineffectual, inarticulate. He took my arm and led me down the hall into his own bedroom. We sat on the bed and Dris thought a long while before he found his voice again. I had never seen him waver at a crucial moment before.

"Davey, you're right. Linda and I got off on the wrong foot. We've never managed to get into step. Love—it takes a lot of ridicule, this love business—but Linda and I—we were in love. Hard in love. You don't know, Davey, what it's meant, knowing her when I was studying law, when I was in that lousy war, when I stood at the bar a member of a great law firm." His rage was rising. "A man isn't a man alone. He's flesh connected with many things and many people. Linda—you, Vicky, Gramp, all have been living tissue connecting part of me and what I want from life. But Linda—she alone gave me most that chemical reaction, that surge, made me do things. This secret drinking, Davey—it's her damn family. Their family pride, position, their social snobbery. I should have married her and lived in a furnished room with her. Eaten in a lunch wagon and tried to show everyone we could be happy on very little. Who wants this rich barn—this barbaric flaring of good taste?"

"Nonsense, Dris. You're a romantic. You know damn well with your law income you could have lived any place

—not in this gilded tomb, maybe, but very well. But would Linda have followed you?"

"Yes," said Dris, calming down. "She would have. I never asked her. But she said, the night we left to get married, 'I'm giving you my life. Take it and do what you want with it. What you do doesn't have to be right or proper—as long as you do it with me by your side. Only one thing matters, Dris,' she said, 'the love I give you and what you do with it.' Davey, it sounds very sloppy—like bad fiction, but I think she meant it to mean everything love is."

"Well—I guess you see where you've flopped?"

"Yes—and no. We drifted into a false position, that dead end that almost tied me forever to the law firm. We drifted into this thing of her sitting here in her glory, making social small talk, while I was away spouting speeches to ward heelers and rabble that were going to vote whatever way Ned Wonderly cracked the whip, anyway. But I mustn't get bitter, Davey—I *mustn't* speak of rabble and things like that. I wanted the people to hear why they were voting for me —even if they had to."

"What are you going to do?"

"I'm taking Linda away for a month. Then we're selling the house—and we're going up to the State capital to live on my salary and on some stocks I have. But I'll be fearfully in debt. Never mind. I'll pay it all back. It will be a fine trip well taken."

"Palm Beach? Atlantic City? Newport?"

"No." Dris went to the desk and took a cigarette and lit it. "No. I'm going to buy a camping outfit and take one of Gramp's pack horses and head for tall timber with Linda. She'll like it."

"I think so," I said. And then, with an apparent want of tact, "And better take along a few bottles. It may be a little hard to taper off after a big bat."

Dris grinned. "You've become very worldly in the last few years, Davey."

"I just have an aunt named Netta who likes the stuff. So have you."

"So I have. And Linda will be all right as an officeholder's wife. You'll see. At least, she isn't as bad as Mrs. Lincoln, who used to chase Abe down the street throwing frozen potatoes at him."

The morning papers carried no pictures of Mrs. Driscoll Ormsbee, wife of the newly elected State Senator. At least not new pictures made with the newly elected Senator formidable in his moment of victory.

They were both high in the hills with one of Gramp's pack horses and a hound, when the house on King George Road was placed on sale. The sign disappeared the same day. Hartley Gould Coppard bought the house and paid cash for it and so some of Dris's money worries were over. Hartley Gould placed the deed in Linda's safe-deposit vault at the bank where she found it a year later. The hall bedroom never materialized. Dris had a house at the State capital.

Vicky, of course, took the election with her usual form. She felt that now that Dris was in politics there was nothing to do but repaint the car and wear her Sunday dress every day. The pot-cheese business had failed. She and Uncle Thoreau had also been interested in breeding rabbits, in a sandwich shop and a bowling alley. I don't think they ever went very far with these ideas as they had no capital at all. Pete was back at the steel mill three days a week, shoveling iron ore and stewing molten steel with a long slice bar. The market had fallen off in his cabinet business.

Every once in a while he had to put aside his tools and put on his burnt, steel-puddler's shoes and go back to the steel mill. He was fifty-five the last time he went back. After that, they wouldn't take him any more. Young buck niggers were appearing and made up most of the open-shop crews.

I was fed up with Antioch. The local college gave me nothing. I had read all the books in its library I wanted to read. I was painting almost every day and the stuff did not please me. I knew nothing about the technical part of art. I could gabble with the best little louse of a critic about Cezanne and descending form and building masses, and of color and line—but I wasn't very good yet when it came to putting it down on canvas and paper. Jake Fry gave me a note to a Boston gentleman who ran an art school—a Christopher Cabot Carson.

I had two thousand dollars, made at the polls and in the office of *The Antioch Advocate* doing pen-and-ink cartoons for the sport page.

One morning before breakfast I came down with my bag packed and my best suit on. Pete was on the late shift at the mills. He was eating bread and peanut butter and stirred a muddy cup of coffee.

Vicky was mashing some eggs together in cold grease and waiting for the pan to heat up enough to char the eggs for Pete's breakfast. She looked at me and rubbed egg off her small pug nose, a nose as *retroussé* as ever.

"*Where* do you think you're going?"

"I'm going to art school. Have a letter to a Boston man now in New York. Then Paris, maybe—Rome . . . Hell, I don't know—but I'm fed up with local elections, with local magazine-cover art, with the taste of local earth and cooking."

Pete put down his bread. "Doug's running oil tankers. Got a card from him at Singapore."

"I'm not going to Singapore," I said. "He'll never get any place with his tubs."

"No, I guess not," said Pete, fumbling in his pants pocket and offering me a little wad of small bills with a look from his liquid, cow eyes as if he had printed them himself. "Here, Davey."

"That's your trolley and lunch money for a month, Pete. I don't need it. I have a little something. I'll drop up to see Gramp and Aunt Netta and Uncle Thoreau and be off. I've got plenty of money—don't worry."

Vicky set the eggs in front of Pete and came over to me after a moment's hesitation. She was suddenly very, very small.

"How much money?"

"Just *enough* to study art."

I got up. Vicky put her arms around me. I looked down at her small, pretty head. She was weeping. "Like little birds leaving the nest. All my big sons—Dennis and Doug and Dris and *now* the baby—Davey."

"Don't worry about me."

She hugged me to her. I could feel the beat and energy of that tiny body. It was as if tocsins were always clashing within her. "Be a good boy, Davey. A very, very good boy, Davey. You'll make your way. I know you will, Davey. Be a good, great man."

Pete looked at me and filled his mouth with the mangled egg. But I could see he could not swallow as his emotions reached dumb, terrifying proportions.

I picked up my bag.

I am sitting on that bag this morning, writing this history. It is old and travel worn. Gramp made it years ago out of a steer's hide. It fits in here among the growing grass and my

[211]

friendly rabbit. He has raised up a rabbit family and they come every morning early to keep me company at breakfast. They are good company and never talk of the state of the world. They remind me of the drawing teachers at the art school. . . .

SIXTEEN

WITH A HUMBLE, beating heart I came to study art. . . .

The brown escarpment of uptown apartment houses frightened me at first. So did the intermittent street fighting of traffic.

The New York City papers were not greatly interested in the political doings from other states. It was rare when I saw Driscoll's name mentioned. And only once until he became Governor did the Manhattan journals run his picture.

I was studying art—or rather, sitting among other young hopeful, would-be artists—planning to create beauty by measuring the distracting rump of an unwashed female with a glance and trying to reproduce the sulky flesh with soft pencil or red chalk on unspoiled paper. And later, to talk too much with other students over a half a liter of bathtub Chianti.

Carson's School of Art was a four-story building in the high Seventies of upper Broadway. Fat gold letters were screwed into the yellow brick front and a groaning cage elevator took one up to any of the four floors painted an austere black and lemon, and to halls into which studios and classrooms flung out the talented youth of both sexes at the end of a pleasant day of smearing colors.

Christopher Cabot Carson, the friend of Jake Fry's, had welcomed me to the school with his little blue cherubic eyes and had sat me down on a red-covered chair and fingered, with very white hands, the few sketches I had brought along as samples. I felt a blathering oaf.

Cabot Carson was a Boston gentleman, once a bosom friend of Henry Adams. He had visited Japan with him, had studied painting in Paris under the wrong masters, had become a designer of country estates for Stanford White and now—in his old age (he was seventy-eight when I first saw him)—he had retired from the business world to surround himself with a group of talented snobs from the right families, all grouped into the Carson's School of Art.

No one really knew why he had opened an art school. Some decided he had won the Broadway loft building in a bet at badminton—others, that he had lost his fortune in Paris through a stable of race horses, and there were those mean people who said he had been ruined in mad, whirling love affairs, first with an Italian opera singer wider than a tea table and then with her manager, a tall, Russian baron with a long blond beard and a habit of inhaling ether. It all sounded not of this world. I don't know. Very romantic and shocking when I first heard it but perhaps it's all stupid and false. Cabot Carson never spoke of his early life, but would wink and tap on his thin nose.

He was dressed in blue the first time I met him. In his lapel gleamed the little red ribbon. He was a Chevalier of the Legion of Honor. He was bald and his skin was very white and polished. He looked at my sketches and smiled like the luminous dial of a watch set at ten after ten.

"David Ormsbee, you're a bad artist at the moment."

I nodded. "That's why I'm here."

"You really want to paint?"

"Yes. Mr. Fry said you would tell me how to go about it."

"Well, this isn't the place for you. Go find a room downtown, *not* in the Village. Buy a lot of paper and go to the

Met and sketch for a year—casts—armor, old masters, the drawings of Michelangelo, Blake, Daumier, Goya, Hogarth. Set up an easel and copy some Turners, Winslow Homers, some Cezannes, a Picasso—but *only* one. Then study some Manet and Renoir and Van Gogh—and go away and repaint them from memory."

"And then?"

"Then you'll most likely find out you don't care for art."

"And if I do, Mr. Carson?"

"Then forget everything you've learned. Pack some paints and canvas and go to a place like Mexico or Russia or Ceylon—any place that will knock you down with amazement at its color and oddness and strangeness. Paint your fool head off for a few years. Come home and see America with fresh eyes and paint your first masterpiece. Sound too much like penal servitude?"

I sat a long time looking at the grinning blue eyes of the little Boston gentleman. Then I said, "But I *did* want to begin in your school."

"Fiddlesticks. This isn't an art school. It's a polite finishing school for society girls and Southern cigarette heirs. For real work we give scholarships to bright farm lads and Jewish boys with fine heads and no social standing. We teach advertising, layout, type designing, stage setting and some trash called dynamic symmetry. But not art. Not what you want."

I fumbled my drawings back into their folder. "I still would like to study here. I—I—well, I like this city and . . ."

Cabot Carson smiled and stood up as if he didn't suspect I was mentally deficient. He was short and wide but carried himself as if he were seven feet tall. "I know. You like the looks of the debutantes painting in life class. You want to be part of the little group of polite drunkards who have those roadsters parked outside. You think there are a great many interesting art volumes to read in our library. You are impressed by the fairies wearing old Harrovian ties teaching here."

"Well . . ."

"All right, David. You go ahead and enroll. Linda, too, sort of asked me to look out for you anyway."

"Linda? I thought only Mr. Fry knew you. I mean . . ."

"Jake Fry and I once chased the same dancer across the Atlantic in 1912. But Linda Coppard—pardon me, Linda Ormsbee—happens to be a great-niece of a great-aunt of mine."

I flushed. "I forgot Coppards are a Boston family—or were."

"Were," said Cabot Carson, looking down at his Shiraz rug. "*Were*. Boston lies low and stews in reaction and mistakes it for a mystic sensitivity. The great days of Adams and Hancock and Emerson are over. They no longer throw Greek verbs at one another—only burn fish peddlers and shoemakers from a judge's bench. How is Linda?"

"All right. I haven't seen much of her. Not since Election Night."

"This brother of yours seems a strange fish—a rather peculiar creature mixed up with those political cats squabbling raucously for power."

"He's sincere and he wants certain things from life . . ."

"Wonderful," said Cabot Carson, "wonderful. I am too foully brushed with the European snobbery and Mayfair's ironic witticisms to feel sincerely about anything myself, but I admire it in others. Drop in any time at all, David— any time at all and you may catch my futility of effort."

But I didn't dare drop in at any time. There were four hundred students and art lovers and craftsmen in the four floors of studios and classrooms. And the talent—as the

[216]

teachers and instructors well knew—formed a solid (if rather bony) rank of flesh around the aging body of the little dandy who was Cabot Carson. And every day he took a sun bath *à l'allemande* on the roof, his head covered.

I didn't dare go up to his third-story study and ask to be permitted to drop in for a visit. His door was guarded by an evil-looking New England spinster armed with a red-hot temper and sour stomach—a dried-up wench of fifty named Miss Snow. She sat at his door and ran the school on Cabot Carson's whispered orders and never was known to bend the three warts on her upper lip into the half-circle of a smile. We called her "the blunt end of a pig."

I was homesick at first. Then I got over it and discovered the novels of Somerset Maugham and Aldous Huxley in the possession of a divorcee from Seattle, a Mrs. Knott. She was studying window designing and loaned me her copy of the novel *Chrome Yellow*. I suppose I was rather a fool, a young fool, as I thought her a *femme supérieure*. I was down to rudimentary biological values.

Mrs. Knott knew everyone who mattered in Europe. She had eaten fried shrimp with a woman named Stein and babbled of a man called Hemingway and she was advanced enough to have smuggled in a blue, paper-bound copy of a book by an Irishman, Joyce. And her late husband had beaten her tender flesh with a Cossack *ngaika*.

In her flat—a delightful place smelling of canned anchovies and Chanel Number Five and the coated paper used to print *Vogue*—there hung several primitive-looking drawings by some modern Germans named Dix and Grosz. She owned a small Matisse which I hated (it was such decoration and so little art) and there was a tray of Russian cigarettes with gold tips. The tips shed gold dust on your lips and the tobacco was part incense and part horse dung. In her flat, as I started to say, I lost my homesickness. She would cook boiling messes of cheese and scented Italian sausage and we would lie on her Bokhara rugs listening to recordings of Sibelius and she would tell me more about her husband. A very remarkable cad.

I suppose it was an education although a rickety substructure for an art career. I learned very little about art, very little about the serious things of life such as most of the people were learning—things like Wall Street and margin and installment buying and the virtues of cheap tin cars made in Dearborn. Yes. I was neglecting my classes in perspective and taking Mrs. Knott to Russian movies when I should have been reading *The Antioch Advocate*.

That is why I missed Dris' first appearance in the New York press. How could I look at the Hearst and Scripps-Howard press when I was translating François Villon into Chicago gangster argot?

It was Mrs. Knott who brought me back to every-day thought. One morning as I was sitting under the chin of a fat female model who smelled of shaving soap, trying to copy the overlapping chins on her rib section, Mrs. Knott, the rings under her eyes carefully covered with face powder, came into life class, sat down and looked at me out of the corner of an eye.

"You related to Driscoll Ormsbee?"

"My brother. Why?"

She opened a tabloid and handed it to me.

REPUBLICAN LEGISLATOR DRISCOLL ORMSBEE CONDEMNS HARDING ADMINISTRATION! CLAIMS BOODLE GANGS OF PRESIDENT'S FRIENDS ARE STRIPPING THE NATION'S RESOURCES!

And then a box with an old picture of Dris much retouched around the chin. I read on among the edifying details.

Breaking suddenly with the party that elected him to public office, it seems that Dris had gotten some information that certain oil men and supply dealers and land speculators were busting the country wide open with graft, corruption and swindles, stealing national resources, bilking the United States Treasury.

I read every word of the newspaper story with a thrill. It quoted Dris as saying:

"I am not a muckraker and I know *certain* press lords will howl 'Red!' I am only an American who sees the resources of our nation being stolen. I could not sit by and I could not reach anyone high enough to stop this pilfering of the public till and pantry. I leave myself open to a great deal of libel in these statements but I have proof of much of what I say. I have facts and figures and places and names of much that is going on. But of all that is being done to undermine our nation, I can only offer guesses. It is too much for me alone. It is up to America. Not the flagwaving slogan-makers and song-and-dance men but up to every person who is part of this nation . . ."

I turned to Mrs. Knott, swallowing aspirin tablets. "He's wonderful, isn't he?"

"He's a wonderful fool. That washes him up as a public officeholder completely."

That night I returned her volume of Huxley.

The news story brought me out of my artistic fog. Uncle Thoreau wrote me all the details. It had been Piggy Tone who had told Driscoll of the vast looting that was going on in Washington under Harding. Dris was no innocent fool, blinded by the table manners of eminent persons. The times were such that no man of business but felt that he could go to Washington, meet the boys who could cut him in for a percentage. So in time there was a great deal of whispering and too many people came to know of what was going on.

Piggy in his new guise of business man had gone to Washington with introductions from the right man in Ned Wonderly's organization. Piggy had set his little red-rimmed eyes on nothing more or less than the millions of gallons of medical whiskey in government warehouses. He had hoped to pay out to certain gentry in power—old, poker-playing friends of the President—and thus get permits signed with fine impartiality by the proper department heads to remove a few truckloads of alki. To Piggy's surprise, he was told that he could have *every* drop of whiskey, bottled in bond, labeled and crated in the Federal warehouse in Antioch, *if* he could meet a certain price.

The sum staggered Piggy who, for all his vices and evils, was a simple soul, mired at youth in a gutter until he grew tough enough to simmer to the top and get nasty in his own turn. He had certain honest emotions. He was proud to be an American and he cried, I know, at sad motion pictures. Vicious, cruel and hard, he still respected certain things. Amazed at the price asked, but knowing also the value of the whiskey, Piggy rounded up some little Italians who had been recooking hair tonics, and added a Polack beer baron, and they pooled their cash and interests and paid—suspecting, I am sure, to be bilked out of their swiftly earned wealth.

But the next day, Piggy's trucks drove to the warehouse, he signed certain legal papers and in broad daylight drove off with every gallon of alcohol in the place. The next week they cleaned out another warehouse and had only to wait until sales were paid for to buy more government whiskey. No one protested this challenging behavior.

Piggy became a millionaire. Which meant he bought a

dozen silk shirts and a new dress for his mother and ordered the Thugs' Special—a Lincoln car. But when certain men in power offered him hospital sheets from Veterans' Hospitals, floor wax and X-ray machines, he said he had no use for it. He was too busy investing his money in Wall Street, he explained.

The gentlemen gave him rich, green-leaved Havana cigars and said that in that case he ought to invest in oil property. There was a neat little group of rich oil operators being formed. They needed right guys and Piggy was *right*, being from Ned Wonderly's backyard. Had he ever heard of Elk Hill? Tea Pot Dome? Oil lands reserved for the Navy but the boys were taking them over on lease and Piggy could make a lot of money coming in on the deal. Piggy said he would think it over. His faithful sub-bourgeois soul was suddenly very angry.

If I were a proper kind of story-teller—one of those bright novelists who creep into the minds of all the characters—I could give a brilliant review of what went on in the mind of Piggy Tone and sent him to see Dris. But I can only say that, while I have known Piggy since childhood and always found him a loud, cruel lout without one redeeming decent feature, I still can't crawl into his mind and explain fully why he squeamishly refused the graft. But he did go to Dris and explain about the great oil swindle.

Dris told me later that he thought that Piggy, deep in his body, felt he was redeeming himself as a law-breaker by exposing this stealing of part of America by a pack of thieves. The pariah had found lower lice. I don't know. I've seen Piggy kick a girl across a room just because he didn't like the way she looked at him. He was repugnantly vulgar, but perhaps like all of us he existed simultaneously at different levels. The patriot in him talked.

[221]

Even Cabot Carson followed the newspaper stories. He stopped me one day in the hall.

"I see the absolute no longer beckons your brother."

It was a time of big business and a time of stock mergers and splitting up one for four. There were ethics in those days, but they were business ethics of the big men who had gathered in the resources of the nation and held them close and played the game in their own way. It was smart to cheat the government. I remember, the day after Dris broke the scandal in the newspapers, I heard men say, *"The dirty bastard, why is he stirring up trouble?"*

It was a strange time. Some men felt that a government was made to be cheated. But not all men. There was a great cry in the press—not with horror but with something as likely to raise circulation, and committees were appointed and much more scandal found. Oil men slipped aboard ships leaving for Europe. And witnesses retired to ranches, and when juries found others innocent the jury men drove by next week with new cars "a block long."

I followed the newspaper stories of the attempted house cleaning, but soon I saw other public actors take the limelight from Driscoll. The miracle happened—the party did not turn against Dris but patted him on the back and triumphantly asserted he was an honest man and dumped their holdings in certain oil companies and handed back their dividends of secret companies set up in Canada to pay some gentlemen a little income. Dris was a hero in the party, for Ned Wonderly had taken no graft, although in his cynical way he knew all that had gone on. The strata of society shook but no cracks appeared underfoot—yet.

President Harding announced he was going to take a little trip to Alaska. A week later eminent politicians were collecting money to hide him in a marble tomb.

I saw little of Dris. He served on investigation committees and fought the liquor interests from swallowing all the medical whiskey in Federal warehouses.

The morning the papers announced the death of Harding and that the little, pickle-faced man was President in his place, Dris called me from the Astor Hotel. He was in town to serve on some committee and wanted to see me.

I found him in a small yellow room floored with correctly measured oblongs, reading reports and smoking cigarettes with two or three draws to each cigarette. He looked pale and a little puffy. He smiled at me and rubbed his tired face, a face in the strong light almost an enamel on silver bones.

"Hello, mug. Sit down. Hungry?"

I sat down. "A little. You look tired. How's the great muckraker?"

"Nonsense, Davey. I'm small fry. The big bellies have taken that all away from me. We'll never put the real big dogs in jail. Fall, Sinclair—may stand trial and get a few years. But the big swindlers are being protected. I'm tired, Davey. Very tired of it all. I feel like a theatrical paranoiac for bringing it all into the foreground."

I was learning to keep my own ideas to myself. "I don't know. It will do some good."

Dris shrugged his shoulders. His animal verve was gone. "I didn't want to do *some* good. I wanted to clean the stables a little. This Coolidge is no better. Honest according to the legal terms—but a penny-pincher while the big chins steal everything in a lawyer's way. Davey, if I felt anything was worth fighting for, it was this oil steal, and now it's out of my hands and being white-washed. Oh, hell! I'm having dinner with Cabot Carson tonight. And he asked me to bring you. You like his school?"

"It's not bad. Not good, either. Carson is no fool, though."

"Linda asked me to see him."

"How is Linda?"

Dris did not answer me at once. He stood up and brushed his topcoat. Then he began to pile papers into brief cases. When he spoke he was very noncommittal, but I knew I had jarred his susceptibilities.

"Linda? Linda is fine. She's home—home resting. I didn't want to bring her to New York in this season."

I looked at Dris. He looked at me. I said, "I see."

"She isn't drinking. I mean overdoing it. Cocktails—a few drinks at parties, but nothing, nothing morbid—you know—in a mood of penitence. Everything is *just* normal. Call a cab."

I picked up the phone. *Just* normal sounded dismal to me.

New York apartments come in many sizes but all seem to have an odor of dust or forgotten garbage and rugs boiled in Lysol. Cabot Carson lived on lower Park Avenue where it was not so fashionable but much more livable and more light pushed through the shifting, growing piles of office buildings.

A black walnut Boston Victorian flat out of Beacon Street. It was a small flat reached by walking up two flights of painted white stairs. The furniture was old and I didn't care for it, but each piece was an original from some Brookline mansion. The walls were painted green and on them hung paintings of old Roman ruins by an artist I have never heard of since. And there were several of those stiff, polite Colonial gentry in silks and laces painted by Stuart and Copley (and all members of the Carson family *and* the Boston Athenaeum).

Cabot Carson greeted us in his usual blue with his red

sliver of ribbon in the lapel. His white bald head was as alert and darting as ever. There were no other guests, no cocktails, and only a manservant with red hair and a scarred chin who spoke French.

Cabot shook hands and we went into another green room in which were many books, a marble bust of George Washington as a Roman Emperor and pen drawings of Bulfinch's state house and Pinckney Street looking to the Charles River for hope—and not getting it.

"Mr. Ormsbee," said Cabot Carson, "I've always wanted to meet you—since Linda first wrote of you, and since you've stirred up that mess in Washington I've more than ever wanted to. I made Linda promise you would call on me when you were next in town."

Dris grinned. "I am a simple example of the village politico. A willing, trusting lad who grew up in the local political machine and is out to make good."

"Ah. That is too honest and I *always* suspect too honest remarks like that. They stink of the endowed asses, the pillared brick and reactionary ivy of Harvard Yard."

"How is Davey making out as an artist?"

"That only time will tell. But I am endeavoring to steer him into becoming a man—a cultured man. But the clay is crude and the mind wanders."

The manservant came in and bowed and saved me a protest. We went into the dining room. The food was good and plain and served with ritual. I didn't care for it. There was too little of it, the sauces were too good and the flavor made me hungry. Candles burned on the table. There were flowers in old-fashioned vases covered with Flaxman drawings and the wine was too subtle for my young, gin-burned palate.

"I eat too much alone," said Cabot Carson. "I eat like a gentleman and am therefore old-fashioned, like the Athenaeum

[225]

where the modern books are kept in a locked room."

Since his death there have been novels written about the last real Boston creature, Cabot Carson. They have some certain merit of catching the crude shadows of a finely drawn etching—but they are not the real man. The men who write them are too full of the idea of dredging up a fragment of the dying New England culture and presenting Cabot Carson as the last of the dodo birds. He was more alive, modern, alert and interesting than the novelists who wrote about him. They missed him badly in their best sellers and I shall not try and better their efforts. I am too shy to try to write the novel that is in Cabot Carson and the dying aristocratic snobs of Louisburg Square and the banking houses on State Street and the old stone street where Ticknor & Field published Emerson and Thoreau.

The dinner ended and we went back to the book-lined room, where we all smoked thin black cigars and had coffee followed by a brandy that Dris said was very fine.

Cabot Carson held the glass of amber brandy in his thin white hand and smiled at it.

"Like Henry Thoreau, I believe there are laws to be broken. This law forbidding the drinking of distilled spirits is one. Driscoll, you were right to refuse to defend the sellers of this stuff, but I think we are again at Concord facing tyrants when we drink it. Jefferson said, and most men forget, that it is good to rise up and shed a little blood every time the people want to change something. But I have forgotten the exact quotation and only fools and fops can always quote correctly. They and those dull young men in crew haircuts at Eliot House."

Dris swallowed his drink. "I have an idea that it is a mistake to quote any man dead over fifty years and expect anything he said then to really apply to present-day situations."

Cabot Carson nodded and puffed at his burning tobacco until it was drawing well again. "If I thought you were right, I would cut my throat—or better still, draw a hot bath and open my indigo-containing veins. You see, I am the egg that hatched too late and can't find a nest that fits my prehistoric rump. No more Brookline mansions are being built on China tea and opium. Boston is dry and in reaction and the juice is gone from it. I see its glory—but the luster is gone. Driscoll, I am an old man with too many manners and old, odd habits of taste. There is no room for me here in this world except to train young people to design advertising to sell milady's drawers. Harvard is full of endowed bums and imported chemical stinks. But I keep hoping there will arise again men like Webster and John Adams to save the nation before we go up like tinder in the flames they are setting across the sea. That is why I sent for you—I wanted to see you. To see if you are one of those."

"Am I?" said Dris. "Honestly I don't think I am."

The old man put aside his cigar. "No, you are not. I am foolish to think that patterns always repeat themselves in the old manner. You are of the newer, rawer people that Mark Twain turned away from and so died of a broken heart. I must push down pride and remember you are the newer pattern but of the same basic cut underneath."

"Let's have some more brandy," said Dris.

"Yes," I said, "it's good brandy, I think."

Cabot Carson laughed. "Listen to the young plowboy speaking as if fine brandy were something he knew from childhood!" He turned to Dris again. "I don't understand everything but this I know: I am very out of fashion. The world I knew is gone forever. *Cabot Carson, Esquire* is just old "Kit" Carson to the press that still remembers me. I am happy to die. No, that is not true. No man wants to die and become the nothing, the foul empty nothing of coffin-worms' food. But it is better I die than see the fashion we set cause our collapse. Driscoll, even your work will go too and after it—what? The hardness, the iron of New England stock has gone to seed in idiot-minded old maids who sputter from rotten teeth of sons and daughters of the Revolution—but know nothing honestly American—who preen themselves in Park Street Church on Boston Common. But the hard men who fought Indians and dammed stony brooks have grown bald counting stock market numbers and their sons are tapped for Skull and Bones or join Hasty Pudding (a place as artistic as a Polish saloon) and then are hidden from life from then on. And those people, Dris, who came here in rags and went West and died in dry soil—they have been pushed off the land by bankers and lawyers and their brood go barefooted on dust-wrecked farms or stand in line at cafeterias smelling Rockefeller gasoline poisoning the shade trees. I have no answer, no cure. . . ."

"Neither have I," said Driscoll, looking very closely at the old man's face.

"I feel," said Cabot Carson, "that I am in one of H. G. Wells's Time Machines and have suddenly awakened in a finished, dead age."

The old man's head grew transparent. I could see his skull—like thin and wonderful worked silver. His brain pulsed and beat against the silver shell—and the lines on it were wonderful and so clear. The eyes were big, swimming in their sockets, turning and rolling. I could see his vocal cords twanging like plucked violin strings. I knew I was a little too full of brandy. . . .

SEVENTEEN

THE BRANDY HAZE lifted. I had been napping.

I suppose Dris and Cabot Carson would have sat up all night talking of the coming social debacle, talking such stuff not meant for little minds like mine—for I am one of those who likes the simplest idea brutally put, a thing, I have since learned, that cannot be done with all subjects. But the doorbell rang. The manservant seemed to have retired. I answered the door.

I knew the young lady who stood at the door with a physical swagger, leaning against the bell button. Her name was Cathy Williams. She taught certain refined young girls from good families how to decorate walls and curtains and mix pleasing colors at Carson's School of Art. She was tall and strong-looking, glowing with an immense virility, built like a slim baseball player in training. She had a frowning smile and very pretty eyes and long dark hair, drawn carefully back into a shiny knot. I had seen Cathy Williams many times before and always she reminded me of those Greek goddesses full of muscle and grace found on certain vases and nowhere else, usually. Her nose was fine—a big, long and very straight nose. Her teeth were large and perfect and there was a strong chin—not that it spoiled her beauty, but it gave her too much character and I felt she had some to spare.

"Hello," she said. "Kit in?"

I knew she meant Cabot Carson. Some of the bolder society gossips called him "Kit" Carson.

"Yes—Miss Williams. Come in."

She was wearing dark tweeds and the fashion of man-
nish felt hats for women was then new; the hat tipped over
one eye.

"You're David Ormsbee, aren't you?"

"Yes. Come in." I felt I was being derisively handled.

Cabot and Dris got up out of their comfortable postures
when Cathy entered and Cabot took her hand and kissed it.

"Driscoll Ormsbee, I want you to meet Cathy—Cathy
Williams. Teaches some fool domestic and decorators' mess
to snobs. A transitory phase, she thinks, to better things."

"How do you do?" said Dris, sinking back into his chair.

"I do well," said Cathy with a nervous arrogance. "I'm
not supposed to be impressed but I've been following your
adventures in the press."

Dris frowned. "Not any more. Bigger minds have taken
over the kill."

Cabot smiled like a polite old tomcat and pressed his lean
arm around Cathy's hips, changing suddenly from Doctor
Faustus to Mephistopheles before my eyes. "Cathy is an
example of New England decay. Her grandfathers walked
with Winthrops and helped bring Yogi to Boston Com-
mons. There were once tea clippers off Hong Kong cap-
tained by men called Williams. They once held much land
and old letters from Cotton and Alcott and others and lived
polite lives in Back Bay. Now this is the last of the breed—
looking very well in tweeds. She has left the nest for an
alien city, *just* to be near me."

"You're a fool, Kit," said Cathy, reaching for a cigarette. "Mr. Ormsbee is not interested in the dead past. He's
a man of tomorrow. *What* are we drinking?"

Dris poured her a glassful and we all sipped. Outside, the

night winds made mouse noises while off in the river the thunder of sea whistles shook the cut-glass reflectors over our heads. The dirty, sulphurous darkness seemed to push into the room.

Cabot put down his glass. "I am an old man surrounding myself with the young and ruddy—and you have interrupted me, Cathy. One of the few times I have allowed myself to get serious. What *do* you want?"

The girl laughed—full, healthy, open-mouthed laughter. "Don't play bear with me, Kit. I couldn't sleep—as usual. I walked for hours—getting some tempting offers from sailors. Then, passing below, I saw your light. I wanted to talk—talk about anything."

Cabot almost yawned, but being too polite for that he turned it into a twisted, grinning grimace. "I sleep like a log of sandalwood. So I'm afraid I'm going to turn you all out. When all pleasures dim—that of flesh and food and drink—when art grows numb and the limbs no longer carry their load with joy, there is but *one* full-blown pleasure remaining—sleep."

"I wish I could sleep," said Cathy. "I never get enough. I toss all night and just before dawn I drop off and, *bang*, the damned alarm clock goes off in my dainty ear."

Cabot kissed her lightly on the mouth and shook hands with Dris and myself. "Good-bye. I shall see you all again. You, Driscoll, and your easy hopes displease me. But not as much as most men. You've let them take this investigation away from you. You still think politics is a fine sport. But you'll grow older and wiser." He winked. "But that is better than growing older and being no wiser—like myself. May your devils be exorcised and driven off."

Cathy patted his arm. "Sleep for me, too. I'm going home to try and bore myself with a detective novel."

Cabot groaned. "To such levels has literature fallen. Pam-

pering the foul erotic nerve-ends of fools. A shallow sim-
plification of eternal death. I haven't read a good one in a
week. . . ."

I stayed that night at the hotel with Dris. Lying in the
extra bed, waiting for Dris to finish brushing his teeth, I
yawned and wished I had drunk more of the good brandy.

Dris came from the bathroom, his mouth puckered in distaste at the tooth powder. He was a little puffy but the
shoulders were squarer than ever. He always went to bed
nude. His head fitted more firmly into the torso and he still
advanced head first, the legs flexed as if ready to give fight
if he had to, but the features were more penetratingly
poignant. Dris was entering middle age.

"A good evening, mug?" he asked, folding back his
sheets.

"Pretty good. Lot of big talk."

"Don't like big talk?"

"No like it, Dris."

"Old Carson is no fool, although a little careless of consistency."

"Cunning old bastard," I said, pulling out the light.

"I like him. Something ostentatiously magnificent about
him."

"He likes you, too. He doesn't shoot his mouth off much
usually. Just looks wise most of the time. He let loose
tonight."

"Yes," said Dris, punching his pillows.

"Wonder why?"

"I think he was trying to tell me something. People have
a habit of doing that to me. But it's no go. I'll just be a
stubborn hothead all my life."

"Huh?" I said, half-asleep.

[232]

"Davey . . ."

"Say something, Dris?"

For a moment there was silence. "Davey, that Miss Williams. What's the matter with her?"

"Ask me tomorrow. I'm sleepy."

"She says she can't sleep. She talks with a boldness not at all becoming and she carried herself all wrong. She could be a very charming person—although she's a little too over-developed and toughened for my tastes. She certainly is familiar with Carson. . . ."

"You're cute, Dris," I yawned.

"Why?"

"The school gossip is that Carson is her lover—more or less."

"I don't believe it. He's an old man. Good Lord, Davey, you're getting a dirty mind. Whatever else may be wrong with Miss Williams, she doesn't look like a tramp."

I groaned at this savourless obvious motto. "Stop talking like a small-town hick. A lady can have a lover without being a tramp, Dris. Anyway, it's only school gossip. It's all pure 'Uncle Cabot' at that, I bet."

"Good night," said Dris. "I regret my respectable notions of decency annoy you, mug."

"Nuts."

I fell back to dream of Cathy Williams dressed in tiger skins chasing me through a rocky field and then the sky parted and red lightning filled the sky and it rained a long time and I was cold and frightened and Cathy Williams advanced toward me smiling—those green eyes smiling and the long black hair flowing wet and free behind her, and I shivered and was persistently harassed and I awoke.

The window was wide open and chill night air was pushing in the curtains. I got up and closed it almost all the way.

[233]

There was just light enough to make out Dris sleeping soundly and deeply.

That night I had no more dreams.

The next morning Dris left for Washington on some secret errand for Ned Wonderly and I was again alone in the big city making my colored marks on good clean paper and wondering if ever I should be an artist and was it worth all the heartstring tuggings and the nerves frayed and the shimmer of distant success when I knew that no matter how well I painted I would never be pleased with what I did and would brood and scowl the rest of my life desiring a perfection that no living man or dead artist had ever reached. But I could try, I said in juvenile confidence.

Just before Dris left, he shyly slipped a folded ten-dollar bill into my hand.

"Work hard, Davey. And play, too. And write Vicky a letter once in a while. Don't get too damn languorous, and bathe more often."

"Sure."

"And if you hear from Doug, let me know, will you? I'm worried about him."

"He's in China, isn't he? Running some sort of an oil and freight service with a lot of Greeks?"

Dris shrugged his shoulders. "I don't know. He was. But I hear now he's picked up some South American tubs and is thinking of expanding into a sort of wildcat freight service. I don't like it, Davey. Where would Doug get money for this sort of thing? A lot of gun-running has been going on in China. I hope he's kept clear of it."

"Funny, Doug should own boats, after all."

"Leaking tramps, most likely. But better than pumping gasoline. You will let me know if you hear from him?"

I looked at Dris' frowning face and nodded, and there was a fervid pressure of hands between us.

Later I went to the Public Library and hunted shipping registry and boat listing but found no Ormsbee ships on the seas.

I felt Dris was worrying too much about the family. That nervous susceptibility to things was growing on him.

I spent Dris' ten dollars on a new second-hand sofa for my studio and a set of Woolworth dishes and whiskey glasses. I was living on East Twelfth Street, four flights up under a slanting roof and a skylight only slightly cracked. I had a view; an extensive esplanade of sweatshop lofts full of poor tired Jews.

In the summers I boiled in a heat out of Egypt that killed the wailing tenement babies around me. In winter I turned blue like early English noblemen in war paint, and I stuffed old drawings in the skylight cracks and hammered on the steampipe with little result. I drank Dago red, the favorite tipple of bibulous art students.

The sofa I bought with Dris' money was, I admit, a bit of swank. But it looked well in front of the huge easel with the unfinished (and never to be finished) canvas of *Invasion of the City*. It showed mounted knights in full armor carrying great banners riding through Times Square. It was an experiment in form and color. Huge whirling shapes, struggling horses and the full cold terror of cold armor against the solid, terrible city of stone and glass, I saw often in my dreams. It was a bad dream that I had tried to put on canvas for two years. . . .

The sofa was a great success. It could hold eight sprawling art lovers of both sexes at one time, the jugs of bathtub-brewed red wine bought from the Italian janitor fitting neatly under it.

I saw Cathy Williams a lot. She stopped me several times between classes at the art school and we talked of nothing important. Somehow she got around to my paintings and I foolishly spoke of what I was painting at my studio.

I don't know how I did it—but I was forced to invite her to come and see them and have dinner with me. There was more to her than appeared on the surface. I borrowed five dollars from Mrs. Knott and decided I would take her to an Italian red-ink place and fill her full of salad and the meat-ball spaghetti special. I love to watch women eat well—and plenty.

We didn't go out to dinner. Cathy showed up wearing knitted green silk and carrying several bundles of food. Potted meats and stuff in glass and a French bread and some greens. And I went down and got a half gallon of red wine and a quart of something called Bourbon, for jest.

She ate well and swallowed the wine and we mixed soda with the Bourbon and sat around later and drank it while I showed her my drawings and she made the proper sounds over them. (I didn't know if they were digestive sounds or if she really liked them.)

"Davey, I didn't come here to see your drawings—but now I have. I think you've got a lot on the ball."

"Thanks. Why did you come?"

"I like the way your family sounds. Your mother—your father. I feel your brother could do something, if he broke with the political ring he runs with."

"Not a chance. Votes count and the machine is the only source of winning then. Dris is all right. He's big—he's got ideas. But Gramp is the real man."

"Why hasn't he done things?"

"Why? Why haven't we had a lot of real big men doing big things? Because Gramp—like all these—well, it's his fate to be forgotten with a lot of other fine people who never had more than two shirts of their own or a few horses and some acres of America. It's wrong, I tell you, and I don't care if U. S. Steel goes to four hundred and Radio splits three for one. When they lick Gramp, they lick everything we really are. Have a drink, Cathy?"

She smiled and took the bottle from me. "No. And you've had enough, too. Are there any more sentimental idiots like you and Dris at home?"

"Huh? No. Dennis—he's worried all the time about the state of God's underwear, and maybe he is right in thinking we are all lost pagans whose churches are empty of everything but fat shouters of dry wind. He says the Church Militant has finished off Christianity. But Doug—you'd like Doug. He's in China, I think. Running freight tramps. Dris thinks he's smuggling guns in the Chinese Revolution. He's like you, Cathy—a muscle-lover. A wind-swept guy with lots of iron in him. They beat his head off at the steel plants once, they drove him out of the independent gasoline business—but he's the real McCoy. Say, am I drunk?"

"Just enough. What about your father?"

"Pete? A wonderful man of good low antecedents. But there isn't much left of him. Just a husk. Once he was a noble peasant with a desire to till the soil and bring the fruits of the fields within his own four hand-hewn walls. But now he sits among sterile shavings mouthing old hopes with bad cooking. He's a rabbit—a human rabbit—just sits and wags his long, long lost hopes. Let's talk about you, Cathy."

The girl smiled, serenely impartial, and mashed out her cigarette. "Like the school gossips do?"

"Don't they, though. I don't believe a word of it."

Her mouth went very hard as she worked a lipstick on it. Her eyes were suddenly full of hate. "Then you're a fool,

Davey. *Not* that I care what gossips say. Tell me about Dris' wife."

"Some other time."

Later I took her home. She parted my mind in the middle. Half of me liked her. She was alert and wonderful and had a hard direct beauty. Half of me suspected her Boston upbringing—those things in her that gave her drive and push and a desire to hold destiny under her lovely firm thumbs.

For some reason I took her to dinner a week later. . . .

EIGHTEEN

CATHY AND I remained friends. Coldly so.

There was a chill wind rising in the world. No one paid it any attention. I took on an extra art class.

A few months later Driscoll Ormsbee was nominated for the office of Governor of the state. Ned Wonderly was no fool. The nation may have forgotten the legislator who had first brought to light the government oil scandals which had been investigated by other hands than his, but the state hadn't. It was a time of wasteful extravagance but everyone enjoyed a scandal.

As for myself, I wasn't as impressed as I should have been at Dris' rise in public esteem. I was still studying art and more than that—painting in my studio a great many things that pleased me alone and to hell with those rising young fools who said that an American artist should paint barns and cows and burlesque queens and Bowery tramps and cornfields and city streets. I took no part in the critics' small, puerile animosities. I was after more than that. I wanted the stuff of life, the color of things and the shape of the eternal values, and I wanted to mix that colored mud and smear it on linen and lift out an atmosphere of pulsing light and moving creatures that would have form and content and be what I saw in my own way and re-created as no paint smearer had done before me. And as I was young and strong and not as bright as I might have been, I worked too long on the canvases and got angry at the failures and tore them up and then started again and spent months on a painting from which I would cut one tiny square, one little shape that wasn't at all bad. I made prodigious expenditures in sweat and toil and canvas. I began to snarl at people.

So I missed the full significance of the power and fortune that had come to us Ormsbees. Dris was going to be Governor of a state. A good Governor, an honest one, created, developed and sponsored by the political machine of Ned Wonderly who, in pious pride and firm, stern judgment could say, and did, to reporters, "*I make the law.*"

Doug, the drifter, was coming up in the world, too. There was solid cold steel in him now. I had letters from him. From South America where he and his Greeks were buying up more old leaking tubs and expanding their pirate and cutthroat price competition to the fancy white-painted ships. Doug's ships would handle anything at any price and would cut any rate to get it. I no longer had trouble finding the Ormsbee Overseas Lines in the shipping directories. But as yet Doug had not invaded the United States. He lacked capital and enough strength to try his hand with the robber barons who were milking Washington dry, getting mail and shipping subsidies from a willing, lobby-inspired board. I saw nothing wrong then in inherited privilege levying tribute.

Doug sent me a snapshot of himself—bigger and wider than ever but the same old Doug—only harder, more slit-eyed than the young steel worker who had been bloodied by the mill company's police. There was something romantic about Doug's business and his life and yet, unlike Dris, he was always an earthy, normal creature like Pete—a little too ready to believe and full of his own dreams. And not at all romantic-looking: a little too heavy of limb, big of jowl and low of forehead. A plebeian-looking, cheerful hulk with an animal directness.

I forwarded whatever I found out about Doug to Dris but the coming campaign was going to be a hard one and he had little time to answer me. The Coppards and Cruikshanks had again broken with the Wonderly machine and were running a "Reform" and "Clean-up" ticket of their own—a ticket of broken party hacks and old patch-pants colonial families down to their last ancestral portrait. A great deal of gerrymandering went on.

I was a little surprised to think of Hartley Gould Coppard coming out against his own son-in-law—but not very. It was a time of mergers and holding companies and Dris was speaking of creating a law for a new corporation tax concept. Hartley Gould would be forced to set up a lot of his schemes under the Du Pont-Delaware corporation hide-and-seek. Hartley Gould liked to do things at home in comfort and not go running to a feudal estate kept by runaway Frenchmen along the Atlantic Coast.

But I was wrong. It was not a corporation law that brought the break. Vicky for once wrote me a letter explaining the real reason for Hartley Gould's turning against Dris.

Like all of Vicky's letters, it babbled and ran on a great deal about what glory the future held and how she had raised up her sons to be great men. But at last she got down to cases—for in the end she almost always became naively logical:

. . . And don't think Dris (her letter read in part) is having things his own way. Great day in the morning, but those Coppards are sure showing their real streak of meanness . . . Why, you would think Dris was spending his money on his own mother instead of pushing every nickel he makes on the back of his wife.

If you ask me, it's Linda that has caused this dirty King George Road trick of starting a Reform party just now when

Dris is going to be the best Governor this state ever had. I mind my own business and don't go stirring other peoples' pots—so what is between Dris and Linda is between them two . . . Whom God had put together in holy wedlock—and you know I'm for that—although I've had a clod of a husband tied to me for over thirty years—but, as I say, God is in his Heaven . . .

But I skipped a great deal, for Vicky had reached the point now where she treated God as an equal; although in her youth she never really believed in Him, she now was cozy with His name and I believe preparing to help Him run the universe. Anyway, I skipped to the third page of her letter, as usual getting a little wild and unsteady in her script. She would start in a small, delicate script like her own little person and then, as emotions poured through her, she would expand and pen-sputter and end up a letter in scratchings that were almost pure modern art and not text at all.

Hartley Gould and some man named Insull, (the letter went on) are setting up some damn-fool utility empire (as your Uncle Thoreau calls it) and Hartley Gould wanted Dris to retire from politics and move away from Antioch and go to Washington and work in something called a lobby for the utilities. It certainly would have been fine living in Washington but Dris would rather be Governor and so would I, and anyway the real reason Aunt Netta says is that Linda is ashamed to be seen in Antioch for *certain* reasons, and then Aunt Netta winks and shakes her head and I can't make much sense out of it. It's all gossip anyway because I don't think Linda flirts or smokes cigarettes in the street.

I wish you would wear long underwear, Davey, and not be so lippy and modern in your health habits. Pete needs watching every minute or he's walking round barefooted nights, and you're not much better and so . . .

I laid the letter away in a table drawer and sat down on my sofa and thought a long time. A great many things I hadn't dared think about came back to me, and I saw Linda's face and the way she walked and the way she held her body when Dris kissed it, and, and . . . I knew I couldn't paint a stick that day. . . .

For two weeks I had been teaching an extra night class the art of finding muscles in the buttocks of a fat model and explaining to grubby little clerks and dandruffed slum talents the beauty of the washed nude human body. It was hard work, for these city people wanted success and not beauty and were painting not because they wanted to do fine things and strike bold new patterns on a canvas. They wanted to make a great deal of money and paint magazine covers and buy new Ford cars and invest in U. S. Steel. I wished I could too.

No, I didn't like the art classes I taught in the Twenties, but I worked hard at it and came home late and fell down on my studio bed and slept minus my pajamas—a habit I had learned from Dris.

I was dreaming vague formalized shapes one night when there was thunder at my door and I got up, drawing my bathrobe belt tight, to find a messenger boy standing at my door chewing gum. The message read—after I had thrown cold water in my face to bring me back to life with genuine reluctance:

LINDA IN NEW YORK USUALLY STOPS AT WALDORF KEEP HER COMPANY DRIS.

I looked at the message and yawned. It was all a normal wire except for the word "USUALLY." Dris should know if she were stopping there or not. I tossed the message aside and went back to sleep.

I got up with the dismal recurrent letters of the wire muttering on my mind.

I was under the shower trying to adjust it so that I didn't boil to death, when suddenly I understood the wire.

In a moment I was pulling my clothes on over my wet body.

There was no Mrs. Driscoll Ormsbee registered at the Waldorf. I tried the Ritz, the Sherry-Netherland and the green-stained bulk of the dove-loved Plaza. Then I stood on the curb, smoking a cigarette, worrying. It was Election Day. They were electing a Governor in New York. Back in Antioch they were electing a Governor, too. Only back there he was my brother Driscoll—I hoped. I brooded over the chromosomes of the race and cursed my brother. What was Linda to me?

There was no use in standing on a street corner eyeing the passers-by with sour looks. I went back to the Waldorf and asked if Linda Coppard had registered there. No. So I tried all the other hotels again. No Linda Coppard. I was beginning to feel tired and blown. I stopped and tossed a breakfast into my stomach, found a phone and pushed away a pint of silver calling every hotel she might have gone to. I even called the St. George in Brooklyn and the Half-Moon Hotel at Coney Island. It was pretty hopeless. The sun shone resplendently and I tried another brand of cigarettes.

The streets were full of election returns, but they were all New York State. They didn't mean a thing to me. I wanted to try the city morgue but felt that if Linda was really there I could afford to wait until after the election. I kept thinking of Linda, her face, the way she swayed when she walked, the way her hand felt in mine, the many times she had called me cute. It was very hard to think something

had happened to her. I walked on, the skein of circum-
stance and destiny dragging after me. I was angry at Dris.

I wondered if Dris had sent me any more wires calling
the hunt off. I went into a Third Avenue bar and had three
beers and a fistful of dry popcorn for lunch and went back
to my studio.

It was only as I stood at the head of my stairs that I
noticed that my door was open. Someone was stirring behind the half-opened door. So she *had* come to me! Linda
had remembered she could always turn to me! I pushed in
the door and rushed into the studio preparing to be the
firm, brotherly shoulder, to be persuasive and very kind and
loving—a little too ready.

But seated on the model's stand was not Linda. A stocky
big man with a wind-tanned face who looked a little like
my brother Doug. He sat pushing tobacco into a pipe with
a square thumb that reminded me of my father.

The man fired his pipe and blew smoke in my direction
and said, phlegmy-voiced:

"Say, you charged in here as if you knew I was here."

It was Doug's voice, a little deeper than I'd ever heard it.
It was Doug. I almost wouldn't have known him. He was
heavy, a scar smiled from the corner of one eye. But he was
as slow and easy in his gestures as the man who used to
pump gas into flivvers. His heavy, dark suit of strange cut
and the solid square-toed shoes didn't hide my brother from
me. It was like him to dress badly.

"Doug! No, I wasn't expecting you! How did you
get in?"

Doug didn't move. He grinned, showing big yellow teeth.
"You must be in an uproar these days. The door wasn't
locked. Christ, you've grown."

"You, too," I said, sitting down and looking at Doug.
"Wider."

"Yes. Been putting it on. I guess I take after Pete. Not after you tall thin ones. What kind of hell hole is this? Looks like a whore's nest."

I blushed for my art work and all the idiotic ingenuity of my studio. "I'm being an artist. But tell me, Doug, what have you been doing? Your letters don't tell much."

"Ships—steel ships, iron tramps, rusting fruit tubs . . . Done all right in them, too. Me and my Greeks. They put up the money and I know how to treat iron and machines and keep them floating and full of cargo."

"And you left home to go into the junk business."

"Yeah." Doug got up and walked around the room, looking at some sketches of burlesque queens I had been making. "Never did junk those ships I went after. Some Chinks wanted me to run guns for The Leader. Ever hear of the yellowball?"

I hadn't then. "No. You still running guns?"

"Christ, no." Doug laughed and rubbed a hard thumb across a strip-tease belly on the wall. "I'm Ormsbee Overseas Shipping now. A very lucrative racket-to-be—I hope. Mostly South American fruit tubs and nitrate and bird-dropping carriers—but I'm coming North. Yes, sir, Davey, the world is going mad and I've found the golden touch."

"You going to fight Cunard, U. S. and the French Lines?"

"Nuts to that, Davey. There is a dirty little street downtown called Wall Street. Me and the Greeks are going to take it for a little ride. We're floating some big-sounding stock deals—fifty million bucks' worth—Ormsbee Overseas Carriers. Ships with special elevators built into them to load export automobiles, tractors, machines. No more slinging them in nets, no more packing cars in crates—just drive them onto our boats and drive them into the hold. Davey, it's my own idea and every motor and steel thief in Detroit

[246]

and Dearborn is sold on the savings involved. Hell, that stock will go like butter on hot cakes."

I looked at Doug and smiled as if he were a partisan of a new cosmic theory. "Well . . ."

"Well, *what?*"

"I can't believe it's you, Doug. You, who got your head cracked for organizing the steel mills. You, who got pushed out by the robber baron gas stations."

Doug nodded and pulled emphatically on his tightly knotted black tie.

"It's me, kid. I've been around. I've seen the working stiffs and the barley bucklers and the seamen being pushed around by a world busting up. It's a time of big lies and larger bluffs and I'm through being a mug. Vicky was right about it being a time for big doings. She knew. Maybe she just felt she knew—but I know because I've seen it, see. It's a time of wolves, Davey-boy, and I didn't like being a sheep. I've the ships and I'll get a thousand more. I'll run them and race them and scrap them on reefs with full insurance. I'll blow holes in them or I'll chase them around the icebergs. And I'll make the old bastards who grabbed the furs and land, the oil wells and timber and copper and coal and waterways and airways—I'll make them sit up and say 'Pal' to Doug Ormsbee."

"If that's the way you feel—you're not angry at Hartley Gould Coppard."

Doug laughed again and knocked out his hot pipe on his horny palm with a solemn, triumphant gesture. "*That* two-bit steel peddler? Hell, he's got no drive, no guts, messing around with art and little refined tarts with soft bellies. I'll have him sitting down with me at his table and glad to—*when* the time comes. . . ."

"You so sure of floating that stock?"

"Don't tell me, Davey, *you* don't believe in the Bull Market?"

"I don't know. What is a Bull Market?"

"A Bull Market is a market when a lot of little people get together and decide working is too hard a way to make money. So they listen to a lot of talk by smooth crooks with little china Harvard piggies on their watch chains and begin to feed the kitty. Then the big guys and the little guys get drunk on a lotta numbers on paper and by the time they wake up me and the Greeks and the bankers and steel boys have swiped all the swag but in a *very* legal way."

"You're too sure of yourself, Doug. So aggressive, pugnacious."

"Sure I am," said Doug, biting off a bit of skin from his thumb. "I've gotta be. I've got this system figured out and it can only play one way if you make it sit and beg. That's the way I want it. I made a million for the Greeks in China —but I made them ten times that in South America. And now my cut is seventy percent. I'm top man. I'm rolling in it—the way Vicky wanted—dreamed about . . ."

I looked at his badly tailored suit, at his heavy shoes. Doug noticed my glances and said, "Don't mind these duds. Next time you see me, I'll be in Harris tweeds and a five-dollar haircut. I'm a little short of cash just now. Bought up a lot of government ships laid up to rot since the war. Just got off a fruit tub, too. Don't worry, Davey, and I'm putting you down for a hundred shares—as a gift. Hold on to it and be as rich as an oil thief."

"Yes. Who are these prodigious Greeks you play with?"

Doug winked. "These Greeks? Hell, most of them aren't Greeks. Mostly Englishmen who are full up on Vickers, and some are French boys of the Jockey Club and the Bank of France, and Germans full of marks and not too sure they like the Republic—and even a lot of real Greeks and Ginzos and Chicago packers, chemical stink makers and oil-well diggers. A lot of loose cash all over the world and a little unsure things are as good as they look. Ever hear of Insull and Kreuger and—— and—— and——?"

"Some place in the back part of the paper."

"Those are my 'Greeks.' Say, isn't Dris running for election today?"

"For Governor. It's all set, with Ned Wonderly behind him."

"I don't get it—a right guy like Dris playing ball with Ned."

"Dris is all right. He takes Ned's backing but doesn't play football with his public office."

"No? That's good. Well, I think I'll be through with this stock setup in a few days and then go down to see Vicky and the family."

"She'll be glad to see you."

Doug winked. I never had noticed that incandescent glow in his eyes before. "Maybe. She's a wonderful gal. But it's Dris that's the apple of her eye. How's the bim Dris married—that Coppard gal?"

"Oh. Well, I guess she's all right. They seem to get along. There is something about her puzzles me—but I like her."

"Not my type. I like 'em like this." Doug painted a picture out of Rubens in the space in front of him. "A little more meat here and there and ready for a rowdy lark, come what may. Well, want to run down home with me when I'm finished doing business?"

"I've got a lot to do—and I'm teaching an art class nights. Linda—she's in town—and—well, I sort of said I'd look her up."

"O.K. I'll give you a ring soon and you'll show me what

the night life in this town looks like. I've been away a long time and I'm in a spending mood."

He slapped me on the back, hugged me to him and I smelled liquor, cheap tobacco and hair lotion. I could see he didn't know what to make of me in this artistic nest. But I *was* a brother. . . .

"Well, take care of yourself. If you need any folding money . . ."

"No, thanks. I'm getting by."

"Well, maybe we'll have a Governor in the family."

"Too early to tell yet."

Doug left and I went down to the corner and tried a few more whiskeys. When I came back, the little dancing teacher next door to my studio said a Miss Cathy Williams had been trying to get me. Would I call her back?

I thanked the dancing teacher and went into the studio and lay down on my sofa and smoked too many cigarettes. I certainly wanted no small talk with Cathy this afternoon. I did not call her back.

N I N E T E E N

In the late afternoon, the radio next door began to howl in election results. I had given up hunting for Linda. Once every half hour I called the Waldorf. But I did not expect any longer to be told that she had arrived and registered. I did it merely for exercise. I was exasperated but numb.

I went out into the streets and bought a newspaper. Radio has never been very real to me. It is always noise— a jabberwock howling in the night. Full mouths and advertised tripe hung along the ether to trap fools and annihilate reasoning. Nothing it says seems as true and solid as letters printed on paper.

But the newspapers were not much help. They were yapping for their particular scoundrel—the one political figure they personally wanted to see in power. There was little out-of-the-state news. Only a small item that a strong opposition had developed to Driscoll. Some sort of "Reform Club" plan sponsored by certain interests . . . The usual thumb fumblers and crackpots taking unknown backing—but a real threat, for certain Ned Wonderly wards were going against the machine. It was too early yet to see if the gathering momentum could reach a peak.

I tossed the newspaper aside and started back along Fifth Avenue. I was fed up—up to the gullet. I wanted to go home, lie down and fall asleep. The blood beat against my temples like metronomes.

A cab bumbled along the curb as I turned in at the corner. The cabby put out his sandpaper-colored face and said:

"Hey, bud."

I felt a lack of interest in the human race. I did not answer. Suddenly a voice shouted:

"Isn't he cute! Hey, Davey!"

I turned to find Linda staring at me over the partly lowered glass from the back door of the cab. Her mouth was slack and her eyes out of focus—the honey-colored hair was in disorder and she kept drumming her fingernails against the dirty cab window with a flippant bellicosity.

"Linda!"

The cabby threw a thumb toward the back of the cab. "You know *this* tomato?"

"Darling Davey," said Linda, at first jubilant. Then she began to sob.

"She's been drivin' me nuts all afternoon. Picked her up at the Penn Station and she refused to get out of me cab. Six-twenty, fella."

I opened the cab door and Linda fell out into my arms. She looked strange, as if from a sleep-walking dream. She lacked shoes. She must have tossed them away. Her bag hung open and I took it and removed some bills from it and paid off the cabby. I had only twenty cents on my own person after a day of phone calls.

The cabby handed me the change and I held twenty-five cents toward him. He waved it off.

"Keep it. Glad to get rid of the lush."

Linda stood, looking very small on the sidewalk in her sleek silk stockings, twisting her head and muttering. She smelled of whiskey and a faint, delicious pungent odor of violets. She was soft and slim against my arm. Her wet mouth hung open. Her muttering took on form as she mouthed monosyllables.

"Little Davey. Little Davey, play on your harp . . ."

"This way, Linda," I said, leading her across the sidewalk and thinking of the four flights of stairs ahead. She walked like a nervous trapeze performer.

"Am I stinko?"

"Yes," I said with wooden Indian stolidity.

"Good—girl—Linda—good for you," she said, kissing me. "Haven't had a drink for three months. But this is a dandy, isn't it, little Davey?"

"Yes. Now lift one foot at a time. Everything is going to be all right."

She threw her hands up and her voice was very high as she chuckled. "Everything *is* all right now. I have my cute little Davey!"

It was dark in my studio. Night was coming down over the heat haze and dust-outlined buildings of the city. I hadn't made any light. Next door the radio was growling out election returns from a tinny diaphragm. Linda sat shoeless on my sofa, scowling into a cup of black coffee. The pot at her elbow was almost empty. Everything appeared so grotesquely inconsistent to me.

She looked like certain shell-shocked soldiers I had once visited at a hospital with Dris. The same loose neck, as if it hung on a thin thread, the same misjudgment of distances and that blinking, unreal focusing of eyes. She put down the cup with a clatter.

"Thanks, Davey. Thanks a lot."

"How do you feel?"

"Not sober. I'm still drunk. But I know I'm drunk, not climbing clouds. Just aware I'm on the knife-edge of disaster."

"You lie down and rest."

Linda shook her head. "Don't want to lie down. Don't

[253]

want to rest. My limbs aren't efficiently organized yet. Want to talk. Cigarette?"

I put one into her grinning, shaking mouth and lit it, and she groaned with pleasure and exhaled smoke, a great deal of smoke. Then she felt her ribs and looked at me with that fluid quality of charm she had always had for me.

"You open my girdle?"

I nodded and looked away into a corner.

"Davey—you're learning *things!* Davey, I want to talk."

"All right. What about?"

"Life. Big, bold, busting life. About life and me, and me and Driscoll, and you, too. You, too, Davey. Oh, sure—us all and life."

"All right. Start with you. Today *is* Election Day."

"Why did I pick on today to get unladylike? Well, I'll tell you. I don't want to be the Governor's lady. I don't want Dris to run for office. I—I knew Papa was going to try to defeat him. And you know what? I like to get drunk. Love it. I've had a cork in my heart too long—three months not even a glass of sherry. Deplorable, provincial—isn't it? For poor Linda . . ."

She began to cry and I let her weep and she sniffed into a handkerchief I handed her and then she looked at me and then at the glowing cigarette end. Her hair in the near darkness had the iridescence of liquid bronze. I drew closer.

"Davey, it's no good to be young and beautiful and be alone. Dris loves me—but not my way. He's normal. He's ambitious—like Caesar in schoolbooks. He has a full life ahead of him. Me—I'm a dark soul, a nasty, sticky person. Some days I feel I've got to grab at happiness, at pleasures, at—at lust. *Yes,* lust—because I'm going to die young. You ever feel it, Davey? Perceptions, intuitions of early death?"

"Sure—when I've been drunk—like you."

"Yes. When you've been drunk. Me, Davey—I've felt

that way all the time—drunk or sober. I'm built for stronger passions and—and greater vices. Oh, hell. I know I sound like a bad Victorian poem. But it's true—true, see? I'm not really Linda, the little lady. I'm—I'm very drunk, aren't I?"

I looked at her. "Not as much as you think. You're getting sober."

"Too bad. At first, you know, I felt Dris and I—it was fine—oh, very fine, going to bed, lying in each other's arms —forgetting, driving out the world with your own home-made lightning . . . But then—then for Dris life held other things. It wasn't the same any more. I wanted to lie around mornings and just—just, *hell*—just let my emotions do what they wanted. Dris—Dris got up every day at six and had a shower and went out to business. Then—then at night— when the whole darkness seemed to crack open and the world wasn't this world and we two were—*anyway*—I guess I got out of hand."

"Look, Linda. You don't have to tell me all this."

"Oh, yes, I do. I'm a swine. A female swine—gotta tell somebody everything. I possess no standard virtues. So. Oh, yes. Then I began to suspect Dris—felt he had other women. Didn't need me as much in the same old way. That wasn't true. I was just a swine, that's all. Then I got drunk one night, waiting for him. And the fire in me dribbled away ingloriously."

"Would you care for some hot soup?" I asked.

"What? No food. My head is full of whistling katydids. I got to like getting drunk. It was better than the nothing of vacillating thinking. Dris always off some place . . . Then I got to hate drinking. But drink liked me. *Understand?* I had to have it but it wasn't fun any more. Dris took me away to the hills and I got hold of myself—and I stopped for a while. But I went back to it. Where was I? Oh, yes. Cure, drunk *and* trip; cure, drunk *and* trip. Dris was good to me. Very good to me. I was under control—under control. Only a few petty defalcations. Get drunk once in a while but nothing terrible. Then—then I suddenly understood."

"What?" I asked, listening to the radio next door.

"Huh?" She inclined her head graciously. "I found I no longer loved Dris!"

I looked at the beautiful woman across from me and said nothing. She smiled at me. Then she went on in a hoarse, quavering voice.

"That hurt. I don't know how you turn off and turn on this passion—this love business. But mine got turned off. I no longer loved Dris. I told him so. I said I was bad for him and I got mean. Oh, Davey, I *can* be mean! But he didn't send me away. He didn't divorce me. Davey, he didn't get another woman or try to get out of the unadulterated hell I was broiling him in!"

I shrugged my shoulders. "Dris is that way."

She smashed out the cigarette on a palette knife. "I hate myself for that. I hate Dris for being so noble. I'm mixed up inside. But I don't know the reasons for it. I loved Dris, he loved me. I guess I'm just not normal. I'm a freak. A dirty, superficial freak. Got another cigarette? You must hate me, too."

There was something on my lips and I said it before I could bite it off. "No, Linda. I love you. I've always loved you—ever since I can first remember."

"Do you?"

"Yes. I fooled myself—like a kid at first—then—then, well, I grew up but it was still there. A look, a touch, the scent of you—and I'm all haywire."

There was morbid, panting indiscretion throbbing in the darkness. We felt it.

She looked at me from under her long eyelashes. I could

see she was sober now. The radio next door was still braying. It was very dark in the studio. The neon sign on the building across the way bathed our faces in blood every two seconds and sent a nebulous delinquent glow over us.

The radio grew louder: *"Flash. The Reform ticket has conceded that Driscoll Ormsbee has been elected Governor by an overwhelming . . ."* Suddenly the words stopped in mid-gurgle. It was very still as some disinterested fingers snapped off the announcement.

I looked at Linda and she closed her eyes.

"Poor Davey—poor little Davey."

I turned away. One moist hand caught mine and I leaned down. The scent of her spun my wits around. I looked into her face and I kissed her. I pulled her to me and the horn of the Judgment Day could not have made itself heard in my ears.

I could feel and taste her, the wonder, the glow, the full fleshy thrill of her shoulders and neck. There is such a thing —there was such a thing—I felt such emotions as I had never felt before. But yet there was something there, too—a full, high wall, a spinning of guarding nerves that could not give me full pleasure, full contact with this new, intriguing, gushing fluttering between us.

I was suddenly pushed aside and a voice—a sharp, fully controlled voice—said, with not a touch of sentimental emotion in it:

"Don't be a damn fool, Davey. I am *now* the Governor's wife."

After I had borrowed shoes and taken Linda to the station, the clouds opened.

The backbone of the hot, muggy night had been broken by rain. Now that the election excitement had simmered down, great knifing rain squalls beat against the streets reflecting madly the green and red lights of the shops and signs. It was all suddenly intrinsically ugly.

I had Linda on a train for Antioch. I think she was sober. She looked very sobered. My outburst of schoolboy passion had shocked her into normality. For me it was a shameful exhibit of feeble fumbling and lack of manly control. I was pretty obviously an animal (for I was trained in my schoolroom reading to take such things as passion with a noble gesture of the head and a tight-teethed grip on my lip). It was popular literature to suffer unreturned love with a wet eye and noble brow—but I felt very unliterary, ardent, but sterile—a sort of aching, grandiose hopelessness.

I was suffering. That I should ever have been in love with my brother's wife—that I should have forgotten myself enough to blurt out my longing to her while she was recovering from a drinking bout and *then* . . . No, I was no hero of popular fiction and I was no gentleman.

Vast bald, shapeless clouds poured water on me.

I walked along the flowing curbs, thinking of Linda's big eyes smiling at me as I handed her her railroad ticket and the cheap, cheerful magazines. And then the *jong-jong* of iron on iron, the puff and putter of steam and the train was away, blinking in rain as it swept by street-crossing tunnels, slashed with green and yellow and red lights, and then the last tunnel swallowed it. Linda was gone—going home to be the Governor's Lady. A wet desolation splashed over me.

There was something I needed. I couldn't go back to my studio and sit on my sofa still warm from Linda's body. No, I couldn't sit alone, a fool for love, a self-pity gnawing at my vitals, just waiting to be broiled on the emotions I could bring up to *this*, the first real tragic affair that had bitten deep under the calloused skin of my youth.

I remembered Doug, home from strange places with a

[258]

most different kind of story to tell. The rain was still coming down. I drained it from my eyebrows with a fist and floated toward his hotel. People, colored black and ochre, passed me like so many neolithic drawings to my wet vision.

It was not a good hotel and it had too much chrome and silver trimming and too many lights and the service was a little too fast and curt. But Doug, I could see, liked it. His rooms—he had two—were a Turkish-red-colored living room in which cigarette-scarred modern furniture stood numbly around, long since used to the misuse of the passing sports and show folk from Hollywood who came here often to sin quickly and loudly.

Doug sat deep in a modern club chair, Scotch in square bottles at his elbow, a fearful cigar smoldering, and many legal papers passing through his fists. He waved at me with his cigar and grinned that wide grin of his and tossed some papers aside onto a torso of a Maya maize god on a table.

"Sit down, Davey, and have something to drink."

"Thanks. Busy?"

"Hell, yes—but there ain't a lawyer living yet that can confuse me with these *whereas* and *withwhos*. Just organizing. Hungry?"

I shook my head. "No. Well—Dris is Governor."

Doug winked, punched his own chin with a short jab and picked up more legal trash. "Yes, sir, how do you like them apples? An Ormsbee up there with the swallow-tail coats and the silk hats. Vicky must be proud to busting, like my good-luck Mayan god."

I looked at the little stone god again, shivered and peeled off my wet jacket. "Yes—I guess so."

"You wet? Say, here. Swallow this. Nothing like liquor to keep you healthy. Here."

I swallowed the raw Scotch and made a face and sat down. "Doug, you remember Linda—the girl Dris married?"

"Sure—a neat little filly—not my type, but I got a low mind and a high hand. You asked me that before."

"She drinks, drinks like a sea bass. Something has happened to her. I don't know what. She and Dris—it isn't working out—I saw her tonight—put her on a train for home. Too bad . . ."

Doug grinned and looked at his cigar, threw it away and picked up a fresh one. "Look, infant. No dame in her right sense is going to turn down a chance of being Governor's Lady—and if Dris plays his cards right with those big muckamucks and political machines, some day he'll be President of these United States."

"You think so, really?"

The cigar was bitten, pushed into form and fired. When it was smoking well, Doug took it out of his mouth and looked at it. "Sure, I think so. He's better than these goons —Harding, Coolidge—they've been hoisting up. Look, me and Dris—maybe we don't see eye to eye, but Dris has the stuff and he can talk and he can stand up and look handsome and he can shake hands and mean it and the big boys like him. He can be President if he wants to be bad enough."

"Is that all, Doug? I mean—what about America and—oh, well, all that stuff we learned in school?"

Doug pushed aside his papers and poured two glasses. He held one toward me and winked at his cubic monolith good-luck god. "Here. Look, Davey. You're young, you're innocent, you're a hell of a nice kid. Any illusions you got— keep hold of 'em. I never read a lot of books. Once I never had any ideas except the normal life. Working and sleeping and having a job and something to do and maybe a few cheerful gals and a case or so of Scotch—some sun and farm land and a good shotgun and the duck swamps early at dawn—very early. But I got kicked away from most of *that*."

I swallowed my drink and looked at my brother.

He poured himself a fresh drink and held his cigar as if it were a hammer. I felt I was near the essential core of the man. "We are going for one hell of a sled ride—the whole world. I don't know too much about charts and history books . . . but everything is all screwy. We didn't knock off the Huns and they are stirring again. We didn't clean house here. The oil and the coal and iron and land and lumber are still being held by the big crooks who swiped it after the Civil War. And now they are dealing in worthless stocks and lawyers' dirty lies. Somebody is due for a kick in the brisket."

I burped and sat very still. Doug's face was very close to me. "I love a ship. Lots of ships. You can't build a ship of paper, you can't work her engines with margin calls or bond issues. And Davey, the whole world is being run in step to stock tickers. The little people, the storekeepers, the farmers and the cabinetmakers are standing around looking at the stuff we should eat and wear go over a cliff. I'm a little drunk, maybe—like your Linda tonight. Maybe I'm just saying what I've wanted to say since they cracked my head with a fink's baseball bat. But it's all over, Davey. Everything we stood for. Everything Gramp worked for and Uncle Thoreau dreamed about in his chicken houses and Pete wanted from his lousy shacks—everything Jake Fry started to do to the law before he defended railroads, everything Dris used to put into those school essays for which some fat crook would give a prize of five dollars and a pat on the head. Davey, it looks to me as if we're going to watch the sea come in now over the land."

I yawned and stirred my wet toes in soggy shoes. "Then

why are you going on with these stock schemes and ship mergers and stuff?"

"Because I'm the first of the new barbarians within the gates, Davey. I like to be with the winners—and until the end comes I'm riding with the boys who are going to hold all the aces—until someone tears up the deck. Come in with me. I'll make you richer than a fat pig in clover."

I felt heavy-headed in the heat. The wet, the Scotch which I disliked, the heavy cigar smoke, the plastic subtlety of the little corn god and all this talk which meant nothing to me had me woozy.

"Thanks, Doug. But I've just made up my mind. I've some cash saved up from teaching art classes and from peddling drawings to the comic magazines and I'm going to Paris to paint pictures."

"Can't you paint here?"

"Yes. But what I want is over there. The painters, the writers and a certain kind of room to swing my arms around in and not knock over anything sacred."

Doug looked at me closely, buoyantly optimistic, amused. "I don't know why every crackpot and paper spoiler is going to Paris. Well, go and have a hell of a time."

"Thanks. So long, Doug." I got my jacket and stood at the door, wrestling with its wet arms. Doug was back with his legal papers—but he looked up as I put my hand on the doorknob.

"You *don't* have to run away if you're in love with Dris' wife. It might be better to keep it in the family at that."

"Go to hell," I said and closed the door behind me.

Outside it was still raining—a misty languor covered the streets. . . .

The city passed me. I seemed to stand still and rain and people and huge buses walked past me; ran, growled and sent up sheets of spray from the gutters. There is a smell and color about New York in the rain. No other city has it. It is a mood and feeling that gets into the bones—and the tall towers seem to nod over the streets and help the pressure that whistles in the eardrums.

Red and green lights were reflected in the oiled, tarred surfaces of the streets. People were not people but shapes wrapped against the rain. People are never people in New York—they are bundles moving in the patterned streets. Their faces speak of a hundred nations in Europe and their emotions are those of ants twitching into their grub holes.

The rain sopped deeper into my body—I had never felt such a stranger in the big cold stone city. More people passed and a few broke the city rule and stared at me. I got home and made hot tea and put the last three fingers of whiskey into it.

I got out my old bag, but did not pack. I sat looking out at the rain-gray city. Lights went on in the sweatshops. The dry drawn meek face of the Wandering Jew appeared in the shop across from my windows. The wisdom of the Talmud seemed to sweat from his brow as his lean hands drove the needle through the cloth.

I began to pack. . . .

BOOK THREE

TWENTY

ALL DAY AND all night the ship had run at high speed. Just before the chair folk went down to dinner the coastline of America was a pencil smudge, a geological labor of land masses, ahead of us.

Three years in Europe, the collapse of the great Bull Market and the devil-twisted destiny of a continent marching toward the gallows were behind me. I was homesick for the American land, the city of Antioch, the faces of Vicky and Pete—and prepared for the newer glory that had overtaken my brothers Dris and Douglas.

They were big with success. There was talk now of Dris running for the United States Senate after two terms of being Governor, and everyone knew the Ormsbee Ships, those fast, alert little travelers to the strange corners of the world, carrying cargo and steel tools *and* passengers looking for romance and escape (at a low rate) from the huge white snobbery of the English cruise boats.

As for myself, I stood that day at the rail while the dining-room steward played his gongs and I wondered what I added up to. I had spent the last few years in Paris, and now the joyous elation was falling into the bittersweet melancholy of time ill-spent.

I knew the town of Paris—its peoples, its artists, its methods. I had sopped up my *bocks* at the Dome, I had lived in a huge square studio with paint peeling off the ceiling and canvas stacked along the walls. I had painted like a whirl-

wind. I had made a tour of Rome and London and Berlin—
I had lived in Munich and seen the gore-red banners of reaction grow in size. I had seen Big Chin strutting in Rome,
and the French and English diplomats had begun to wear
my temper thin.

Paris was fine. Paris was an education. Dinner at Maxim's
—but by Metro to save taxi fare—late brawls at the *Bagatelle*
in Montmartre, or the fun in Place Clichy—and the small
boîtes and the Opera.

But where was the brake that was to stop this mad rush
to hell going on all the time? Evil was coming. The mad
cruel clown strutted and no one gave him a crack across the
back of the head. I had been there, had seen the failure of
the Beer Hall putsch and had seen the Hero toss himself
against the street stones in fear as the bullets whined into
the flesh of his followers—in such haste that he threw his
shoulder out of place. And then I had seen the mockery of
the trial, the selling out of justice and I didn't care any
more for *Mittel Europa*.

I had painted a few hundred paintings, my sketchbooks
bulged. I was penniless. Hoover and Morgan laughed off the
depression—but whatever holdings I had were worthless.
The Ormsbee Overseas stock I had sold to get *"in on a good
thing."* And so, the market for pen-and-ink sketches—cartoons—falling, the little art magazines folding, the dilettantes
beginning to withdraw and go home to eat fatted calf in
the Wastelands—I burned a lot of my early work and
booked passage away from Europe's colonnades, triumphal
arches and cupolas.

The sea was very calm and the huge ship slid in joy toward its home port. The turbines whined and the very shell
of the boat seemed to strain for the shore—ached for it. This
floating world would soon make land contact, the passen-

gers would spread out and leave and I would stand on my native soil. If I was sloppy with emotions, I didn't feel ashamed of them. This was my own, my native land—the land I lived. I stood staring—revisiting my past on an emotional archaeological expedition.

Home! It lay numb with pain. The Stock Exchange a shell of mocking echoes of paper fortunes. It bled at a thousand small bank wounds that tore up farms and broke up fields and forgot at times the people who still saw in this dust their heritage. The little investors again sat in darkness —and I swore I would never save or invest anything again. The ship sailed on, beating, for me, toward the navel of the universe—toward Antioch.

The last gong for dinner sounded, but I was too full of a puckering emotion to eat at the huge tables or to listen to the second officer telling again his affairs of the heart.

I went into the bar and drank an old native Bourbon. And when I ordered another the sapient barman shook his head.

"Be inside the twelve-mile limit soon. Locking up the bar."

I looked into my empty glass and thought of freedom and the right to get roaring drunk at seeing my native land again. No dice. I went on deck to see the green copper goddess float across the dirty waters of Gravesend Bay—a scalloped evening sky rode pink over the up-pointed buildings. Ferries passed with precarious gentility.

Below the passengers were singing, "Auld Lang Syne."

I went a little foolish and sloppy. I didn't mind.

To see again after a long period the land of one's birth, to look from new angles at endlessly repeated, old, remembered patterns is worth all the turmoil of travel.

As the train tossed and groaned on toward the city of

Antioch, I could only think of childhood and boyhood and those shapes and colors that are always so strong in the tired traveler.

The station looked smaller than I remembered it. The streets were narrower. The people were just people—yet I knew them. This street, that tree, the fat cop directing traffic —all were such stuff as my dreams had been made of these last three years. I saw it all with the blank, watery eyes of a bad poet.

The city had changed. It was stiller. The cars, the people were shabby (for a Bull Market exploding in one's face does a great deal of damage). I dragged my bags to a taxi and the old, remembered face of one of the gang stared at me from over the meter, starting again innumerable dazzling ripples in my mind.

"Hya, Davey."

"Hello, Turtle . . ."

"Been away—*huh?*"

I nodded. The cab started and I saw new buildings and old ones and empty stores and new signs and known faces, so much older than I remembered them. And far off past the mills, escarped slopes of green corn growing. And the hills and slag heap.

"How come you're driving a cab, Turtle? Weren't you with Piggy's boys?"

Turtle turned a sad face toward me. "They got Piggy about a year ago. The Lanzanzo mob. They highjacked us and Piggy happened to be along. . . ."

"Too bad."

"Yeah. He died hard. Shot away most of his stomach. He screamed in the cement barrel they threw in the river. You been to *U*rope?"

"Yes. All over it."

"Whatcha think of it?"

"Haven't made up my mind yet. Things pretty tough here in town?"

"Everyone on the bottom of his fanny. Town's broke."

"Coppards, too?"

"No. Not them. Only the people. Going into politics, Davey, like the Governor?"

"No. I'm an artist."

Turtle spit into the road and moved around a huge truck labeled COPPARD STEEL CORP. "Well, I guess it's as good a way of starving as any. . . ."

"Not much election excitement," I said.

Turtle nodded. "Ned Wonderly has the state sewed up —as usual."

"You still working at the polls?"

Turtle shook his head. "I'm all washed up with that. I'm voting for this here guy Roosevelt—*and* the Governor, of course, if he runs some day for the Senate."

Certain things weren't the same in Antioch after all. I watched a labyrinth of alleys pass. Turtle gave me a secret satanic smile in his mirror.

"How *was* the French broads?"

I saw the yellow house of my father while still far down the street. It looked as I had ever remembered it. As I came closer I saw that the tall gaunt oaks and shade trees in the yard had been cut down. Tin garages filled the once long yard where Pete's garden had flourished. A sorrowful remnant remained, marking the undisguised disaster.

There were dust and peeling paint about the place—yet I saw it now as something dear and close. The trick of nature that forces us back to our early nesting places held me.

I walked across the yard and remembered a hundred images and scenes. The grape arbor still floated over the kitchen door and an old man sat there reading a newspaper with meticulous, methodical care.

It was Pete.

The hair at his temples was retreating fast. The rust-colored hair was full of silver and his arms appeared weak and thin. He turned and looked at me through brass-rimmed glasses and rose and knew me suddenly in ecstatic jubilation.

"Davey! Davey, boy!"

We rubbed cheeks and held each other's arms and he was as shy and remote and as easy to hurt as ever.

"You're looking well, Pete—as well as ever."

"Sure. Come in and see your mother."

I sat at the table and knew that Vicky's cooking had not improved. Had, as a matter of fact, grown worse. But I lecherously licked my lips over the cake.

Vicky sat looking at me, and I swallowed the burnt offering and smiled back at her. She was much older now—a surprise I hadn't expected. Yet several years had passed since I had seen her last. Time moves. Her hair was full of gray now—but she herself was as busy and as alive as ever. Her tiny body seemed smaller—and she had, by some process that I could never figure out, grown shorter. Her face, as small and perfect and pretty as ever, was heavily lined now. All those delicate features were marked with fine wrinkles, as if in an etching. But the fire was still in her. The primal force that ties a city to the earth—she had it.

"Hell's bells, Davey. You haven't learned table manners yet. Gobbling your food and using your fork as if it were a hay lifter. Eat slow."

Pete sat watching me. He was more silent than ever, ingrown to a degree I had never seen before. Only his pipe was alive—gurgling and glowing. Vicky sniffed at it and turned on him with a cherubic tint in her excited cheeks.

[271]

"Get that reeking furnace out of here. I declare, I've a good mind to throw all your carved smoking broom handles into the garbage."

Pete knocked life out of his pipe and sat calmly staring at me. I pushed away the plates (a habit I had also been warned against) and smiled about me with a confidential intimacy.

"It's stupid and childish to say—but I've been very homesick."

"Those Frenchies—cooking up sauces and horse meat. How's your stomach?" asked Vicky.

"Pretty good. How's Dris—and Linda?"

Vicky poured coffee from a hot pot and I saw how rough and hard her little hands had become. "Fine—Dris is fine—the best Governor this state ever had. Everyone says so. Not just his mother—everyone."

Pete came alive. "Except Ned Wonderly."

"Don't tell me Ned and Dris have broken up?"

Vicky shrugged her shoulders and made a low, corrugated forehead. "Not yet—but Ned doesn't like some laws. Some higher income tax laws with things called surtax. Hurt too many of his rich, grafting, contractor friends. And this law of Dris' to take over all unworked land and give it to some sort of homesteaders—*well!*"

"Why, that sounds," I shouted, "as if Dris is doing something for the people who elected him!"

Vicky nodded. "That's why Ned isn't getting too lippy. Dris is a mighty popular man these days with the voters. Of course these things aren't laws yet."

"And how is Linda?" I said, sticking my nose into the coffee cup.

I looked up. Pete was staring at his now cold pipe. Vicky was staring at Pete. Then she turned to me with patronizing triumph.

"If you must know, *no* damn good. Never was, never will be, and not *even* any use as a wife. Two nurses guarding her day and night. Drunk as a Wonderly judge all the time, they say—*and* doping with needles until I hear her backside and arms are just *one* big mess of wounds. How do you like that for poor Dris to carry around with him!"

"It's very tragic," I said, watching Vicky's little nose dilate with scorn.

"Tragic, my foot!" said Vicky. "She's a stumbling-block to Dris, that's what she is. And to think that I gave up the pot-cheese business to keep the Ormsbee name off the streets! While *she* staggers in the gutters. Or used to before they got the nurses!"

Pete rubbed his stony, inflexible mouth. "Now you know you gave up the pot-cheese business because Douglas started giving us a weekly allowance."

"Anyone ask *you!* Sitting there while his sons slave to support him. I should see the day when I have to beg my bread at the doorsteps of my children!"

I grinned. "I hear Doug gives you enough to have butter on your bread, even. I think I'll go see Gramp—I missed him."

Pete shook his head after a deftly restrained glance at Vicky. "Gramp is pretty low. Can't move his arms any more. He's living with Thoreau now. Cap Roc—madder than ever—takes care of the Range. That man's going to kill someone soon."

Vicky was rattling the dishes off the table. Then she sat down next to me after glancing at Pete long enough so that he got up and began to wash the supper things.

"Tell me, Davey. Is it true—all Frenchwomen are tarts?"

It was strange to take up my life again in Antioch. It was as if I had missed a few chapters in the middle of a book.

Everyone was older and had lived through a few crises. Uncle Thoreau was about the same—his Kipling mustache was longer and more tobacco-stained, his baldness went farther back, he was a Marxist now and deeply convinced the world would be saved by the Kremlin. His old brood was scattered and he lived with a few new babies that Aunt Netta had spawned from her opulent fertile curves since I had seen them last. Aunt Netta was larger and wider and her nose was red all the time now. But there was no obscure frustration about her.

I asked her about Linda.

Aunt Netta rubbed her cherry-colored face and pushed back a stray lock of hair. She spoke in subtly nuanced tones.

"Don't you believe all you hear about her. This talk of dope and needles—it's lies. I go to see her a lot. We get along fine. The doctor's got her on a quota—and we sit around sometimes and sip our wine and talk. She is a *perfect* lady."

"You mean Linda isn't at the state capital with Dris?"

Aunt Netta narrowed her good-natured eyes. "He may be your brother—and the best Governor we ever had—but like all men—I tell you the best of them—and Thor is an angel—isn't to be trusted to suck eggs, let alone live without a woman."

"Don't tell me Dris is running a harem in the state capital?"

"Well, no. But you can't pull any wool over my eyes. That Miss Williams that travels with him and types his speeches. She's *too* pretty and well dressed to just hammer on a typewriter. . . ."

"Williams? *Not* Cathy Williams!"

"Tall, golf-playing girl with a lot of muscles?" asked Aunt Netta.

"Yes, but . . ."

"But, my foot! Here comes Gramp—keep him company

until supper. I want to make an onion stew. He likes them."

Gramp came slowly down the street, his arms held life-
less at his sides. He looked almost transparent. The long,
white beard was neglected—windblown and clipped by alien
hands into a square mat. He walked slowly, his head down,
as if displeased with the lyrical immensities of space ahead
of him.

"Hello, Gramp."

He lifted his head as if with effort. The eyes were still
eagle eyes and very bright. In them there was no dreary
desolation.

"Davey—you've grown up."

"Sure, Gramp. You look about the same."

"Don't lie, boy. I can hear the grave worms sharpening
their teeth. Let's sit in the garden in solemn immobility. A
torpor is in my arms; help me."

It wasn't much of a garden. Uncle Thoreau called it
Walden (a book he had never read, I was sure). I found a
bench for Gramp and filled his pipe and put it in his mouth
and set fire to it. He puffed and nodded his head—and made
confidential, ominous sounds.

"I miss my hands, Davey. Need them for a hundred silly
little things every day. How is the art world?"

"About the same—fools knocking ideas about and trying
to show the world what boils in their heads. Academic
chores and brandy vices. I had a fine time in Europe—but
the whole place is going mad. Like seeing a dog you love
getting distemper and getting ready to bite his best friends.
How's your hound dog, Major?"

"Captain Roc shot him three months ago. No teeth to
chew with any more, couldn't get enough nourishment on
pap. He was the biggest dog I ever had. The last, too. There
is an austere simplicity about a dog. Tolerant, kind and tem-
perate."

[275]

"He loved the hills and the trips we took to the tall timber."

Gramp puffed his pipe. "Put out the pipe. No taste to it any more since I can't prepare my own pipes."

I knocked life from the pipe and put it on the bench to cool. "Is Dris' new land law going to damage you much in the hills?"

Gramp grinned. "You damn young fool, you think Ned Wonderly is going to let him take away all the unworked land at an honest cost from the big estates? Why, they even failed to do it in Mexico after a revolution! No, my land is safe. Funny, I should be suddenly listed with all the rich publishers and bankers running hunting preserves and breeding places for trout, and gardens to murder deer in blood, diarrhea and glory."

"It sounds like a good law."

"That's the trouble with laws—they all sound good to someone. Politics will see that the land-grabbers get the best homesteads. It will never pass. But Dris is turning out better than I thought."

"I always liked Dris' ideas. It's Douglas that surprises me. He's even weathered the collapse of Wall Street and snapped up a dozen busted lines and about a hundred new ships. The thrust and jostle of the Stock Exchange are home to him now. Our Doug."

Gramp chuckled. "Doug amazed all of us. He passed through on his way to Washington last month. Bought me some perfumed tobacco I had to throw away. Stood there bold as brass and said, 'Gramp, they call me a sonofabitch on Wall Street. Before I'm through I'll be the biggest bastard that ever licked them. You wait.' I said I didn't have much more time to wait. Haven't. The envenomed night, Davey, and then one of Pete's best long cabinets. Soon."

We sat in the little scrubby garden, watching people pass.

I felt Gramp had calmed down a lot. A man dies easy, I guess, when he sees his grandsons stirring around and raising hell in a world of their own. I suddenly remembered what Cabot Carson had once said to me among the slashed Assyrian marbles at the Metropolitan. "A man's children and grandchildren are his revenge tossed on life."

I turned and told it to Gramp.

He smiled, and the wind stirred his beard tenderly into the old, bold-patterned ringlets I remembered.

"Davey, what you hoard is lost forever—gold, land *or* children. What you toss away is yours. You don't understand that yet. You may, some day. Let's try the pipe again."

TWENTY-ONE

THE DAYS PASSED quickly, multicolored and normal. I was back in my old bedroom again. It was all mine now. I moved in my painting tools and bought a great deal of canvas. I was up at dawn and packed two thick pads and a small box of water-colors. I would eat an early breakfast at the truck drivers' lunch wagon and then spend the morning along the river, sketching, blocking in ideas for oils, and coloring square bits of paper with little color notes that I hoped some day to design into huge canvases. I finished some paintings of the Protestant Cemetery in Rome by the Porta San Paolo. I had begun them so long ago.

I invited my spirit to loaf and with the sketchbooks filling up fast I really delayed doing anything serious in the way of new finished work. I enjoyed that hot stab of sun—an intonaco of Pompeian red—growing higher and higher until it boiled over and I took shelter in some beer parlor along Polack Point or Jefferson Basin and filled myself with the beer and thick sandwiches. Vile beer, too. Then I would go tramping into the foothills—listen to runner birds in the newly cut fields and measure with cheerful eye the distant mountains and the leaning oaks and the line of farm buildings and elm trees and the full rustling flow of the streams. With immeasurable conceit I painted farm girls in the manner of Sienese Madonnas, and farmhands shooting crap in no style at all.

The slag heaps and slate piles were longer, wider, spread

out more. The air stank if the mill wind was behind it and the furnace gas and the bitter purple and yellow dye of manufacturing were flowing deeper and deeper into the land. It was a time of slackness, yet a great many chimneys spouted sable soot and the coal mines were always surrounded by little black ants of men attacking the bowels of the earth. Steam shovels practiced their cataleptic grip on the rocks.

It was strange to walk across a field of wheat stubble and feel stirring under me the mine shafts—and hear muffled the distant blanket thud of explosions as the man ants tore at the black coal almost a half mile below me.

I would run quickly from the dark, blasting sound—following the leaping Merry Andrew grasshoppers—until with one spring they would go over the edge of the world and I would drop after them, clinging to gullies and bush, dropping at last into a lower field. I would lie, mouth open foolishly, grinning, my heart tossing like a land-tossed fish—and I would feel escape from the power of darkness. And then —*then* under me I would hear it again . . . the deep, dull drilling of coal-cutting tools. The extraordinary, penetrating groans of coal slides.

No, there was no escape from it. It was cutting up the earth under the fields and under the river bottoms deep in maidenhair ferns. Day and night the perceptible pulse of blasting went on.

Coming home at dusk, I would pass the little bent-over man ants—soiled, ebony-masked—and they would politely stand aside to let me pass. They talked little—chewing on small pipes—their white eyeballs gleaming in black faces like minstrel men until I expected them to ask Mr. Bones, *"Why does a chicken cross the road?"* But when they spoke it was with a deep dust-hoarse voice—a hard black voice. . . .

"By damn, Joe—that coal get harder to get out every day. By damn . . ."

At night the voluminous dimensions of neon would flicker like fairy fire downtown, and poolroom and movie palace and lunch wagon and tea room and cheap clothing sellers would hide behind their red and green and blue ribbons of light and lure the few coins that still jingled in the shabby pockets of the night into their tills. Oblong feline electric pupils blinked over every busy street.

The Antioch underworld was a dim shadowy place that spotlighted green felt billiard tables—or spun bowling balls in polished alleys or ran crap games behind moldy boxes of unsold cigars. The tarts were bold and brassy with lemon-colored hair. Irish and Polish and a few Hungarians and Yankee old stock down on its uppers. Laughing loud in bold respirator sounds—twitching . . .

There was no glamour to any of this. Vice was plain and labeled. I sketched away at this, too, filling more notebooks and bought beer and stale beef sandwiches for slatternly whores dressed as Clara Bow and Garbo. I played Kelly pool and heard again the saga of Piggy Tone who died game with his kidney and stomach torn to shreds and leaking gore like a mashed bag of strawberries, and dying alive, set hard, in a barrel of new cement.

Midnight the streets would be almost stilled—but there were many trucks doing their bit to keep the night sounds full. The midnight movie palaces took on a vicious glitter. Bums snored in the balcony while lovers (with no parlor at home) sprawled together in amorous love-knots while the screen showed Hoover's baby-face uttering some rambling remarks about the fine state of the Nation.

It was usually almost dawn before I would start toward the yellow house of my father. The wind was cold and wet

[280]

from the bay, and fog most likely was weaving halos over the last dying traffic lights. I would ride the milk wagons— the big-rumped horse cheerfully drumming against the road-way while I sucked a pint of good, cold, stabbing milk from a dripping bottle. And the driver—a member of the old gang, most likely—and I told each other legends and fables, or muttered foul slander about the bodies of certain women we claimed we knew.

The yellow house under the flickering arc light was like a torn shred of old motion-picture film on a wavering screen. Far away the steel-plant whistles were testing the dawn for sound echoes. Across the river the freight trains were mov-ing. Old memories stirred in the few trees that still fought gasoline odors and the bark-stripping gangs of dirty brats now sleeping in their underwear with unwashed feet all around me in the silent houses. In devotion and humility, I bowed to the doorway.

On such a dawn the first damn fool sparrow was already making sounds in his chest, clearing his throat to keep time with the whacking, walloping clangor of the church bells about to call the pallid pious to early Mass. And then Vicky in a too long bathrobe would open the door and eye me with distaste and many words.

King George Road had not changed much. The trees were as tailored as ever and iron deer still stood timid and rigid in space. Dris' house—or rather, Linda's now, by a direct gift from her father—slept in its hedges with a de-tached elemental indifference.

A large Irish nurse opened the door to my ring and looked me over, heard who I was and nodded. I went along to the living room. Two more, larger, Irish nurses sat there knitting. One had a wonderful mustache, the other ran to oversized moles. They looked at me, and the one with the mustache approached as if to search me for contraband, but took in my shape instead and decided I wasn't harboring a quart of whiskey on my person. She waved me through the door with a feverish abrupt gesture.

"Hello, Davey," said a voice, and Linda stood there smiling at me. She hadn't changed at all. She was as slim and pale as ever. The nurses gathered their wool balls and retired somewhere in whining irritation.

Linda came toward me, took my face between her hands and kissed me on the mouth. She smelled pleasantly of rye whiskey and a pungent lilac darkness.

"It's good to see you again, Linda."

"Yes, I'm sure. I've been waiting for you to call for a long time."

I made no excuse but just stood there smiling. I was still in love. Closer to her, I could see a few little wrinkles around her eyes, and the eyeballs were finely etched with red veins. She gave me a fixed, abstracted look.

"Davey, oh, Davey—it's been a long time since I've seen you." She sat down at the piano and looked at her well-cared-for fingers. "The last time I saw you, you tried to make love to me—remember?"

I lied. "No. Did I?"

She smiled. "Don't stand in hypnotic immobility as if you'd slept with *every* pretty tart in Europe. *You* remember well enough. I do. . . ."

"Yes. How are things with you, Linda?"

"Just dandy. The earth endures—and I with it." She looked at me. "You wouldn't have a—no, I suppose those battle-axes searched you. Huh?"

"Not a drop."

"Damn. They keep me on a pint every eight hours."

"Play something."

"What do you like?"

I sat down and looked at her, slim and lovely, the sun moving in her honey-colored hair. "It doesn't matter."

She began to play—Chopin's *Polonaise Brilliante*.

She stopped playing after a while suddenly and looked at me. "Your brother—my husband—is a damn fool. He's in love with another woman and acts like a saint in a hot fire about it."

"Dris is a pretty right guy. Very honorable. An inflexible puritanical nature."

"He's a fool. I'm not worth a pin to him. I don't love him —don't love anybody any more. I'm dead inside—dead all over and only whiskey stirs me now. Davey, you've got to talk to him—tell him it's no use. I'll never change—never. He's got to get rid of me. He's a good man and a big one and I'm no good for him."

"You know how far I can get with that kind of talk to Dris?"

"Davey?"

"Yes?"

"You know Miss Williams?"

I nodded, looking out of the window at the spring-feathered trees.

"You think *they*—Dris and *her*—that *is* . . ."

I was rather brutal. "I don't know if they sleep together. I don't give a damn. You're taking everything wrong, Linda. You are building up mountains out of a dust mote. You'd think you were the only woman in the world who liked her liquor. Look at my Aunt Netta. Hell, you've got to pull yourself together and see that Dris wants to share his life— his everything—with you. You can't act like a leper and feel there isn't going to be any tomorrow. You're wrong, Linda —wrong as they come."

"I'm wrong—all wrong—but there isn't any future. Ever hear of a brandy heart?"

"Nonsense."

She looked at me, penetrated nakedly my look, and began to play again. I heard some chatter at the front door and my Aunt Netta entered, brushing away the nurses with grotesque terrible gestures.

"Back, you swabs. It's just a friendly visit and the back of the hand if you try any fancy tricks. Hello, folks."

The nurses rubbed noses and made small talk among themselves and fell back. Netta closed the sliding doors and barged down on us, confidential, conspiratorial and grinning.

"Well, I knew Davey was coming but I didn't expect him here today."

I grinned. "You're looking well, Aunt Netta."

Netta kissed Linda, kissed me and sat down on a white sofa, fanning herself with her blue velvet hat in solicitous exquisite gestures.

"Lord love a duck—what a day! I just knew my Linda might be lonely and so I decided to drop in."

Linda looked down at her hands, then at me and then at Netta. My aunt rubbed her rosy nose and bit her thumb. Then she looked at me, frowned, smiled and slapped my knees.

"Davey, I raised you from a pink-forked carrot to a man. I fed you and wiped your nose and I'm sure—very sure— you'll not be a Boy Scout with two ladies dying for a snifter."

I held my hands up, palm up. "I haven't a drop on me."

Netta, her face in suave smiling reassurance, slapped my knees again. "That's all right." She dived a fat hand down between her great breasts and came up with a quart of whiskey. She looked at it with a cocked eye, pulled the cork and poured a swallow down her throat. Then she winked at me, wiped the neck of the bottle with her palm and handed it to Linda.

Daintily Linda took a swallow, closed her eyes, smiled nicely me and handed me the bottle after scrubbing the neck with a small handkerchief. They both sat looking at me. I took the bottle, looked at it, smelled the strong bootleg rawness and took a swallow in turn.

Aunt Netta's hand banged me on the small of the back with deep solemnity and respect.

"Davey, you're a *gent*."

The three of us sat on the long white sofa. Linda swallowed a drink and passed the bottle to me. An unbelievable aura of desire, a soft amiability, held me.

"Davey, dear—you read a lotta books. *What* is life?"

I looked at the low level of the bottle and passed it to Aunt Netta. "Life is something drunks shouldn't talk about. Life? Life? Oh, hell—life is a lot of things that mean nothing—a lot of emotions that are painful to have and worse to forget. *Kennst du das Land wo die Citronen blühen?*"

Aunt Netta nodded. "You got a brain, boy. Always said you had a brain. Told Vicky that time and time again. Davey is the runt and fool of the litter, Vicky always said. No, I said, he's gotta brain—a fine human beem—that boy. A drink, Linda dear?"

I watched Linda drink. "Davey—sweetest little boy, grew up to be a big man. Very big man. Loves me, Netta. Loves me madly. Passion under pressure. Controlled emotions. Very romantic, huh? *If* I wanted the peculiar erotic intimacy of saints."

I took the bottle. "Yes, I love you—I love everything. Pictures, books, sunsets—even bad ones—dark nights, clear dawns, and the patter of naked feet on unswept floors. The taste of whiskey and the bite of well-dressed food. I like the young girls walking, the trees in spring, all the silly, daffy stuff that's so easy to see—the lewd, delicate tidbits—the great stone hills . . ."

Netta shook her head. "That's—that's bad. No man worth his salt loves too many things. Gotta love one thing. Gotta work hard. Wanna be a success, don't you?"

"No. I have seen success—seen it plain, seen it fancy. I just want a little corner of the world and you ladies to look at. I love you both very much."

"Damn fudge," said Netta. "You'll be kissing our hands next. Europe spoiled you—kissing our hands . . ."

"Davey," said Linda, "you can kiss my hand—my body— my soul. Kiss my hand, Davey."

I did. Netta snorted. "Show me a hand-kisser, I show you a man no good at all. I like a man who doesn't waste time. I like—a lot of love, a lot of whiskey—I like everything good and solid and strong and when I like to—I like to tell everyone about it."

Aunt Netta began to whoop like an Indian. I pulled her arm. "You'll wake up the nurses."

Linda shook her head. "Doesn't matter—bottle empty."

Aunt Netta began to weep. I wiped the huge tears. I kissed her cheek. Linda came over and hugged her. Arms together, the three of us swayed on the sofa. We laughed and wept, we giggled—and suddenly there was a knocking at the doors.

They opened. There stood Driscoll and behind him Cathy Williams, clear-eyed and more solid than ever—and in the background the nurses, like witches from *Macbeth*, bubbled and boiled in whispers. I hunted assurance and poise— and failed.

I stood up, unsteady. I was unused to bootleg whiskey after Europe. "Hello, Dris. Just dropped—dropped in to *say* . . ."

Then I fell down, tripping toward the rug in one full, launched fall, the swift thrust of space carrying me on. I passed out.

When the late spring hill rains stop their dripping dirge, there are new green buds laughing from the old trees. I am snug here, camped in the arms of an old tree, and the fish are never done doing their dancing in the stream.

How much paper I have covered and how little I have said and how much more I have still to tell. What to put in? And what to leave out?

When the rain let up I went for a walk. The lake was very still—as if punished enough by the rain and now willing to lie smooth and slick until a wind came stirring and ruffled its surface. Some place across the water someone was burning wood and I could smell the wet smoke. The distances were purple and old gold but soon they will be spotted with green dots and the tender apple green of new-born leaves will thicken and turn emerald in color and sap with pulse in the shaggy brown tree trunks. All the daffy wonder of spring growth will take place around me and I will still be writing.

TWENTY-TWO

SOMEONE WAS giving me some dreadful stuff to smell. I looked up and saw the wide smiling face of Douglas. I shut my eyes and groaned guilelessly.

"Open up, Davey—no playing possum."

I opened my eyes and sat up. I was still in the living room of Dris' house—but alone with my brother Douglas. Doug had grown wider, grayer—and his eyes were harder—but the corners of his eyelids laughed, like old times. There was a coarse humid serenity about Doug.

"Sorry, Doug, it's that bootleg stuff. After Europe it hit me hard. Is Dris very angry?"

Doug, lacking any feeling for proprieties, chewed a cigar and shrugged his shoulders. "Aunt Netta confessed she smuggled the liquor in."

"How's Linda?"

"Sleeping like a child by now, most likely. She *can* hold it, can't she?"

I looked up at the shaking walls, a piercing spur of pain in my head. "Yes."

Dris came down the few steps from the hall. He was neatly dressed, a little too full in front but a very handsome figure of a man. He looked at me calmly with a terrible, intent silence. Then he spoke.

"Hello, mug. You're still the damn fool, I see."

"I'm sorry about—about the drinking. . . ."

Dris sat down and looked at me, smiled and patted my shoulder. "Things will happen. Glad to be home?"

"Glad to be home among my more successful brothers. It looks as though I belong with Dennis—one of the low and normal ones—almost normal, anyway. How's the Governor's chair fit you?"

"Like a glove," said Doug. "Like a white kid glove around his pompous fanny."

Dris smiled and patted my shoulder again. "You have a habit of arriving when I'm about to break once more with my past."

"Going back to law?"

Doug grunted, winced as if he had pulled a tendon. "The big lug—he's breaking with Ned Wonderly's organization."

I sat back and looked at my brothers as I calmed my prancing nerves. "That sounds fine—but in a mood of fantasy. . . ."

Dris stood up and walked over to the small, locked bar, opened it, came back with three tumblers and a bottle. I shook my head and he and Doug had a drink. Dris looked down at his empty glass. "This is the kiss-off, as Doug would say. I've got enough popular approval behind me and have scared the local grafters and officeholders into a body that will back me in the land and corporation law reforms I'm sending up to the state legislature next week."

Doug groaned. "Little Rollo, the fifth Rover Boy. Kicking himself in the behind and out into the ash can for a lot of monkeys who will not be able to hold on very long to whatever benefits you give them. The loan sharks, bankers and real-estate wolves will take it all away from them."

"Perhaps," said Dris with a gesture of rueful humor. "But I remember you with your head banged open for howling about the little people."

Doug grinned, elfishly, mockingly. "You can't do it with laws. When the mugs get good and tired of being kicked in the rump, they'll be like me—they'll take things, like I have."

Dris shook his head. "I want to keep them from that. Ned Wonderly will smash me flatter than one of Vicky's omelettes—but all the empty barren land in this state is going to be broken into homesteads. We will pay the landowners a fair price when the farmers pay us. I'm going to have honest corporations paying honest taxes with no bilked stockholders, no bond-issue scandals—and then it doesn't matter what happens to me."

"Jehovah," I said, "God of Israel planning some new Commandments."

Doug, with perplexed, scrutinizing eyes, looked down at me and ate his cigar. "Isn't he an innocent bastard! Dris has got it all figured out. As *if* Ned Wonderly can't elect a whole new setup and kick this whole reform in the ash can!"

"He can't," said Dris. "I wasn't a lawyer for nothing. I can be as audacious and cunning as Ned. The Driscoll bills are so worded it will take years to break them down, and Ned wouldn't dare. He can knife me—but he needs the people's votes. And the people like these bills. Oh, let's forget politics. How's the great painter coming along? Proselytizing a cult of cube-makers?"

I said, "Not as bad as most people expect."

Doug turned to me. "Want to paint river and ocean stuff? I've got a new yacht I bought and I'm taking Dris and Linda down river tomorrow morning. Come along and bring a gal."

I shook my head. "No, thanks. I'll come alone. Who you taking?"

Doug looked at me, then at Dris, and I felt suddenly a

strange taut feeling between them, an infinite patient wrath. Doug was never subtle—never one for secrets in the family. He grinned stalwartly at me and winked.

"I'm going to impress Dris by dictating million-dollar orders to his secretary."

"She must be pretty nice," I said, without thinking.

The Governor of the state bent like a couchant lion over the bar, looked at me and said without smiling, "You've met her, Davey. You remember Cathy Williams?"

I remained for dinner. Linda did not appear. Doug went to see that his boat was ready for the morning. I sat looking at Dris.

"I forgive you, you young fool," he said.

"I knew that, Dris."

"What else do you know?"

"You've grown to love it."

"What, Davey?"

"Politics. It no longer bothers you—rubs you. You like the bustle and bump of practical politics."

He rubbed his chin, looked down at the cloth and nodded. "I've been afraid of that for years. You can't fight, I used to think, you can't really begin to change things if you fall into the pit of admiration and desire for the sordid details of political life. But now I don't know. I don't know, Davey—I think I've changed my mind. The drive, the cunning words, the driving, taut moving of men against men— the feeling that you are doing things skillfully—it's got me."

"It gets everybody, I guess."

"Yes. Ward heelers and hangers-on, the smallest, the biggest. Yet the bottom of it all is low and evil. The whole thing is built now on the bosses and the machines getting out voters who don't care much for what happens."

"That's why you are scared of liking it?"

"No. I just admire more those men who like politics and remain honest to their hopes. Well, see you tomorrow on the ship. It's a big boat, I hear."

"Doug always liked size."

Dris wasn't listening. He asked me again if I remembered Cathy.

I said I remembered her faintly.

The sky was a sapphire sparkle over the docks.

Doug's boat lay tied up against the bulkhead at Coppard Basin. She was very long, very thin and gay-looking with polished masts and trim booms and much done over in teak-wood and bronze and polished brass. There was nothing about her that reminded me of Doug's sturdy steel cargo ships. *Sea Witch* was built for pleasure, for speed, and was a little too well cared for, a little too trim and neat, like those upper-class harlots I had seen in Lady Astor's circle in Mayfair during a trip to London. I didn't like her. She did not fit among the bronze sea-green hills near by.

A neat little man with blond mustache, dressed in white, met me at the gangplank with a sensual, dubious bow.

"How do, *sir?*"

"I am David Ormsbee. I'm expected on board."

"To be sure. May I show you to your cabin? When is your luggage due?"

I looked down at my frayed paint-dabbed pants, my French fisherman's shirt and my soiled canvas tennis shoes and shook my head. "I travel light."

The little man took a dislike to me. The deck crew were polishing brass, the most worthless work I ever saw. I turned to the little man.

"No one on board yet?"

"The Governor and the master are both a little delayed.

Shall I show you to your cabin?" He rubbed the amoral sleekness of flesh that was his flabby chin.

"Later."

I went forward and looked down river over the tired slant of overworked fields. The Jefferson was in flood—it passed, lipping against the white sides of the boat. Far-off brick barges shouldered their loads and a freight train picked its way across the lower railroad bridge. The smudge of steel furnaces and mills, like the ground of a good etching, gave tone and atmosphere to the day. I loved this river, the very smoke that soiled it. There was something good in a river that could still flow happily while men soiled it and sent their filth into it. It flowed on to the bay, cleaning itself and I hoped we would soon sail and reach the full blue belly of its cleaned depth. The pollen of a golden day danced on the ripples.

The sun went higher and the river was a finely organized painting—a well-colored, trustfully painted picture by—by someone like . . .

"Like Cezanne, isn't it?"

I turned to find Cathy Williams grinning at me. A sun-drenched Valkyrie and yet too cool for a Norse goddess.

"Yes," I said. "How did you know what I was thinking?"

She smiled and sat down on a deck chair. She was as solid and tall as ever—more the Greek goddess than the Norse.

If my brothers were coming to blows over her, I could understand why. She was a little too sure—too full of that hard animal wonder for me to love her. I was still the victim of the mystery of woman as seen secondhand through the fingers of painters who caressed a mystery both cerebral and physical into their flesh tones.

Cathy, in her neat white shorts and well-filled sweater, set off with blue cloth stars, was a realism I was yet to like.

Cathy grinned again. "I know you painters. Nothing exists but other painters. Your best girl is a Titian or a Matisse. Your home is a Picasso arrangement and even your food is a still life by some Paris tramp with a way with disorder. Come on, Davey, forget painting and enjoy the trip. Who said life is worth more than mere happiness? Never mind. It's a fine day ahead."

"If we ever start. You have left art in the lurch, I see, and have entered politics."

"Why not, Davey? Art is dead—smeared on linen by dreamy fools. Politics is full of the most suave harmonies. Oh, hell! Let's not get too worked up. Too nice a day. I suppose you want to know how I managed it—all this casual familiarity with your brothers?"

I shook my head. "No, I'd like to know how you're going to manage it from now on. I saw Dris and Doug almost leap at each other's throats when your name was brought up. Or does the erotic spectacle please you?"

Cathy frowned. "A fine how-do-you-do. What would *you* do?"

"I'm just a droopy little dreamer spoiling canvas—remember?"

The little blond man—he was the steward—a Cockney named Hayes—came cheerfully toward us with a perfectly neat servile smile.

"Everyone is coming on board. The Captain asks if you would care to join him in the chart room?"

Down river the waters cleared, grew blue. The boat pitched as we hit solid bay waters, and then the land on either side drew away and there was the sea. *Sea Witch* took it like a lady shivering in a shower, then settled down as Doug put the wheel over and ran along shore just outside the teeth of the rocks waiting to snap at a foolish stranger passing too close to their black kelp-covered teeth. Sea gulls gawed idiot repetitions; the sun boiled golden waves.

From the stern the sea foamed and sizzled and threw back a white wake and sea birds dipped low with guttural tones and floated a long time on silent, unmoving wings.

Linda sat back, wedged into cushions on a low deck chair. She looked too pale to expose to wind and sea and sun. I thought how like one of those creatures of Poe who never, never go outdoors and always live in candlelight. But then I rebelled against the thought. She was real and troubled—and I was a phlegmatic, literary dope.

She looked at me. "You still angry, Davey?"

"Over the drinking?"

"Yes."

"No, Linda. Frankly, it isn't the first time I've been blotto. I was a rather gay fool in Europe."

She smiled and probed me with a small shod foot. "Yes, the wolf of the Latin Quarter, I'm sure."

I looked at her pale face and her nervous hands. "You shouldn't have come, Linda. You need rest in bed."

"I had to, Davey. I'm afraid to stay home alone. I have the most ludicrously inappropriate ideas alone."

I looked out to sea. "You came because you thought Dris and Doug might come to blows."

"How did you know?" There was sharp anguish in her voice.

"Neither is being very subtle about it."

Linda and I sat, holding hands, watching the sea.

The freight ships were tossing their wide rumps high over the plunging waves and a whole family on a brick barge stood up and cheered as we passed, swift and white. Doug gave them two toots on the whistle.

"Strange thing," said Linda, rubbing my brown wrist, "I'm not worth anything to anyone. Yet here I am setting brother against brother and most likely breaking that bitch,

Cathy's, heart. And Davey, I *don't* mind it at all. I hope she suffers—*suffers*. I hope her insides turn to ground glass —that she can't sleep and takes drugs. Why am I so mean? I'm no good to Dris—to anyone. I'm not giving Dris a home or a family. That cold Boston slut could. And *how* she'd love to. How easy it would be to make them all happy—if I just stood up and walked off the boat and let the sea gulls sing their guttural Mass over me—and I floated, fish-bitten, in subterranean basements of the sea."

"That's just lousy prose, Linda, huh?"

"Davey, a Coppard doesn't kill herself. Brandy heart and all. I'm here to stay a while. You pity her, don't you—that Cathy—that archaic New England goddess?"

I shook my head. "I don't know. I don't think so. She's one of those strong people who bend horizons and force their will on the world. She has character and brains and great beauty—but she's too firm to pity, too sure of herself to feel sorry for. There is too much intense ambition in her."

Linda said, "She sounds like just the kind of wife Dris needs. Somebody to bow with him from public platforms— to feed unwashed Baltic ambassadors and serve tea to English lecturers—to bear him strong children in that tennis-playing body—to be a mate to a great man—perhaps the greatest political figure of our times."

"You're kidding, Linda. Dris is finished, once he cuts loose from Ned Wonderly."

"You think he will cut loose?"

"Yes. Dris has that tight mouth—firm and thin and hard to change. I saw him set it the other night against Ned Wonderly."

Overhead the bell began to ring. Doug stuck his head out the pilot-house window. His yachting cap was heavy linen and gold but it didn't fit him. He did not look like the millionaire owner of a yacht. He looked, as always, like a steel puddler dressed and uncomfortable outside his working clothes.

He waved a red flipper at us.

"Lunch time. Come on, I've got a tub of caviar on ice and a naked roast turkey bigger than Herbert Hoover."

Out of the corner of my eye I saw Cathy and Dris come up from below deck, both arguing very loudly over some wires that should have been sent to Washington. They looked like two people who had been writing letters—dull business letters—all morning. *Life is worth more than mere happiness*, Cathy had said, I remembered.

I ate too much lunch. I ate too much dinner. I saw too much sea. I lay down and slept for three hours. I awoke with a start and banged my head into the low chestnut rafter. I tripped over a Cafaiolo vase set in a rack.

It was very still. The motors hummed with a lowered pitch. Outside, the sea night was very wet and cold and dark. I screwed shut the porthole and held my head and had a drink of stale yellow water from the water cock. It was warm and tasted of rust. I gagged as if I had swallowed the sea teeming with slimy creeping life.

It was too far to the galley for the fresh ice water. My head ached, the rust-warm moisture rasped my throat. Doug had a water cooler packed in shaved ice in his cabin. I went down the shifting hall. The golden nimbus of little ceiling lights made shadows.

It was very still and I could hear the clatter of bronze bolts as the ship shifted and the creak of timbers as the sea twisted her. A ship is never really silent. Always she moans against the twisting seas—and the sound of the screw is like the deep alto of blackbirds. . . .

A thin thread of golden color flowed out from under

Doug's cabin door. Without thinking much about it, I opened the door and went in with a dull, sleepy nonchalance.

Doug, in the bottoms of red pyjamas, lay on the wall sofa, while Cathy, in some wispy sort of thin sleeping suit, stood over him with a tray of little sandwiches, feeding him and tickling his bare brown torso, which he took with enduring patience.

I stood very still. "I'm sleepwalking—just passing through to haunt the next cabin." It didn't sound amusing.

It was a stupid sort of wit at best, but I was too shocked, for all my moral wideness, to say anything more serious.

The two looked at me and Cathay set down the tray of sandwiches and licked her fingers. Doug chewed and looked at me without rising. He said, with a rising inflection:

"I *always* forgot to lock doors and Davey *always* opened them."

Cathy picked up a blue wool robe and put it on. "Sit down, Davey, before God sinks the ship with a lightning flash before your staring eyes."

I sat down. She put some sandwiches into my hand. Doug rolled over, got to his feet and found his pyjama top and elbowed his way into it with unrelenting hostile glances at me.

I chewed sandwiches and said nothing.

Cathy lit a cigarette and sat down on the sofa, licked a bit of tobacco off her tongue and said, "You're just the man we want to see, Davey. Doug wants me to sail to England with him."

I reached for a bottle of spring water and drank it all; wiped the wet beads from my chin and nodded. "That would be fine. Better than a lot of malignant secrecy going about."

"Fine, my foot," said Doug with cold venom. "She keeps telling me she's in love with Dris—what's so fine about *that?*"

"Are you going to England with Doug?" I asked.

"No," said Cathy. "I'm going to stick to Dris."

Doug ate more sandwiches. "But Dris will never leave Linda—you know that. He's an old auntie about life."

"Maybe," said Cathy. "Maybe he isn't like the rest of us. But I've got to stick. Maybe after Ned Wonderly cuts his throat I'll go with you to England, Doug. Be your girl—the way you want."

"No," said Doug, his anger rising, "I'm just as happy Davey walked in here when he did. You're not the kind of gal I want to take to England. You're as much of a Boy Scout as Dris is. You *don't* fool *me!* You've got the New England purity of body and soul as bad as he has. This little drama of walking in here tonight with a tray of food *might* have led you to my bed—but it didn't, my ice-cold virgin—so now clear out! I'm washed up with you. Go spend the rest of your life blowing Dris' nose!"

Cathy did not move. Her voice sounded very husky. "I guess you're right, Doug. I'm a cold-nosed Boston virgin and my morals are cut from tin and hurt me as much. Don't be angry. I tried—*didn't I?*—to be—what is it—a sport?"

I lost my thirst and hunger. I sat, arms folded, yawning. I was very sleepy suddenly and a little shocked.

Doug stood up in curt, arrogant dismissal and hunted for Scotch, drank some and didn't offer us any.

"All right, Cathy. I'm not angry any more. Hell, it could have been a lot of fun. We would have knocked holes into Europe and picked up enough loot to set every Boston uncle of yours back on his ears. But let it pass. I don't say what I do, how I do it, is right. It just suits me fine. I don't even offer the excuse that I was hit on the head by steel mill thugs and can't think proper and moral. The trouble is, I think too straight. Go on—go blow Dris' nose for him. I had hopes for him, but he's getting as noble as my cracked brother, Dennis."

We went out together. She did not weep.

TWENTY-THREE

I DIDN'T SLEEP too soundly the rest of the night. Somehow I had a feeling that I wasn't the only one who knew about the scene in Doug's cabin. Dris was up at dawn, prowling along the deck, scowling and smoking too many cigarettes. At breakfast he ate little, looking at Doug and Cathy and rattling the dishes. He left to see that Linda ate her breakfast in bed—but I felt there was going to be an explosion and even a little knocking of fists against angry faces. Perhaps greater damage.

It was the weather that saved us from something pretty ugly. It had been clear. With a tin plate sky of blue, a few lazy clouds scudding far down. Then, as we cleared the last bar to the open sea, *Sea Witch* heeled over, the wind caught her sails full on. She recovered. Doug had his hands full giving orders. We bore east with a course set at southeast. I watched Doug bite his lip at the charts, and he stood by to help with the wheel while the sailors moved the fluttering canvas.

A black squall came out suddenly from northeast. There was a jamming of new, untried gear and the jib and mainsail split with the sound of the world tearing apart. The barometer read 30.26 and Doug banged it with his fist. Below I could see Cathy and Linda staring up while the steward locked the portholes. There was an ominous pause. Immense storm-weathered sea came by.

We began to labor heavily and the mate came and said

she was leaking on the starboard side forward in the chain-plates. And through her new paint. A nagging warfare of waves began. Doug had all sail taken in, howled down to the engines for steady speed, and as the whole world of wind tore at us he said:

"Nothing to do but run for it—unless I turn around and head for the mouth of the bay."

"Will you?"

"She'll go over and never right again, maybe. Hell, I'll try it. Full speed."

It was a scene of something out of Turner with a sea you could not believe and a wind you could not breathe against. *Sea Witch* went slowly around. The grandfather of all waves hit us broadside. Boats, deck debris and all loose gear went over the side. But Doug had her now, pointing into the wind and while she took green water over the bow all the time, she kept pushing ahead to the stirring weed beds where the coastline should hold the bay mouth. It was all too sudden to have full fear grip us.

It was fearful hours until we got under land and the wind's force was broken. We made it with the water gaining on the pumps. I wondered what glory, romance and thrill anyone could get from the sea. It was cruel. Showed no mercy, gave little chance once it felt the upper hand. I was happy to see a yacht-club-landing.

Except for one other time, I never set foot on *Sea Witch* again. The wind blew and I saw a nebulous half-guessed horizon.

But the fight was gone from Doug's red face and Dris was busy helping Linda and so a fearful row was avoided. The storm had been some help after all.

Cathy avoided me on the way back to Antioch. She took another hired cab and traveled alone, saying we were too crowded.

Linda was very ill. We got her home and to bed and a good strong tot of rum did wonders for her white face. When she was asleep, snoring slightly from parted lips, Dris said he wanted to see me in his study. From his window I looked down at the monstrous sprawl of the storm-swept city.

I sat behind Dris' desk, watching him walk around his pale Bokhara rug. I suddenly knew I didn't know him at all. It is strange to grow up and live with a person, read of his exploits, and yet know nothing of the inner him—nothing of the deep and full thing that lives within him, nothing of all that stirs him and makes him tick. The Dris I knew was a surface creature. I knew his wife. His home. His public office. His ideas and his hopes. But the real, multicolored, cataleptic core of him—nothing.

Dris turned and looked at me, one eyebrow high.

"Well, mug—want a job with me?"

"What are you offering?"

"I need a private secretary."

"You're letting Cathy go?"

"You're a smart boy. And take that morbid fixity of an eye off me."

I said, "You are a fool."

Dris smiled weakly. "Getting pretty big for your breeches, aren't you? Know a lot about life now, don't you, Davey?"

"Enough."

"Want the job?"

"Yes. You might as well have me with you when Ned Wonderly sinks you."

"Think so?"

"Yes. If you pass those reform bills."

Dris nodded and walked around his rug again. Then he

stood over me, infinite apathy, confusion on his face. "You know I love Cathy Williams."

"She, too, thinks a lot of you."

"Damn."

"You both going to let it go at that?"

"Yes, Davey. I can't leave Linda and—there is something in me I can't force myself to do; certain low things. Oh, hell, Davey—I've *never* slept with any woman but Linda in my life!"

I looked down at the desk and picked up a paper knife. "You're impressing me with your rigorously observed moral etiquette. But what now?"

Dris didn't even look at me. "Some men—it doesn't matter to them. They have a naked philosophy of lust. Drunk and happy—it's all one. Any woman will do if she's pretty and laughs at their jokes and . . ."

"And if there's a bed handy."

"Yes. You know, there must be a lot of old Dennis in me. He's no freak. Some of the family heritage is in him— and in me. I'm as noble as he is about the wedding bed."

I said, "Too bad Doug doesn't have any of it. Your case looks like Desdemona strangling Othello for a change. I'm sorry, Dris, this is no place for my foul wit."

"How about you, mug?"

"Let's not talk about me. I'm not married and in love with another woman. All right, you've fired Cathy. You both must have been very noble about it and cried and said it was for the best and you would both wait for each other if it took a million years. Now what? A man must either rigorously believe in everything or nothing. Where does all this leave you?"

My brother sat down and rubbed his weary face. I saw suddenly that there was a lot of slack gray skin along his cheeks. His eyes were bloodshot. His hand shook. He wasn't as secure against calamity as I had thought.

"Now, Davey, we're going to put the bills through—and not think too much about what will happen. Don't think I'm a fool—but Linda is something I can't leave now, forget —get rid of. She's a part of everything I am. She hasn't failed me—I've failed her. Do you understand her—the innumerable, immense complexities of her being?"

I looked at Dris. "No, I don't. But you might as well know I've loved Linda since I put on my first pair of long pants. When it comes to it, I can be just as honorable a bastard as you are."

We looked at each other. My brother was no longer such a stranger. He took my arm and smiled.

"Davey, I'm counting on you!"

I was a lot of things the next few months.

The corporation and land reform bills were called the Norton-Burton Reform Measures. Dris had planned them, worded them, fought and sweated over them—but two dull, earnest, plodding members of the state legislature introduced them and pushed them while Dris called in old political warhorses and talked turkey to them and hinted of things to come if they failed the voters now. Blue Peter— now a lobbyist called Mr. Peter Blue—gave secret help.

Dris was mad, mad over this bill. He was up at dawn and I would sullenly dress in gym clothes, for I never took exercise, but I would watch Dris punch the bag, be rubbed down and eat a full breakfast. He always seemed to retain a complete public integrity even in gym drawers.

I would sip coffee and gag at the sight of food and then at eight-thirty we were at the capitol. Dris hammered away at messages, read all the mail I thought fit for him to see, called long distances. Then we moved over to the Governor's chambers. Little groups gathered in fine cigar-ash and planned battles in cloak rooms. Dris was everywhere. Patted, howling, scolding, showing a hard forefinger, waving a fist and lining up votes. He had a disciplinary manner and fearful invectives.

Lunch was eaten out of paper boxes. I watched a battery of stenos take down dictation in many little books. After lunch we would go to bars and secret drinking places and to political halls and there Dris would again pound away at his bills to indifferent political fools. And then to pep up the bill's stepfathers.

Mr. Norton was very fat and sweated, and Mr. Burton was thin and sneezed a lot. Afternoons we would sit in the Governor's office or sneak into the public galleries and hear Wonderly's tools denounce the bills. And I saw some of the honest men, joined by those in fear of their voters, defend Dris' ideas.

At dinner, newspaper publishers and D.A.R. girlies and Union leaders sat with us and we talked them softly into public backing of 6758B—the Norton-Burton Bills. Night was hell. Gambling halls, vegetarian meetings. Old Fire Laddies. All were pushed and prodded by Dris to support publicly, loudly, the measures.

Then at midnight the leaders on the floor would appear to sip whiskey and break good cigars together and talk over tomorrow's plans and Dris would put iron cores into them, throw them out at two in the morning. My head would feel like a tremendous detonation of rockets.

I would rub his aching back and feed him hot milk, and he would lie hugging the pillow and groaning. There is no archaic simplicity about passing a bill.

"I'm a damn fool—mug."

"Sure. Here, drink this while it's hot."

"I hate to think of tomorrow. Ned is winning the power lobby over to him. I've got to talk to Blue Peter in the morning."

"Here, drink this."

But he was asleep, moaning—his eyes shut. I pulled off the lights.

Mr. Peter Blue came to see us the next day, long before any of the other political fish were stirring into the dawning day. I was always happy to see Mr. Peter Blue. He had come far from the beer-garden and speakeasy days. He was older, more solid, more square—a figure out of a wood carver's shop. Roughly hewn in big square strokes as if by a sharp knife and never taken up again for a final, detailed finish. Dris called him a sweet barbarian from Ultima Thule.

He was a strong Ned Wonderly man, sat high in his meetings, was deep in his trust and was a lobbyist for the Polack and Hunky and hillbilly wards in the matter of old-age pensions, sick pay and other forms of meager social relief that Ned Wonderly permitted. Mr. Peter Blue admired Dris and sorrowed that he should be now battling Ned Wonderly.

Mr. Peter Blue mopped his square low brow and sighed as Dris shook his hand. He spoke in a confidential bull's voice.

"By damn, Dris, I think you one foolish sonofabitch. But I like you—I like you fine—like—like my own son—if I have any sons. You big damn fool. Why you fight Ned Wonderly? Why? You tell old Blue Peter?"

Dris looked at Peter and smiled. "I've told you twenty times, you old square-head and you never get it in that beery mind of yours. I asked you here to tell me what chance has my bill to pass?"

Peter Blue groaned. "Not a lousy chance—by damn—*not* one."

Dris looked at the solid man, right into his blue eyes. "And you'll not get any of the lobby boys to help me?"

"By Kee-rist, Dris, *not* one. Not a finger I lift for you now. I love you, Dris. Old Jake Fry, just before he die, he say to me, 'Keep an eye on Dris, Peter. Keep a good eye on him.' And by damn, I do. But I don't see no sense in this reform bill. Little people get land maybe from your bill— real estate sharks take it away. Corporations ever pay honest taxes, you think? They run away to lousy Delaware. Dris, you big fool—I crazy for you—love you—but no. I do nothing for you now."

"Now, Peter, let's not part enemies."

Peter Blue looked into his empty square derby hat. "We *never* enemies. I know your father and your old grandfather. By Jesus, that old bastard one fine fellow. And *don't* you forget it. Great big man and you, too, got plenty of his stuff, his brain."

"Thanks, Peter. We're still friends, then?"

Mr. Peter Blue stood up and looked at Dris. "You betcha. I always your friend. This bill business mean *nothing*. You take good beating and come back stronger than ever. People like you. And then, Dris—some day—some day I surprise you. By damn, I make you proud you got old friend like ignorant immigrant—like Blue Peter. You *see!*"

"I'm sure," said Dris, patting the square man on the back.

"This is *nothing*. Some day bigger thing come to block your path. Something national—you see—and then nothing stop me. My mother, my father—my daughters—nothing stop me from doing a big help for you. You see."

"Not even Ned Wonderly?" I asked, watching the exultation creep into the square face.

"Nothing. I tell you I God-damnedest fellow you ever

see when I want to do what I think is right. You betcha on that!"

They shook on it and Blue Peter, his old self, clapped his iron hat to his head with the sound of a clap of thunder and walked out. Dris watched the door close and then turned to me.

"Turn on the cold shower—ice cold. I was sort of banking on Blue Peter's help."

The day was spoiled. Dris wasn't helped by the shower, by breakfast, or by a fast walk. He ran ahead and I followed at a slower pace.

After three miles he gave up and we entered a little park and I sank down on a seat puffing and panting. Dris watched me, wiped his face and grinned.

"Davey, this is doing you more good than it is me."

"I'll thank you some other time."

We sat smoking. Dris looked at his cigarette, tossed it away and turned to me.

"You know what's the matter with me? I'll tell you. I hate to be beaten. That's one of the things wrong with me. Some men take beatings and go on. I'm a poor sport. I like to win."

"Is that bad?"

"Of course it is. A man should take defeat with a certain amount of grace. I don't. Winning is very important. It always was. Even when it was only trying to get a new washroom at the capitol or voting on the color of car plates. But this thing I'm behind now—it's big—it's important—and I'm the world's worst loser about it. That's the flaw in me, Davey—one among many. I'm just common Ormsbee clay. Hell, I better get out of politics and run a bowling alley."

"You might like it."

Dris stood up. "Come on, we'll run back. I've got a few tricks to pull out of a hat."

"Let's walk back."

"No time to walk. Run, you mug."

We ran. . . .

The history of the Norton-Burton Bills is the history of Driscoll Ormsbee discovering his political maturity. I saw the bills gather force. I saw them almost sink from sight. I saw the tactics of those who attempted to kill them. I remember no mellow reminiscences of those times.

It was not a dull period. It was hidden behind the loud voices of the political hog-callers, dirty politics yammering of Home and Democracy and Freedom and Old Glory. It was a serious moment in the career of Dris. The world of the early Thirties was moving and I saw the fearful mess the world had made begin to frighten certain people. People like Dris, Gramp, Cabot Carson and—yes, Cathy Williams.

I was walking down the halls of the state capitol building and while passing an open fumed-oak door, I heard her voice on a phone. I went in and found her bent over a typewriter. She looked as healthy and bold as ever, that solemn immobility of features still there.

"Hello, Davey. Shut the door and sit down."

I did. She hung up the phone and put paper into her machine and began to pound the keys with those long, rhythmic fingers of hers.

"What are you doing here, Cathy?"

She stopped typing, pulled the sheet of paper from the machine, made a ball of it and tossed it on the floor. "I'm doing publicity for the Norton-Burton Bills. Norton got me some sort of public functionary's clerk's job—but I'm really sending out press releases on the bills."

"Dris know you're back?"

"Yes. We're all fighting hard for these bills. Even you, I see."

"Sure."

She looked at me and grinned that puissant, goddess grin of hers. She laid her head down on her firm brown arms and stuck her tongue out at me. "*That* for your dislike for me, Davey. I wanted to stay away. But—well, if this beats Dris, I wanted to be around."

"Any chances of winning?"

"Rather good. The state is behind Dris and the politicians are too smart to pull anything raw enough that he can expose. The machine boys are scared, too. Dris is giving out names and districts and how every man votes and if they go against these bills they will be afraid to go home. Blue Peter is wrong, I tell you."

"What then?" I asked.

"Then *what?*"

I looked at her. "After the bills are passed. What happens to you?"

"I could go to Palm Beach with Doug—in his boat. He's asked me again."

"It's a very society town there. You'd like it."

"Maybe. Let's wait until the bills are voted on before planning anything."

I looked at her and went out. I certainly didn't want to talk to her about her morals.

Dris was showing the strain. I got him away from a citizens' meeting and bundled him into a car and drove out along a country road. The wheat was high and heavy-headed, young calves ate green grass and the hills seemed always to follow us and never fall behind.

Dris sat beside me and I drove along, stirring up a long column of dust behind. A state patrol car followed us, ready to arrest us, I suppose. But they saw Dris beside me and waved and fell back.

Dris looked at me. "Is this a snatch?"

"We've been hitting a hard pace."

"I'll get them to vote on it soon or bust their fat heads."

I pushed the gas down a little farther. "Hungry?"

"As a matter of fact, I haven't thought about it. I could eat something."

I nodded. "Fine. Remember, Dris, the first big meal we had together at Ned Wonderly's headquarters? Steak and fried potatoes and fresh rolls and coffee in silver pots—and the black boy giving us eighteen-carat service?"

"Sure, mug—and the fingerbowls. I will never forget the horror on your face at all the lewd luxury."

"Well, I'm taking you to a place I found. A farmer runs it—hangs his own steaks for six months in a cold cellar—then brushes the mold off them and rubs them with salt and garlic and puts them over a charcoal fire."

"Sounds like a dream," said Dris, smiling.

"You'll see."

The road fell away and crossed a white bridge, the old Campbellite church pointed its finger at God, and then there was a series of waterfalls and woolen mills grinding their looms, then sheep and beef herds and soon many oaks and at last the brown frame house and the neon sign: STEAK . . .

Dris got out first and sniffed the air full of the odor of meat on coal. Feathered striplings of elms were on all sides.

"Think they have any left, Davey?"

"Plenty."

We went in and found out. We had two huge cuts of top sirloin and we ate like old times, chewing the meat in grinding mouthfuls—pouring down cider, cold and strong, and then buttering the white wheat rolls and adding the fried onion rings and attacking with sharp knives the rest of the yielding beef. We ate a long time and by the time it was night we could only grin across the table at each other and sip coffee and moan with pleasure in imbecilic catarrhal tones.

"Davey, it's the first real meal I've had in months. Once this bill is through, I'm going to buy a trailer and a sharp axe and load Linda and a side of beef into it and cut my way up to the top of Gramp's Range. No car has ever been up there—but I'll make it."

I looked at Dris. "*If* this bill goes through, it will not be Gramp's Range any more."

Dris grew serious and rubbed bread crumbs together. "It isn't, anyway—the mine people have injunctions out to seize the land—got a lot of condemnation proceedings through. Claim they need it for mine timber and slag piles. They have a lot of old land grants bought up some place for title too. This bill has to pass. At least the homesteaders will get Gramp's Range instead of the mine people."

"Gramp doesn't seem to mind. He'll get a pretty good amount from the state for it. Only Cap Roc doesn't like it. He's threatened to shoot *anybody* trying to take over title to the Range."

"Davey, I don't know what to do with Cap Roc. Gramp can't take care of him any more. And I can't put him away. It would break Gramp's heart. But we'll think of that later, Davey. I want you to go back to Antioch—and watch Ned Wonderly's boys. Ned is too smart to show his face at the capital, but I hear a lot of the officeholders are going down to Antioch to get orders from him. Get a bunch of the old gang you can trust and report to me who the backsliders are. I'll scare the daylights out of them."

"That all?"

"That's all, Davey. This is my swan song."

"You could run *again* for Governor."

"I don't want it again. I might get the popular vote once more—this time—but why fool myself? I'm a political corpse."

"Why not run for the United States Senate?"

"We just elected old Ironman Connors again. He's in for a full term. By the time Senate elections come around again, I'll be a dead and forgotten pigeon. No—when my term of office is over in three months, I'll just retire and collect postage stamps. I'm a has-been. Like a winter moth, I shall fall ponderously athwart the cold earth and stay there."

The torn and tattered steak bone looked up at me and then I looked up at Dris.

"I'll take you back and start for Antioch at once. You sound like a teacup reader in a gypsy lunchroom."

It was after eleven the next morning that I got home to my father's house. Vicky was standing at her claptrap garages, arguing with a fat little man leaning against a fliv-ver. She won some sort of verbal victory—the fat man handed her green bills and Vicky came toward me as alert and alive as ever.

"Hello, Davey. You got here just in time. That no-account Wop thinks I'm running a bootleg hideout and has been storing bottles in my garages."

"Did you make him move?"

"No. I raised his rent three dollars a month. They are *only* wine bottles, and Pete and I like a sip of wine. How's Dris?"

"Very busy. We're getting this bill in order for passing, and it's hell on wheels. I've got to get some of the boys to-gether and do some work here. But I'll go see Linda first."

Vicky looked up at me and pursed her small lips. "Well, all right. But promise me you'll not tell Dris how she is."

"What's up?"

"She had a sort of stroke. Oh, nothing much—Doctor Watson told me. But Linda made us all promise we'd keep our mouths shut. She doesn't want Dris to leave the capital now when the bill is so important."

"Was it a serious stroke?"

"Well, no. She's still drinking."

TWENTY-FOUR

LINDA LAY in sunlight that cut diagonally across the bed, and looked up at me. I smiled and held her hand and felt very foolish and more than a little sad. It was a time in me of fevers burning, of great things about to be done: such painting to make and thoughts to think. I was dust, I felt—left here to spin my short time—and I had dreams to catch and put down forever on small walls. And I stood here holding a small, lovely, drunken hand, mixed to the hilt in some political ballet, mired by some crackpot scheme—tossed about for votes and plans of little men in fat-bellied power. *What the hell was all this to me when I could be painting?* I felt intellectual self-indulgence.

"You're frowning, Davey."

"Was I? I was lathering my soul in self-pity."

"You look so cute when you frown."

"Don't you think we ought to let Dris know that you're not feeling well?"

"I feel fine—or about as fine as I always feel. No—this is big stuff to Dris. His time and place. Let him win. It's his finish too, Davey."

"He knows it, Linda."

I sat and smiled down again at her—such a small body—pathetically small—in the big bed and all the pink and old-gold odors too much for me—dusty, sweaty, in my traveling clothes. The door opened. Doug came in. He looked at me and made some sort of greeting to Linda, and I went out after him into the hall, the cream-scented humidity of her body still in my head.

The great shipping king looked worried. He ate a cigar and tossed the fragments of it on the floor. His glance held me ominously rigid.

"There is hell to pay at Gramp's place on the Range."

"Fire?"

"Worse. The mine lawyers got wind of how hard Dris is working to pass his bills. They jumped the gun and went in with writs and injunctions and their fake land claims to take over with a sheriff's group."

"What happened?"

"Cap Roc was up there with some field hands, cutting hay. Cap went raving mad—stinking mad—went right off his nut."

"Hurt anyone?"

"Killed three deputies with a sawed-off shotgun and blew most of the stomach out of the fourth. Then he packed up all of Gramp's guns and gear—loaded up a pack horse and took to high timber with half the town bums after him with their deer rifles."

"We've got to stop them. Cap isn't normal—we've got to get him down from those hills and safe in an asylum."

Doug nodded. I could see the sweat and talcum powder on his jowls. "I'm pickin' up Gramp and we're going to try and lure him to safety before the mob tears him apart."

"Isn't Gramp a little too old for the trip?"

Doug threw away his cigar and started on a new one with physical distrust. "I know, but Gramp is raising hell and ready to *walk* up to the Range. So come on. You know the trails and can save Gramp a lot of extra hiking."

"How will this affect Dris' plans?"

Doug grinned like an imbecile child and held his cigar in his usual grip—like a hammer—and waved it at me. "This will just *about* pass those bills! It was the last master stroke needed to hoist them into place. The whole nation is aroused at these killings brought on by the lousy mine-grabbers. But I don't want Cap Roc to cap this climax by losing his hide."

The land rose as usual, and the big car moved, upward and forward. Gramp sat between us, the pale red eye of his pipe glowing excitedly in the dark interior of the car. He seemed neither pleased nor annoyed. His limp, useless arms lay folded in his lap and his pipe bubbled. The car moved upward over jarring ruts. Doug and I sheltered Gramp from the worst pounding of the drive. He sat like a proud serene Lucifer, fire smoking in his beard.

We had said little since starting. The whole nation was foaming at the mouth. Reporters and cameramen were moving in, and the connections of these murders and Dris' reform bills were smeared in cheap ink across the worst pulp paper. The melancholy stupidity of a foul, smearing press was in full cry.

All the sheriff's relatives were forming posses and swearing in deputies—state troopers were breaking out tear-gas bombs and mooing hounds tugged on leather leads, ready to take up the hunt. It was a sort of sporting stack. A hunt for man—better than tearing open a mangy fox or standing in muck blasting wild ducks apart with steel balls.

Gramp's house rose before us, and after a close examination by men with tin stars we passed on—brushing clinging journalistic lice from the running board of the car.

The sun was very high and the land was checkered with cultivation. The car stopped and we helped Gramp out. On the lawn lay three torn shapes, among which blue-steel flies buzzed and sang as they gathered in black-streaked puddles in the grass. Men were taking pictures of the bodies. The bodies were nothing—just torn meat, rags drained of their red fluid, waiting for someone to hide them in the earth. But the cameramen were busy taking angle shots of these things lying among drifting dandelion seeds.

The flies buzzed and sang among the soiled grass roots.

It had started at dawn, we found out. The living deputy with the torn stomach told them about it between shots of drugs into his tattered gut muscles. The big lawyers had hired three of them at ten dollars each to serve the papers on Cap Roc and a little lawyer came along. The sheriff was to wait at his phone and if Cap resisted, he was to appear with a squad of state troopers and beat him to a pulp and toss him off the land.

The four bloody fools, happy over this easy money, had stopped on the way up and filled up on beer, played a few tunes on the juke-boxes and had arrived at nine-forty in front of Gramp's house. The field hands had breakfasted and gone to the fields. Cap was worming a fox hound puppy when the men opened the door and the little lawyer threw the legal papers at his feet. Cap stood very still for a moment and made no formal acknowledgment. Then he picked up the sick puppy and turned and placed it in the wood basket by the fireplace. This done, he swooped down, pulled up a short, sawed-off shotgun lying among the hickory fire logs and, firing without aiming, blew off the head of Pinky Fadiman, the little lawyer, at the close range of three feet.

The three remaining deputies fell back. Brick Benet reached for his service pistol, and the other barrel of Cap's shotgun took him in the ribs, opening him up like a barbecued side of steer. Cap dropped to one knee, calm, hard and precise, pulled with his teeth at his jacket pocket and swiftly loaded two new shells into the smoking barrel of his shotgun. It all took four seconds from the time he put down the puppy.

The two unwounded men grabbed the screaming Benet and dragged him out of the house. Thought failed them. They started across the lawn toward their car. Firing from a smashed window, Cap finished off Benet, the slugs catching him in the buttocks and spreading out to mess up his torso. The two men dropped the butchered shape and Chuck Garnett suddenly alert and thinking again turned back to fire at Cap. He never had a chance. Cap was a dead shot, and a shotgun with its barrels sawed down can't miss. Garnett went down with a red spray replacing his throat, and Cap ran out as Chick Morley, the last of the deputies, indulged completely in blubbering fear and opened the car door. Cap dropped to one knee at fifteen feet and Chick—as one field hand later said—shouted:

"Christ, Cap—*please* don't!"

Chick turned away from the car, opened his arms wide and walked slowly toward the kneeling man, shouting pleas of leniency.

"Cap, listen. You know Hazel and the kids—*don't!*"

The shots caught Chick under the breastbone and removed almost all of his inner man. He died twelve hours later in fearful agony, begging Cap to think of Hazel and the kids.

The field hands did not dare approach too close to the house. Cap walked around the bodies, sniffing, his shotgun ready. Then he turned back to the house, beating his head with his fist, and came out again, tossing the first man killed among the rest of his friends. Chick lay very still. He was unconscious, bleeding gouts. But Cap paid him no attention, his scorbutic visage twitching.

One of the field hands, a colored man, started across the fields to phone for the police. Cap went into the house and got him from an upper window at a hundred yards with a Remington. Right through both thighs. The colored man fell down and lay there. He wasn't badly hit. But from them on he lumbered awkwardly the rest of his life.

After that the field hands stood beyond the pasture gate, not daring to move, holding whispering conclave among themselves.

Cap appeared in the open at eleven, loaded with guns and bullet belts and many packs. He caught a pack horse, mounted Comet, the black stallion he always rode, and galloped off, shouting something the field hands couldn't make out. The sun went higher.

Chick had recovered consciousness and began to scream, but the field hands were too frightened to come near him until Cap was out of sight on the upper trail.

The sun stood at high noon, a blazing ball balanced in the hot brass heat of the day, as we stood on the soiled grass looking down at the bodies. Men stood tactfully anxious, throwing glances over their shoulders at the hills.

Gramp, his helpless arms by his side, looked away from the huddled, broken shapes and he, too, eyed the ridges which men were now climbing, their rifles held carefully before them, the dogs sniffing the ferns and pine needles. The great manhunt was under way. High in the hot sun an airplane rested on blue wings, as it watched the thickets and the silver ribbons of the brook.

But Cap Roc—mad, murderous and evil—was a cunning creature of this Range world. No one caught any sign of him until four o'clock. He had ridden up Big Bend Brook, swam his cattle across the sandy shallows of Big Pine. At four, his black stallion spitting foam and his pack horse, its poor ribs collapsing from the hard traveling, pulled into Pine House, a hotel not yet opened for the season.

The caretaker, an old Swiss with a twisted nose and slight limp, gave Cap Roc water and fed his horses and brought him a side of bacon from the spring house. All would have been well, but the Swiss was oily with greed and insolent assurance, and had heard of the hunt over his small radio. Cap Roc, sitting on the hotel porch changing his work shoes for hunting boots found in the hotel, heard the tinkle the old-fashioned phone made as the Swiss ground it into life.

It was a foolish gesture. Cap howled derisively, pushed the barrel of Gramp's best army Springfield through the window and drilled the Swiss just below his ear. He lived for two hours until a posse found him and gave him whiskey. He told his sordid story and died claiming the reward in an avid voice. Cap was miles away. Clanging up and up toward the tall firs.

The reward was not official until six. Then the mine people offered five thousand dollars, *Dead or Alive*.

Cap lost his head as darkness fell. He circled back down trail and hunted a blacksmith. The stallion had cast a shoe. Ben North at Black Corner fitted a new shoe and took two silver dollars for it, but he didn't say a word to Cap and Cap said nothing to him. Cap knew Ben knew. His mad eyes almost dared him to comment on it; standing at the bellows, puffing like a sulphurous demon.

Ben said nothing. Cap moved on. In the four days of the manhunt, Ben North was the only man Cap could have killed or mangled whom he spared. Fierce, indomitable, some mysterious potent poison seemed to flood Cap's body to blood heat lust to kill.

A band of slaughterhouse workers armed with skinning knives and revolvers heard the sound of horses crossing the wooden bridge below the Coppard Power Company water station and hurried forward. A blast of buckshot stopped them. They fell into the dust, bleeding from small hurts, but none were very much harmed.

That was the last anyone saw of Cap Roc that night—Monday.

Gramp and Doug and I went along with the sheriff's car until Rock Point. There we left the car and camped out in a farmer's hay shelter on the peak of Rock Point where the early hill hay was stored.

We lay in the hay, cuddled cozily but shivering, listening, but heard nothing but cars arriving below, the ballet of hunting feet and the bark of dogs. I slept, Gramp bunched up against me, and twice I awoke and felt Gramp stir in his sleep, muttering something I could not understand. Once I went out and got him a drink of well water in a rusting tin dipper. The sky was excessively chaste, the water, ice cold.

It was very still. The hunt slept, the wind whispered in the tall firs, and there was no moon—only a milk-white mist over the sharp crags. Somewhere Cap Roc watched or snored.

Dawn was wet, inscrutable, tense. Then the sun came and burned the day into life. It etched the great hunt all around us. The hills were full of men. Deer hunters, sadists, nosy parkers, fools, thrill-seekers—patchpants journalists, hangers-on, revenging relatives, scowling fresh-made orphans. We heard that Chick Morley, the last man shot at Gramp's place, had died. The county was offering another five-thousand-dollar reward. The National Guard was asking if any help was needed. Boy Scouts had been posted with signal flags on certain ridges. All for one mad, contemptuous misanthrope bearing death.

It was a ghastly thing to see how eager all the people

were to hunt man. We ate with many others, thick bread and butter, bacon and fried eggs and strong coffee.

Doug's beard was black on his face. He ate huge mouthfuls and watched me while I held Gramp's coffee cup and the old man sipped. Doug picked up another wedge of bread and looked about him into the dark, cumbersome woods.

"Damn goons, look at them. You'd think they were going to get free candy instead of their heads shot off."

Gramp nodded as I wiped his beard. "Cap is a dead shot. Can hit a dime at two hundred yards if he took the telescope attachment with him."

I said, looking up at the soft russet, pink and gray hills, "Think they'll get him alive?"

Gramp blew air through his beard. "Cap isn't alive. Hasn't been since they put those silver bands on his cracked skull. He's just been going through the motions of living, madly."

Tuesday passed. We went higher into the rosy-gold and indigo silhouette of the mountains, walking now, alert and watchful of all dark clearings. Gramp kept up fine. Doug and I helped him some, hooking our arms under his. The hours passed with not a sight of Cap Roc that day. The sunset was like the Day of Judgment. We were very high —almost up to the last tall pine. Above were enormous cavernous socketed stones.

The signal flags stirred across the crags at dawn. The cadaver of the black stallion had been found at Devil Ridge, his fractured leg doubled back. Cap had shot the horse and gone on, leading the pack animal.

Wednesday was the posse's lucky day. Cap was too high to find any level streams to wade. The dogs picked up his scent and followed him, their wet noses protruding bleakly, their throats rasping.

Ahead I heard the howl and the puzzled shouting of the dogs. Then suddenly four shots, close together, like chain thunder. We moved forward. The dogs talked together no more.

The trail dipped here and went down about fifty feet before it rose again between huge rocks shaped like broken stars. I could see the dip and then the bodies of the dogs lying on the trail. A furiously angry man with a welter of dog gear ran forward, cursing his loss, and then something snapped and the dog-lover lay in the trail, his thigh shattered. A sickness and lassitude churned in my stomach.

We moved down behind a ridge of small stones.

The fat sheriff rubbed his swollen neck glands and shouted from his red face in exasperated tones:

"Come on, Cap. You *ain't* got a chance."

An echo answered. The dog-lover moaned and rolled about in agony. The sheriff shouted again, perplexed, violently earnest.

"You ain't got a chance, Cap!"

Suddenly overhead a small voice, derisive and cold, said, "I'll count three. *Then* I'll shoot."

We looked up. Balanced on an overhanging rock lay Cap Roc, his bare, red skull hatless, his hands holding the Springfield aimed at the sheriff's body. For the first time I saw the pack horse lying dead in a thicket.

Gramp stood up and walked forward to where the dog-lover still moaned. I watched Cap Roc's mad little eyes take in the thin, bent figure. Gramp was very calm, austerely classic and grave—not hurrying, just moving slowly forward.

"Come down, Cap. It isn't any use—all this."

"Don't worry, Gramp," said Cap kindly, taking a long,

tremulous breath. "I'll get every last one. I never miss. You know that."

"Come down, Cap," said Gramp kindly. "It's all right. They know you aren't right in the head. They'll not hurt you. They'll . . ."

There was a short, sharp bark of the Springfield. The sheriff had moved forward very skillfully for such a big man and had been trying to flank Cap by climbing a higher rock. Cap had turned and fired, and almost before the sound of the shot had stopped resounding from the rocks, the big body of the sheriff fell at our feet and seemed to collapse like a clown's bladder.

There was a small hole over the sheriff's right eye—and a blue foam came from it. No blood. The sheriff's other eye was open and he was staring into the direct rays of the sun.

He was obviously very dead.

After an hour we went forward and picked up the dog-lover. His thighbone stuck out of his flesh like a fragment of a white comb, but he was still alive.

Cap killed two more dogs that day and blew the arm off a colored man who refused to come along with him into the high rocks and cook for him. Cap hated tenacity or stubbornness in other people.

That night it was very cold. Gramp and I slept wrapped in many blankets. But still we shivered. We lay close together in the open, not speaking. Then when the full darkness came, we lay listening to the great clatter of the growing hunt. Flares dotted the mountainside. Big fires burned—and someone rigged a loudspeaker and gave many orders until a slug came out of the darkness and shattered the big voice of tin and wires. Then the hunt slept. But there were so many dogs now that sleep came only in snatches.

Morning was a white mist. I could not see a foot ahead

of me. The white world of blindness echoed with clashing men and clattering gear but no one stirred from their camps to try the almost sheer walls of the Devil's Castle in the white soup. The hunt waited that day.

I combed Gramp's beard.

TWENTY-FIVE

Cap Roc killed his last man on Thursday.

All day on foot he had been creeping deeper and deeper into the wild rocklands, climbing almost three thousand feet by two o'clock in the afternoon. The hunters, with insatiable desire, followed him. He was near the snow line now and the hunters sent back for coats. Cap had cut himself down to only what he could carry and travel with. He had discarded all guns but the army Springfield. He had a blanket, a coffee pot, a side of meat and perhaps a canteen of water. The trails of hunted and hunters paralleled each other almost indefinitely.

Gramp refused to be left behind. Wrapped in wolf pelts, carried by four men, he went on, Doug and myself assisting. Gramp's tenacity and stubbornness were almost like Cap's.

The hunt was deadly now. Men slipped and cursed but no longer talked too much. There was an acid, sweaty scent about the men, an almost distilled odor of hate and fear and desire to kill coming from their skins. Their tongues coated, their eyeballs were yellow and they drank raw whiskey and tore food, gulped, swallowed and went on. A grim, miscellaneous mob of hunters.

Devil's Castle was a sheer wall. It leaped up—and no one living had ever climbed it. Beyond it lay lush, rolling hills leading to great forests, spinning streams and such broken twisting ways that once over the Castle, Cap Roc would be safe. Word was shouted down to send men up from the other side—but it appeared that the hunt was lost.

At four, across a thousand feet of space, the tiny figure of Cap Roc could be seen moving slowly up the steep face of the Castle. A small dark blot on the nacreous silver and iridescent color of the rocks . . .

Through strong glasses he appeared, a rifle and bag hanging from him as he picked his way by toe and fingers up, up along a wall of terror.

The day would be dying soon—the blue ice fields reflected from the steep mountains to the north chilled the air. Shadows walked quickly to blot out the remaining light. A great, phosphorescent sea of twilight began to annihilate the day.

The hunters fired—but the Castle was out of range. It was almost deep dusk when they got into range. But, finding a level crack, Cap ran ahead, bent over, running fast and, soon again, was out of range—and almost free. Only three hundred feet stood between him and freedom.

A party of hunters started across an ice field to flank the Castle in a last hope of destroying the madman. There was a sense of taut hope and a sense of impending calamity in conflict.

Gramp was done in. The high air, the full throat-stabbing struggle to keep moving, were too much for him. I went on ahead with the flanking party, hoping that at least I could get a word to Cap. He had been fond of me as a child. Perhaps I could bring him alive from this bizarre incoherent situation.

We moved slowly, slipping on the ice. Then descended and turned around and went creeping along. The last faint tone of the sun still touched the top of the Castle. We could see Cap closer now—steadily climbing like a human fly, up, up, across a face of stone—the hardest patch he had struck yet. But always moving. At times the wall seemed to over-hang him—force him out into space until he hung only by his fingers, his heels kicking free. Always he found some-thing to touch, to haul himself in to safety and go on climb-ing. The high place gave me a gagging feeling of boisterous, headachy intoxication.

Through glasses I could see his red face. It was no longer mad. No longer angry. He was smiling. Enjoying the hunt. And slowly climbing.

Then he saw us—about two hundred feet from him, sepa-rated by a broken field of great stones. The hunters were panting, too breath-broken to steady their rifles and aim well. Some fired and missed, knocking off stone shards above Cap's head. Gramp shouted below. I listened to the echoes of the walloping dactylic meter of his voice.

Cap took it calmly. I never took the glasses away from him. He found a projecting stone, tested it with his weight, found it holding, tossed his legs in a grip around it and pulled the Springfield from his shoulders. He aimed.

The light was bad. We stood somewhat protected by broken stone. Cap leveled off again and I saw his teeth snap together as he pressed the trigger. Behind me someone made a little thudding sound, diabolically wicked. A body rolled past me and, still rolling harmlessly, as if a ball in a child's game, bumped from stone to stone and fell away into dark-ness with absurdly simple ease.

Cap aimed again. For the first time on the hunt, he missed. I saw him in the gathering darkness shift his position, twist his legs in a new hold. Then the rifle barrel banged against the granite wall and fell from his red hand. He made one lunge to recover it, failed, the Springfield fell swiftly away from him. He was unarmed. He laughed. Simian mirth came from his big throat.

I stood up and waved my arm.

"Cap! Cap! It's Davey! Davey Ormsbee! It's all right! Gramp is here."

His voice floated across to us, malignantly hostile.

"Go to hell, Davey."

"Cap, listen!"

Behind me the hunters were firing now—their gun barrels held steady against the big stones. I tried to stop them and was shoved aside. I picked up the glasses again. It was hard to focus in the fast-oncoming darkness.

The shots were coming closer. The last shred of day left the granite wall. Darkness confused the hunters. It looked as if Cap had made it. He was fifty feet from the top of the wall. The way was the hardest yet—but Cap moved on, very sure he could top the sharp wall.

At ten feet from the top, the going was very easy, broken up into huge cracks. Cap pulled himself erect and thumbed his fingers to his nose. Behind me they were still firing, blindly, the slugs making plaintive musical sounds.

Cap wriggled his fingers. Three rifles cracked together. Cap staggered—fell—recovered. Bent way over as if very ill. Then he began to walk up the cliff. He stopped, slowly turned—fell to his knees and began to fall.

He held tight in a truculent attitude to a projecting stone. Then calmly he pulled himself erect and leaped forward into space!

I saw the body fall in a long, graceful arc.

It took a long time falling. We just stood and watched. When it had fallen halfway, complete darkness swallowed it.

Someone below was firing shots in celebration.

They found him later in the light of pitch flares, lying in a stream bed. He was not damaged much. The skin was torn from his mad skull. Two small, red holes spoiled his wide, red torso. He looked very calm. When they brought him down, Gramp looked at him and said:

"Poor Cap. He only served in his loyal madness what he believed was right. He was a good man. A fine creature— once."

"He never had a chance," said Doug. "Poor bastard, they almost called in the whole United States Army to hunt him down."

A newspaperman drinking raw corn whiskey shook his head. "Once over that cliff and he could have held out for months in those badlands. Well, he got his just in time to make the bulldog edition."

We went on to a farmhouse halfway up the mountain. It was too dark to try and descend. The sheep farmer's phone had buzzed down its news, and now we sat around Cap's body, with its covering of feed sacks, drinking raw liquor. A fire burned among the stones of the fireplace. Men rubbed their brushed heels and counted their toes. We could hear the cows outside squeechily forming cuds in steadily chewing jaws.

The climax seemed to have left us all very feeble and weak. Only Gramp, smoking his pipe and watching the rag-covered corpse of his servant, seemed to have purpose and character in the flickering light. At fixed recurrent intervals, he sucked his pipe into fire. A reporter hung up the phone and came and sat down.

"Well, Cap didn't die causeless. His going wacky against the mine owners got action at the state capitol, anyway."

Doug stirred the fire and asked apprehensively, "What happened?"

The reporter bummed a cigarette and looked out at the rare, absolute black of deep night. "The state legislature called a sudden unexpected session and after hearing in outraged dignity of the tragedy caused by the mine interests trying to beat the law, passed the Norton-Burton Bills. With fifty votes to spare . . ."

Gramp gripped his pipe in his thin mouth and grinned. "Well—that makes me a bigger pauper than ever. I guess I don't mind."

We didn't go down with the hunters and their lump of meat in the morning. Gramp was suddenly very tired. We took our time reaching the spot where we had left the car. The imbecile rapture seemed to have left the posses. The thrill of licensed manhunting was over. They spoke of Cap as a great guy.

We rode back to the city saying very little. There was little we could say to each other. At my father's house, we found Dris. He looked tired and worn. He had traveled all night after seeing the bills passed. He had signed them and started for Antioch at once. He did not look very happy over his new hypothetical better world.

Vicky and Pete sat and looked at Dris. When we arrived, Dris came toward us, his voice still under control but blurred at the edges into the relative tranquillity it took on when he was very tired.

"Terrible thing to happen to Cap."

Gramp looked at him, seemed to look into the heart of his grandson. Then he lowered his head.

"Dris—Dris, we haven't been as close as we once were. This thing wasn't your doing—they've been after my land for years. Dris—it's better the homesteaders should have it. Dris—I want to shake hands with you—but can't. . . ."

Dris stood very still and then he smiled. His hand came down and lifted one of Gramp's dead hands, he looked at the thin, pale wrist, lifted it to his mouth, kissed it—then hugged the old man to him.

[333]

Vicky sniffed and looked proudly about her. She wiped her tiny nose.

"It's a picture, *isn't* it?"

The Norton-Burton Bills were law. There was, of course, at once the usual test case brought forth by prepared leering lawyers to take before the Supreme Court—but Dris had planned well and knew all the tormented phrases of legal bickering. The laws held water and were hard to spoil. The lawyers brought out loggy, legal erotica as evidence. The laws held.

Corporation and land reforms began—and the courts slowly but firmly backed them up. The lawyers howled and spoke of doom. Dris had won his fight. In three months his term as Governor of the state expired. He came home and took Linda on a West Indies trip. What he was going to do now, I did not know. He was deep in middle age—still as firm and solid as ever. There was gray in his close-cropped hair. But he looked as handsome and firm as ever. And no one—not even his family—could claim an excessive intimacy with him.

He had offers to go into law firms—head corporations—serve on interstate committees. He accepted none of them. He went away with Linda on a white ship and with a package of novels by Smollett and Frank Norris and Balzac that I had picked out for him and which most likely he never read. He liked history and was in the habit of quoting Gibbon.

I was free again. I hadn't cared much for my work with Dris. I am not of the stuff of which faithful public servants are made. I was between painting sprees and looking for interesting dimensions to multiply. There had been a show in one of the Fifty-seventh Street art galleries. The art critics had said all the wrong things about my work—finding in it merit I didn't have, and damning with foul and high-browed praise its faults as virtues. I was fed up with the tremulo-throated gentry of the art world, the Westchester social queens leering sexually at the artists, the Hollywood gallery groups talking prices as if they were selling rump steak by the pound. The buyers of the six paintings I sold were interested only in those things that would match their living-room drapes or creep with sweet melancholy into a tart's heart when she was brought home at night.

Antioch College offered me a class of young people at which I could talk of art and art history, and I took it. Young, corn-fed children who sat in classrooms and listened while I spoke of the days of artists who painted holy ceilings and designed great public buildings and painted only for the glory of God.

"Just like the WPA murals in the Antioch Post Office, Mr. Ormsbee," said my class, and I cursed them for ecstatic fools taken in by the bad illustrators spoiling good walls for political reasons.

I was sitting over a dull book of logic one night. I was tired. The classes had been nasty in their reaction against the drawings of Gillray and Rowlandson—as compared to the brilliant stuff found in the pages of *Collier's* and *The New Yorker*. I closed the book and picked up the newspaper, *twenty-two comics, count'em.*

Senator Connors. Ironman Connors had dropped dead in Washington. Fifty years in Washington—never made a speech—never introduced a bill—always went fishing and when an important social bill was up for votes he didn't know the answer. A warhorse—battered by cigar smoke and tamed by free whiskey—a friend of the lobbies and the Chambers of Commerce and manufacturers. A full-blown fool and a damn crook. But, noble now in death, the news-papers were telling his accursed life story in detail. And what man could be appointed to fill his uncompleted term? *Who?*

A star fell and hit me. This was the time for Dris! I had figured it all out suddenly. Logic—schoolroom logic. What was lacking in the world was faith. A faith like old-time religion. A faith honest, earnest and true to all those things handed down from a mountain in Sinai. Religion, some would call it. A return to a faith—not a return to the ugly stone boxes with their mumbling fools treating God like a classmate. No—but a return to a faith of the little people, a love of mankind, an understanding, a tolerance of the rights of people. Of the rights of lovers and children and fields and . . . Perhaps my head was a little hollow, my stomach empty of everything but whiskey and schoolroom logic. But I knew that this was the chance for the return to the faith in the little people. I wondered what unquenched, just-found spiritual craving burned within me.

I walked from the college grounds thinking, Dris *must* get that appointment to fill Ironman's unfinished term. But how? Ned Wonderly—*not likely*. Jake Fry was dead and buried—*deep*. Gramp was tired and very old. Cabot Carson —old, too—and away somewhere lecturing on how to dec-orate store windows.

Cathy! She was running a press bureau—a press service for debutantes and authors and packing-house products. Cathy could see it. I found a drugstore and hunted through a phone book for her number while I mouthed a tune from "Don Giovanni," *Dei, Vieni alla finestra.*

Cathy said, come on over.
There was something strange in the success Cathy had

had putting the faces and products of people into the pages of the daily press. Her offices were gray hardwood and silver and indirectly lit and full of tall handsome girls on wonderful legs. No one talked above a whisper, and the chairs in the waiting room were soft and the magazines very well printed but dull.

Cathy did not keep me waiting long. Her private office was gold and gray and hung with better pictures than I had expected. Cathy was slimmer but as firm-looking as ever. Her hair was caught back and waved into some fairy's idea of charm. Her clothing was slick, sporty in cut and a little too out of *Vogue* instead of closets. But she had not painted her fingernails blood-red and she still smiled widely when she saw me. She looked, I thought, like a burning Japanese lantern. Out of character for her.

I sat and poured words for about a half hour. Cathy lit cigarettes, handed them to me. I puffed on them several times and then mashed them out and went on talking.

After a while, I ran out of words. I looked up. "Well?"

Cathy sat back and took a ringing phone off its cradle and did not answer it.

"Well, Davey—you couldn't have surprised me more if you had taken the veil. This idea of bringing Dris back is something I should have thought of. You're right—I'm not happy here advertising lard as cold cream."

"It's not going to be easy."

"Don't be foolish, Davey. It's a pushover. You don't think Ned Wonderly is going to raise a finger against Dris getting the appointment. He wouldn't dare go that far against public opinion—yet. Since the land and corporation reforms, Dris is a public hero."

"A hero out of office."

"We'll fix *that*."

I shook my head. "Ned Wonderly will fix it. You know he controls all appointments. He doesn't have to appear against Dris, but a few *hints* and it's all over."

Cathy began to fill in a cable blank with those abracadabrical absurdities for sending messages across seas.

"Davey, you *are* an innocent. I hold the filthy throat of almost every newspaper in the state open and pour advertising down it. I can shove *anything* down their gullets. Ned knows what I can do to him. Nothing to hurt his machine, perhaps—but Ned has gone holy. He attends Mass—he takes the wafer and is building stone grottoes for novenas all over the city. A little of the wrong kind of press now and his noble efforts will backfire on him. How do you spell Cap Haitien?"

"What are you doing?" I asked, watching her as she went on writing on her cablegram blank.

Cathy looked up and flipped the cable sheet across to me. I read:

DRISCOLL ORMSBEE ROYAL HOTEL CAP HAITIEN HAITI COME HOME BY THE NEXT PLANE STOP YOU ARE GOING TO FILL IN THE REST OF THE TERM OF THE LATE LAMENTED SENATOR CONNORS IN WASHINGTON.

"Come on. I want Ned to sign this."

TWENTY-SIX

I NEVER FOUND out what Cathy told Ned, but there was a note from her the next day. It said that Ned Wonderly wanted to see me. It didn't say about what. I went down to the club and I did not have to wait in the hall cooling my heels among the dark, cumbersome furniture. I was shown right in.

Ned's office had not changed much since I had first seen it years ago when Dris and I were hanging up Wilson posters over the town. Ned had changed. He sat behind his desk dressed in his gray suiting, the pearl pin as black as ever in the dark tie under his tall collar. But the face was almost muddy in color, the hands were thinner, deeply scarred by yellow spots, and when he rubbed them together they trembled just a bit. But his eyes were as cold as ever, the mouth as thin. He had thinner hair, almost white now—a parting plastered to a bony skull.

He looked at me and half turned in his tall-backed chair until he was a flat silhouette—as always, dapper and profound.

"Hello, Davey. Sit down. Your folks all well, I hope?"

"Gramp is getting very old. Otherwise we're all right."

Ned nodded and rubbed his dry lips with a thin, well-cared-for finger. "I'm going to have Dris appointed to fill in the vacant seat of Senator Connors in Washington."

I said nothing. Ned went on in a magnanimously dull

tone: "After that, I shall support him for the Senate seat as long as he wants to hold it."

"Why?"

Ned fingered his black pearl and said almost violently, automatically, "You believe in God?"

I said, "*Why* are you backing Dris again?"

Ned frowned, spoke low, as if studying his personal fidelity. "I believe in God. I always have. What I have done, I have done with fear of evil and hate of Hell."

I looked at Ned. He was old. He was tired. He was as proud and stern as ever. But this heavy, martyred, cold earnestness was new.

"Davey, what your brother did was something no man has ever done to me. I have served well those who served me. I haven't shot my mouth off about it. I haven't claimed to be as pure as the lily. I'm what they say I am—a powerful political boss. They talk of reactionaries, oppressors, monopolizers, too. I'm cruel, I'm ruthless—until I have my way—but I'm no God-damn fool." Ned leaned across the desk toward me. "I don't think anything can beat Dris—not even I. Something—call it luck, faith—what you want —is behind him. I play my hunches."

"Frankly, Ned, all this means that you can't face the voters if you give anyone else this Senate seat. They would howl you down in the next election if you did. You may believe in God, in faith, and Dris—but I think you're also smart enough to believe that your political power comes from a lot of people who will only string along as long as you can hand out gravy and win elections."

Ned did not answer me. His thin nose protruded grayly. He looked at me calmly. I went on. "It doesn't matter if you back Dris or not. You can appoint anyone else you want to the Senate now—but Dris will beat you at the next election."

Ned stood up and held out his hand. I took it and we shook hands limply. He was almost smiling—there was a lassitude—a chronic anxiety—about him suddenly.

"Good-bye, Davey. You may be sure Dris will fill Connors' seat as long as he wants to. Anything I can do for you?"

"No."

"Too bad. I like you, Davey."

I nodded and went out. I suppose Ned Wonderly did like me. I couldn't make him out. Villains are all black, I had been taught for years—but there was a lot of gray in Ned—a chemically cold virtuousness I couldn't ever understand.

I walked over to Cathy's offices and told her about my interview. She did not appear to be surprised and said she had expected it to turn out that way.

"I don't get it," I said. "Ned has taken the worst beating of his life from Dris and even if he *is* forced by popular opinion to put him in office now—why should he talk as if he really loved Dris?"

Cathy shook her head. "Don't let it worry you. You know the old bromide about we've never heard the Devil's side of his story. All men like Ned are and stand for may be the cause of the world breaking up. There are thousands of people like Ned Wonderly. They were in control in Germany, they sold out France, they weakened England. Through hands like Ned's pass the orders of the fat bellies and the dividend kings, the steel trusts and the D.A.R. gentry and the hunters of mangy foxes."

I grinned. "That's not *you* talking—that's Cabot Carson."

"All right—so it is. But what do I care? It's Dris' chance now. . . ."

"For what?"

[341]

"I don't know, Davey. I'm afraid to think. Suppose I'm wrong? Suppose we've all been wrong?"

"About Dris?"

"Suppose Cabot Carson, Jake Fry—all of us—are wrong about him?"

I got up, took one of her scented cigarettes and lit it. "I don't get it, Cathy. You—Ned Wonderly—all of you seem to think a great faith is going to sweep through your world and make it clean again. Something—no one knows what—is going to come up over the horizon and dust off the world and everything is going to be hunky-dory."

"Don't you? If you don't, what is there for the world but suicide? A jungle-eating of fresh-killed brothers . . ."

"Oh, hell! Maybe I felt that ardently pure stuff yesterday, but, Cathy—history is full of times like these. I don't think we're now going to have anything new in the way of faith—I don't think anything is going to change. The same cycles will go on repeating themselves. You're all soft in the head—Ned, Cabot—you—and even I am—at times."

Cathy grinned. "Get out of here, you old cynic. I've got to arrange some press hoopla for Dris when he lands."

At the door, I turned. "Cathy—listen to me—getting back to earth from the furiously intense wishing. What's in all this for you?"

"I don't know. Everything and nothing. Get out of here, you gloom hound!"

I went out.

It was strange, this ominous eagerness for Dris.

When I saw Dris he had already been appointed to finish the term of the late Senator Connors. The events of Dris' life from then on are such public property that they are almost not worth recording. It was a popular appointment. The national press carried it, featured it, photographed it and overdid it.

Dris made a speech in Antioch that I suppose someone will one day dig up and explain as the beginning of his faith and hope in a world gone mad, his hopes for a new future for a foul world of madmen and dishonor. I heard it sitting in back of the platform among the stale banners and the dim powdery light.

It was a fine speech. Dris was tall and tan and healthy-looking. He spoke low, earnestly and with a voice that seemed to catch every ear. The First Speech is too well known for me to repeat it. I sat watching a sweating little man take it down in shorthand—I saw the radio engineer twirl his dials to send it out over airways cluttered with sales talk and soap serials. In this pinnacle of turmoil I just sat and wondered if any of it mattered.

Dris spoke that speech of hope and strength for a world that could be saved only by firmness, by a pureness of purpose and fullness of understanding and tolerance. It was the first simple new note among the hates and smiles and meetings and snarlings of the leaders. I felt it—the people felt the new simple note.

I didn't feel the greatness in Dris that Cathy and the others did—I suppose, being a brother, I never could see it as plain as they could. All I could feel was that clearness of his point. There was no confusion, no bickering, no mental, vocal debris. He felt that with a firm show of our desires for a better world we could bring back an era of kindness and understanding to the nations. That seemed to me to be the importance of what he said. He was sure that kindness and understanding would return. He said it with no political discretion, with no philosophical generalizations.

Whatever else the editorial writers and the drum-banging patriots have read into it since, I did not feel. It was as simple as that. After the meeting there was a gathering of people in Dris' King George Road house.

Vicky and Pete were there, stiff *and* proud—Pete disappeared and was found smoking his pipe in the kitchen. Doug showed up, loud and cheerful, banging backs and howling "Senator" at the top of his voice. Cathy handled the press and Dris refused to make any more statements. Someone turned on the radio and there was the usual small talk of storm trooping and double-crossing at the diplomatic tables.

I went upstairs and knocked on the door of Linda's room. She was sitting at the window, staring down at the cars in the drive. She looked well. There was a thin tan over her pale features and she rose to greet me with an avid look.

"I thought you had forgotten me."

"Of course not, Linda. I just had to brush off all the seers and star gazers below."

"Davey, you coming with us to Washington?"

I shook my head. "No, I'm going to take some cash I've made selling some paintings and take a trip to China on one of those big white luxury boats. Pretty soon they'll stop making trips and I want to go around the old apple at least once before the curtain falls."

"Oh, Davey—are *you* going to talk world conditions, too?"

I took her hand and kissed it. "Honest Injun, no. I feel feverish."

"You will write me—from Bali—about the girls?"

I promised.

Perhaps I ate something wrong. Perhaps I read the wrong books. But I spent the next week in bed with one of those

[344]

fever upsets I hadn't had since childhood. I lay and knew I lacked the faith in faith.

And I saw etched on the back of my eyeballs the fact that all that happened upon this planet was but a short shout before the coldness of space and the eternal earth covered the few fragments of bone that had once been the two-legged, hairless ape. Fever drove my mind . . .

And when I awoke I was a man again and the fever was gone. I knew I was going away. There was a school of painting in China I wanted to study. Yes, I told Vicky, when she came to rub me with alcohol, I was going to China.

She looked at me and sighed. "Only one damn fool among four sons was not a bad record." For she had joined the church again and thought more of Dennis than before. "A painting is a pure waste of time."

But I already saw the pleasure dome of Kubla Khan.

There is no use writing about China here. Its clanging militarists have nothing to do with Dris—and perhaps I shall write of China some other time when I am writing about myself.

I was there three years. I tossed away everything I had learned about art. I bought a badger-hair brush with ten hairs in it, and some ink stone and I sat down and poured water on the ink stone and made black ink and then I rolled up my sleeves and began to paint anything I wanted with a delirious solitary objective—pure form.

At the end of two years, I had been every place I wanted to go to in China and I had thousands of drawings—some of them almost as good as I could ever make. None of it ever became very real to me. It was calm. It was strange.

During those years I kept a scrapbook. Vicky would

send me newspaper clippings, and now the time was past when only Antioch and local state papers mentioned Dris. He had become a national figure. When he had finished the late Senator Connors' term of office, he was elected to a full term. His friends nominated him. The Ned Wonderly machine was not invited to help—but it did and Senator Ormsbee made a speech thanking everyone who was interested in good government and went back to Washington planning his bills to draft resources. Once in a while I had a letter from him. And there would be a few lines added to it in a weak, wavering hand. I would look at them and know that Linda was very ill. What credulous, plastic things emotions are when seen in handwriting.

There were two pages of pictures of Dris and Linda in the rotogravure sections of the national press the month the Ormsbee Bank Reform Bill came out of committee. There were viewers-with-alarm who wrote long and dull screeds when Dris approved the nation going off the gold standard. I still have before me the text of his Senate speech on the menace of new evil forces in Europe backed by British and American loans. And the half-witted remarks made to it by a nasty, bumpy-faced Senator.

Not all of Dris' bills were passed. His legal reform measures to curb the habits of corporation lawyers failed. There was his very bad defeat by the advertising agencies when he tried to put strength into an honest pure food and drug act. And his battle with bishops over child labor. The Romanists won.

At the end of the second year in China, I pounded colored earth with water and bought a new brush and began to tint my drawings. In six months I lost all track of a real world and was painting away on special paper and linen, scenes of people and plains and buildings. I started a huge book about my boyhood and filled it full of drawings of my father's yellow house—of Vicky shouting down Pete, of my father's grape arbor, of Antioch mills and Polack Point, of people in the park, on the river at dusk and the high hill beyond Gramp's range of mountains.

Sometimes I would find I could not sleep and then I would remember I was a short candle and that sleep was almost death and I would grin at such sloppy thoughts. Then I would sit under the oil lamp and paint Cap Roc with the bullet holes in his head, and Linda and Aunt Netta and myself getting drunk. And Doug on the bridge of his yacht and the mad blue waves . . . I would paint Piggy and Turtle and faces from the art school, and I would lie down by my paintings and fall asleep.

And suddenly I wanted to go home again.

The houseboy came out on the terrace. He walked with a limp, and one side of his face was very scarred. Chen had been through the Shanghai trouble. He had been beaten with a steel whip, and his sister had been thrown alive into the fire box of a locomotive.

Chen bowed and from one sleeve he took a letter.

I took it and turned it over and over. From Washington, and Dris had put a stamp on it—although he didn't have to. I looked up at Chen and behind him the scarlet geraniums were in full bloom.

"Where do you come from, Chen?"

"Up river thousand miles beyond Tai-Yuan, Kaifeng. . . . Maybe two thousand miles."

"Ever want to go back home?"

"Home here now. Mother—father—all dead—sisters all dead—grandfather grave gone—river wash away. Chen has no home."

I opened the letter and did not read it. I was wondering how long it took to catch the essential quality of this race.

"Chen, don't you ever want to see the places you remember as a child? The green fields, the silver streams, the little fences, the cobblestones—the house you were a kid in?"

"All same to Chen here or any place. Fire-war and much famine come and then flood and smallpox. Nothing in China ever the same again."

"Maybe—mix two gin slings and have one yourself."

"Oh, no. Never drink when I am houseboy."

I looked up. "You a Christian boy?"

Chen rubbed his scar and spit. "Leader, *he* Christian. I am only a Christian for rice. When I work I am free—then I am Chinese and the gods of my fathers are enough. I smoke some joss stick and gilt paper before them. They help me—I take care of them. They fail me—I toss them in corner." He spit again. "I am not good Christian—sorry."

"Make the gin slings, anyway." I began to read my letter.

DEAR MUG: (I read in Dris' handwriting)

Your last letter was amusingly mad. I hope the sun hasn't hurt your head. We are very proud of the paintings you sent us. Linda has framed the clouds and river scene and lies all day looking at it. She is not very well.

I am busy but it is good to take up a pen and write to a brother far away. How far apart we are all these days. I saw Dennis in Chicago about two months ago. There was some sort of independent church conference. He looked old and tired. His hair is all white. The world still puzzles him more than ever. I couldn't give him much hope of a brave new world to come.

I suppose you have seen by the press that Doug has pulled another of his Wall Street miracles. Ormsbee Overseas Shipping is now Ormsbee Overseas Steel and Shipping Ltd. A vast strange monster of interlocking holding companies and mergers that has combined almost all of the steel mills, rolling mills and steel ships in the nation and now he is spreading out to

[348]

Europe and Asia. He had his wish last week. Hartley Gould Coppard was happy to sit down with him at dinner.

I can even tell you what they talked about. About that damn bill I was preparing to bust wide open all these holding holding holding companies and trusts and stock swindles. Frankly, their lobby is so strong and the men who sit in Congress so tainted by their payrolls that I'm sure my measure will never come out of committee.

Vicky and Pete—they never seem to change. Vicky is as talkative as ever and still scheming to make a fortune. Gramp is very old. He wants to see you soon, he said. He can't write but he begged me to.

When are we going to see your ugly face again?

Your brother,

Dris.

I looked up. Chen stood at my elbow with the drink. I took it and sipped. There was a line of shaking, inky scrawl under Dris' firm script. It read:

"Please come home soon, Davey—— L."

Chen still stood over me, the empty tray in his hand. His scarred face spoiled the pleasure of the cornflower-blue sky.

"Get me a packing case for my paintings. I'm sorry, Chen, you have no home to go back to. Very sorry."

Chen nodded and took the empty glass and said in a reconciled voice, "You are going home?"

I looked at the writing of the dying woman and nodded. Across the street the sing-song girls were still putting aspic on their blueblack hair. T'ang Li, the Pekingese, barked at a spotted mouse.

It was the last painting I made in China.

The color here in the hills is slipping into the golden-umber range and I am still writing. The summer is high and the heat that reflects off the fields is stronger now than any winds. I sleep in the open and my skin has the color of good unsoiled leather.

For weeks I have not been able to write a line. It just would not come. All week the heat was heavy and wet and the little animals sat in the shadows of tall stones, panting, their little mouths open, the pink tongues flickering. I caught a squirrel today and held him in my hand. He was too tired to protest and his little pumping heart was quick and full through the fur and bones of his body.

The sky grew dark and heat lightning came spinning across the backbone of distant hills. The first raindrops soiled the dried earth and the earth sucked them in and soon everything was wet and smelled wet; the grass, the old dead wood, the tender herbs and the heat-tormented meadows.

The lightning hissed and sang heavy bass over me. Big grape-like raindrops hit the skin of my tent and rattled off. After that the fury of the storm wiped out in a glassy, oily curtain all the world. I saw the big oak die as the lightning hit it and its topmost leaves just brushed my tent in passing. The bottom of the world seemed churned up. I smelled the burning ozone of lightning-made trouble, and mud formed under me and I no longer tried to remain dry.

Suddenly it was over. The drip-drip *fell away to gurgles as the streams lipped over.*

BOOK FOUR

TWENTY-SEVEN

I WALKED INTO Linda's bedroom following Doug's big bulk, thinking of my journey home. To this day I remember nothing of it except the stamping of my passport.

To all homeward-turning travelers, no matter how much they travel, the fullness and bigness of the world are never too real. Yesterday is now today and today would soon be tomorrow and faces and places all look alike even if some are brown and some are yellow and some are white—but none of it is too real.

The nurse let go of the soft wrist and went out of the room. I looked down on the white face of Linda. The dark eyes were looking up at the painting I had sent her from China. The mouth tried to form something into words, failed. Tried again. Got over its indecisiveness. Vicky, sitting by the bed, sniffed. Linda tried again.

"Davey . . ."

"Hello, Linda."

Her tiny hand hovered over my fist and touched it at last. Her fingers intrigued in my palm.

I bent over the bed, touched my lips to the hot brow.

The face bent a weak smile into place, then firmly held it there—even in pain.

"Doug too—nice—very nice . . ."

Doug swallowed hard. "You mustn't try to talk."

"I know—I'm running down—no centralized control any

more. All dignity, pride, shot to hell—I'm ice to the hips—right now—half underground . . ."

Vicky wiped her little wet face, put her lips together hard.

"Let her talk."

The woman on the bed let the corners of her mouth drop, gasped, a shiver of pain ran through her. Then her eyes turned to the painting again, drew sustenance from it. Dris entered on tiptoe. Linda's voice was low.

"I don't mind—too much. Except . . . Throws our perspective all out of joint. Poor Dris. It's been a long time. Now, well, I don't take this in my stride. . . ."

The pain passed. Dris turned away to weep alone in a corner, tremendously sad, overwhelmed. Vicky sat, her arms folded, far off, unstirring. I held the hot hand. The woman on the bed swallowed. Words, sentences, rushed piecemeal from her.

"Always promised myself I'd take this like everything else—with my chin up—but it's frightening to think of. You raise a body, feed, pamper it, give it love and art and music —give it a retrospect to kick around and then—this—and then you have to throw it away. Yes, the silly inner thing —the soul—the noble emotions—the thoughts—the whole daffy drift through life doesn't matter—it's just the little cells and the gases and tissues dying, stenching up. All I've been, all I've hoped . . . Well, I'm out of this interminable turmoil—no regrets, Davey—no regrets—hold my hand tight —it's so—so *easy* to slip away. Excuses and subterfuges no good now—no—none . . ."

The nurse came in, fingered a pulse and went out. It was growing dark but they turned on no lights. Dris was sobbing out loud.

Linda turned her head on the wet pillow.

"Friends cry well—from the heart—they have had long practice. We've seen to that. Poor Davey—poor Dris—you two forced to stay and remember—me, I'll be well out of it—it's cool, calm, restful in the ground and the sun never burns—cool in the soil with new growing forces surging by. No! Promise me—to scatter my ashes in the sea!"

The head lifted off the bed. The deep dark-pooled eyes looked about her. Imponderable, then liquid sensuality tinged with pity, fear. Dris came to her. She looked at him.

"If this no love can be like this—oh, Dris—don't can do this for forgetting a man . . ."

The head fell back, lay disheveled. The air rushed out of the lungs, hissed past the numb vocal cords, the breasts fell, the insistent blood stopped flowing around the limbs, messages faltered in their rounds, the last spark left the eyes and the little air rushing from the mouth left the tongue across the throat. The brain could not get even a momentary quiver through the still passages and valves and stilled nerve ends.

Linda was dead.

I dropped the limp hand.

I looked away and cried, and then I looked at the painting of hills and a long road and full-feathered clump of trees and I knew some of what Linda had thought and all she had wondered about while she lay dying here.

She had thought of me. Thought of me among those green Chinese fields—*and what else?* I did not know. I turned back and looked at the calm face. It did not look as if death hurt much.

She had asked to have her ashes cast into the sea. That would do no harm, either.

"Man that is born of woman hath but a short time to live and is full of misery. He cometh up and is cut down

[354]

*like a flower; he fleeth as it were a shadow and never con-
tinueth in one stay . . ."*

The Vicar looked up from reading the burial service. Hartley Gould Coppard scowled at him. The steam yacht *Sea Witch* rolled slightly as the mighty river tugged against the mooring ropes. The dimpling waters, a deep purple-green, ran on and, far off, the disquieting sun was a low great disc of orange pasted in the sky.

The urn stood on the small plain pine table set on the sloping deck. Around it were grouped Vicky, small, standing very straight and dry-eyed, Aunt Netta, veiled, unresistingly limp, leaning on Uncle Thor, Pete, Doug, Dris—and a dozen others—I never asked who. They were here to see the urn opened and the ashes of what had been Linda cast into the swirling, sea-drawn river. The river rocks watched from the shore like great stone griffins.

Dris nodded his head at the Vicar and looked into the sinking sun.

"It will be down soon. She wanted to go out with the sun and tide."

Far out a river boat hooted, the wake left great swells that came across the waters and tossed *Sea Witch* into a heavy roll.

I kept my befuddled, fixed gaze, caught a deck chair and held myself erect.

Aunt Netta sobbed aloud, mouthing her veil. Dris stood watching closely the small, shiny urn that held so much of his life. Ashes. All that was Linda, his old plans and old laughter and old lost love were in there. A handful of dust. Doug's arm tightened around him. I tried to probe my tired mind, to synthesize all experience. I failed.

Vicky stood unmoving. A wind slouching in from the sea gathered momentum.

Sad, plaintive dusk came down. The wind was cool, and

Doug draped his jacket around Vicky's shoulders. The Vicar reopened his book.

"Forasmuch as it has pleased Almighty God of His great mercy to take unto Himself the soul of our dear sister here departed . . ."

I took the urn when Dris failed to pick it up. I pulled off the lid and looked at the oily mouth of the Vicar.

"We therefore commend her body to the deep, to be . . ."

I tilted the urn.

The ashes fell into the river, a long, loose streamer of gray dust spinning, flaking apart.

". . . turned into corruption, looking for the resurrection of the body . . ."

I threw the urn and the cover into the glassy, glaucous water, watched them sink, white, flashing. And so that was that. The world was a strange place. But they still buried their dead, wept for them, thought of love and tomorrow and remembered sorrows. Perhaps there was hope for the world yet.

The Vicar closed his book and bowed his head and finished quickly in the chilly blue-black night air.

". . . when the sea shall give up its dead . . ."

It was my brother Doug, directly after the services, who suggested I spend a few days with him in New York. I jumped at the offer, to escape sitting with mourners. We went direct from *Sea Witch* to the train. Dris was in good hands. Gramp and Pete were taking him home and I didn't want to stand around, another source of gloom.

The ashes had belonged to no wife of mine—I had never gone to bed, felt love and passion with her—yet like some foolish medieval poet I was broken by Linda's death. Logic was no help. A drunken society woman, the muckrakers would have called her. A beautiful woman, too rich, too spoiled, too little to do, they would (and did) say. To me she was Linda and I couldn't be very explanatory about what she was or meant to me. Perhaps I didn't want to.

Doug was fine about it. He fed me whiskeys and told me bawdy stories and asked me to buy another painting for his office on Broadway and Wall Street, which I had helped furnish (until Doug decided I wasn't spending enough money on it).

It was raining in New York. The taxi skidded among the traffic, and near the Battery the lead-colored waters were restless under wind and rain.

I wondered how far ashes could float. . . .

Doug's office was something to make a Medici gasp. It was big, it was paneled in a rare yellow wood, the drapes were hand-blocked linen, the rug was a special woven spruce-and-cobalt-blue Persian with Savonnerie runners. The desk was twenty feet wide, circular in shape, and covered with three phones and plate glass. No papers, no notes, no files were to be seen. There were a huge Tudor oak cupboard that opened into a bar, a Florentine cabinet of Paul Lamerie silver, six chairs—real Chippendale and Sheraton and Hepplewhite furniture—too wormy, ratty-looking and patched to be anything but priceless. On the walls were only three paintings—I had bought them with Doug's money.

Cezanne's *Self Portrait*, side face, Titian's second version of the *Venus of Urbino* and a remarkable *Third Class Carriage* by Daumier. A Flemish tapestry covered a door to a private bathroom. The rain beat against the tall windows as we entered.

Under the *Venus* sat Maggie, the chief charwoman, a favorite of Doug's, reading the *Daily Mirror*. She was smoking a reefer, drawing the drugged smoke into her

[357]

lungs with crackling gusts of mirth over the comic sections. She was a horrible sight, a pure hobgoblin, in the daylight. Old, bent, twisted, a face of purple-veined flesh, her mouth full of black snags and her bald pate shining through the few strands of dirty gray hair twisted under into a knot behind one mole-grown ear. Her feet were in old broken ski shoes and she wore no stockings. When she lifted her wet brown skirts to scratch her knees, her varicose veins lit up like a road map of neon signs. She sat on copies of *Burke's Peerage* and the *Almanach de Gotha*.

Doug was very fond of her. He was a believer in charms, in omens, in lucky signs. And Mad Maggie was the best broom rider he had ever found. Her appearance alone, he would say, was enough for him.

"Good day, Mr. Ormsbee," said the creature.

"Hello, Maggie," said Doug. "This is my brother, Davey. You've seen him around, haven't you?"

The witch held a bent finger against a red nose. "That I have. His head—now have you noticed the way it widens above the nose? It's a sign of a great importance. Ah, and that frontal sinus . . ."

Doug winked at me. "Maggie is a seer. A teller of fortunes, a reader of stars, a great drunken liar."

The creature came near me and took my hand. "Let me see the life line, Davey. Let me look at the inner secrets of the universe."

I looked down at my fingers in her claw-like grip. Doug laughed. "Watch it, Davey! She's on the make. She'll sue you yet for breaking her dirty old heart."

Maggie peered into my palm. "I see a new sorrow and that you aren't going to ever like what you're going to do. Nothing will be fine or good enough for you. You'll never be rich, you'll never be a ruler of men. You'll just do yer work and find happiness at last in knowing you've failed. You'll . . ."

Doug came up behind the witch and swung his arm across her rump. "*What* kind of fortune is that, you frowsy pixie! Get the hell out of here and clear out the john. You've lost your touch, you hag!"

I shook my head and handed Maggie five dollars. "It's all right, Doug. That's the best reading anyone could give me. I like it."

Doug looked at me closely. "Huh—how about coming to London with me?"

I watched Maggie drag her pails after her out of the room. I shook my head. "I'm going home to help Pete sit under his grape arbor."

Maggie turned at the door. "You have the head for vine leaves."

Dris came to help us sit under the grape arbor. He had lost weight—he wore a black band on his arm. We didn't speak much about Linda.

Gramp came over, and the old habit of reading aloud came back to us. Dris read best. One night—under the yellow electric eye of one dangling bulb—he read from an old tattered book of La Bruyere. From the tool shed we could hear Pete sawing at some cabinet length—and Gramp's pipe made gurgling sounds.

One sees certain savage animals, male and female, scattered over the countryside, black, livid, burned up by sun, rooted to a soil which they furrow and dig with invincible doggedness. They have a sort of articulate speech and when they lift themselves upright they show human features: in fact they are men. At night they retire to their hovels, where they live on dark bread, roots and water. They spare the rest of mankind the

trouble of sowing, laboring and harvesting, and thus deserve
not to be deprived of the bread they have earned. . . .

Dris closed the book and we sat listening to Pete in the
tool shed saw at a plank.

"That," said Dris, "was written a century before the
French Revolution, Gramp. Have you noticed that the
'savage animals, male and female . . .' are again being treated
to the kindness of the machine masters? They are again 'not
to be deprived of the bread they have earned.' As if those
for whom they sow, labor or harvest were taking over
God's right to provide for them."

Gramp laughed. "You'll get over that morbidness, Dris.
Wait until you have a lot more problems to solve—a lot
more urgent things to decide. . . ."

"Maybe . . ."

It was good to sit under the grape arbor and smoke and
watch the moths and night insects dive at the light. Then
Aunt Netta came for Gramp and led him away—and Dris
and I sat very still, listening again to the dull-pitched voice
of the saw.

Dris stirred—I could hear the loose rungs of his chair protest as he moved.

"It's all right for Gramp not to feel morbid, Davey.
Think of his life—the good and the bad—the sorrow and
the joy. He watched something grow—and now he's too
old to see it may take a turn for the worse."

"Gramp is no fool."

"Davey—when Gramp was fifteen he remembered the
vast sea of buffalo grass—twelve feet high. He saw the birds
in passage darken the sun, he saw buffalo by the hundreds
of thousands. When he was twenty he was driving his own
wagons East again—a pioneer resettling the land he had
come from. When he was twenty-two he was a captain in

Union blue—at Cold Harbor—in the Wilderness with Grant. When he was twenty-six he owned a mountain range and built a house by hand and raised a family and planted fields and broke the sod and saw a free river through fern bottoms move toward a sea. When he was thirty he saw the first steel mill send up its smoke, and then came the stone bridge and the new railroads and he didn't mind. It was his country growing up.

"When he was forty the first hordes of new, seasick Americans came inland from the shore and he welcomed them and saw them take up land. And then more came and he cursed the day they were waylaid by the mill owners and sent into sour evil slums to live out their lives for dividend making. But Gramp at fifty knew he, too, was in danger and he fought back. He saw the cheap-jack ironmonger and the oil and lumber and coal and land thieves take over a great deal of what belonged to others.

"At sixty, Davey, I think he knew he was going to be licked—but he went on fighting. Well—that's all right for him—he had a lot to look back on that was good. What have we got, Davey?"

"A dark night for you to get moody on. Hell, you've gone through a lot, Dris, and you shouldn't think of a lot of things right now. I don't know any answers. That isn't my business. What you need is a rest—go off some place and fish and dance and get drunk a few times. Then come back and it will all look hunky-dory."

Dris grinned and patted my shoulder. "Thank you. You'll be suggesting I should take up water-color sketching soon. No—I'm pulling out in the morning . . . I want to see what boils in Washington these days. And you—what are you going to do?"

I relaxed against the back of the chair. "I'm just going

to sit here awhile—a long while or a short while and watch the grapes grow."

"Well, Davey—I can't call them the grapes of wrath—these are just grapes. But in other places—in other grape arbors—tonight—tomorrow—next year . . ."

"You've got it bad, Dris . . ."

"Sure, mug—you just sit here and watch these grapes."

"I intend to. . . ."

TWENTY-EIGHT

Dʀɪs ᴡᴀs ɪɴ Washington.

It was another spring. The little grape leaves were puckered and very apple-green and Pete pointed out to me with his pipe stem where the bunches of grapes were forming. I nodded and thought of Linda and how no one living could adequately feel death.

My father had withdrawn further and further into himself. There were almost no things of the old Pete left in him—for public view. He still looked as always—solid and square—but was grayer and showed more of his brown scalp. His hands shook a little when he lifted a gardening tool, and it was almost an effort for him to fill his pipe. The forest creature had vanished long ago, irrevocably.

He was dead to all that the world held and perhaps it was better so. The world was in a bad way and getting worse. The storm-trooping, the Oxford yammering at green tables, the decay of international trust and faith were hard to look at and remain full of a hope of the goodness of mankind. Soon the shocks passed. An enormous ennui set in.

All the next few summers I sat with Vicky and Pete under the grape arbor and we watched the British Empire and France sell out the Spanish Republic and Ethiopia and Manchuria.

We watched the smudge-nosed Antichrist come out of a Munich beer hall and sputter his mad, cunning way to power over the confused little people betrayed on all sides.

We saw the slow rot of France start, we listened to the Liberty League, the bankers, the Republican beef trusts, to the stupid ex-air hero *and*—but this is no history of our times.

Enough we read and stirred uneasily under our grapes and then no longer cared very much.

It was fine to sit in the mottled sunlight, great bunches of grapes hanging over us.

Vicky was older—but no wiser. She had slipped somewhat inside her small skin and seemed to grow smaller and more wrinkled with time. But the small mouth, the tiny pert nose, never changed. Nor her tongue. She still felt that *she* herself had failed to win that reward that was coming to her. No matter how much the papers condemned Douglas Ormsbee and his holding companies or wrote of Senator Driscoll Ormsbee and his reform bills, she—Vicky Ormsbee —felt out of it. I think she would have been pleased and happy to sit on all of Doug's boards and directors' meetings, attending Dris's committee battles and posing for all the newsreel cameras.

Pete and I would sit and smoke and look at the grapes, and Vicky would boil and sputter to herself and then relax her tiny body and join us in our staring, our intimate self-abandonment. So we stared away the years—at least three, I think—for I no longer cared to paint. I hadn't touched a brush since I tossed the ashes of Linda into the sea-borne river current. Some stupid penance—a mortification of too eager flesh held me.

I was a damn fool. I was no romantic, I didn't go in for mystic Platonic love. Linda had always been something far away and briefly remembered—but I just didn't feel any urge to paint pictures.

So we sat—and around us the world curled up on the

edges and began to smell, while men armed and shouted and tossed words and steel at each other and prepared to blow up the planet in one vast, walloping bang.

And the bright boys went on rubbing metaphors together for weak little literary sparks.

At four Gramp would come—with Aunt Netta to help him over the curbs and fill his pipe and set fire to it. No one knew for sure how old Gramp was. He had reached a gnarled, twisted old age and never changed after that. Netta would open the gate and come toward the back of the house where we sat under the grapes, the crescendo of church gongs a block away making headachy noise.

Gramp, red sparks threatening his white curls, would puff up and sit back into his chair—as if crouching on horseback.

"God-damnedest traffic—every bastard and fool in the world and his uncle getting a flivver on credit and driving like mad to wreck it before a payment is due!"

Aunt Netta would sit down beside him, rub her red nose, take a drink of "cough medicine" which she carried in an old Father John's Throat Tonic bottle and flex her big fat fingers. "Ain't it a humdinger of a day? Out our way the aromatic pines are like a punch in the nose."

Vicky would sniff at Aunt Netta's medicine. "How is Thor?"

"Fine and dandy. He's got a new party to join—the Union of English-Speaking Nations."

"Goosing his morale," Gramp would say as his pipe died.

Pete would repack his pipe and hand it to Gramp and set fire to it and then take up Gramp's old battered briar and begin to clean it. Pete got along now with about ten words a day. Never a large speaker, he had cut down his quota.

Gramp would suck and listen to the fresh pipe gurgle

[365]

and clear his throat. "I told them the German savages would rise up again. They aren't civilized and never will be. White Zulu niggers, that's what they are, and the time will come when, like the old Islamic tribes, they will boil over and spew out their filth over all of us. Always said so."

Aunt Netta sighed and took a swig. Vicky sniffed in disdain. "We'll not live to see it—no *siree!*"

"I will," Gramp would chuckle. "I'm old and there isn't much marrow in me—but I've got a cracked leg bone that split at Cold Harbor when Grant took us into the Wilderness and it's twitching like old Harry. It means that the trouble will come soon for the luxurious buttery gluttony of our times."

"Nonsense," Vicky would say. "Just a mean old man who lost every cent he had to leave his children by bad management and now he sits here telling dirty stories to scare children."

Gramp would grin and nod to Aunt Netta to knock ashes out of the pipe. "*What* a hellcat I spawned! Vicky, you get fuller of the damnedest things the older you get. I tell you, you're as bad as Dris and his ideas that there are enough brain cells in Congress today to think us out of a world muddle. Grapes coming fine, Pete."

One day we sat like this, making our small talk and eating the grapes because they were ripe, when Gramp looked about him and seemed big and inflated with some secret. "I've been hearing *things*."

"What things?" asked Vicky, picking grape seeds from her small mouth.

"I been hearing Dris—Senator Driscoll Ormsbee—is going to get married again."

I turned around and looked at Gramp. "You sure?"

"Very sure. I went down to the corner to get a beer—and all the barflies knew it. What's surer than that kind of gossip?"

Aunt Netta nodded. "I've heard talk. I was going to—to my druggist—to get my medicine refilled—and I heard it, too."

Vicky rolled in mirth but I could see her jealousy aflame. "Well, well—I still don't think that Miss Cathy Williams will put it over. No siree, I don't think it will come to marriage. She's too full of fancy ideas and stuff for Dris. He likes his old way—his own way—and she has plans—always plans—and she's too smart and pretty—smart and pretty like I was at her age."

I shook my head at Vicky's egotistic naive manner. "I don't think Dris will marry her."

Gramp winked. "There is talk, anyway."

Aunt Netta sighed. "No. Dris' heart lies on the river waters."

Suddenly Pete turned and cleared his throat. We looked at him. Was he *really* going to offer comment!

He was.

"Dris is marrying Cathy. Got a letter from him that says so."

We just sat and stared at Pete, who was again looking up at the grapes. Vicky shook—but for once her rage made her silent.

The wedding took place in Washington. The President came, and Vicky in red silk talked to him until they led him away. It was a huge wedding, a great many people were there. Intricate social negotiations had gone on a long time.

There were society reporters who proved that the Ormsbees went back to the creation of Adam, and that the bride was much *more* important, being a great-granddaughter of a Boston minister from Back Bay. She had a Crusader forefather. A *Fidei Defensor*.

Cathy in a pale-yellow silk dress looked like something noble and polished from a fine Greek period. She was firmly happy. She did not talk much but hung on Dris' arm and nodded. Dris looked very amused and allowed his joy to pour from him in happy banter. The couple stood for the cameramen and smiled and bowed and then everyone drank too much and the Maryland fox hunters broke a few vases and the Russian noblemen in patched ribbons and orders of St. Tarmar spoke of the Tsar and the whole thing degenerated into a Washington political wedding with the English Ambassador speaking through a cold in the head and wishing them well. A few virulent disreputable skeptics made remarks about it and Pete stood in Yankee impassivity.

The only face that was not a member of the family that I enjoyed seeing was Cabot Carson's. Small, white, dressed in his usual blue with his sliver of red ribbon in his lapel as usual. While Cathy retired to dress for going away, he took me aside and told me what he was doing, which seemed to be nothing more than brooding over a lost past. But on the matter of the wedding he seemed to be pleased.

He winked to me in hardly disguised satisfaction over the largest champagne cocktail I had ever seen.

"Davey, my dear lad, Cathy is the one ingredient that your brother has been lacking."

"That so?"

"She has a cold purpose, Davey. Whim of iron and a desire to sit high. She will bring out the best in Dris—and soon."

"I don't think Dris will change much."

Cabot picked up another cup. "He doesn't have to change. Only his surroundings will. A toast—some sanguine prophecy."

"You name it," I said. "All I can think of are Hugo's lines: *'Dieu était ennuyé avec lui.'* They don't fit."

"No. I am still old-fashioned enough to believe what I wish for must be kept to myself. So I've wished. Let's drink."

I had never seen such a gleam in Cabot Carson's eye as I saw when he swallowed his drink. Yes, I had—a smaller version of it that gleamed just as bright. It had been in Cathy's eye when the organ welled up into *The Wedding March.*

I reached for a big drink myself.

I had a great many drinks.

Too many.

Cathy and Dris went away. A great many people went away. I got back to my hotel and lay down on the bed without undressing and felt very ill and unhappy.

I was foolish—foolish to lie here like a sotted swine reeking of strong drink—thinking of a dead woman who had once, too, been a bride—who long ago had lain with Dris on just such a night—and that night, too, I had felt odd emotions stir me.

It was not desire, it was not lust, it was some strange chemical reaction in my blood. And now *that* was all it ever would be and I was one with fruity poets and those who worshipped visions and saw love only at great heights.

I slept and awoke and felt worse and drank black coffee. And Cabot Carson, after a sleepless night, as gay and alert as ever, came to see me. He sat on my bed and grinned.

I scowled and cursed him. I was in a nasty mood.

[369]

"And now," said Cabot Carson, while my head still spun, "you're going to come to Boston with me. I am arranging your Chinese paintings for an exhibit there and I shall let you help me pick out the ones you want to show."

"Where did you get them?"

"Your mother asked me to remove them from her attic before she threw them away. They are too good for that."

"I haven't painted in ages—never will again, most likely."

Cabot nodded and rubbed his pale bald head. "Come with me. I'll tell you the story of my life and how to become as wise as I am."

The Boston butler had left the toast rack, folded the *Times* and opened the stiff linen napkin. Cabot Carson came slowly down the grand stairs, not noticing the colonial oil paintings, the waxed trash of early Americana that had once been his long-dead wife's delight. He ignored the heavy cherry breakfronts, the Chippendale and Sheraton highboys and tables, the shelves of Georgian silver, the great, faded rugs, the canary-yellow drapes and the battered pewter and brass tools in the Adam fireplace. It was all cold, handsome, expensive.

"Good morning, Davey."

"Morning."

The butler appeared with a great pot of coffee. Cabot liked his coffee brewed in pots. He hated the gadgets of glass and drips they were marketing. Absurdities.

"Morning, sir."

"This morning, Davey, I shall tell you the story of my life."

"Why?"

"Because, Davey, you must understand and forgive Cathy for what she may do to your brother. I trained her and she may rub off some of that training on Dris. It may do him good."

When he was still unborn (Cabot Carson told me), just stirring in his mother's womb, she began to prepare the world for him by playing Chopin for hours. She tried to read Plato, to put her mind and blood stream into the proper tempo, although she weakened at times and opened Dickens ("which her family thought very vulgar. *Cockney humor, you know!*").

When Cabot was very small (he went on), they hung art studies over his crib. Michelangelo, Corot, Maxfield Parrish, Botticelli, Burne-Jones' *Galahad*, Delacroix's illustrations of Scott's *Ivanhoe*. He had his own bowl of goldfish in his corner of the garden.

When he was six he played the piano ("played it neatly, without emotion but with a good touch and a built-up pedal"). Chopin, of course—Mama's favorite—and bits of Verdi and Gounod, Gilbert and Sullivan "up to here" and lots of nice little songs and lilting Offenbach and cute things like *A Russian Sleigh Ride*, *Turkish March*, Liszt's *Hungarian Dances*. Even years later he would still whistle them while sailing his boat into the wind and when the boom would come banging around, while the brine, knived by his keel, went passing by white-spumed and angry.

At ten, Cabot was taken down to State Street to meet the firm. ("I was called Master Carson, handed a noggin of port for a toast and given a pen to play with.") He was now a member of the firm. He also went to dancing school, wore white gloves and held little girls **very** close and learned to waltz and polka and wondered **what** little girls were like under their dresses.

"I still brood over it—although now, of course, I really know."

At twelve, demure, tonnish, languid, he went away from home to a very swank prep school ("which Carson 1st had built a gym for"). He was hazed and beaten by other little gentlemen and *next* year *he* beat the boys and took delight in hitting his own fag over the genitals with a wet, knotted towel. He learned much that year. Life was a lot of fun that year after dark—under the sheets. ("This was long before Ellis and Freud, mind you.")

He worked just enough to get good marks. He didn't pimple up like the other growing boys, and one summer a tall, blonde serving maid with splendidly tapered legs seduced him and his joy was complete. He came back to school with a leer and a full report and after that joined the older boys when they went on beer-and-girls benders in town. He thought of himself as a scintillating, aristocratic fellow.

He went to Harvard, set in a mold but still not completely jelled. The Gold Coast welcomed him ("Carson II had built a training annex for the school"). He took another hazing but broke a freshman's shoulder blade the next year in revenge. The freshman was only a Jew ("and his father had never done more than give a million-dollar research lab to the medical school. It was hushed up"). Carson III did not appear deeply penitent.

Harvard chilled him. Marriage dulled him. Business bored him. Life irked him. Drink made him ill. There was still sex, but it had gone muggy on him. Life was dull. Eat, excrete and wind the clocks for sport. Copulate, propagate.

On the third morning of Cabot's life story, I tapped my egg with a dull silver knife and looked up. "Why tell me all this?"

Cabot Carson pushed back his bacon and grilled kidney.

[372]

"I rather enjoy shocking you younger people. You imagine you alone have ever had shocking things to tell. No—I am really leading up to Cathy. One day I left everything—Boston, the old firm, the Harvard bores at the club—and went to Europe. You have heard legends of what I became. I wrote a book on them for the *Wiener Nationalbibliothek*. I will not disillusion you about those myths. I enjoyed creating them. There is even some truth in some of the milder ones. You've heard the one about Baroness K? *Elle sera couverte de diamants*."

"I've never bothered to believe any of them."

The old man looked at me. "Too bad. I rather liked them. Made me appear more of a man than I am. Well, when I was old and dry and rather penniless, I found myself owning a veritable gold mine of a New York art school. I don't remember how I got it. I filled it full of Boston frumps and good names and it was a fine success. It bored me and I would have given it up—only one day a young girl walked in. I can still remember her standing there—the sun from the windows behind her wonderful body—that solid, well-carved, beautiful head haloed in sunrays."

"Was that long before my time there?"

"About two years before you joined us, Davey. I took Cathy to live with me. I don't know how I broke down her Boston training. Perhaps I am a better talker than even I think. Anyway, everyone soon said she was my mistress."

Nester, the butler, appeared with more coffee. He refilled our cups and left. Cabot Carson sighed. "That, too, my boy, was a myth. I was too old. It was just an old man feasting his eyes on forbidden fruit while he munched the artistic graham crackers of mere painted nudes on the walls."

I looked at the old man and began to laugh. "You know she told me once she really was your mistress."

[373]

"Yes. She told everyone that. She wanted to have people believe she was not iced with noble New England characteristics."

"My brother Douglas once said she wouldn't sleep with anyone unless she married him. He was right—as he found out once."

The old man closed his eyes and rubbed his brows. Then he looked at me again. "But I haven't told you all this to rack old memories. Cathy is full of something—something as hard and solid as the rocks of New England. She will become a driving force now that she has your brother—and I hope she does not shipwreck his life on her ambitions."

"What does she want to be? The wife of the Ambassador of the United States to the Court of St. James's? I can't see Dris in knee pants."

Cabot Carson sat bent over his coffee cup, playing with the dull silver in his hands. He seemed smaller and older than ever.

"Davey—she told me the night before the wedding that she will make Dris the President of the United States."

I should have seen it all long ago.

We did not talk of Dris and Cathy again nor did I hear any more of Cabot's own myths and life. The Boston show of my paintings was a great success. The most popular picture was the painting I had given to Linda, which Dris had returned to me when I asked for it after her death. It had grown secretly. It was no longer only a simple road between tall elms with a red, eroded hill and rock pines growing between black stones—and a sky all chalk-blue and violet— and a river the color of an eggplant—two old tired tree trunks bare of leaves. And that's all. All done simply with a broad brush stroke and no detail. It was now really the story of a boy who once loved a woman very much.

I came to look at it every day. And when the show was over I took it down and sent it to Cathy as a wedding present. The hurt feeling went with it.

When Dris and Cathy returned from their wedding journey, Cathy wrote me a short note of thanks for the painting. Three months later on new letterheads of rare linen paper the color of chrome-yellow straw, I was invited by her to attend and design the British Victory Ball she was helping to sponsor in Washington.

It appeared a little premature to me. The broken British ranks were just then piling up on the nightmare of a beach at Dunkirk and no mercy sat in clouds over London those days. I wrote back I would be happy to attend. I was in the mood for it, having been again caught reading a poem:

> Unto the Death gois all Estatis,
> Princis, Prelatis, and Potestatis,
> Baith rich and poor of all degree;
> *Timor Mortis conturbat me . . .*

TWENTY-NINE

I HELPED DESIGN the ballroom. Such sweet people helped me. When spring actually broke, society had to prepare to scurry away to Newport and little green islands off the coast of Maine or the cutest little dude ranches you ever saw or the old family house in St. Mary's county of Maryland.

Before all this the right people got together and gave the British Victory and War Relief Ball for the poor little battered countries of Europe getting their ears pinned back. Fine, mannered gentlemen living in hall bedrooms, who represented Prague and Warsaw and Vienna (the gay, the old, the Strauss *Wien*), Norway, Denmark, and other old broken crumbs of Europe, pressed their frayed tails and came to the Ball to shake many hands and eat and drink too much free fodder. Marquis, marchesas, supply buyers, dancers—all were there and I sketched them at five dollars a throw. Cathy made me.

Later I joined Doug and Dris and Cathy at their table. Dris looked very happy and Cathy grinned at me and had the waiter pour me a drink. She bowed to an Ambassador's wife and said I was getting fat. I said she was filling out, too, and she smiled and thanked me again for the painting.

Doug bowed to a scrap steel buyer, a hissing, evil-looking little Jap. Doug told us he had worked a capitalization of fifty-five million dollars for him on a rolling mill that could have been rebuilt and re-equipped for nine million.

Three bands played. Society passed, chattering. Waiters, walking on their toes, went quickly around with trays of drinks and there were many people—most of whom mattered. There were accents and French and Dutch with holes in it, and toasts and tears to fallen tyrants, tattered governments and much remembering of things past and glory to come. There were nobs from Beekman Place, Russian Hill in Frisco and the Episcopal bishop of the diocese enjoying his wine with no nonsense of the Blood of the Lord.

The tabloids had sent cameramen; feature writers roamed at will, snaring big names and the glamour girls. Yale cartoonists in white ties clutched at each other and gave great horse laughs as they told one on Peter or Jules or Jaro or Jockstrep or that *swine* Maurice (who was admiring the taut buttocks of the passing waiters).

Doug knew a great many people there and there was much laying on of hands and directors and vice-presidents giving each other the office as Elk met Elk. Residuary heirs bowed to sole executors. Everyone drank.

Dris greeted everyone coolly but politely. Cabot Carson came over to join us and said, "Oh, this sideshow of ecclesiastical, financial, legal and artistic glad-handers."

"Why?" asked Dris.

Cabot shrugged his shoulders. "It's easy to see, Dris, you don't know how to give money away. One comes not only to help what he thinks are dirty peasants bombed out of their sties but also to be known as a person of a great and open soul—one who aids with a lily-white hand while posing, with the debutante legs showing for the press photographers. There will be no real honest giving, just to help, until they take the name Rockefeller off the foundations, Mellon off the museums, Carnegie off those ugly red stone libraries, Harkness off the college ivory and bedbugged towers and—but let's drink! Man is a swell-headed little ape who feels that if he sticks his name on bronze or stone or marks it on the outhouses of history, his bones will rest better among the shards and worms and no one will remember his crooked franchises of public service corporations."

Doug held up his glass. "No fair, Carson. That was almost a speech. You've been drinking before we joined you. Let's get this one down and have a toast to Dris and Cathy."

Cabot stood up, held his glass high. "Well, *that* is something to toast."

We drank the toast and sat talking, and watching people pass. Cathy went away to bag a millionaire for some free milk fund, and Dris told us about the state of the nation and the far west and the dust bowl he had seen on his wedding trip. He spoke of the plow that had broken the plains and set the dust storms free to make grain surpluses.

"Plato," said Cabot, "has handed us over to Henry Ford. It's the only answer."

"Davey," said Dris, "you look as happy as a fat old tomcat with a whole block of backyard fences in your domain."

Cabot said to Dris, "Davey is all right now. I pulled him out of his blue funk in Boston."

I said, "You make me sound like a Greenwich Village drunk."

Cabot twirled the stem of his wine glass, sat somberly contemplating it.

"You lack the tragic sense, Davey. For all your intellectual licentiousness, you are always trying to be a soulful Philistine."

Dris said, "He needs castor oil."

I nodded, full of too much brandy. "The mysticism of microbes will get Cabot Carson in the end and all his whoring after heroics and lusting after spirituality will end with his whimpering at the feet of Rome, if for no other reason than that they know how to soft-soap and sedulously organize nervous, ghost-haunted stomachs."

"You're unfair," said Cabot. "You're trying to kneel in prayer and kick me at the same time. The colon—not the heart—is the seat of the soul. I see you know that, Davey."

"Sorry," I said, "maybe I'm drunk."

Cabot got up and patted me on the back. "Think nothing of it. I want to talk to Cathy."

He went off into a mulling crowd of Washington Society. Doug swallowed his drink and made a face. "Well, here we Ormsbees are—if Dennis were here we could take a group picture of the Ormsbee boys in clover."

"How is Dennis?" asked Dris.

"Pretty good," I said. "He's got a church of his own now. Invented it all by himself—but he's too honest to make anything good or rich out of it like Mary Baker Eddy."

Dris looked about him and nodded to some oil men in ill-fitting tails. "The next time Cathy gets on the committee of one of these jamborees, I'm going to have Vicky down for the cheering. She'd love this."

I said, "Cathy seems at home in all this glitter and broad-A talk."

Dris grinned. "She wants to take in all of it she can—before the baby comes."

Doug and I looked at each other, then got up and began to slap Dris on the back until he coughed. People turned around to stare at us. Doug howled, "Hey, waiter! What's the oldest wine you've got?"

More people turned to stare. Even the bishop saying grace at a far table stopped and looked at us and then went on quickly—the cigar placed in the tray before him smoking up like incense in his face. "*WethankAlmightyGodforwhat weareaboutto* . . ."

It was almost dawn when we all got home. I was too taut to sleep. I went out on the little open balcony and looked at the river fighting its way into the mist that hid the coming day.

Dris, dressed in a loose robe, came out too—pulling the belt tight around his hips. He looked at me and then at the river. He spoke—but did not look at me.

"Well, I was offered a bribe tonight. One million dollars, cold and solid *and* in cash. . . ."

"I didn't know you were that important."

"I'm not, Davey—it's just that I believe that America is the land—the trees, the gold, the oil, the river and spillways, the power dams and the earth they plow—*and* I'm planning to say so in the chambers. I'm going to say we can all save all of America or none of it. Not just the part on the Stock Exchange listings or in the vaults of the land grabbers."

"A million dollars. . . ."

"Either a million dollars as four years' salary as head of the Interstate Business Groups of America—*or* they will bust me wide open and send the bits through the mails to warn other fools."

"Who made the offer?"

"Doug. He said he knew he was wasting his time—but that his 'Greeks' wanted a refusal first."

"How did Doug take it?"

Dris grinned. "He said he would have busted my neck if I had taken the bribe he was offering me."

"I think he would have."

The river ran on slowly, making plashing sounds. Dris yawned. "It's going to be a busy time. I think I'll stay on here rather than resign and head a lobby of cutthroats and pirates. Even if I were weak enough to fall, I couldn't right now—I want my child born while its father is a member of the United States Senate."

"*Its?* Cathy is sure it's going to be a boy. Says so all the time."

"Cathy is very sure of herself—but this one time something bigger is surer of things than she is. Even a Boston grandfather in heaven—or wherever Boston grandfathers go —can't ask the Great Giver to see that his granddaughter below is given what she asks for. Good night, Davey. I've got to get a little shut-eye. Tomorrow and tomorrow is my busy day."

I watched the river mist turn to sun a little while, and then I, too, went to bed. I had no busy day tomorrow or any day after that.

THIRTY

I HAVE NEVER seen any man work as hard as my brother Driscoll. He was up at dawn and away in his car to the Senate offices. Almost all night he dictated projects for bills. All day he sat in the Senate chamber and tried to lead a few men against a mob of dullards. He was on two committees, he served on commissions, he interviewed buying offices, howled down stiff diplomatic backs and made much noise against the greed of the market place.

He slept little and that little he tossed away in agony. He felt there was little time left to get anything done and he tried to crowd more into his days and hours. He went with Cathy to parties and meetings, he addressed many groups of eager-eyed listeners. He sent out much official mail and wrote many people and made plans. Always he made plans. . . .

And when he had seen everything and found out how it worked, he planned his great bill. A bill which, in time of confusion and darkness, would unite all the resources and all the plants and all the projects of men and machines of the nation into a unit, a solid form with only one desire, one will and one purpose: to save the cause of the nation, to keep it as direct and honest as it had been while first formed.

He slept less, he saw more people and twice had to be put to bed by force. As time passed, the glow went from him. The eager look left his eyes—but he never slowed his pace.

He refused to admit that men would put personal interests first in such times.

Harassed and stalled, he drove on. But I think in the end he knew he could not win. Senator Ormsbee became known as a serious grind. A man to avoid.

Lean, haggard and with red-rimmed eyes, he went on along those stone corridors of Washington. There was so much cold marble in the city, he said one night.

That summer the heat walked close to the ground in Washington. Secret ramifications, feeble press witticisms aided the heat. A fire, damp and itchy, seemed to have entered men's souls, and there was so much talk and so little sense that I began to fear for the sanity of the world every day after my five o'clock highball.

France died—the hands of her own leaders on her throat, and the French Ambassador and his court rioted in tears and drank rare wine and shed public sorrow for their betrayed nation. The English business men came to town and rented the best houses, and the rich noble Gentile refugees from the Lowlands and Kentish moors and French watering places came. In good cigar smoke. And many diamonds. To wait out the war and let the beaten little people back home who lay captive, but ready (they hoped) to leap up and gain back the landed estates and mines and business holdings of their masters when the time would come for the Antichrist to have lived out his political life span. They all got little sympathy from me. Times would get worse before they got better.

It was only Cathy who kept me sane that summer. She was heavy with child. Dris had taken a house in Maryland. A house set in a green salad of trees and bluegrass, and there were silly, long-legged colts and red mares and spotted panting hound dogs almost like the ones I had known at

Gramp's a long time ago. It was fine to see something that was not the embodiment of those iniquitous times.

There was a steel core to Cathy that I never grew to like. There was about her the scent of history—something of those vast brooding qualities one found in once-famous women who had their heads axed off, or who swayed empires or piled up fortunes for their drunken foolish families. That part of her I didn't like. But when she was ill in the summer heat, when the child inside her stirred and life pulsed under her belly, I could pity her and say soft pleasing things and take her rowing in the gentle stream that purred below the white farmhouse. Her pregnancy made her cowed and apprehensive.

I would row and Cathy would trail a hand in the cool water and far off in heat haze the dome of the Capitol could be seen like a throbbing white headache over the bickering, foul, humble, fat, foolish, tired, honest, bored, crooked men who were the law of the land. It was a tiring time. Men were hard-pressed to believe in this fine thing Jefferson and Jackson and Lincoln had built up. The little malicious undertones with butter faces stood in bitter rank tearing at the leaders with slimy hands.

Church fought church, and the tinsel and smoke of Mass entered into the arena. Some came to the defense of old white churches that had seen Bunker Hill. There was a colonel, Cabot Carson told me, "and he was a colonel until his country needed a colonel. And those Wall Street playboys who dreamed smoky dreams in time to the beat of Wagner's music that had made drunk other empty, burning heads of savages across the sea."

"Yes, I know."

"There is a burning little fool—who sits near Dris in the Senate—small, rat-toothed, who hates the elected President and who would be willing to commit treason to tear him from office. There are others—oh, so many others."

Rowing the boat in the purling stream, I escaped Cabot's long list of fools. I knew that I must not be bitter. I must not let the little lice who soiled the curbs and halls of Congress build fires in my own head.

"How you frown," said Cathy, looking up at me.

I let the boat drift and rested on the oars. It was very warm. The insects spun on the waters. There was the smell of lily pads and frogs and the cold, cool waters from deep springs. The rush and rattle of canebreaks.

I said, "I'm confused. My values are all lousy—gone. I lack the taciturn Wall Street solidity."

"Washington is like that," said Cathy. "It's not at all like the civic books we read in school, is it? Here a theory of government is being put to the test. It's now or never to make it work."

"How do you feel, Cathy?"

She looked at me and smiled. "I feel fine when I'm not mad. Why shouldn't I feel good? There is a lot of heat and I'm a little tired with this biological trickery of breeding— but I'm all right. I'll have a son—a big, fine son—you'll see."

"I see—or a girl. . . ."

"*No* girl."

"I like girl babies better. . . ."

"No girl," said Cathy in the tone of a seeress brooding. I began to row again. The sun reflected on the stream and sent shards of light into my eyes. The dome of the Capitol was gone now in heat mist. The banked fern bottoms danced in haze. Slowly I rowed back to the landing. Red colts saw us land and lifted wet velvet noses from the stream to stare at us.

Four hours later Cathy's labor pains began.

The doctor said I had better find Dris and bring him. He was a society doctor and delivered future Ambassadors, grandsons of oil thieves and the best of those people who had made their pile and held on to it. I liked him but didn't trust him. His manner was too professional.

After we got Cathy to the hospital, he had to give her something to stop her screaming.

"Hard case—very hard," said the doctor, looking down his aquiline nose. "A little old for child-bearing. And her *pelvis . . . Well . . .*" He showed me between two lifted hands the shape of a small trout.

"It's all right, isn't it?"

"Oh, yes. Not going to be easy. Have you contacted Senator Ormsbee?"

"He's at the Capitol. Some committee. I'll find him."

I went down the Lysol-smelling stairs. Behind me Cathy was screaming again. The heavy breath of thunder stirred in the heated air. I began to run.

Washington is a hard place to run around, looking for a man. The heat bakes down. The saloons are many. There are a score of good clubs a man might be at. The British were having a garden party. The Germans and Japs were holding a jamboree of local spy clubs (the corner cop told me) and there was always an airport to open or some general at the War Office to knock down into his proper place among his stale volumes of tactics. Dris could be at the War Office.

I had two iced beers and went to the War Office. Early heroes of mine looked down from spider-etched walls. Lee, Grant, Longstreet, Sheridan. How I wished they were alive today. The West Point glamour boys (as Cabot called them) with sunlamp tans testing new desks with their new spurs did not please me. I sat waiting, brooding. (Was there, some

[386]

place in Newark, New Orleans or Detroit a drunken officer, kicked out of the army, who would develop new methods of fighting coming American battles? Was there some sleepy old college that held a new Lee or Sherman? As yet only a name on the files filling this vast building—but soon...)

"What can I do for you?" asked the slim Tarzan with the toothpaste smile.

"Is Senator Ormsbee here?"

"Left hours ago. Brother of his, aren't you? The Senator doesn't think much of our new tanks."

"Too bad."

I went away and tried the biggest club. Hillbillies in shoes and patent medicine kings and oil millionaires, corn-growers and Texas band-leaders, big-name cigarettes, sat around reading the afternoon papers. Cabot Carson sat in a dark corner at a small radio listening to a news bulletin.

He snapped it off and turned to me. He exhaled the antiseptic odor of old brandy.

"Hello, Davey. You look pale. Let's take on two Old Fashioneds."

"Has Dris been here?"

"Not this afternoon. Cathy—it's come?"

"Yes. At the hospital—soon—I've got to find him."

"I'll go over and keep Cathy company. Fitting. The last Bostonian—holding the wet, pained hand of a woman in labor."

I gulped my Old Fashioned and went along into the hot city. It remained a hot, empty town, receding according to perspective.

I thought of the new airport. Some British Buying Commission was due. Dris was interested in forcing the Empire's upper classes to declare their American holdings as loans. He might be there.

I found Dris seated at the airport bar, a bottle of Bourbon at his elbow. I sat down, poured three fingers, scooped in ice, and plashed in a little soda.

"Cathy is at the hospital."

Dris wiped his brow. He was a pathetic spectacle. "I know. Been calling every twenty minutes. I'm a coward, Davey."

"She'll be all right. Been looking all over town for you."

"Am I drunk?"

I looked at him. "Not yet. You will be soon, Senator."

"God, it's dreadful stuff. This birthing. This damn stupid spawning. Better anything—anyway—than this. You take something lovely, something you love, and you twist it, deform it—drive it screaming mad with pain, fear. Davey. Davey, don't go away."

"You need another drink. Hell, Vicky had four of us—big, bouncing babies and no doctor or soft hand rubbing her belly, either. Think of all the pioneer women lying in covered wagons while Indians whooped. Think of lonely pine clearings and dirty work-worn hands. Think of . . ."

"Oh, shut up," said Dris, "you God-damn pioneer."

We sat and finished the bottle. Planes came and planes went away. Cameramen photographed imported legs. Newspaper reporters took down expert statements by Czechs and little fat diamonded Dutchmen—all sure Hitler would be beaten—from the safety of the Ritz Hotel. A Hanoverian school tie explained Lady Astor.

The afternoon passed. I grew tired of phoning the hospital. It grew darker. But not any cooler. Green and red lights blinked on the field. I tossed in my last coin and tried the hospital again and spoke to the doctor. I went back to the table and took Dris' arm.

"Come on, hero! Your wife wants to talk to you!"

"No—no."

"Come on. She wants to tell you about your son."

[388]

That night Greece died and certain Balkan nations. That night Sewall Ormsbee, named for Gramp, slept well, rolled up, his arms interlocked with his thin legs, a red raw bundle of manhood—in the position he had so long held in the womb of his mother.

Cathy slept smiling.

Babies improve quickly. Too quickly. In a few weeks they become more human, take on some of those strange and amazing details of their heritage. Sewall Ormsbee grew quickly. He made strange sounds, he took his nourishment and looked up at his father and smiled. Although the nurse would say *nonsense the poor darling has gas*—and toss the child on her shoulder and joggle it up and down until the little man blew a small, grunting bubble of wind.

"Let me hold him," Dris said, handing me his cigar, smiling with restrained pleasure.

"Well," said the nurse, sniffing the burning tobacco, "*just* for a moment."

"I've held hundreds," Dris said, taking his son in his arms. "You forget I'm a political figure."

"Care of his head," said the nurse. "*Don't* let his neck wobble. Support his back—higher. *There!*"

In panic Dris handed the child over to the nurse. "Here. You'd better take him. Soft, aren't they?"

Dris watched his son blink his eyes and made no pretense of his joy. "It's pretty wonderful, Davey. I never would have thought it. Something so small—*so* full of weaknesses —to get such a grip on a person."

"You sound like all fathers, Senator."

"Let's go see Cathy, mug."

Cathy lay in a huge white bed surrounded by hothouse fruit and best sellers and knitted trash that some people always give on such occasions. She looked well but paler than

I had ever seen her. She also looked proud and absolutely justified in her hopes.

"Hello, gentlemen. How is the heir?"

Dris kissed her on the mouth and pressed a nude shoulder. "He's wonderful, Cathy. Damn delicately made and cunningly wonderful."

Cathy grinned. "You forget I'm a perfect breeding machine. If my grandfather ever found my grandmother *not* pregnant, he always suspected the fall of America—and *that* was rare."

Dris smiled. "They are naming a destroyer after your grandfather in two weeks and wanted you to smash some wine on its blunt nose—but I begged off for you."

"Nonsense. In two weeks I shall be strong enough to play golf again. I'll launch that destroyer."

"But Cathy . . ."

"Dris, the President is making a speech in the shipyard. And *his* family is launching a battleship. I've just got to sail my own little boat. It will mean a lot to you, Dris—even if he is only a Democratic President."

I looked at Dris. He kissed Cathy again and whispered loudly, "Keep up making society items out of me and I'll break that strong slim neck of yours some day."

Cathy launched three naval units that summer. It was a world of loud talk and much spending of money on paper. The hotels were full of oily-mouthed steel salesmen, merchants of pipes and canvas and canned beans and hash stood around pledging to do their bit at only an honest hundred-percent mark-up after writing up costs.

Doug was in Washington. He had formed a dozen new companies, was hammering together oil tankers. Buying up old tubs and refitting them with cement patches and condemned bulkheads. He was bigger, wider, than ever. He came over to see the baby and stayed for dinner and drank a lot of wine and then when it was over he took me aside.

"Look, Davey. I want to see Washington. The tourist's Washington. All the lousy oil paintings of generals, the Monument, the Lincoln statue—everything."

"I thought you came for business?"

"*That* starts tomorrow. Come on. I've hired a big car. I've wanted to see this since I was a kid."

It was one of the biggest cars in Washington. I showed Doug the classic junk. Bad Roman imitations of Halls of Justice, Treasury and Departments of State. Then I showed him the beautiful things. I showed the river banks deep in green dusk, the full moon behind the Capitol and the slender birch trees and the stately elms. We drank root beer in the shadow of the Washington Monument like any tourist and sailed along at a cooling pace to Arlington. But it was the giant Lincoln, remaining stonily awake under his floodlights, that moved Doug. He sighed and shook his head with affectionate awe.

"Some night he is going to get off that big stone bench and go back to the mountains they cut him from, kid. This is no place for anybody like him these days."

"Why, he belongs here, Doug. We are re-arming, getting ready to defend what he kept together after Gettysburg. This is his town."

"You make me sick, Davey. You sound like the big mouths talking for history books. Is Washington full of Lincolns or fat steel salesmen trying to pile up dividends? Davey, the only way to save everything now is take over the factories, just like they're taking over the young boys, and work them day and night. No big mouths taking or refusing orders, no windy press agents promising better cars in 1949, no board of directors' meetings. Davey, I've just come back from Europe. This is the death rattle of the world if we don't build and build and arm and arm and no monkey business about sacred ownership. The time for that tripe is past. It's all of America we've got to save—*or nothing*. Got a cigar on you?"

"No. You sound like Dris."

Doug grinned, gave me a raffish, side-eyed look. "Sure. Why not? We both know what's the matter with the world. Only he wants to save it. I don't know if I do. It's lousy. It's low. And yet the little people are all right. Hell, I'm down here on purpose to see we keep that ten-percent profit mark-up in war profits going."

"That's a lot of profit—if you really hear the death rattle."

Doug rubbed my face with his big fist. "Innocent little bastard, aren't you? This eight- and ten-percent profit we're getting on war defense orders is *after* and above costs of manufacture are added. We have deducted all kinds of costs. With a little bookkeeping we can list that after cost into a hundred percent profit—salt it in certain forms of investments and come out of this crisis bigger than anyone did in 1919. If there is anything to come out to."

"What's it to me?" I said, trying to be hard.

The big black car purred on. I sat watching a peaceful landscape. I was learning every day about the world's ways. It was all becoming a pattern. The Utility Wonder Child had been for drafting men but not for drafting industry. Everyone was for preparing for the foul fires coming closer but no one who had seized the resources and methods of making things in the Robber Baron days was willing to give them up. The fools in Congress yammered and played politics and the mills and plants sent their lobbies to Washington to keep their little greasy mouths filled with their personal percentages. And all over the land the little people worked hard and faced a rising sea of prices while the

Army broke strikes for owners with West Point tactics. That was hell against steel fitters, Doug said, but stale empty threats to any panzer ideas of murder. Doug who was so wrong in everything he did now—was so right. All of America would be saved—or none of it.

"Thinking?" said Doug. "Thinking about the funeral without plumes the world is having?"

"Why should I?" I said. "I'm an artist, a painter of pictures. What's all this matter of dividends or the mark-up the oil, flivver or steel thieves get? Let them fill their gullets— choke and strangle—they can't paint a landscape, can they?"

Doug was suddenly very serious. "The hell they *can't!* I *saw some* they painted in France and in England. *Jesus!*"

I went to the Senate chamber the next day and yawned away an afternoon. These men were not saving America or any section of it, it seemed. They were medicine men, sellers of cure-alls, dealers in little hates, and slow verbal poisons. Some hated the leaders. Some hated each other. Many hated themselves and bit at their arms. They stared defiantly at the clock with the eyes of a blind horse.

Dris sat at his desk and made notes. He no longer made speeches. I thought of Webster and Clay and the giants that were on the American earth in those days. Some were still there. Men like Dris, and certain older men who dressed neatly and tried to stem the minor bickering of foolish minds and unreliable faces.

I had lunch with Dris in a corner of the vast dining room. "You didn't make much comment today."

Dris looked at me and waved his fork at me. He was tanned and healthy-looking. The birth of his son Sewall seemed to have lifted ten years from his age.

"Davey, you see a defeated and broken man before you."

"You don't look defeated."

[393]

"But I am. This morning the committee buried my bill for the nation to take over all war industry—and pay for it in Victory Defense Bonds. And set it working in three shifts turning out materials of war. I even, thinking of our dear brother Douglas, tacked on a ten-percent profit—but *not* above cost sheets of the manufacturer—only above raw materials and labor. This to be paid in the future of America—in the same Victory Defense Bonds. The bill was strangled at birth. Well, I'm finished. I'm still a young man —in emotions anyway. I have a son and a wife and a few, *too* few, years to enjoy them. I'm retired as soon as my term is up and I'm going far away from this turmoil and shouting."

"Good Lord, Dris—you can't. Not in a time like this. The Germans are opposite Brazil!"

Dris frowned. "Half measure is not enough, Davey, to save the world we love. We here are only trying quarter measures. I want to sleep with my wife, play with my son and sit in the sun a few times—feel my marrow stir, my limbs dance—before the deluge comes. . . ."

"Will that be all?" said the colored waiter, removing the pie plates.

"That will be enough," said Dris, signing the check.

Pools of sunlight checkered the tablecloth. From some place there was the scent of drenched violets. . . .

I recited:

Et je verrais mourir frère, enfants, mère et femme.
Que je m'en soucierais autant que de cela.

Dris frowned and handed some silver to the darky. "What are you feeling so good about? You forget I haven't had the practice you've had in French."

"It's something Molière says in *Tartuffe.* Translated:

My brother, children, mother, wife might die!
You think I'll care; no surely, no, not I!"

Dris said nothing.

*The pack horse has slipped badly twice and I've almost
finished writing. The snow has been sighing down for two
days now. Only a wild wind has kept the trails clear. But
in some places it has drifted thirty feet deep. I am tired of
plodding around the drifts. I am very cold and somehow I
feel I should make permanent camp and stay here resting in
this white world. That is foolish—I would freeze solid and
next spring they would find me here with a lot of moldy
pages scrawled over with a family history almost finished.
I will stay here until dawn and then move on alone. The
horse is done for and he knows it. He does not seem to care.
He stands in wind and slash—dreaming of the fat summer
he has had. The wind has risen—I can feel it running across
my sleeping bag with icy feet. There is no sky and what
does grass look like?*

*How still and white the night is. Nothing is alive but my-
self and the nodding horse. Never have I seen such a snow
in November. I must hurry away in the morning. The snow
came early and ate away the last brown fields and smothered out the streams and now it is advancing like a dreadful
king to the low, populated lands. At home, the yellow house
of my father must have some hints of the coming whiteness.
A chill breeze must nuzzle the weathered chimney bricks.
And in the city they are voting at the polls! I suddenly
remember!*

Tomorrow I will know. I will reach the first phone lines.

A new kind of snow is falling. Its flakes are almost as big as tennis balls. It is soft and sings a whirling silence. There is no feel to it. The wind whips the few hairs of the horse's tail and the creature still smiles, remembering old pastures.

With this wind it must just have begun to snow outside the election polls.

THIRTY-ONE

THE DUTIES OF a normal Senator were few. He either stood up and tried to spoil as much of the defense program as he could, he signed stupid little tirades with such discarded public figures as still soured in dark corners, tirades showing that only these few neglected reactionary geniuses of the land could properly handle a crisis. And if they couldn't then better it were not handled at all, they said, with a sleek ecclesiastic show of feeling.

In this confusion and counter-confusion, Dris did his duty, sat in his seat, supported those things that helped somewhat the national condition. But the big bold days of his plans for all-out effort were over. He was settled, he was solid, and his wife and son were enough for him now. He had stood in sand, had had his say and they had strangled his ideas in committees. The red-nosed bumblers, the small fry, the accursed spirits, and fat mouths of special interests.

Dris was finishing his term and thinking of a place where the sun shone and the grass was very green on a small farm near Antioch.

Vicky and Pete came to Washington to see the sights, and again I hired the big black car and took them around to the piles of stone and the files of stale official paper and the public hog-calling chambers full of corn-fed loafers. Pete soon disappeared, to spend his time in the Department of Agriculture, hunting pamphlets on grape diseases and crop rotation but Vicky, small and gray now, but pretty as ever, although wrinkled and not too sure of her steps, went rushing on so that I had to catch her as she tripped down the many useless steps of public buildings.

"Davey," she said, "you're a fool not to be an office-holder. Look at them—everyone as happy as a bee in a flower show. Nice fine people in pressed suits. I never seen such busy places and times. It's like the war boom during the last war."

We were seated in a fine dining room and Vicky was ordering dishes with whipped cream on them. Like a small, well-bred cat she would lift the confection to her tiny mouth and eat off the whipped cream with a genuine animal pleasure.

"Davey, I tell you, if I were twenty years younger, I'd start in again and make a fortune. Buy up a lot of foothills near Polack Point and build houses for the steelworkers. . . ."

I grinned as she examined the measured squares of more cream. "You did that once and lost your shirt."

"Watch your talk, Davey. You're *not* too big to get a slap in the face from me right here in public. Anyway, if your father hadn't ruined us, we'd be rich today, rich as a Mick street contractor, and don't you deny it."

"Pete never had any head for business. Besides which the postwar collapse wiped out all you pin-point speculators."

The waiter passed with a tray of Danish pastry. Vicky motioned to him and helped herself to three bits of castle (molded in whipped cream) with indulgent facial gestures.

"Have some, Davey. Good for the kidneys—all this cream."

"Since when are you a doctor?"

Vicky licked off a cup of whipped cream. "No use for doctors. Most ignorant people alive. Always wanting to open you up like a spring broiler and meddle with your liver and lights." She licked her fingers daintily and looked at me over a fresh, undevoured pastry. "What's this talk of Dris not running again and settling down on a farm?"

"It's true. Unless he changes his mind. He's fed up with the whole bunch of fools here, and these tedious generalizations."

"H'm—well, he's made his mark. I'm proud of Dris. His land laws saved the state. Everyone says so. But what about Cathy?"

I looked at Vicky, picking up her pastry fork for the first time. "Don't be so damn subtle, Vicky. You know this will bust her heart wide open. I think she wanted Dris to be Ambassador to England or something fruity."

"That all?" leered Vicky. "Well, I never said I liked Cathy. Her nose is always too high in the air. But she *is* a lady and gives Dris a better home than poor little Linda ever did. Will she be living on a farm near Antioch? Not after these newsreel pictures. No, siree. She's the restless, wanting kind."

"So were you, Vicky. You always wanted the world on a red ribbon. You've gotten used to living in Antioch."

"Have I? Another kind of a husband and I'd be living on the fat of the land with a maid to wait on me hand and foot. But . . . Where is Pete?"

"We left him looking at pictures of prize hogs. Remember?"

"Let's go find him—after *one* more of them high fluffy cakes."

"*Just* one more, Vicky."

The visit of Vicky and Pete to Washington was a great success. I planned to go back to Antioch with them. Washington held nothing more for me, either. I wanted to mark up canvas again, enter a last phase of my fight with space and tone and color. This time I knew I would come out of the right end of things, for I was free of youthful precocity and the fear of death gnawing at my vitals.

Cabot Carson arrived the night before we left for home. I knew Cathy had sent for him, had begged him to fly down and try to keep Dris in office. I didn't think he had a chance of changing Dris' mind. He knew it—but he tried. In subtle ways—in methods polite and polished. But Dris just grinned and knew that neither Cabot nor Cathy would use anger or rage with him.

Cabot Carson attacked after dinner. Cathy had left us alone and we were drinking tall cool drinks on the verandah facing the river. Dris said something about having learned his lesson reading history.

"History," said Cabot Carson, "is an old slut showing her withered breasts and asking us to accept them as omens of what once was and what will be again."

Dris went to the table and poured himself another drink. "You ignore a great deal. What once was is here again. The age of the savage streamlined and cruel. We here do not think of this new war of the world as a great religious-economic war—so much more fools we."

"The eaters of blood and flesh have perhaps carried to its logical limits the breakdown of what we called our civilization," said Cabot, "because there were men like Darwin and Marx and Wagner and Freud and Henry Ford who took away the sticky silly soul and gave us machines and classes and savage songs and primitive emotions."

"Good Lord," said Dris, grinning, "are you linking up the *Origin of Species*, *Das Kapital*, a dream book and a stinking flivver and blaming them for the breakdown of the Western world?"

"The savages of Wagner's operas, the bloody, incestuous murdering thugs in Wagner, from Siegfried to Wotan, are nothing but poetic storm troopers in mangy pelts. Biological and cultural dogma have replaced the superstition of the Middle Ages but the result is the same. Dris, my boy, if you must have history, see it that way. Wagner, Darwin, Marx, Freud and Ford."

"Maybe," said Dris. "Maybe we did create a world of materialists, a scientific, literate world of dog eat dog. Perhaps this love of oil systems and steam heat and advertising, this abstract science and our foul habits of seeing nature as claw and fangs. But no, Cabot—I can't believe it and remain honestly sane."

"Look. We see war and famine and death creating in Darwin's books a higher animal. Carry it one step higher and you have the fool who sees *more* war, *more* death, and *more* famine creating a bigger, better race. In this case, a German race. And Wagner is nothing but the damn fool idea that blood and slaughter and war are the natural expression of the normal blond he-man. You see, brutal force is stylish."

"Cabot," said Dris, "you have a trick of quoting the wrong truths."

"Marx created the theory that history is the battle of the classes, competing classes. Man therefore was to be a machine responding to physical necessity. A perfect society that would do away with classes and history could work only *that* way or a stone wall waited for you. I haven't gone too deep into the *Critique of Political Economy* to say how wrong—or how right he is."

"You have me waiting for what you see in the *Ring of the Nibelungs*," said Dris, looking out over the river.

"What but a lusty packet of sexual muscle-flexing, a tribal social system and a sort of slimy twilight art—like a very scented whorehouse where the lights are always dim and the women very blonde, horsy, beautiful and willing. The *Ring* celebrates the return of the supersavage—the fall of the old gods because they love gold and the triumph of the Hun race in a long, marching, goose-stepping story of blood, lust and lies."

"Oh, come," I said, suddenly interested, "let's have it in a few words and less artistic trimming."

Cabot put down his drink. "All right. Instead of being human beings living, eating, enjoying life and spending our time in our gardens, we have been sold on the ideas of the survival of the fittest, the theory of value and surplus value, the beauty of and the need of physical struggle, a religion of libidos and Ford cars and the regeneration of mankind by *heils*, oil kings, steel furnaces, chemical stinks and fornication with blonde goddesses in or out of armor."

"You have a cure, of course," I said.

"No," said Cabot.

Dris turned. "Maybe if we sent science back to technology and not to superbombers, if we could write off all of the nineteen centuries' materialism and had less cynicism and pessimism among the so-called leaders, we might have some hope for humanity and posterity. But . . ."

Cabot Carson knew he had failed to change Dris' mind. He set down his glass. "It's damp out here. Let's go indoors."

I have filled a great many sheets of paper. Last night I felt the ice-cold wind of real winter come raging down between the hills. There is a stronger chill in the icy azure liquid sky. It means even deeper snow coming.

I shall re-pack my gear and go down to the world of men and battle and turmoil. Turmoil, turmoil. *How often I have written it on these sheets. Turmoil and lament. How I must amuse the facile, glib, clever people below me.*

I started to tell the story of my brother Driscoll. In that I have failed—and it does not matter now. Failing, I have created a picture of some of him, of his mind, his ideals and his hopes and his defeats. I have drawn a full picture of those people and those things that made him. The story of Dris is the story of the Ormsbees, the story of Antioch, Linda, Cathy, Washington, America.

I know now he himself cannot be drawn. The core of the man is too red-hot to examine and study and write about. What I have done is better. I have pictured his family, his beginnings, his wives and his political career. All in the past tense, you see. The test for him is yet to come. I like the story better this way.

When Dris and his family returned to Antioch he was finished politically, everyone around Ned Wonderly said. His national bills had never come out of committee. Many foolish visionaries had written of him hopefully. And a great many public figures had condemned him.

Dris didn't mind. He was sure the whole shooting match was going up in flames anyway. He wanted to have a few happy years before the madness came.

Ten miles above Antioch he found a small place with old trees massing self-consciously around flower beds. A rambling farmhouse of stone and pine planks, and he whitewashed it and refloored it. Here he set up his bookcases, his collections of public papers. All that there was to show for his years of public office. Here, under a furled bank of clouds, he cut his grass. At night under a covey of stars he smoked his pipe.

I will admit Cathy made the best of it. She picked the grapes and helped clear the lawn and even permitted Dris to repair the river dock and buy an old yawl over which Dris and I pottered. We patched its sails, scrubbed its keel, repainted the hull and set a mast. Rotund, pompous pigeons watched us, and the patched sail was recut and dried.

The baby lay in the sun and grew. Dris drove the haying machine for the farmer who had rented his meadows and sowed sorrel and alfalfa there. Dris made no move to act like a grower himself. He didn't call himself a farmer. Just a retired, political has-been. Twice a week he drove Cathy to town in an old coughing Buick, and once every month Dris and I dropped down toward the bay in the yawl, fishing for tide runners. And when people asked Dris if he was bored, he grinned inscrutably and winked.

I had repaired the old barn on the place and was painting my head off. Finished painting followed, one after the other. But the fishing trip was the best part of the month for me. Dris and I didn't try to fool each other. I with my painting, he with his wife and son, hadn't locked out the worries of the world. We heard of them between advertisements for trash on the radio, we read of them in newspapers and magazines between demands that we chew gum and wear two-pants suits. All was not well. But Dris and I kept up our game of hermit.

I had slept late. Dris came into my room, his face looking very sad. I yawned and sat up. He looked at me and said in a low voice, "We are at war. The Japs have been attacking at Wake and Midway. And at Pearl Harbor there is great damage."

I rubbed my eyes. "I came back from China and saw our lines of defense, Dris. They are very good, only ..."

"Only, what?"

"I didn't like the higher officers—fat, whiskey-drinking snobs—looking down at the little warped monkeys from Nippon—and now they've been caught and hard hit—huh?"

"Yes ..."

"Americans don't know the real Japs. They are not very human—just hissing little yellow monsters bred too close

[404]

together for thousands of years into bent little apes. Ask any Chinese."

"This means a real big war, Davey—going on and on. I'm too old to fight—I'm too out of trim to do anything but sit on a farm and think how different it all could have been if we hadn't been so foolish. Davey—these men who are dying—these Americans—who is killing them? What? American gasoline in Jap planes. And the planes and warships? Built of old Fords and scrapped U. S. steel. It's hard, Davey, to know all that and know it all could have been avoided. Well, we've a war to win."

"What are you going to do?"

"I don't know—organize some sort of civilian defense hereabouts."

I got into my pants. "Let's have breakfast and you'll feel more hopeful. Remember what Cabot Carson says—'The oil crooks, the steel kings, and the jalopy-benders are not America.'"

Cathy came in, very pale, holding the baby very close to her. "It's dreadful—I can't help thinking of the baby—he's only a future hero of the Fifth World War."

"Let's not be so lousily dramatic on an empty stomach," I said.

Later when the Nazis and Italians declared war, Dris sat at his radio and listened a long time. Then he sent off some wires to Washington. But he was a dead duck. No one had a place for him on any board—his knowledge and background were not wanted. He was a has-been. He tried in Antioch —but the Wonderly machine had its orders too. Dris rubbed his jaw and scowled at the baby and went off to a farmers' meeting.

The first national civilian defense group was formed, and Dris and his farmers drilled in our hay field, and read books about blocking roads and putting sand on bombs.

Cathy knitted; Vicky sat under the grape arbor and cursed and knitted. I painted posters and offered my services, but I was told to wait until I was needed—and when I was called they looked at a stiff knee that was no bother at all, and which I had banged on a rock in the swimming hole—but it was no go. I came back to the farm and sat with Dris and looked at the fields and trees. I knew if the going got tough I would get in it—a little stiffness in a knee is nothing when there are German savages and yellow warped monkeys to be killed.

Gramp took it hardest—he was very old and his old war wounds ached. One day he and Dris and I sat drinking hard cider after an afternoon of drilling farmers to fight off tanks from behind stone walls. I knew Dris felt bitter at this sterile task—but the Washington and local machines would have none of him.

Gramp swallowed his drink from the cup I held for him. He looked like one of those Greek gods—the golden cider dripping from his white beard.

"Well, I said it in 1917—you *can't* make peace with a savage. But *they* tried to—they said, 'be a good savage—we will spare you—go home and starve.' You can't say that to blood-drinking savages. They rose up in their hunger and broke out to foul a world. Well, all right—are we going to do the job right this time?"

Dris shook his head. "It's not that easy. You can't condemn a people like that—*any* people."

Gramp snorted in his beard. "You're a fool, Dris. I'm not a blood-drinker—I'm an old man—but I've killed timber wolves and rattlesnakes and barn rats—and you can't say all animals are good. Some are evil and nasty—and we must break up Europe so that the German savages can never rise again and slaughter other people. We must burn out the

[406]

Japs from those rats' nests of islands and teach them table manners. This is no time for feeling that all people are good, only that they lapse from manners. Nonsense—there are perverted people, warped people—and when you find them you must heal them right or lock them away."

"Isn't that what Hitler says?"

Gramp looked at the cider. I gave him some. "No. Dris— what Hitler wanted was a master race of blond savages lording it over everyone. I'm talking about the poisoned little people of the world who have been conditioned to march like grasshoppers over green fields. The Germans, the Japs—sure they once had a fine honest outlook—but in them poison stirs and they are mad.

"Ever have a horse eat loco weed—a fine good horse— and then suddenly he's a killer? Well, that's the Germans and the Japs—they are full of loco weed and if you try to pat them on the back and say 'be good little boys,' they will turn and tear out your throat. I used to shoot loco horses— but maybe you moderns have a better way of curing these things. I don't care *how* you do it—but clean up this world of loco eaters. . . ."

Dris looked into the jug and refilled the cups. "To me, Gramp, it isn't only the war. *If* we throw out the fat bellies, America can win any war. What's coming after? Who is going to have everything here? How are the war profits, the spoils of arming going to be divided? Who is going to sit in Washington? Another Hoover, another Harding? Are people going to stand in breadlines, play stock markets, see the big crooks in power again—or are we going to lie rusting, rotting, dying because we can't mesh the gears of war into gears of peace? That's what I think about."

Gramp grinned. "Vicky always said you'd sit in the White House, Dris—so maybe it's your headache."

"No—I've lost my chance—lost my path. I went walking

through little-used paths and I'm out of it all. But I think about the war and the peace and I shiver for us all. Winning wars is a bad business—on the winner more than the loser. Look at the last one. . . ."

"I've looked on half a dozen."

"So you have."

"None are anything to be proud of unless you know for sure what you are fighting for. This one has clear-cut issues on the surface. *They* snapped at *us*—but behind it stands a lot of low dealing and stock markets and world trade and juggling of holding companies and what you call the 'safe twenty-percent lovers.' "

"Let's eat lunch," I said.

The jug was empty. . . .

Dris worked hard. He made speeches—he toured the farm lands—he planned the growing of needed crops. It was good to see him busy. Time passed.

It's strange. I look at some notes I kept of those war years and they seem so unreal. Events that marched in headlines meant less to me than the corn and cows we grew. Dris and I worked out a rubber-saving plan and had two cars service every farm road and cut down on the use of cars.

Cathy worked with farm wives, and jars of foods went into cellars. Seasons passed and started again. Time went on —war details were printed. Dris grew thinner and grayer and I went to enlist every time I felt my knee get better. Nothing happened.

The trees grew, the boys grew—the times were hard and tight, but no one lost heart. It was a time of work and a time of looking ahead. When the looking ahead looked bad Dris and I would take the yawl down to the harbor and fish out our bitter outlooks. But as time passed we went fishing less. The task was hard.

Almost everything of that period is like a haze before my mind. Work, eat and think as little as I could. I remember the last fishing trip Dris and I took. That is a clearing—a clearing suddenly in the haze of my memory.

One night someone stood over my bed. I pulled on the light. It was Dris, looking rather shamefaced and sleepy.

"What's up?"

"Nothing—and everything. Move over."

"Why?"

"Why! I have just been tossed out of my rut in my wedding bed. My wife will have none of me tonight."

I moved over and Dris slid under the covers.

"It's like old times, Dris."

"Women, Davey—I know nothing of them. I love her—she loves me. We get along well. The sex business—the way we feel about it suits us fine. But say something wrong—say something she doesn't like—and you are up against a stranger."

"Well, a lot of men—smarter and dumber than you, Dris —have found that out."

"Tonight it was about the Presidential convention. Why didn't I get myself an invitation."

"You couldn't get a good answer?"

"Not any she liked."

"And then?"

"Then I was standing on the cold floor in my bare feet."

"Many an old married man has stood there before you."

"Tomorrow I'm sure it will be all right. We'll act as if nothing has happened. Tomorrow night we will go to bed together again. We shall lie very close—and even make love if the mood moves us. We shall sleep close and be very much in love. Yet who knows? The next night we shall talk in darkness—and *bang* I'll be back here with you."

[409]

"You're always welcome. Let's go fishing tomorrow if you fear you're getting into a jam over this convention."

"That's running away."

"What smart married man doesn't?"

"Where did you learn all this wisdom, Davey?"

"My friends talk when mellow."

I pulled out the light. Dris stirred. "I don't want you to think anything is really wrong between Cathy and myself."

"Of course not."

"A man can be alert and educated—he can have a lot of so-called worldly wisdom—but there comes a time when he feels that a woman has stopped his thought processes and his blood stream."

"What you're trying to say is that you wish you were a ditch digger and could blacken her eye for her—much as you love her."

"Oh, no—not that. I love her too much for that—ever."

"How about the fishing trip?"

"I don't know."

"Sea bass running."

"Might be strong weather."

"Fair and calm. The yawl is all ready."

"Well . . ."

"The *first* sea bass of the season."

It was a good cold dawn. At four the first flush over the hills was still weak, but clean and cozy. I loaded the beer cans, the basket of food, into the tiny cabin of the yawl. I shivered, lit the first cigarette of the day and decided I wouldn't bathe this early in the river. The hills rose, like in a painting by Piero della Francesca.

Dris came across the lawn, dressed in soiled white. His battered linen hat was full of fish hooks, and he was just lighting his pipe as the rooster on the next place awoke and

stretched himself in a howl at the dawn. I could hear Dris'
rubber soles on the wet, dew-marked grass. There was a
delicate aura of promised sun behind the elms.

"Well, mug, enough wind to get us down to the bay?"

"I think so if the old sail doesn't split."

"Shove off, then."

The yawl had good lines. She moved away from the
shore and I got the mainsail up and the wind filled it and I
tucked the tiller under one arm while Dris fussed over the
rigging. The mystical crumbling blue day gave way to sunlight.

I yawned and Dris opened a vacuum bottle of coffee and
we drank it. Black, sugarless and strong, from tin cups. Below the freight basin the bellow of tugs came to us and the
low hanging mist broke from over the river and tattered
away into nothing. Soon we were under the railroad bridge
and Dris got up and reset the sails. The water fowl were
crying stertorously and the *put-put* of a motorboat drifted in.

Antioch came yawning across our bow. The factory
chimneys were beginning to puff up and near the steel mills
the all-night shifts were stumbling homeward. Great gouts
of flame shot up when they tapped a furnace. But the rest
of the city slept, lay wrapped in silence except for the early
clatter of milk wagons. Soon we ran into eddies and dirty,
rainbow-colored muck from the mills and plants. The wind
fell away and we drifted and then a puff spun us along and
the city thinned out as we passed the packing houses with
a faint redolence of grease and beef.

Tugs were waking; like bad swimmers the oil tankers and
lumber scows were beat upstream as we passed. Then
they, too, were gone. Below Antioch were miles and miles
of grain elevators, and lumberyards and brick works and the
many foolish shapes of storage tanks. Then the open country again, broken here and there by a spot of weathered

[411]

huts' red roofs and a clapboard hovel, or river farm in torpid indecision clinging to the rich muck in a confusion of
garden patches.

The sun was up now and in force, but slanting too much
to give off any great heat against the triangular noses of
passing islands. A fish leaped and broke the oily swell of
bay-pulled tide. Dris had been brooding, his back against
the cabin, but he stirred himself now and came up from
below with thick egg sandwiches which we munched and
swallowed with the help of coffee now sweetened but not
creamed. The last neat, precise star had long since fled.

The little yawl beat ahead. The shapes of the bay buoys
and lights took on color and solid shadow. The yacht club
hung on a red, bleeding cliff and I made out the anchored
shape of Doug's yacht, *Sea Witch*. I hadn't been on her
since—since Linda. I could still get a melancholy quiver out
of the thought.

The sea swell took us and tossed us and I watched the
patched sail, but it held. Dris had the fishing gear out and
we sailed south along the coast into the sheltering bay where
the full force of the sea was broken and calmed by the
many sand bars and mud flats. A subaqueous glow came up
from the weed bottoms.

Here careful steering was needed and here the big tide
runners came past swiftly at certain secret routes that every
fisherman was sure only he knew. It smelled of kelp and
brine and opened clams and old wood and sun-soaked
winds.

Already other boats were in place, drifting by, casting
shrimp chum out behind them. Dris had the lines ready and
baited with the twisting bloodworms. We sat soon, drinking
cold canned beer, puffing foul black pipes, the floats and
lines dragging behind us. The reefed sail gave us just enough
headway to stir against the tide.

None of the boats seemed to have caught anything yet.

I relit the heel of my pipe and looked at Dris.

"Have you heard those rumors about Hartley Gould Coppard?"

Dris pulled on his line and knocked a twitching crab off his bait. "Same as you have. He would make a fine President."

"Think the convention will really nominate him?"

"Why not, Davey? Nobody expected them to nominate Willkie that time in Philadelphia. Strange things happen in those convention halls."

"You going?"

Dris shook his head. "I'm out of politics for good. I don't even know the delegates. Times are strange and will get stranger. The next man in the White House is signing away his life."

I joggled my line. The pastel-textured sky grew hotter. "I guess so. It's a job for a Jackson. Somebody big and strong."

Dris pulled on his line. The reel sang, the rod danced in silly motions and the line went wetly taut and a fighting sea bass came in over the chipped paint and lay dancing on his fins. Dris grinned and unhooked him, taking care not to touch the long ugly spine. Heavily, mechanically, the bass flapped his tail.

"Six pounds, Davey—*if* an ounce."

I threw the bass into the ice hole. "Four—*maybe* four and a half."

"Five anyway, you mangy artist!"

Dris rebaited and we drank more cold beer. Far out at sea, over the bars, the last grayness was turning the pink of the inner skin of a grape. A great many boats were out with chum lines around us and they were also beginning to catch fish. Male voices crossed to us in loud, enthusiastic tones.

[413]

"Dris, if Hartley Coppard is the next President of the United States, it will be just what they deserve. He'll run the country like a holding corporation. Play it like a Wall Street stock pool and end up by putting it into receivership with any lousy group of adventurers who suit his needs when the moment of break-up comes."

"Mug, you sound like H. G. Wells at his worst. Hand me another worm—a lusty one."

I picked up a long, evil-looking worm. "Here is one who looks like Hartley Coppard at a board meeting."

The sun was higher.

We caught more fish. Dris turned to me and said, "You think I gave up too easy, Davey?"

"I don't know. Nothing is ever all surface. Hell, you may have gone through a fearful stew of emotions before you decided to give up public office."

Dris rebaited his hook. "I did. No one ever knows what goes on inside a man and sometimes not even the man himself. You think it is easy to beat down, as if with a club, all the hope you've had within you for a long time? You think it doesn't hurt to see lesser men make a mess of everything you have tried to do? Davey, I'm all sore inside. I'm hurt and I'm a little numb from the pain of it—but I'm curing myself—healing myself in the sun. Gramp gave me a volume of Thoreau to read. Ever read him?"

"A little, Dris. A little too windy and chilly for my tastes."

Dris cast his line into the water. I could not see his face. "Davey, I found a passage in Gramp's copy of Henry Thoreau. It says what I've been trying to say to life and put into action. It isn't windy or chilly, Davey. It's as honest as childbirth. Henry Thoreau says, 'I wanted to drive life into a corner and reduce it to its lowest terms, and, if it proved to be mean, why then to get the whole and genuine meanness of it . . . or if it were sublime, to know it by experience . . . If we are really dying, let us hear the rattle in our throats and feel cold in the extremities; if we are alive, let us go about our business.' "

We sat looking at our bobbing lines. I said, "Yes."

THIRTY-TWO

IT HAD BEEN a good day for fishing.

Darkness was beginning to smudge the hills and the farm fields when the yawl slid against the dock. I loaded the sack of gutted fish on my back, Dris following with the gear. My face smarted from the burn of sunlight reflected on the water, but I felt clean and warm and full of a poignant outdoor zest. Fishing trips always left me like that.

Dris and I stood behind the barn, scaling the fish on the old work table while the cat watched us and politely ate tidbits. There is a knack to scaling sea bass. The spine bristles, sharp as needles, are grabbed by skillfully held pliers and the whole backbone is then pulled away from the fish. In a moment the fish is clear of all spines and ready to fry —but it takes skill and practice and close attention.

I was pulling spines. Then I was suddenly aware that Dris had stopped cleaning porgies. He was looking up at the house and at a man coming down the path toward us. It was Ned Wonderly, looking as gray and well-cared-for as ever. The long narrow head, the tall collar, even the usual black pearl in place through the tightly drawn gray necktie. The same efficient satisfaction in himself, I thought.

Ned did not hold out his hand to be shaken. We were too full of fish scales.

"I saw the boat come in and Mrs. Ormsbee said you always cleaned the catch down here. You seem to have a good day of it."

"Pretty good," I said. Dris hadn't made any move to welcome Ned. He placed the cleaned fish on the beech leaves.

"Dris, I came here today to speak with you."

"Speak," said Dris, picking up a small porgy.

Ned sat down on a chopping block and lifted the creases in his trousers to preserve them. "Dris, you and I have been friends for a long time. All right, then—we've worked together for a long time."

"That's true," said Dris, scaling the porgy.

"Yes," said Ned, kicking his heel into the heather and moss. "What you think of me—well, it doesn't matter. I made you a public figure and when you felt you could get along without me—I *still* supported you anyway."

Dris tossed the fish aside and said, "Thank you."

"Oh, damn it, Dris! Let's talk. You know me—I am what I am. I started in politics with two ideas—to get rich and to get a lot of power. I don't change much. I'm rich and I've got a lot of power. I like it—and if I get more of both—fine. If not, I've done all right. I've done fine."

Dris began to wash his hands in the water bucket. "You always were honest with me, Ned. You never claimed to have any high ideals. You still don't."

"I'm just Ned Wonderly, the political boss, chairman of the state party, leader of the states in our section. Well, you know me—who I am—what I stand for. I don't have to wave a flag for you. But, Dris—I want you to stay in public office." Ned wiped his brow with a gray silk handkerchief. "These are mad days. It's no time for a man like you to hang up his hat and stay at home."

"You're wasting your time, Ned. I'm finished. I want no part of you, your organization or the offices you can hand out. I don't like your setup. But the main reason, Ned, is—

well, it's too late. It's all over but the firing squads—you and your kind have fixed everything fine. History will now be an incoherent scrawl of bloody brutality."

"I don't agree," said Ned. "I can't feel like you. Things can't be that bad. Dris, I'm an old man—no kids, no kin—nothing but money and a big fist. Well, I like this country, too, in my own way. It's been good to me and my friends."

"No flag-waving," said Dris.

Ned got up, paced sedately, and stood very close to Dris.

"Dris, you fool, I'm offering you the party's nomination for President at the coming convention."

Dris did not bat an eyelash. He tossed off the stale water in the bucket and began to refill at the old pump. "You can't offer *me* anything. There is something sacred about conventions for all their drunks, whores and lousy speeches. It's a gathering of wild happy people going to appoint someone to speak for them."

"You amaze me, Dris. You know how the party is run. We can put in anyone we want."

Dris grinned. "Remember when the Utility Wonder Child was wished on you by the hand-picked mob in the gallery?"

"*That* isn't going to happen again. I've buttered my pride, Dris, in coming here like this. Hat in hand, I've asked you. Do you want the highest office in the land?"

I looked at the fish. They lay in a long row staring at Ned Wonderly. I began to pack them in the pail.

Dris helped me. Over his shoulder, he said, "You'd better back Hartley Coppard. He'll make you a fine President. He was created to be God's ventriloquist."

Ned shook his head. "I wouldn't have believed it. You—acting like this. You know me. I've always said every man has his price. I thought this was yours. And I would not have asked for anything—maybe."

"No," said Dris, simply. "I've got a price—it's one you can't offer. It's a little price. But only little people can give it to me. Well, it doesn't look as if the little people can give anything these days. So, good-bye, Ned."

"Good-bye, Dris—Davey."

Dris and I walked up the grass-grown path to the house. It was dark now and the orange squares of windows looked very cheerful. We carried the bucket of gutted, cleaned fish between us. I looked back to see the yawl resting against the dock, tugging now and again at her moorings. Then I saw Ned Wonderly cutting across the field to the road where a black shape of a car waited for him. The talk had been vague there in the extremely unreassuring stillness.

For the first time that I could ever remember, Ned looked tired. He walked bent forward, not at all his slim, rigid self.

Full of fried fish I sat, sated, at the huge fireplace, watching blazing pine knots flare up the chimney. Dris was sitting, arms folded, grinning, while Cathy, face flushed, tried hard to keep from letting her temper run away with her. She sat as if lightly anesthetized.

Rage, anger, humiliation, and at last as I expected, she could no longer remain still.

"Dris, look at me. Tell me. You really turned *it* down?"

My brother turned and, still smiling, said, "I'm looking at you, I'm telling you—I turned Ned Wonderly's offer down."

Cathy shook her head. "It's—it's fantastic—you're a young man yet. You can't sit here on the farm the rest of your life."

Dris frowned and his fingers nipped the hawthorn blossoms in a vase. "I shall sit here as long as I can, Cathy. A man can only stand so much of anything. I stood it for a long time—that public apathy, that stupid machine perversion of defense. I had to come here. I'm built that way—born that way. I stayed there until I saw it was hopeless."

"But Cabot Carson doesn't think it's hopeless! Ned Wonderly doesn't think it's hopeless! Davey, do you?"

I stirred the fire. "I thought it was—I didn't give a damn. I guess I was like a lot of people Dris spoke about. But when Ned came here today—well, I suddenly saw Ned was frightened, scared out of his skin. Ned is honest in his way. He's loyal in his way. Remember Piggy Tone, Dris?"

"Yes, of course."

"Piggy was no good—to his people, to his friends, to himself. They shot him full of holes and planted him still alive in a barrel of cement and threw him into the river in those berserk days of the Twenties."

"How dreadful," said Cathy.

"But remember, Dris, how he came to you when he got wind of the Tea Pot Dome swindles and the oil scandals? Well, Ned is coming to you, too. He's gotten wind of something and it frightened him."

"What?" asked Dris. "Fifth column plots—Dies Committee yammering? Or do the new tax ideas hurt his bank balances?"

"No. He came to you because he can't put a name to it. But he's in fear. And he knows he can't lick this fear—this terror. Hartley Gould can't. All the big faces and loud voices can't lick this fear."

"And Dris can! Can't he?" said Cathy.

I shook my shoulders. "No one knows. Ned—I—or—or Dris. But I think we would rather try to lick it with Dris than with anyone else in the world."

My brother looked at me after this storm of absurdities and tossed wood on the fire. "Davey, you're a fool—just like

Ned is a fool. You can't buy me with flag-waving or with talks of terror to come. You've always impressed me as a conceited egotistical artist. Not giving a damn for the world. And now you're acting out Pollyanna mottoes like Ned Wonderly. I can't accept Ned's offer. I can't listen to you, Davey—or to you, Cathy—because you're both emotionally upset."

"Who will you listen to?" asked Cathy.

"I don't know. I know I could hear *it* if *it* called. But it never will now. Come on, Cathy—let's go to bed before we talk ourselves into nightmares. Night, Davey—lock up."

"Sure. Night."

I sat a long time watching the fire spin patterns. Then I kicked out the cat and locked up. I suddenly realized the intolerably narrow limitations of my mind.

I did not sleep well. I was up at dawn and went down to the dock and pumped out the yawl. Dris had little to say at breakfast. He read his newspaper and talked to young Sewall, who was getting bigger and eating and making efforts to talk like a human being with exquisitely proportioned features in a rosy face.

After breakfast we went out to the fields and helped the farmer load hay. It was fun at first. The great amber-colored mounds looking so light scenting the air. But the sun grew higher and the loads heavier and I no longer envied those who earn their living in the fields. By noon we had loaded three wagons and the horses had moved them across the short stubble. There was a naked look to the fields. Like a plucked chicken.

I was too tired to eat and so I sat at the radio listening to the mumbo-jumbo of the opening convention speech. Dris went back to the haycocks but Cathy and I stayed and heard the dull speeches, the tattered talk of God and Country and Old Glory and at last the full flow of jabberwocky that would nominate a candidate for President of the United States.

A few trained seals and perpetual officeholders, tax-evasion bankers, were mildly greeted and given a few votes. Then the convention got down to booming serious business. I could feel the heat, the dust, the rasping throats as they banged and shouted and cheered through the radio. Senators were nominated—utility lawyers—crackpots and reactionaries—but it was easy to see that the main business was slow to start. *Then* someone nominated Hartley Gould Coppard. The ovation lasted fifteen minutes. It was well planned and well carried out. A solid pyramiding of sound.

Ned Wonderly's State Governor got up and read a long screed to that man, that noble man, that great builder of steel and jobs, that hero of production, that noble business man—Hartley Gould Coppard. Again the bands played. The ovation went on. It was very impressive. A dubious bankruptcy of cracked voices and stiff minds.

Suddenly there was a roar, and a faint ticking sound puckered in the radio's metal throat. Over the shouting ovation I heard, *"Driscoll Ormsbee . . . Driscoll . . . Ormsbee . . . We want Driscoll Ormsbee!"*

I looked at Cathy. She was very pale. I turned on more power, but the shout was very confused and made no sense. Then the chairman's whiskey voice was heard in official displeasure.

"If there is any more unwarranted shouting from the galleries I shall be forced to take action. This is a duly appointed body to do the people's will—and it will not be dictated to by mob voice. And now it is my honor—great honor—to introduce that noble law-giver—that great legal giant—Senator . . ."

[422]

I turned off the radio. Cathy stood up and folded her arms.

"It's stupid of us to listen, Davey."

"I hope you mean it, Cathy. Don't hold any false hopes. Ned made it clear this convention isn't going to get out of hand and force them to nominate anyone but whom the political bosses want."

She went out to see how Sewall was doing under the big oak. I tuned the radio on very low but the great law-giver's voice was bubbling through a speech about nothing at all. With a guilty feeling I clicked off the set before Cathy entered the house again. There was suddenly a delicate, compelling intimacy between us—a foolish hope.

It was a hard-fought convention. The party lacked a real figure to capture the imagination of the people and knew it. The political bosses, the press lords, the oil and steel kings were in conflict. Ned Wonderly was the strongest, but I knew it was taking time before he could promise everyone everything in frowsy hotel rooms and could get enough votes to put in Hartley Gould Coppard.

For two days the struggle rattled on and then Coppard's delegates began to forge ahead.

A chief delegate was Blue Peter—he who had once owned Blue Peter's Beer Garden and later a speakeasy—but who was now a public figure, head of the True Republican League and chairman of the National Manufacturing Committee. He had come far since the days of bung-starting but was as loud and hard as ever and time and again I could hear his deep thunder over the airways. I remembered the time he had almost killed the Norton-Burton Bills.

Dris had regained his interest and listened with the rest of us to the radio—listened with repugnance but with a growing interest.

[423]

"It's hard to see what's going on," he said. "Ned is strong. But not strong enough to get the two-thirds vote for his man. Now a dozen cigar-smelling conferences are going on in hotels all over the city. Men are sitting in bathrooms drinking Scotch, lying on beds waving big cigars. And through them the real convention is doing its work. Ned is promising everything to get delegates. Judgeships, jobs as ambassadors and captains in the Air Force. Blue Peter—I always liked his hard edges—he's doing a lot of talking and back-slapping and lining up a bloc to support Ned's Old Guard when Ned thinks it's time to finish the farce. But Blue Peter will ask and get a high price."

"Suppose somebody slips up and double-crosses Ned?"

"Who?" asked Dris. "And why? Hartley Coppard will please them. Ned's men are all loyal to him."

"Well, let's get dressed and go to town. It's Vicky's birthday," said Cathy sadly.

"I forgot. What good is a birthday," I said, "when Vicky no longer admits to her right age?"

Dris shrugged his shoulders. "She still claims she is sixty-five—sixty-two if you pin her down."

"She's over seventy-five," said Cathy.

"Shhh!" said Dris. "That's *foul* slander. That would make Gramp near a hundred."

"He must be," I said. "But I never thought of him as being that old."

"We never do," said Dris. "No one is that old until some day someone makes a silly remark. Turn off the radio, mug. They are yelping stertorously until they get real orders."

The machine was still bumbling but it had a more sinister tone.

We found Vicky glued to the radio with a ferocious grimace. Pete was setting the long table and in the kitchen

I heard Aunt Netta and Uncle Thoreau quarreling over the proper way to mix a chef's salad.

Vicky turned and eyed us in the doorway. "Damn it, I think they are going to forget about you, Dris."

"They have," said Dris kissing her. "Happy birthday. You're the damnedest youngest woman I ever saw at sixty."

Vicky grinned, her small wrinkled nose perked way up. "Stop fooling—you know I'm older. Why I'm—I'm—over sixty-two—*a little*."

So we all kissed her and handed her some bundles and admitted she looked her age—sixty-two—or over—a little. The house looked smaller. Every year it grew smaller when I saw it after long periods of time. The living room still had the same coal-burning stove and the silver, very worn now, retained that buttercup pattern that I had chewed my first teeth on. I suddenly saw time, like a night beast, drinking in the rain. . . .

Pete came over. He was gray but solid as ever—just a little slower in his gait and a little stiffer in his joints, looking like an old peasant who had plowed too many wet fields. Strange how his character had never changed. Even his appearance was what he had once been meant to be. He accepted life without heroics, rancor or passions. He held up a jug.

"Wine. Made it myself—toast Vicky in it. Huh?"

Vicky grinned up at Pete. There was nothing she could scold him about. Not while he made such a huge speech and offered up a toast.

"Silly fool, that Pete. Always thinking up excuses to soil new, washed cups. Oh, well—don't spill any on the fresh tablecloth. Let's eat one meal without sitting down like pigs."

Aunt Netta's red nose smelled the wine, and Uncle Thor

followed her, his face still a copy of Kipling's—but of a white-mustached fullness that had survived the bigoted poet's own warped lifetime.

We stood, glasses filled (almost all of them from the same set). Aunt Netta looked into hers and smiled, then lifted her head.

"Wait for Gramp," Dris said. "He's in the garden with Dennis. Get them, Uncle Thor."

"Dennis?" I said. "I didn't know Dennis was here."

Vicky nodded. "Dropped in. Collecting funds for some fool church thing. Come on. It's *my* toast!"

Gramp and Dennis entered. Gramp was the same—small, twisted and white-bearded. But I would never have known my brother Dennis. His bald head was trimmed with white cotton fringes. His face was redder and fuller than I remembered it and the eyes were very peaceful. There were scars around the corners of his mouth where in youth there had been small white pimples.

"Well," said Vicky, "let's have it over with."

Dennis picked up a wine glass and fitted another one into Gramp's hand and held it there. Gramp looked about the room and said in something like his old voice:

"Thank you. Let us drink to Life. All the other toasts are now stale and out of date. Ferments of wrathful dissenting opinion. Nothing—wealth, prosperity and the hopes of races and families seems worth much now. So to the wonder of living—of being alive—to *Life!*"

Dennis lifted Gramp's arm.

We all drank—even Vicky with that greedy little polite pleasure she took in all things.

Pete got out a fresh jug.

THIRTY-THREE

THERE WERE MANY toasts after the first one.

We were still eating when Douglas arrived with great bundles and many sealed bottles. He stood at the head of the table, pushing his packages onto the cloth and shouting at the top of his huge voice with incessant clamor.

"Happy, happy birthday, Vicky. A hundred and twenty more to you—and then some."

"Drunk," said Vicky, grinning as she sniffed at Doug's mouth and kissed him. "Drunk as a wet smack and twice as ugly. Who do you think you are, coming in here like this? This is no honky-tonk. Respect, Douglas—that's what I want from you!"

Doug winked and Vicky smiled and he lifted the tiny woman in his arms and kissed her again and again until she howled in protest. But we could see that she was enjoying it more than ever. She gathered her breath and tore open a package and draped silver fox across her small shoulders. It was a paean of triumph. *She* in silver fox!

Gramp shook his head. "Enough pelt there for Vicky to bathe in."

Doug nodded and began to pull corks out of cognac bottles with his big teeth with that over-elaborate graciousness of his.

"Come on, drink. This indeed is a surprise—an evening of gaiety. A time to laugh and a time to guzzle! *We* are to be honored tonight."

Dris, with a piercing sense of some secret, said, "What are you talking about?"

Doug was very drunk, sweating profusely. He staggered, hit Dris a happy blow on the shoulder and winked, and then turning on a spinning heel he winked at everyone until Aunt Netta began to laugh so hard she sputtered into her whiskey mug. But Doug went on clowning, closed one eye and opened it and then snapped his big thumbs and switched on the radio.

"Damn it—sitting here like valley mudsills when big things are about to happen. *Where* do you think I've been all day? On the phone—listening—talking. Revolt is happening! Revolt! Listen!"

We looked at one another with ridiculous patience, and even Pete leaned forward in his chair. The radio bawled into sound. A great confusion of shouting, a clatter of chairs and a braying of voices in battered rhetoric filled the room.

Dris slowly went up to Doug and placed a hand on his shoulder.

"*What* are you raving about?"

"Raving?" said Doug, almost losing his balance as he pointed to the radio. "Raving? Listen to *that* raving."

Vicky moved quickly across the room and placed her head against the shouting loudspeaker. "What're they trying to say?"

"Surprise," said Doug, with a warm red face and sat down swiftly, too drunk to go on.

Cathy stood very still. Doug winked at her, then got up, turned and fell into Dris' arms. Dris sat him in a chair again. The radio was still shouting, but nothing that could be understood came through. It was a dropsical sea-shell drone of far nothing.

Doug sobered, gagged, wiped his wet face, gathered

breath and choked back a full throat. An overwhelming imminence of emotion at last poured from him.

"Listen, Dris—listen—you didn't think your friends, your pals, the people, ever forgot what you did for them? State legislators—the people you helped in court. *No, siree!* Well, a lot of them are delegates—and Peter Blue—good old Blue Peter—he organized them—*see!* Always hated Ned Wonderly for the price he had to pay for liquor protection in the old days—and now Blue Peter has voted a wedge of delegates for *you!* Dris—for *you!*"

There was hammering on the loudspeaker. Someone was trying to whip the convention into order. The name *Ormsbee* came over. Then more hammering. We looked at each other. Dris stood, a hand on Cathy's shoulder. I could see his fingers grip her flesh cruelly. She did not notice. Gramp sat smoking. Pete puffed his pipe calmly. Only Dennis and Vicky and Doug were excited. Aunt Netta and Uncle Thor were numb. Blind, inchoate, the radio redoubled its virulence.

With great care Vicky moved the radio needle a tiny bit. The voices cleared and a great booming took over.

"Order! Order! The name of Driscoll Ormsbee has been properly placed in nomination. The clerk will call the roll again and begin a new tally. ORDER!"

There was sound of cheers and protest. Doug smiled and rolled his head. "Ned Wonderly's boys trying to start a riot. Do them no good—none at all."

Dris did not move. Gramp asked, "How many delegates does Blue Peter control?"

"Thirty-four," said Doug, sombrously contemplating his thumbs. "Just the beginning of the snowball. Watch it pick up on this round. Just you watch."

The clerk's voice, flatly amplified and nasal, came over the air, *"Alabama six votes. Alabama . . ."*

Alabama voted its six votes for Hartley Coppard.

Vicky groaned. Dris shook his head. All of us felt a too intense consciousness of tautness in the room.

In the ten states next polled Dris had one and a half votes. Suddenly the big neighboring states of the Midwest came in. Things picked up. Dris had twenty-two votes. The roll ended. Dris had fifty-seven votes. Hartley Gould was still leading with a hundred and four. Dris was fifth on the list of nominees.

Someone got up to make a speech. We heard the galleries begin to hoot and whistle. Doug looked about him and took a long pull direct from the neck of a bottle.

"Damn their scurvy souls. They've *got* to do better than that. They have got to. It's honest now, Dris. It's the people who know you—it's the people who had office with you. It's the people you helped in court. Listen to the gallery, Dris—listen to your people there."

Dris sat very still. Gramp coughed and Dennis took the pipe from the old man's mouth. "Dris—don't hold too much hope. Sometimes the people get a voice in this—but mostly they are beaten down. There is an elusiveness about this. And Ned Wonderly will fight you all the way."

"It's all right," said Dris, very pale, and shaking off Doug's offer of a glass of whiskey. "I am very proud to think my friends will try and fight for me. I don't expect to win here—I knew everything I wanted to do was hopeless when the fools and fat mouths in Congress killed my re-sources and defense bills. I knew there was no use fighting a tide of hate and greed once it had passed the border into dividends. But even if I knew it, then, I don't believe it *now*. Nothing is ever hopeless. Oh, they'll beat me down tonight. *That* doesn't matter. I was foolish to think no one cared. Don't you see? All those people who turned on the machines and stock peddlers and steel kings and the bosses

—they've all committed political suicide to shout my name for a moment in the noise there. It's all right—I'm all right. I'm grateful for small favors. Shut off the radio. No use eating our hearts out."

"No," said Doug, getting up and barring the way. "The hell with taking it like *that!* You still think there is hope. Well, there is hope tonight. Let's hear one more roll call— I've got a hunch. It's the mugs and little guys getting up on their hind legs and howling tonight."

"Damn your hunches," said Dris.

Gramp looked at Dennis and said, "If you get down and pray, Dennis, I'll recover enough strength in my arms to pull your legs off and beat you to death with them. Light me a new pipe."

"Shhhh!" said Vicky. "They are trying to get another roll call started. Slowpokes! Why don't they go ahead!"

It was hard work. The galleries were shouting *Ormsbee, Ormsbee* in long rolling chants. But at last the thing was begun. It began no better. Alabama was still six votes for Hartley Gould. Then things got better. Dris picked up a vote here and there. The roll call finished with Dris still far behind—having sixty-two to Hartley Gould Coppard's ninety-eight. Doug began to shout with strained vocal cords.

"A sign! A sign! Dris hasn't gained much but Hartley is dropping some of his strength. The delegates are scattering in confusion."

Vicky was almost inside the inner secrets of the radio. She stood directly against the loudspeaker and her small hands tapped its cheap, veneered surface.

She closed her eyes and nodded. "It's going to come out all right! It's going to come out all right! It's going toooo . . ."

It was very warm in the house. I opened the windows. People stood on the sidewalk and cheered as I opened the windows. News had spread. I went back to the radio. A new roll call was showing better results for Dris. Hartley Coppard was dropping votes badly. A senator with a foul mouth and no mind was gaining the lead.

Uncle Thor groaned. Aunt Netta shed tears in her drink. Only Doug tore open his collar and cheered. "Let 'em keep it up! Keep it up! Dris will lead on the next roll call, *you'll* see!"

"Nonsense," said Gramp. "That bastard big mouth will pile up a lead. Every newspaper owner in the land has fed him."

Doug danced around the room. "No! No! Don't you see? Suppose you *were* Hartley Gould Coppard? A smart, modern business man—and you see the nomination going against you to a windbag. What would you do? Forget old scores? Only think that—well, at least Dris used to be my son-in-law. A fool about certain things but better him than this dirty dog and his tobacco chewers who will ruin steel and factories and play games for power. Sure—better Driscoll Ormsbee—a man he helped mold and who married into the family once—than this lousy clod of a shoe-wearing hillbilly!"

Cathy stood up. "He's right. He's right, Dris! Coppard will release his delegates and throw them over to you! Ned, too! Ned hates the Southern crowd and their madmen. You're the only man they have, now that Blue Peter has split them up!"

Dris said nothing.

Dris led the next roll call. He gained on the next two. At two o'clock in the morning he polled two hundred and thirty votes and was the party's nominee for the office of President of the United States.

I turned to look at my brother Driscoll. He was gone.

[432]

The family sat as if numb. Vicky recovered and was hugged by Doug and was too breathless to talk. The first and last time in her life. Dennis muttered a prayer, diligent on the Lord's business.

Gramp stood at the table. The old man let the tears fall down his beard. A somber obedience held us as we looked into his eyes. He spoke low, long.

"Well, here I stand where I never should have been. Maybe a long time ago I might have been proud of all this. But now in these times I can only regret it had to come to Dris in this hour. Maybe he is the man. Like Lincoln. Like Jefferson. Like Jackson. Like them perhaps he was made, created for the time that would try men's souls. I don't know. I never had much truck with souls. I shall be dead soon. I shall insignificantly die and dust away. I'll never know how it turned out. If he met the Thing and beat it down and saved the little people. Yes. I shall be dead. Davey . . ."

"Yes?"

"If you're around or your children are—when it's over —come to my grave and tell me. Tell me it's all right—then —then I'll know—I'll know I didn't follow Grant into the Wilderness for nothing. Promise, Davey . . ."

"Sure, Gramp. I promise."

I was tight inside and I could not face anyone. I went out through the kitchen and under the grape arbor my father had raised. The hot night was very dark. Very few stars showed. I could just make out the curiously symmetrical hills.

Then I saw Dris. He was leaning against the great, gouted grapevine—the main and shaggy trunk that grew so well over the odd yellow house of my father.

He was weeping with the inquiring grimace of a questioner. The way a man cries.

[433]

Deep. Strongly.
Unashamed . . .

The sheep herder found me lying in the snowdrift and rubbed snow on my numb ears. He says I'll live to make a damn fool of myself again some other day. I lie in his snug hut and bring this batch of writing to an end. There is no phone and no radio here. The sheep herder reads his Bible and smokes his pipe, and his lean, wise collie patrols the drifts.

Outside the window the white world hurts my eyes. Below, the white meadows lie still and dazzling. Perhaps tomorrow I shall go on. Find out. Meanwhile the sheep herder stirs his oatmeal soup and reads out loud from his frayed Bible:

"Thy rowers have brought thee into great waters: the east wind hath broken thee in the midst of the seas. Thy riches, and thy fairs, thy merchandise, thy mariners, and thy pilots, thy calkers, and the occupiers of thy merchandise, and all thy men of war, that are in thee, and in all thy company which is in the midst of thee shall fall into the midst of the seas in the day of thy ruin. The suburbs shall shake at the sound of the cry of thy pilots . . ."

Even through the thick sod walls I can feel the cold outside. The snow still drifts. The land is covered with a sea of white.

There is no sky. . . .